Angel of Mine

MOST IMPRUDENT MATCHES
BOOK FOUR

ALLY HUDSON

Angel of Mine Copyright © 2024 by Ally Hudson. All rights reserved. Printed in the United States of America. No part of this book may be reproduced in any form or by any electronic or mechanical means, including information storage and retrieval systems, without written permission from the author, except for the use of brief quotations in a book review.

Digital Edition ISBN: 979-8-9882181-8-0

Print Edition ISBN: 979-8-9882181-9-7

Cover design by Holly Perret, The Swoonies Romance Art

First edition

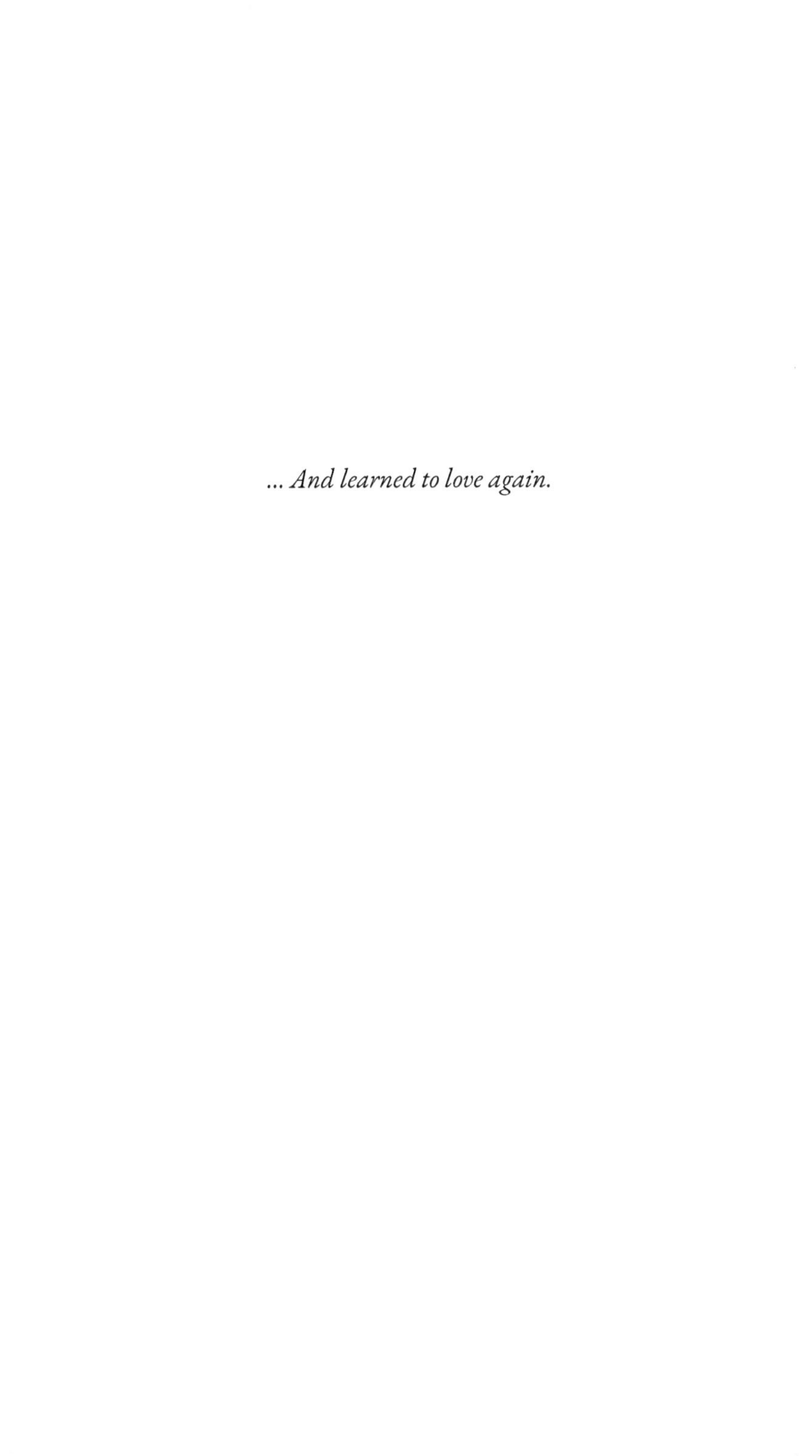

... And learned to love again.

It's a love song / It's a tale of a love that never dies / It's a love song / About someone who tries

— AAÏS MITCHELL, *HADESTOWN*

Angel of Mine

Introduction

Dearest Reader,

Welcome to Angel of Mine. While this book directly follows Devil of Mine—in fact, the epilogue of the first is the prologue of the second—it is not necessary to have read its predecessor to understand or enjoy this story.

The heroine within these pages is a young widow. Devil of Mine is the story of her first marriage and is not a traditional romance in that it ends with the hero's death.

Angel of Mine is a traditional romance. There is a happily ever after for Celine and her love interest to come, no matter how fraught their journey.

Both Devil of Mine and Angel of Mine were passion projects. I adore them and couldn't bring myself to release Angel of Mine without putting Devil into the world. I also couldn't bring myself to hack Devil to fit the traditional romance mold.

While I think each book is better for having read the other, I understand that not everyone is interested in reading or in a place to read a love story that doesn't feature a happily ever after.

That is why I worked very hard to ensure that everything you need to know to understand Angel of Mine is contained within its pages. You will not struggle to understand or enjoy the story by not having read Devil of Mine first.

All that to say, please enjoy the following tale of grief, healing, and new beginnings.

Love,

Ally

New Beginnings

CELINE

It was a ritual now, pressing a kiss to my fingertips before dropping it to him. Spreading the blanket above him and settling down, my back against his cool, broad form. On days such as this, he was a balm against the oppressive, damp summer heat.

"Bonjour, mon amour. Et joyeux anniversaire."

I allowed myself a moment for the grief to come. It was always particularly sharp on these kinds of days. It had once been an open wound, gaping and bleeding. Then it burned with fever and infection. Now it was an old, familiar pain. Some days it was a dull ache, easily ignored. Others, like today, it throbbed in reminder, but it was manageable.

More and more frequently, the pain was shrouded in guilt. It should not be so easily biddable. At one time, I could not open my eyes without thoughts of him. Last week I made it until luncheon before a bite of cheese reminded me of his teasing expression. That my earlier greeting was hindered only by a lump in my throat instead of the all-encompassing sobs of years past—that was perhaps the greater hurt.

It was a nonsensical thought. My husband had been gone for seven years. I had been talking to his headstone for four times longer than we had been married. A lone tear escaped, and I brushed it away.

My sorrow was quiet this year.

Gabriel had not been a good man, not by anyone's definition, but he had been good to me, loved me. He would not wish my wraithlike existence of the first few years to continue.

With that hopeful thought, I continued with my ritual. "I don't suppose you know what one wears to a masquerade held in a gaming hell. A masquerade hosted by the wife of one's former lover, even." The only response was a light breeze brushing through my curls.

"I thought not. Perhaps the deep plum with the beads? It's a bit outdated, but there's a certain theatricality to it that might suit for a masquerade." The fluff of a dandelion danced across the tip of my foot on its journey to somewhere new.

"I'm glad we're in agreement. Your mother is planning to wear something in the style of Marie Antoinette. For all I know, it's one of the woman's actual gowns. You know your mother would not consider it to be overdone." A great tit landed on the nearby oak branch, chirping its usual two syllables at me.

"I do not know what your sister will wear. Perhaps something she stole from that pirate captain your brother and I had to barter her return from last month. She is determined to vex him into an early grave. Are we certain she is not in line to inherit?"

A cloud shifted and the sun found my face, bathing it in a pleasant warmth. Somehow this warmth was peaceful instead of muggy as it had been earlier.

"Michael told me that Lord Champaign may be in attendance tonight. No one has seen him in some years, and it's all very mysterious. You know how I love a mysterious man... Perhaps he will favor me with a dance. I know how you appreciated his attentions toward me before we wed."

The breeze picked up slightly, clouds returning to veil the sun, and the oak leaves rustling their discontent at the disturbance.

"I wish you could come with me. Can you imagine the fun we would have had at a masquerade? And at a gaming hell? The *ton* never would have recovered from our mischief. There are a great many darkened corners in Wayland's. You wouldn't have been able to resist dragging me to one and having your way with me. I would have let you think you were the seducer, but in that plum gown, I would have seduced you."

One of the irises I had planted around his resting place brushed against my arm as the pale-blue butterfly inspecting it moved on to the next.

I was not delusional. My husband was dead. I knew these events were happenstances of nature and nothing more. That breezes and butterflies happened every day all across the country. I knew they happened around me without notice. A regular, uneventful coincidence when I promenaded through the park or stepped into the carriage.

But here, in the little Hasket family plot, they felt different, special.

They were an enticing awareness down my spine.

They were Gabriel.

One

HART AND SUMMERS, SOLICITORS, LONDON - JUNE 5, 1816

WILLIAM

DROWNING IN PAPERWORK, what a way to die. My epitaph would read: *William Hart. He survived an entire war only to be crushed to death by contracts. Dearest nothing. Beloved to no one.*

My hand gave a pathetic seize in protest as I signed the topmost copy. That was the bargain I made with my body, the cramped way I held my quill to write with my favored left hand in exchange for recognizable letters. No amount of knuckle raps from tutors had been able to force legible penmanship from the right.

"Finished yet?" I glanced up to see Kit Summers leaning against the doorway in his customary manner. My partner's dark, curly mop of hair was overgrown and he hadn't bothered to shave in several days. Propped against the door, his arms were crossed and his perpetually disgruntled mouth was turned unusually far down. The brow was furrowed too.

"You look like shite," I retorted, ignoring the question.

"Thank you. So do you. Are you finished with the contracts?"

He was likely not wrong about my appearance. I had run my fingers through my hair more than a few times today. And my spectacles were smudged beyond all measure.

"No, I mean it. You look even worse than you usually do," I insisted, refusing to acknowledge the evening's agenda.

He ignored the slight. "You've forgotten haven't you?"

Tragically, I had not. I laced my fingers in front of me, pushing them away in an attempt to loosen the tension in my shoulders. "Would you leave me be if I said I wasn't finished and I had forgotten?"

"Absolutely not."

"Then no, I am not finished. I will never be finished. Also no, I have not forgotten. In spite of my best efforts, I might add. Why do we need to attend this again?"

"Wayland's is our best client by far. Wayland and Ainsley each invited both of us personally. And Katie begged." All valid reasons. Except for Lady Grayson. The man could manage his sister's meddling on his own.

"But if you'll recall, it's a masquerade. If we're not there, who will know?" I bargained.

"Will, please don't make me attend alone." Kit often wore such a gloomy countenance. I'd quite forgotten the effectiveness of his whining when he feared the glower insufficient.

But the thought of attending this damned ball... "Think of all the ladies you'll attract as an earl. Titled ones too. You won't be alone for long."

His scowl deepened. Reminders of his newly acquired earldom had a way of doing that. There was a fine line between teasing him and upsetting him, and I'd tripped over it.

"Fortune and title hunters who wouldn't have looked at me twice months ago. And Katie has been in a matchmaking mood since lil' Henry was born. Wants a cousin for him. And now she has *options*." He added a dramatic shudder to the last word. A reflection on the horrors he would face—gently bred young ladies chasing after him with ribbons twirling in their wake.

I sighed and rose from the scarred oak desk and stretched my back. When we were busy, I had a tendency to forget to move. It hadn't been a bother when I was a lad of twentysomething, but now, in the midst of my thirties, my body protested.

"All right," I grumbled. "Let me get my coat and we can be off. At least Mrs. Ainsley will have made something delicious." It was easy to console myself with thoughts of baked goods. They might be enough to make this torture worthwhile. *Perhaps*. If she'd made the Shrewsbury cakes. Or the cardamom buns. Or those little cake things.

"No. We need to change first," Kit insisted.

"What?" I glanced down at myself. I wore the same serviceable white shirt and brown, tweed waistcoat as always. In the afternoons, when the sun poured into the window along the side wall of my office, heating the air, I tossed my coat aside and worked in my shirtsleeves.

"Kate's orders," he added by way of explanation.

"You jest."

"I never jest about Kate's orders. Also, you have ink all up your sleeve. These are our patrons. We should probably pretend to be professionals."

Damn, all the way to the elbow.

"My patrons," I grumbled. Kit may loathe reminders of his new title, but it was only a matter of time before he was forced to accept the inevitable. And I would be forced to do the work of two solicitors—busy solicitors—while training up a new partner.

"Will..."

"Fine, but you'll help with at least half of these tomorrow." I gestured toward the precarious stack of financial documents on my desk.

"All right, but you have to wear this." He tossed a scrap of black fabric my way and I caught it with ease. It was a scrap with two evenly spaced oval holes in the center. *No.*

"Absolutely not."

"Kate insisted."

"She's not *my* sister."

"I'll tell her you're looking for a wife," he threatened.

"Won't work. She doesn't know a single lady who would look twice at me and you know it. The lack of fortune and title alone are enough of a deterrent. Then there is the temperament. And look, there's someone with both title and fortune right here—"

"Three-quarters of the stack," he countered in a desperate attempt to quiet me.

"Whole thing."

"Done," he agreed.

"Really? I would have done it for half. This is why you should be off... earling or whatever it is earls do. A solicitor's life is not for you." I capped the ink and began wiping off the quill.

"As far as I can tell, earls attend ridiculous parties and hop about with silly girls."

"It's a perfect life for you." Quill clean, I tugged open the rusty drawer of my desk and dropped the stack of papers inside before locking it.

Kit's scowl deepened but he pressed off the doorframe. "Meet back here in an hour? We can hire a hack."

"Just enough time for you to remove the cat that seems to have taken up residence on your face."

"One hour, Will," he said, ignoring the slight as he dragged a hand across the fur covering his jaw. He *was* serious.

"Fine." I snatched up the ridiculous mask and shut the door to my office behind me. I strode past the two rows of wooden desks that faced the center aisle.

Those desks were long empty; our clerks only called them home between the hours of nine and four. Kit and I often arrived earlier and stayed later, and tonight was no exception.

He opened the glass door and waited for me to pass as the bell above offered a disgruntled clang. We really ought to replace it one of these days.

Kit took off down the street with a nod toward his bachelor lodgings.

This part of town was always quiet at this time of the evening, after the shops and offices closed and people returned to their families. A delivery boy rested on the milk crate that never seemed to return to the dairy. It resided permanently at the corner of the alley between my office and the milliner's shop across the way. The boy covered his eyes with a cap as he leaned against the wall. Two seamstresses from the modiste a couple of shops down strolled past, their giggles startling an elderly gentleman who often rested on the bench across the street.

I locked the door before making the arduous two-step journey to the entry of my flat directly next door. Inside, I climbed the stairs, wishing desperately that I could collapse onto my bed until my stomach protested and I was forced to put something together for supper. Instead, I would need to change into my least comfortable breeches and my overly starched shirt. And then I had to attend a ridiculous ball with ridiculous people. I could feel the headache forming behind my eyes with each step.

Why the devil had I agreed to attend tonight?

Two

WILLIAM

IT WAS WORSE than I had expected. The whole of the *ton* jammed together in a maelstrom of glittering absurdity.

As soon as we arrived, masks dutifully donned, I found my way up the stairs that wrapped in a spiral around the edge of the gaming floor to the offices upstairs. The crush remained below, utterly unaware of my existence, and I could breathe.

I intended to spend the minimum socially acceptable amount of time at this event. That goal required a stratagem, mapping the battlefield, a plan of attack. Otherwise I could be caught unawares in some tedious conversation with a dimwitted lordling.

From my vantage leaning against the railing above, I surveyed the entire floor. The gaming tables were pushed to the outskirts of the massive hexagonal room. The change made way for a dance floor that had been installed in the center. To one side, an orchestra played sensuous tunes, though the effect was negated somewhat when punctuated by hoofbeats of the gentry as they stomped about.

Wayland and Ainsley—or more likely their wives—had set up a refreshment table, piled high with Mrs. Ainsley's best offerings beside the well-stocked bar lining one wall. If I hadn't made it a practice to visit her shop daily, the sight might have been enough to tempt me into the fray.

The dancers below split into two rows and somehow, in what I was certain was an accident, Her Grace, the Duchess of Rosehill, found herself between two groups. It had been years since I last saw her, but she was unmistakable.

She had taken advantage of the theme to pull something ostentatious from her closet. A gown from her youth that had presumably been gathering dust in the back of her wardrobe now spilled out from her hips. The dress was nearly as wide as she was tall, with gold ruffles puckering across the cornflower blue silk. The massive wig atop her head wiggled when the dance called the partners back together.

How a woman that frivolous managed to secure a husband as sensible as the late Duke of Rosehill was still a wonder. The thought caused a familiar pang of guilt at the reminder of that loss. His Grace hadn't been pleased when I abandoned the law for the army. He'd withdrawn his support, emotional and financial. We were estranged for years before he passed, but I respected him. Rosehill was sensible—sensible and stubborn.

Kit began the climb up the steps, a glass in each hand. One containing a whiskey he favored, and the other a lemonade for me, if I had to guess. I didn't drink as a rule, and as tempting as it might be to begin tonight, I didn't intend to start now.

He handed me the lemonade, which was shockingly refreshing instead of cloyingly sweet. He took a sip from his own glass before leaning against the railing beside me.

"Did no one tell her it's the male peacocks that have the fancy feathers?" Kit asked, gesturing with his glass toward a lady covered in peacock feathers at one of the high-stakes tables farther into the room.

Lady Davina—Kit would find her. He always grumbled loudly when her brother arrived, requesting a rescue for her. The girl was determined to see herself ruined or dead in her quest for an adventure.

"She looks nonsensical," he added, fooling only himself. Kit might complain, but it was plain from the flush of his cheeks that he was fond of her.

I did have to agree with his assessment, though. She wore a turquoise gown with shorter feathers peeking above one shoulder. They trailed across her front before angling along to her opposite hip where full-length feathers angled away. There was an embroidered peacock across the bodice connecting the two plumes of feathers. Her mask was simpler, a few feathers cut short curled up on one side.

Compared to nearly every lady here, the dress was overdone and fussy. Compared to her mother, the Duchess of Rosehill... She may as well have been wearing a sensible cotton day dress and a matronly cap.

"How did I know I would find the two of you up here?" A familiar dark head called from down the hall. The pale-blue domino did little to hide his identity. That choice was almost certainly intentional.

Michael Wayland joined Kit and me at the railing, surveying his kingdom. Though he had abdicated the day-to-day running of the club a few years prior when he married, it still bore his mark in every way that mattered. And retirement hadn't made him a jot less rich.

A commotion arose at one of the high-stakes hazard tables, a few groans punctuated by the perfunctory claps of those who lost. A few feminine giggles carried over.

A lady had won a hefty sum, her dark curls bouncing with delight. Unlike some of the other ladies, she was not costumed, merely masked. She glanced about, searching for someone, before tipping her head up. Her eyes found Wayland's and she grinned—his wife.

In response, he tilted his drink, toasting her success. "Jules wouldn't let me play for coin tonight. Said it wouldn't be sporting. She'll probably take them for the lot and they'll thank her for the pleasure." A proud smile slipped over his face. He shook off the adoring admiration when his wife returned her attention to the table.

"You're not playing?" he asked, turning to lean his back against the rail.

"Will has no vices, you know that," Kit retorted.

"And you? You've got coin now."

"I'm not about to lose it all to your wife." Kit took a sip. "Or worse, my sister. Where is Kate anyway?"

"She probably snuck off to a closet with my brother." Wayland posited, taking a hearty sip of his own drink.

"Why would you say that?" Kit groaned.

"At least you've never found them in one." Wayland gave an exaggerated shudder.

"I thought we were here on your sister's orders." I reminded Kit. "If she is otherwise occupied with her husband, we can be off."

No sooner had I made the argument than one of the doors behind us opened and out popped the aforementioned Lord and Lady Grayson, slightly mussed and giggling like children.

Like her sister-in-law, Lady Grayson had forgone a costume in favor of a deep-red gown. In her hand was a gold mask with a rose and some other baubles attached to the side. Her husband had dressed to match in a red-and-gold brocade waistcoat.

"Damn," I muttered.

"Oh, Kit! What are you doing up here?" His sister questioned, smoothing a curl back into her coiffure.

"Needed air."

"You're an abysmal liar. Come, I have a lady I wish you to dance with." She grabbed his wrist and dragged him, still protesting, down the steps to the main floor.

"Does he know how to dance?" Lord Grayson asked, seemingly to himself.

I shrugged in response. He'd taken a few lessons at his sister's behest. Not enough to prevent his inevitable humiliation.

Grayson grinned as he leaned over the railing to watch his wife tow her brother about, pausing occasionally to rise on tiptoes to attempt to see over the crowd. Neither of the siblings were tall enough for that endeavor to be successful, but the attempt was amusing.

"How long before she has him wedded and bedded?" Wayland questioned his brother.

"Well, in spite of her desperate desire for a cousin for Henry to play with, she's a romantic. She'll spend years parading him around every lady of her acquaintance until he falls in love with one out of sheer desperation to end her matchmaking."

"Might have news on that front," Wayland answered. His tone was tentative, low.

"He's in love with someone?" Lord Grayson was not the brightest man I had ever met.

"Yes, obviously I know where your brother-in-law's romantic inclinations lie."

"Oh... Oh! But?"

"She hasn't told me yet."

I didn't often wish for something stronger than lemonade. Presented with the choice of continuing to stand idly beside what was clearly a private conversation and the option of facing the masses below, either would be more bearable with something alcoholic.

Determined to find a way out of this situation, I surveyed the crowd. Perhaps I should offer Kit a rescue. Lady Grayson was now determinedly dragging her brother to every eligible young lady, save the one I suspected he would have been pleased with. He was making a valiant effort to frown them away and it appeared to work on the less determined ones. But what was a frown compared to a title and fortune? Nothing, if the bosomy one in the golden poof of a dress before him was any indication.

In France, I had never left a man behind. The war would have been much shorter if it had been waged on the dance floor. I was more than prepared to abandon my friend to his fate. After all, I had been noted by one of our hosts. Surely I could retreat from the field without repercussions.

Using my vantage to scout for an exit, my eyes brushed across her petite form with disinterest. Just for a moment. Just for the single second it took for my head to catch up to my heart, to recognize the interested, heavy thump the organ gave.

I needed only a single breath to reorient to true north.

I was halfway down the steps before I realized I had moved. She had already found her place on the dance floor by the time I made it to the floor and the crowds parted. A little thing, she reached just to her partner's shoulders—though he was overly tall. She was lithe, graceful in her movements. Her smile was bright, teasing and overly familiar. Perhaps a brother? A husband? My stomach gave an instinctive wrench at that thought.

Her hair was pulled back from her face to twist down her neck like spun gold. It was not an entirely appropriate style and the sight of the loose waves felt... intimate. Her skin—a not insignificant amount on display—was a light golden shade, tanned, perhaps. My mind conjured a brief flash of her, head tipped back and eyes closed, allowing the sun to worship her. Her loose champagne waves would flow down her back, free as they brushed her shoulders in the breeze.

A laugh burst from her, throaty and sensual. What would that voice sound like, pressed against my ear, whispering the words of her pleasure?

My gaze was predatory, I knew that. But I could not have torn my eyes away for the world. My circuit around the dance floor was more of a prowl than a walk. The air was thinner now that I was closer to her, in her orbit. But not close enough.

I could not make out her eyes, not from behind her mask. It was a flimsy, lacy thing. What other flimsy, lacy things was she wearing?

Her gown was fine, finer than anything I'd ever worn, touched, seen. A mauve gauzy material overlay plum silk. It offset the golden kiss of her skin. All across the gown were tiny embroidered iridescent butterflies and flowers. Delicate little decorations to entice. Some had beads to catch the light and draw the eye. Others were textured in some mysterious way that ladies were taught to achieve and lords were taught to feign appreciation for. They were denser at the hem and up the center of the gown, growing sparser at her sides and bodice. She had no need for adornment there, nothing need distract from her face. She was shining, resplendent.

Another step, closer still, I could see a delicate metalwork butterfly on her mask as well. At last, her eyes slipped from her partner's to catch mine. They were a greenish color in the candlelight and framed by lashes a shade darker than her hair. They widened briefly with something I could not name. Interest? Alarm? Lust?

As quickly as it arrived, the expression was shuttered away, leaving behind a self-satisfied smile. She turned back to her partner.

Dismissed.

I was well used to being disregarded by the *ton*. This one stung, perhaps a bit more than usual, but it was nothing I could not manage. It served as a stark reminder of what she was; a pretty jewel, shiny and useless. Just like all the rest. If she shone a bit brighter, well, that was all the more dangerous. I was all too familiar with beautiful baubles. And I was not in a hurry to repeat the experience.

Freed from her entrancing presence, I searched the crowded floor for an escape. My past visits were confined to Wayland's or Ainsley's office. My comings and goings were always through the main entrance. Surely there was a back door though.

I stepped back, nearly tripping into an oversized skirt. Clearly some of these ladies had missed the panniers and hip pads because they'd made full use of them at the slightest of opportunities. I would have thought the slimmer silhouette currently in fashion would be more comfortable.

Finally, a few of them parted and I caught sight of a pair of French doors. Presumably—hopefully—they led outside.

After wrenching the doors open, I found myself on a lonely, rain-dampened stone balcony. Trapped. Trapped but at least free from the cacophony inside. And the mocking verdant eyes.

It was an uncharacteristically unkempt area of the club. Ainsley was nothing if not fastidious. But vines and flowering weeds had wound their way between and beneath the cobblestones, reclaiming the balcony for nature. In front of me was a stone balustrade overlooking an overgrown garden a few feet below. It was a more than acceptable perch for my elbows while I nursed my wounded pride.

As I contemplated the garden, weariness settled into my bones. Lord, I was tired. For a moment, I had felt like a young man again. The same giddy infatuation I'd felt the first time I saw Adriane had consumed me.

Now though, I remembered the aftermath, and I felt every one of my six and thirty years in my bones. I was a man grown. There was no reason to compose sonnets to every fancy bit of muslin I came across.

Now that I had looked away—blinked—I could see. She—the lady—wasn't nearly as breathtaking as my impulsive heart had insisted. She was short, with a slightly pushed-up nose. Her effect was a trick of the light, an illusion of fabric and thread and hairpins. She was nothing special.

None of them were anything special.

Behind me the raucous sounds of the gaming hell rose and fell with the door opening and closing. I made no effort to turn, hoping the intruder would reevaluate their choice of location.

The even-paced tap of shoes on the stones, the drag of a gown, assured me that the evening's luck remained precisely as unfortunate as it had been a few moments before.

The intruder stopped just a few feet behind me. She swallowed audibly and still I did not turn.

"You know, when a lady smiles at you, it is an invitation to ask for a set, not to run away."

Three

CELINE

THE DRAWING ROOM of Hasket House was redecorated annually. It also looked precisely as it had the first time I laid eyes on it more than a decade ago. The extravagant furnishings had changed, but the sharp angles and stark colors remained. My late husband's mother knew what she liked.

"Sit down, Xander. If you pace any more you'll wear out the carpets," Davina demanded. My sister-in-law loved to needle her elder brother, and it was never an easier task than before a ball.

"Technically, they're *my* carpets, Dav," he grumbled, reaching a hand to run it through his perfectly styled hair. He remembered himself inches from the coiffure and pulled his hand away. Behind his back, his sister let a frown slip.

"Do you suppose they'll play hazard tonight? I find myself in need of funds."

Xander's pacing ceased for a moment as he turned to stare incredulously at his sister. "Davina, you cannot—you must behave with decorum tonight. And these people will be playing for real coin. And what could you possibly need funds for? Your pin money is more than generous."

"What on earth else would they play for? And it is hardly your business." She crossed her arms petulantly over her chest, mussing the peacock feathers billowing from the embroidered bird across her bodice.

"Davina—" Xander's tone had jumped an octave, the way it always did when he had reached the end of his patience.

"Davina, darling, perhaps you might go see if your mother is in need of assistance?" She rolled her eyes at my suggestion but shoved herself off the settee without complaint.

In her absence, Xander collapsed across from me, head tipped back to stare at the ceiling. He took after his mother when it came to fabric selections, his black waistcoat, shirt, and cravat standing in contrast to the white damask of the settee.

"What has a bee in your bonnet?"

His head rolled to the side so he could eye me warily. "We're taking my mother and my sister to a gaming hell. To a masquerade, no less. Mother will certainly expose herself to ridicule, and Davina to ruin—and I shall be left with nothing but the scattered pieces of my dignity."

"Surely it will not be so bad as all that."

Xander shifted to sit up properly, though his posture remained relaxed. "You have, in fact, met my mother and sister, yes? Gabriel always made it a point to arrive far later than fashionable, merely so he would miss Mother's grand entrances. And that was before Davina was in society." He wasn't wrong about Gabriel, though that was hardly the only reason for his perpetual tardiness.

"It's a masquerade; a certain amount of pageantry is to be expected."

"Remember that sentiment when you see her," he retorted ominously.

"I've been warned. Is something else wrong? You seem…"

"Agitated?" he supplied.

"I was searching for a more tactful choice, but yes.

"I ran into Parker and Beaumont—at the club."

"Always an unpleasant state of affairs."

"There were some… insinuations bandied about." Xander's hands always danced in front of him when he spoke. But they were pinched and agitated now, held tight against his form.

"What did they say?"

"Nothing fit for a lady's ears."

"I was married to your brother. I've heard a great many things not fit for a lady's ears."

He sighed, looking at the floor. "There was an implication that I would be better able to secure a wife if I feasted on a lady's… flower the way I feast on a man's… well, you know. Then there was the generous offer to demonstrate the proper technique on Davina."

I could not have contained my gasp for the world. "Which one?"

"Does it matter? They may be the only ones brave enough to voice it, but they all think it."

"Of course it matters. At the very least, I shall spread some unflattering rumor. Perhaps something about pustules on the member."

That, at least, earned me a chuckle. "It was Beaumont. But you needn't spare Parker. He was too busy informing every man there that Lady Charlotte James is in too delicate a condition to bother with me."

"But the baron passed several months ago."

"Precisely. Parker insists that the babe is not his," he added, leaning in. Nothing was so diverting as truly scandalous gossip.

"Who else would have her? She is a shrew."

"Some might say the same of you." His lips twisted to one side in the familiar facsimile of a smile that was so unique to Xander.

"I may not be nice, but neither am I cruel. And why must you always defend her? It is one of my greatest reliefs that you did not wed her."

"She is—her life is not what it seems."

"I haven't the slightest idea what you mean by that."

Before he could explain, Davina slipped back into the drawing room pressing back against the wall. When my gaze returned to the doorway, I understood her desire for a wide berth. Her mother followed her into the drawing room. Or, rather, she attempted to follow her daughter into the drawing room.

It was difficult to say which was more impressive, the circumference of the skirts or the height of the wig. Despite both the wide entrance and high ceilings of the room, the skirts caught against the doorframe. Clementia backed up and turned side face to sidle into the room. As she did, the wig caught against a—fortunately unlit—chandelier.

Clearly having expected this inevitability, Xander rose with a sigh to extricate her. Davina leaned against the far wall, her shoulders shaking with silent laughter.

Once freed from her candelabra prison, I offered the duchess the sincerest compliment I could muster, which was that her ensemble would be the talk of the evening. Clementia may have taken the compliment with sincerity, but one look at Xander and Davina confirmed that they perfectly understood my meaning.

A few more strategic complements had us out the door, masks in hand, and to the carriage only for all of us to simultaneously recognize the necessity of a second.

Eventually our party split, Davina and me in one, and

Xander and his mother in the other. We were on our way and only three-quarters of an hour later than originally intended.

MUCH AS I hadn't particularly wanted to attend tonight, I was enjoying myself.

That had often been the case since Gabriel left me. I never wanted to put forth the effort to ready myself for society. The thought of stomaching the peculiarities and absurdities of the *ton* was exhausting. But I was a social creature by nature.

The beau monde was out in full force tonight. Gentle ladies were delighted to see inside the notorious gaming hell where their husbands made and lost fortunes.

No explicit rule prevented ladies from attending. But it simply wasn't done. Oh, the occasional widow like myself, and more frequently women in the profession made an appearance, but tonight was something different.

The excitement was palpable and the ensembles more than rose to the occasion. The hostesses, Lady Juliet* and Mrs. Ainsley, had done a lovely job turning the club into a ballroom. Somehow they had managed to make it appear as the room's intended purpose instead of debauchery.

The tables ringed the room, with a dance floor placed in the center. A side table served as home to numerous delicacies, courtesy of Mrs. Ainsley. Tarts, pies, and fairy cakes towered atop it, each more delectable than the last.

I dipped that way, hoping to nab one of the cheese tarts before they were all gone. Finding my preferred treat among

---

* As an earl's daughter, Juliet retains her title even after her marriage to a commoner. She can be Lady Juliet or Lady Juliet Wayland. She cannot be Lady Wayland because that implies her husband is Lord Wayland, which Michael is not.

the other delicacies proved to be a greater challenge than I'd anticipated. I was inspecting the selection when a warm form appeared at my side, holding a glass out for me.

I turned to meet familiar dark eyes and a crooked grin. "Celine," Micheal whispered in a honeyed tone, a pale-blue domino doing little to conceal his identity. "Good of you to come."

"Michael Wayland hosting a ball. I would have thought the sun would cease to rise first. I would not have missed this." I took a sip from the proffered drink, finding my favorite scotch. I didn't often choose such masculine indulgences, but when in Rome.

"*Host* is a strong word. Acceding to my wife's demands might be a more apt description." He shifted on his heels at the mention of his wife, a proud sort of maneuver.

"As you should. She has made only improvements."

"I will tell her you said as much." He turned his gaze on the feast beside us, pointing at a tart. "Those are the cheese ones. I assume you still favor them?"

I snagged the referenced tart and bit into the delicate pastry filled with warm, rich, buttery brie and groaned.

Michael chuckled beside me. "In two years, I don't believe I ever managed to drag such a sound from you."

"It does not speak well to your skills in the boudoir, does it?"

"Or does it speak quite well of the tart?" he countered.

"Perhaps both."

He shrugged before selecting a different tart, devouring it in three short bites. Dark eyes flitted back to mine. "Have you made your way to the tables? I'm certain if you merely flutter your eyelashes, you could bankrupt half the men here."

"Only half? I must be losing my touch."

"My wife is bankrupting the other half at present." His gaze flitted toward one of the higher stakes tables where a young woman draped in embroidered blue silk that matched his mask confidently rolled the dice with a graceful flourish. Her dark curls were gathered elegantly at the nape of her neck. Lady Juliet Wayland.

When I turned back to Michael, his expression could only be termed one of awe. Besotted suited him. Love for his wife had smoothed some of the sharper edges he wore during our time together.

"You've taught her well."

"She is... remarkable." His tone was wistful, and his gaze hadn't once left her statuesque form.

"I am pleased for you."

He turned back to me. "I never thanked you. For encouraging me her way."

"One encounter and you were smitten. Anyone with eyes could see you were hers."

"Yes, well..." He dragged a hand through messy waves, his gaze flicking to the side before meeting mine. "I am still grateful. I know we are not... close, the way we used to be. But we were friends of a sort. I like to think we are still."

"Of course."

"Excellent. Then you will take it in the spirit intended when I draw your attention to your mother-in-law and leave you to disentangle her from the railing." He gestured to the staircase wrapping the room where Her Grace's wig was caught in the banister.

"*Merde*," I muttered. "I lied. We are friends no longer."

"A tragedy I shall be forced to bear," he retorted, backing away up the stairs, studiously avoiding eye contact with the duchess.

I found my way to her side with a barely suppressed sigh. "May I be of some assistance, Your Grace?"

"I am unsure, darling. Are you able to reach?"

It was a fair question; she was a full hand taller than me

without the wig. With it... Fortunately, she was trapped in the stairs and not the chandelier again. I climbed the steps, refusing to acknowledge curious gazes while I unhooked her.

Once freed, I began the laborious process of guiding her to the ladies' retiring room, ignoring the snickers that followed.

I left my mother-in-law in the hands of a haggard ladies' maid and returned to the ballroom before I could be expected to unhook her from anything else. The wall was particularly appealing in that moment. I was not a wallflower by any definition, but even I could only manage so much shame without reprieve.

Couples had found their way to the makeshift dance floor, laughing through the ends of a lively jig. That had never been my preferred dance, but the sight pulled a smile to my lips.

Movement beside me drew my attention. An unbearably tall blond man had sidled up to me in silence.

"If I remember correctly, a woman as graceful as you belongs on the dance floor. Not along the wall." His mask, black with gold detailing, covered the entire right side of his face as he peered down at me. The other half was bare and familiar.

"Lord Champaign, it has been an age!"

"Best part of a decade. We last spoke on the eve of your engagement, I believe. I am sorry for your loss."

The memory of that night, the night I made Gabriel mine, always left a confusing swirl of lust, love, and sorrow in my heart.

But he was right. I had not seen Lord Champaign after that night on the terrace where he caught me in Gabriel's arms.

"I heard you suffered a similar loss. I am sorry for you as well."

I could not recall his late wife's name. But, if memory served, she died around the same time Gabriel had. I was far too lost to my own grief to send appropriate condolences at the time, and I regretted it now.

"Thank you. Would you care for a dance?"

"I would be delighted." He swept me in his arms, every bit as strong and graceful as he had been when we first danced a lifetime ago.

"You seem to have misplaced your accent," he commented.

"Just for tonight. I think it adds to the mystery."

"Oh yes, I'm certain there are two, perhaps three people in this room who do not know you on sight. Even in the mask."

"Four at least. Do give me credit."

"I'll be generous and give you a half dozen. How have you been?"

That was a question. I went to dances, parties, luncheons, and concerts. I read and practiced with my sword. I chaperoned Davina. I played cards with Mama and our friend Marie.

And several times a week I sat against a cold headstone and spoke to my dead husband.

"It wasn't meant to be a trick," he added, his fingers tightening gently on my waist. There was nothing sensual about it. It was merely a comfort offered from a widower to a widow.

"No, I know. I just wasn't... I wasn't sure which answer you wanted."

"Whichever one you want to give me is more than fine."

I sighed, parsing out an answer somewhere in the vicinity of the truth. "I am well enough. Most days, I am all right. Some days I'm fine, marvelous even. Other days..." I cannot breathe. "Well, you know..."

"I do."

"And you?"

"The same. More or less. Mia—Amelia—and I, we were good together."

"I cannot imagine you being anything else. I should have told you—I always meant to tell you—it was never about you that night. I— Gabriel was... all-consuming. You were—*are*— a wonderful man. I never doubted that you would make a good husband. It was just..."

"I never thought that, but I appreciate it all the same," he assured me.

As Lord Champaign and I slowly turned on the floor, my eyes met a sharp blue gaze across the room—cobalt, royal, azure, sapphire, the bluest of blue eyes.

They were half hidden behind a black scrap of fabric knotted behind the man's head in a lazy facsimile of a mask.

His expression was one of interest. Or perhaps something more intense. It was a headier gaze than those I was used to receiving from men. Ice spread through my veins, cool and drugging. I offered him an enticing smile, hoping to summon him to my side.

In the days before Gabriel, I'd made a game of that. Drawing men to me only to dismiss them moments later when they became tedious.

Instead of crossing the floor at my invitation, rather than grabbing me in his arms and whisking me into a waltz, he scowled.

A man scowled at me.

My eyes trailed him from my position on the dance floor. He stalked around the hell. The man wasn't overly tall, perhaps a hand taller than me, but no more. He was compactly muscled and his movements were confident, purposeful, and irritated. I followed him all the way out to the balcony before he closed the French doors behind him. Shutting me out.

As the last strains of the song drew to a close, I turned my gaze back to the man who held me in his arms. There was something amused in the way he held the corner of his mouth.

"Enjoy yourself tonight, Lady Rycliffe. I think it's time for both of us to live a little," Lord Champaign dipped his head respectfully.

"Thank you," I whispered as he backed away, disappearing into the shadows. Spinning on my heels, I strode toward the French doors the gentleman had slipped through.

I slipped out before pressing the door closed behind me. When I turned to face him, his back was toward me as he leaned against the rail of the balcony overlooking the garden. The muscles of his shoulders coiled tighter, rising as I took first one step, then another onto the balcony.

I paused just a few feet behind him. My mouth suddenly dry, I swallowed harshly.

"You know, when a lady smiles at you, it is an invitation to ask for a set, not to run away."

He spun slowly on his heel, wrapped in shadows and moonlight.

Oh my.

Four

WILLIAM

I SPUN SLOWLY, certain I would be faced with a phantom. It would be some other lady behind me. Or, if it was her, she would not be nearly as enchanting up close.

I was wrong.

The light that spilled from inside the hell through gauzy curtains was minimal, but the moon was full and the clouds had parted after an earlier rain. It was more than sufficient to see, even without my spectacles.

Every attempt to convince myself that her beauty was a lie had been a pitiful exercise. She was breathtaking. She stood before me, her hands clasped in front of her gown. A gift wrapped in the finest of silks, her gilded mask the bow on top.

She called herself a lady and that was evident in her carriage and gown. Not just anyone could afford fabrics that fine nor the pins scattered in her hair topped with glittering stones that caught the light.

A frown graced her face once again. It was a sharp

reminder that I'd been staring, awestruck and silent, for far too long.

I exhaled, breathing a minuscule bit of my anxiety into the night. And then I replied, praying it would be the least bit sensible. "I'll make a note. Smiles for a set. What does it mean when a lady follows you onto an abandoned balcony?"

An unexpected laugh burst from her. Her hand found her chest, where she traced a glinting chain that dipped beneath the bodice of her gown.

"In my experience, it means she intends to seduce you," she retorted, her voice was full, midrange and sensual.

She was a forward one. There were no unintelligible riddles to decipher here. I feigned a casual air, leaning back against the rail. My success was debatable, but at least she did not laugh outright. "And in this instance?"

Her slippered feet were tiny when they took a step forward. With another, she positioned herself beside me. She braced herself on the balustrade with her forearms, preserving her gown. Her forearms were bare.

Now close enough to touch, her scent enveloped me. A warm, spiced vanilla overpowered the suddenly cloying cacophony of flowers below.

"Perhaps a conversation? A set? I hadn't intended a seduction." She turned her head toward me, capturing my gaze.

Now that I could see clearly, I was certain. This was no debutante; she was a woman grown.

Amusement crinkled at the corners of her eyes, barely visible at the edges of her mask. But those lines were a worn and familiar track across her skin.

"Tragedy," I replied boldly. My heart tripped when my head caught up with my mouth. But what good was a masquerade if I couldn't be someone different tonight? Someone better, braver. Someone worthy of such a lady's flirtation.

Her shoulder brushed against mine in a motion that could only have been deliberate.

"I haven't ruled it out entirely," she teased, a smile crossing her lips.

I raised a brow in deliberate interest. Of course, I had no way of knowing how effective the effort was with the mask.

"You do not attend these events often," she added, moving to slightly safer topics.

"No, not if I can help it."

"What happened tonight?"

"The devil's schemes. It's the only explanation." That earned me a smile and another shoulder bump.

I considered for a moment, before deciding to get the next bit out of the way so she could be off. Then I could nurse my disappointment in silence.

"Wayland and Ainsley are clients of mine. It's good for business. And my friend's sister is dragging him about to every single lady within until one agrees to wed him. I'm moral support, I suppose."

"A tradesman? I am intrigued. What do you do?" Her gaze was thoughtful as she eyed me.

"Really?" I asked, incredulity seeping into my tone. "I expected that to send you running back inside."

"You did not answer my question. And I'm still here." Low and provocative, her voice was so different from the childlike ramblings of *her*.

This lady's accent was slightly stiff, formal, as if it were an affectation. *Interesting*.

"Isn't that the point of a masquerade? The mystery."

"Evasive," she pointed out. "Not my favorite quality in a man. Still, I'll allow it. Until midnight." The scold was brief, airy, and there was no heat behind it.

"I'm an open book. What do you wish to know?"

"Your occupation, sir."

"Your guess, first," I retorted.

She straightened, half turning to face me. Her gaze dipped to begin at my toes before sliding up my legs, then to my waist. There was a tightening in my breeches due entirely to her scrutiny and I could only pray it wasn't evident in the dim light.

Her preoccupation was an opportunity to study her as well. She was thin but her arms and shoulders were muscular. She carried herself with strength too. Clearly she had other interests outside of those usually afforded to ladies.

She was as small as I'd thought, and I had a few inches on her.

Light spilled through the doors and window catching in her curls. Up close, I noted the gold strands were tamed with amethyst pins. Swirls of honey, caramel, sand, and ice, mixed to form golden, champagne ribbons.

The skin of her neck and chest looked velvety soft and my fingers itched to brush across it.

Her lower lip was just slightly fuller than the upper and it was quirked in a half smile. And her eyes awaited mine. They were more olive for the dim lighting.

She was amused. That was clear from her expression and I felt the blush forming, but there was nothing to be done for it. Besides, she ogled me first.

"Solicitor."

My brow lifted of its own volition, impressed. "I must know how you found me out."

"A lady must have her secrets, sir."

"What if I guess one of yours?"

"Be my guest. Only your best shot, of course." She could not possibly suspect my military service. Not from just this.

The desire to impress her welled within me. She had danced with at least two gentlemen, so she was likely unwed. Her countenance was lived in. She was no newly presented debutant. That left her as an independently wealthy lady or a widow of means. While I was generally socially inept, even I knew not to mention deceased husbands when flirting.

"Do you acquiesce?" She questioned, offering me my answer. Something about the way her lips pursed forming the word...

"You're French."

"Remarkable," she confirmed.

"How did you know my profession?"

She smirked, mischievous behind her mask. "I hope you will not consider it outside the bounds of gameplay. You mentioned your friend's sister was dragging him about, matchmaking. That could be none other than Lady Grayson. The matchmaker is always my dearest Kate. Which made your friend her brother, Lord Leighton, whom I know to be a solicitor. While I had already supposed solicitor, I also noticed that you have ink in your nail beds. It was a safe guess."

"We never established rules. I am impressed."

"Was the way I said *acquiesce* what gave me away?" she asked.

"It was. And your accent, there is something forced about it."

"That is a disappointment. I thought it was quite natural."

"I have one for you. If Lady Grayson is always matchmaking, why is she not trying to match *you*?"

I earned a half-hearted chuckle. "Oh, she has tried. Though, I suspect she has washed her hands of me."

"Why is that?" I had missed the slight stiffening with my last question, but now she turned statue-like beside me—her smile nowhere to be found.

"Are you trying to determine what, precisely, is wrong with me?"

I bit back a curse. How had I managed to butcher this? "No! Of course not. I was, rather clumsily, trying to determine your marital status."

"I see..." She drew the word out, long and slow. "What were you intending to do with that information? Once you had gathered it?"

"Probably find a different manner in which to bungle this."

She huffed a single chuckle. "I have no present attachments you need be concerned with."

That was very precise language.

"Do you, sir? That is, do you have any attachments at present?"

Sallow, impossibly pale skin, charcoal hair, and sunken eyes, the clearest of blue, flitted through my mind. It was strange. I had thought of her more this evening than I had in months. My instinct was a decisive yes, but... Was it ever really an attachment? And if it was... it had been seven years.

"The question was not meant to be a trick," she added.

"No, I have no attachments."

"Are you certain? The answer required a great deal of consideration."

"I have never been wed," I assured her.

Her eyes narrowed behind the mask, studying me, testing the truth of my statement. Perhaps she parsed my own overly exacting language. She returned to her perch against the railing, this time leaning her back against it, risking the delicate fabric of her gown.

"I see. No attachments for either of us. I ask again, what did you intend to do with that information once gleaned?" Her bare hand settled against the railing. Her littlest finger an inch, maybe less, from my own. My skin hummed with interest at her proximity.

"I don't... I hadn't considered that far." Jade eyes bored into the side of my head. The flush was sliding down my neck now. She straightened abruptly.

How had I ruined it this time?

"You're shy!"

"What? No!" I protested.

"No, you are. That is delightful." Even though it was at my expense, her grin was infectious. "You were all right at first, when you were peeved with me. And when we were playing our game. But now that you've established that I'm flirting with you..."

"Are you?" I asked before I could think better of it.

"Am I what?"

"Flirting with me?"

"You cannot tell? I am losing my touch. I suppose I should make it more obvious then." Her hand slid atop mine. Soft, gentle fingers slotted between my own, pressing us both into the rail below.

My stomach gave a pleased flip.

There was something lovely about the sight of her small, well-manicured fingers separated by my blunt ones. My nail beds were perpetually stained with ink, and they stood in contrast with her immaculate ones.

Summoning my bravery, I asked, "What else is involved? With the flirting? I want to be sure to do it properly."

It occurred to me in that moment that I'd never really bothered with flirting. When I met *her*, I was too young, too naive, and too much of a dolt to attempt it. And when I found *her* again... well, there was no point in flirting.

It wasn't even an atrophied muscle, my attempted flirtation; it was one I'd never used at all. For the first time I wished I had exercised it.

"That was an excellent start," she offered. "I am especially vain and susceptible to compliments. Perhaps you should try there."

"Oh, but I should like to tread new ground. You are so lovely, I doubt there is a compliment in existence that you have not received already." The praise spilled out so easily, so naturally, that it required no thought at all.

"Well done, you!"

I had intended it as fact, not flirtation, but she was pleased with my success.

"I appreciate the effort. Shall I speak plainly and stop this torturous assignment?"

"Yes, please."

Her laugh was genuine and unaffected. "Very well. I hope you do not think too poorly of me after I have finished. Where to begin... I am a widow, one who has been more than two years without a... companion. Tonight, I am feeling especially lonesome. You are particularly handsome. And there's something about a masquerade... So, if you'd like, I can return inside, leave you to your hedgerow skulk—"

"Don't!"

She smiled, satisfied with my outburst. "We could also continue our lessons in the art of flirtation. Or—and this is my preference—we can determine if our interest is mutual and something more than intellectual."

She could not possibly mean...

"It is. Mutual I mean." She pressed herself off the railing, leaving my hand bereft of her warmth.

I did not have long to mourn its absence before that same hand cupped my jaw, drawing me down to her.

"Well then. I suppose all that is left is to see if this is a purely scholarly attraction."

The hand cupping my jaw held me steady as she shifted to her toes. Too afraid to move, to shatter this illusion, I waited as she closed the distance. My eyes fluttered shut as her impossibly soft lips met mine. Pressing once, twice before she tilted my jaw to suit her needs and settled into the kiss with the quietest of moans.

Blood rushed through my ears, throbbing with my

pounding heart. A second, perhaps two passed without comprehension. Then the reality of the situation came into sharp focus. The most beautiful woman I had ever seen was kissing me.

And I was disappointing her.

Frantic to prove myself, my hand moved to her waist of its own volition and instinct took over. My free hand found the back of her neck, pulling her closer. Not close enough. The one on her waist tugged too.

Finally, I had all of her, every beautiful inch, pressed against me. Soft curves found a home, purchase, against my chest. Lips parted, breath mingled, and tongues danced, and I wanted *more*. More of this. More of her.

More of everything.

Five

CELINE

I HAD NEVER BEEN DEVOURED before, kissed with the single-minded determination this man possessed. He kissed with his whole body, with his entire soul.

It was nothing like the simple press of lips I had intended. I had never, ever been so thrilled to be wrong. There was a clumsy eagerness to his movements that revealed his inexperience, but I could not bring myself to care. The lack of finesse was charming, flattering, arousing. What could this man do with a bed and a direction or two?

Gabriel had always kissed me with intent. He had a purpose to make me feel loved, desired, teased, desperate for him. I adored every single kiss. Even now, I guarded their memory like precious gems, taking them out one by one to admire as needed.

Everything about this was different, but it was every bit as wonderful. He was completely out of control, wrecked. This kiss stole my breath and refused to return it. That was all right, I had no need of it.

Distracted by his raw, unpracticed passion, my hand slipped from his impossibly sharp cheekbone, hidden from sight but not touch by his mask. I traced down his neck to press against his chest, above his pounding heart. And oh, what a chest. Those middling fabrics hid defined, taut muscles. Muscles that flexed and pulled against my hands as he worshiped me with his hands, with his lips.

How was it possible that a man who looked like *that* and kissed like *this*, was unwed, unattached, seemingly unwanted?

My feet protested the extended time on my toes and I dropped down to the ground. He followed for a moment, seemingly content to kiss me forever, before pulling back slightly. His shocking blue eyes met mine, searching for permission to continue. Oh, he had it, just as soon as my heart returned to a reasonable tempo.

"I think it's safe to say there is a physical attraction as well." My smile was weak but only because my head was too flustered to ensure cooperation of my muscles. "Slow down a moment, I need to catch my breath. You need to catch your breath."

His answering smile was sheepish, and I could make out the hint of a flush slipping down his neck. The boyish eagerness and reaction belied his countenance.

He was my age, perhaps a few years older if I could judge by the few gray strands peppering his ash finger-tousled curls. His lower lip was full and reddened by my attentions, the upper nearly nonexistent.

His eyes still captivated. His pupils were blown with the effects of our tryst. But he stared at me with something akin to awe. The shade had something of the midnight sky on a night when the moon was more of a suggestion than a presence.

No one had ever looked at me with such an expression of reverence, of naked wonderment. The sensation was heady. I could become addicted. Something about those eyes, that expression...

A spark of familiarity flashed. It nearly took flight before fizzling out when he determined that we'd enjoyed more than enough breathing and crashed his lips to mine once again.

He was more confident this time. He took charge, chasing the sensations he wanted, and oh, it was incredible. I had not felt like this, this aching need forming inside me from a mere kiss since perhaps that first.

Since Gabriel.

I brushed aside the thought of my late husband in favor of tangling my fingers in soft curls.

Somehow, without my notice, he managed to press me back against the stone balustrade of the balcony. The soft perfume of hyacinths below wrapped around us, mixed with his herbal, woody scent in a way that should have been discordant but instead balanced into something enticing.

In spite of his seeming desire to devour me, his hands remained respectfully on my waist, and my jaw. Only occasionally did they slip to my neck. He had taken care with my coiffure and gown.

The part of me that was equally desperate for him wanted them higher, lower, anywhere less appropriate and more thrilling. But the minuscule pieces of my heart and head still processing anything beyond sensation gave a pleased flip at the care he was displaying. The deference he offered, even half lost to passion, was sweet.

It was a wonder we had not been interrupted. Between his infrequent, gasping breaths, and my unrestrained moans, we weren't quiet. The curtains covering the French doors could not possibly be sufficient to conceal the silhouette of our tangled forms. But I couldn't bring myself to care overmuch.

My fingers fisted in his hair in response to the nip he gave my lower lip. It was the only distraction I could offer them.

They itched to untie his cravat, shove his overcoat off those muscular shoulders and strip him bare before me.

Voices from inside rose in unison, penetrating our sanctuary, ripping his lips from mine.

"Ten, nine, eight..." *Midnight. The unmasking.*

The realization that I was having this revelation with a nameless stranger ought to be shameful. I was too wrecked for such thoughts, though.

Navy eyes sought mine, seeking guidance, permission.

Offering a half-hearted shrug, my fingers found the fabric knotted on the back of his head. The ends were tangled in the curls I had thoroughly mussed in my enthusiasm.

In response, his hands found the ribbon holding on my mask.

"Three, two, one!"

Two simple tugs, one each from each of us.

That was all it took to douse the flames, to fill my veins with ice and crush my heart in a single punishing grip.

It took him longer, ten seconds, perhaps fifteen, for realization to set in, for the ecstatic wonder to fade with recognition.

I was face to face with the man who murdered my husband.

# Six

WILLIAM

THE HIGHER A MAN ROSE, the farther he fell. But what happened when he nearly touched heaven and had to come back down?

Probably something like this, this crushing, aching revulsion that overwhelmed me, slipping through my veins like ice. It wasn't sorrow. Nor was it a tender melancholy for the possibility of tomorrow, a tomorrow that tempted me in a way I hadn't known before. Though that pitiful dream lay smashed at my feet.

It was disgust. Pure and simple disgust.

Her name escaped me, even as I stared at her wide, aghast eyes.

I had been distracted the only time we spoke, a lifetime ago. More important things occupied my head that day. Matters of life and death were more essential than the name of the slip of a girl in breeches who scolded me in an abhorrent accent.

She was *his* wife?

That much I remembered with absolute certainty. This captivating creature before me, the one whose hand had found her kiss-swollen mouth with shock. Her fingers caught there on her lower lip.

She was that bastard's wife.

Her unfairly beautiful eyes were filled with disgust and loathing. Mine almost certainly reflected something similar.

Without a word, she turned. She ripped both the doors open and disappeared into the discord inside. Silken butterflies and embroidered flower petals chased her, trailing in her wake.

Her delicate golden mask remained clutched tightly in my grasp.

~

EIGHT YEARS earlier - Yorkshire

"Mr. Hart! Mr. Hart!" Every bleeding time I sat down she started squawking.

"What is it, Mrs. Talbot?" She rushed through the doorway, all flushed, ruddy cheeks and cotton skirts.

Breathing heavily, one hand pressed to her ample bosom, the other supporting her against the doorframe, she panted, "She's missin', sir! Miss Adriane, she's missin',"

The first time, I had managed to temper my reaction.

The second had been a struggle.

But when she fell into a chill after the third time and couldn't rise from bed for a week, my patience had abandoned me.

"Damn it all! Not again. I pay you to watch her when I'm not able to!"

"I can't make her do nothin'," the woman protested. "There aren't enough pounds in the whole country to pay me to sit there when she's bein' all unnerving like."

"That's exactly what I pay you—generously, I might add —to do. If you cannot, I will find someone who can. Have you checked the kitchens?" A frustrated hand tugged through my unruly curls.

"Humph."

Oh, bleeding hell. I did not have time for a sulk. I tossed my spectacles onto the desk, onto the law book I had been attempting to read. Pinching the bridge of my nose, I steeled myself for the coming megrim.

"I'm sorry, Mrs. Talbot. I did not mean to imply that you were replaceable. You're far too important for us to live without you. You know how I worry about Miss Adriane. Have you had the opportunity to check the kitchens? I would not wish her to burn herself."

"She was layin' on the table that way she does when she's bein' vexin'. Talkin' 'bout the darkness and the worms and the stars again. Actin' like a child even though she's a woman grown. An' I told her she wasn't to talk like that no more, but she wouldn't have it. So I said, I don't have to listen to this no more, an' I went to the drawing room. Just for a minute so's she'd stop. But I came back and she weren't there no more. And the door was wide open, so I came to find you."

The speech was delivered in one breath and poorly enunciated, so it took a moment to glean the most important bit of her story.

"Which door was wide open?"

"The front one. Why would I be tellin' you about it if it weren't the front door?"

The front...

Before I finished the thought, I was up and shoving past Mrs. Talbot whose only moment of good sense the entire day had been to get out of my way.

The offending door swung on its hinges in the cool breeze as I raced past, grabbing my scabbard by the door while calling for Adriane. In my panic, I somehow managed to spot a bare footprint in the frost-covered mud.

Toward Rose Hall.

Were I thinking more clearly, I could have reached that conclusion on my own. She was always trying to go that way. She wanted to see *him*. Convinced that one look at her and he would fall to his knees, beg forgiveness, and wed her instantly. As though he hadn't scoffed at that very notion years before. As though he hadn't thrown her away with the rubbish and left her to the wolves.

My heart pounded and my lungs rejected the cold, damp air. Belting the sword to my waist while running was more of a challenge than I had anticipated and I slipped in the muck.

"Adriane!" Again and again, I shouted for her. Enough times that I began to despair of ever finding her.

"Here!" A throaty feminine voice called out. Not Adriane —but someone. And thank Christ that someone wasn't *him*. I crashed through a row of overgrown hedges, desperately trying to drag air to my lungs.

And there she was, still pallid and wraithlike on a bench in the clearing. Barefoot in her nightdress, her hem covered in several inches of mud. But she was alive and whole and as lovely as the first time I saw her.

"Adriane! You should not be out, sweetling." She gave one of her pained tremulous moans, clutching at her head.

My knees gave out just before her. I caught her hands in mine, pressing a kiss to my designated place on her temple. "How did you get so far? You must be chilled."

Now that I had found her more or less safe, I recognized the cool, late-winter morning seeping into my shirtsleeves and breeches. Her paper-thin nightdress was surely no protection.

"I wanted to greet the sunshine." Not the celestials again... I wouldn't have to fire Mrs. Talbot, she would quit. The sun and the moon and the stars always left Adriane rattled. That talk brought out the worst of the disquieting tones of her voice and the swaying motions that made the older woman uneasy.

"Of course. But you know I worry. Perhaps we can meet the sun on the veranda tomorrow?" I offered, pressing a silky curl behind her ear.

Lord, her hair was lovely. No matter how sick she got, it never lost its sheen. It fell in a black gossamer curtain around her shoulders.

"The sun won't come out tomorrow."

Her eyes were the clear blue of ice and her tendency to stare from under lidded lashes unnerved even me on occasion.

"Your sun would not dare hide. Not if you wished to see it. I won't allow it." I had no such power, but in her less lucid moments she sometimes forgot that no one could control the figments of her twisted imagination, not even me.

"Pardon me..." A small voice called from behind me.

I finally recalled the feminine voice from earlier. Bone-deep exhaustion had set in while I soothed Adriane and standing was a trial.

She was a pretty thing, all blonde hair and green eyes. Her Grace had never hired girls so lovely when I had been invited to the house. She had probably been worried about what her son would do to them.

"You're a new one," I quipped.

"I beg your pardon?" she asked. Her accent was vaguely French. Where in France she was pretending to be from was anyone's guess. The London cadence was there, hovering just underneath, begging to be freed from its indistinctly Parisian prison. I could no sooner restrain the resultant eye roll than I could stop the sun from setting.

"Oh, good Lord. Does Her Grace pay you extra to fake the accent?"

"Excuse me?"

"*C'est probablement le pire accent que j'aie jamais entendu.*" My French was impeccable, accent included. Nearly five years on the continent fighting Napoleon had done that. I would eat my hat if she understood even half of what I said.

"*Peut-être n'avez-vous jamais parlé à une française.*"

Fortunately, I wasn't wearing a hat and therefore wouldn't have to eat it. In the language itself, she was slightly better, but the accent was still heavily English.

I was so distracted by it, I had failed to note the breeches she was wearing. That was particularly absurd.

"I've spoken to plenty of Frenchwomen. In France. Where I was stationed. Perhaps you should speak to one. Your French is worse than your accent," I lied. "And the breeches? Is that some ridiculous fashion plate told Her Grace was in style?"

"I am not a servant! I am Lady Celine Hasket, Marquise of Rycliffe, and you will speak to me with the respect I am due."

Instantly, my spine hardened to steel. Adriane was still on the bench, no worse than she had been this morning. Instinctively, my hand fell to the hilt of my sword as I scanned for Gabriel.

When had he married? Why had he married? And this bit of muslin? How had he entered the country without my knowledge?

"Where is he?" I bit out.

"Who?"

"Hasket! Where is he?"

Behind me, Adriane let out a trill of the blackguard's name. My stomach sank, even as I surveyed the landscape for the rake.

"London," Lady what's-her-name answered in a choked whisper.

London, days away. There may still be time to pack up. Time to get away before he returned and nothing in the world could keep Adriane from him. The weather had been warm for March, but wet. Roads would be slower for mud.

"How long?"

"A few more days, perhaps a week."

Time, enough time. Which direction? North, perhaps? He was unlikely to go north. But London would be easier to find work. Perhaps if he never learned of our presence and Adriane never learned of his...

"You never saw us. Do you understand?" Our gazes met as I willed her to understand the seriousness of my direction.

I shouldn't leave her here. It was too risky... But she had helped Adriane. Perhaps she did not know. Perhaps she was a prisoner in her marriage, only throwing his name about when she was frightened.

I turned back to Adriane, urging her to stand. She let out another wordless cry but permitted me to fold her in my arms and carry her back to the house. Later she would fight, desperate to see her beloved Gabriel. But for those few minutes, her frail form wrapped in my arms, I could pretend I was the one she wanted.

As I stood there alone on the balcony, reliving one of my worst memories in a sea that ranged from bad to hellish, the heavens decided to increase my misery. They erupted.

Within moments, I was soaked through to my skin. The idea of returning to the ballroom was made even more unpalatable than it had been seconds before.

The garden below was not so terribly far—a foot, perhaps two. The balcony was more to deter patrons from doing precisely what I was contemplating. Not allowing any further time for consideration, I hoisted myself up and over the railing. Landing on too-old knees, I crushed a few of the fragrant purple flowers beneath my feet.

I had undercharged Ainsley and Wayland when they first opened because I liked them. They could repay me by not hassling me about the flowers.

Free from the trappings of the masquerade, I made my way quickly through the London night. The streets had emptied in the downpour. At last, I made it back to the little apartment above my office.

With a reverence it did not deserve, I set the petite gold mask on the dining table before flinging my wet things into a corner to deal with on the morrow.

Too tired, and too distracted, I didn't bother to dress for bed or close the curtains. Instead, I flopped on the mattress in a thoroughly undignified manner. Then, I memorized the ceiling.

I could just make out a few little rainbows swirling there on the shadowed plaster. It was an effect of carriages driving past the lamps that poured through my uncovered window. They illuminated the farthest corner the same way the sun usually did at dawn.

And then I understood what Adriane had spent all those years babbling on about—the sun, moon, stars, and the play of the light.

I fell asleep trying to determine whether that thought was comforting or entirely horrifying.

Consciousness left me before I could make a decision.

Seven

CADIEUX HOUSE, LONDON - JUNE 6, 1816

CELINE

THE SERVANTS WOULD WAKE SOON. I needed to set my study to rights before that happened. I needed to change out of my gown. I needed to stand, to move off the hard wood floor. I needed to do anything but stare at the old slip of parchment.

> *Hyde Park, 6:30*
> *-W*

There were months before I could bring myself to enter Gabriel's study at Rycliffe Place. In the end, it was only after the late duke decreed that his heir, Xander, would have his rightful bachelor lodgings that I left. Only then had I abandoned the house Gabriel and I built a life in. That had been a blessing, in the end.

At the time, it felt like a death sentence. Pack up or abandon every beautiful memory I had with the love of my life. It was not a simple undertaking, nor an easy one. And one of the unpleasant tasks had been haphazardly stuffing every remotely incriminating document into a trunk to be moved to Cadieux House.

For all his faults, Gabriel had been a loving brother. He would not have wanted Xander to know of his more disreputable dealings. And so it fell to me to hide the evidence.

For nearly a year, my husband's documents yellowed in three trunks. They resided in the corner of my makeshift study gathering dust for the maid to whisk away every week or so.

I had a great many trunks of Gabriel's belongings. Some were easier to open than others. Some had not been touched in seven years.

To this day, I could not explain what possessed me to crack open the trunks that day, thirteen months after he left me. But that was the day I found the note.

That was the day I remembered the missing piece.

At first, all I could do was relive his final moments. All of the things I'd needed to say but could not manage to choke out. The inane thoughts of those moments haunted me—that I hadn't felt him leave our bed that morning. The beautiful words I desperately wanted him to leave with, the ones I was too distraught to verbalize. The way his handsome face had been obscured by a veil of tears. And I could remember every single one of his last heartbeats.

But Gabriel's last day had been full of laughter and love. We had enjoyed a morning luxuriating in bed, an afternoon of teasing at the races, an evening spinning around the dance floor, and a night spent in worship and being worshiped.

Later, I recalled the desperate nature with which he clung to me that final night. He had been insatiable, frenzied, and adoring. Reverent hands cupped cheeks. Impassioned words of love rasped between strained breaths. Infinite kisses had no end or beginning. Adoring lips and tongue tasted every inch of my body. Our lovemaking always had glimpses of those elements, but that night was something else entirely. Again and again, he took me, with a veracity we had not managed even in the earliest days of our marriage.

Then I opened the trunk. Months later, I found the note in his things. In retrospect, it was obvious. Gabriel had known. Maybe not how, or when, or for certain. But the possibility was forefront in his mind that night.

He had known each kiss might be our last.

Once that dreadful understanding made its home in my chest, the recollection of Gabriel's evasive answers at the races that last day gave way to the memory of a wiry form, umber hair, and impossibly blue eyes.

William.

A man with whom I'd had but two—less than pleasant—interactions. We'd spoken but once, and we'd shared a single glimpse across a crowded field.

The first meeting left me frightened, insulted, and vaguely threatened. His love had stumbled across me practicing my fencing in a damp field between Yorkshire moors. Adriane was strange, skeletal, and unearthly beautiful. When William came for her, he came with nothing but biting sarcasm for me and adoration for her. His eyes, so full of desperate love for the strange, barefoot wraith when he fell to his knees before her, were cold and dead the next time I saw him years later across that field.

I racked my brain for days after I found the note. I fought desperately to recall the vague, euphemistic conversation Gabriel and I shared more than a year before, that day at the races. He was certain that Adriane was gone, that she had succumbed to her illness and insanity. And William wished to speak with my Gabriel later that week.

Then I understood. I realized the truth of that conversation. It had been my husband's last evasion, his last half-truth.

The *conversation* he claimed was to take place later that

week almost certainly occurred the next morning at dawn—with pistols drawn.

Beyond that supposition, I had only guesses of my husband's final hours. The moments between him leaving our bed and collapsing on our front steps, a knife in his back, were a mystery.

Presumably, Gabriel went to Hyde Park at the designated time. Whether he stood there alone or whether pistols were fired was anyone's guess. But there were no swords or pistols on his person. Perhaps his challenger supplied the weapons.

At some point, Gabriel stopped by the florist, likely on his way home from that dawn meeting. The irises he brought for me fell with him, scattered by the wind into the pool of his blood. A horrifying reminder of his killer's cruelty.

The rest of my love's final moments were filled with pain and chaos.

W could only be William Hart. I was more certain of it than I was of anything else in this life.

William, with the magnetic cobalt eyes, once filled with love, then filled with death, and finally last night, lust. He was the man on the balcony.

He had kissed me. The thought left my stomach churning with bile, spilling up my throat to leave a metallic tang on my tongue.

Worse still, I had kissed him. Hell, I had been the instigator. Gabriel's killer had his lips on mine. His hands caressed my cheek, traced my neck, and dug into my waist.

Those hands had blood on them.

My husband's blood.

I choked back a gag at the thought.

I was wretched. I had liked it—*loved it, even*. William Hart's kisses were inspired.

And repulsive.

I had lain with men—a man—since I lost Gabriel. And I

had enjoyed my time with Michael. But our encounters had been a means to an end for us both. We had been lucky to forge a friendship on the side of that.

But last night—those kisses…

They hadn't been merely pleasant. I had been filled with bubbling delight, bathed in lust. One kiss and I was… I felt like I could breathe again.

Emotions and sensations so long dormant I thought them lost to time and Gabriel had roared to life again. Feelings that had abandoned me so long ago that I no longer knew the name for them, swam to the surface once again.

And for *that* man to find them—to break them free—to bring them back to me… It was sick. It was disgusting.

It was wrong.

Once the hall clock struck five I recognized the world beyond the slip of parchment pinched between my thumb and forefinger.

The wooden floor of my study was cold, particularly in my once beloved—now loathed—plum gown.

From my vantage, I could see an oversized clump of dust under the bookshelf in the corner that the maid had missed— for at least a year if the size was any indication. The sun was rising, a coppery, fiery slash across the horizon spilling on the wood panels before me. And there was a little gray spider that had made its webbed home between the window and the curtain.

When the hall clock struck six, I finally managed to move, first one foot, then the other. At last, I slid myself up along the wall to stand. Carefully, I returned the ledgers, then the loose documents to the open trunk. Finally, I set the incriminating piece of parchment on top of the pile before shutting the lid with a decisive *thunk*.

In my distress the night before, I had knocked over the chair and I set that to rights as well.

Last night may have been the most disturbing of my life, but I had a mission now—a purpose. I had found my husband's murderer... After seven long years. I was going to see him punished for his crimes.

And absolutely nothing was going to stop me.

Just as soon as I found someone to remove the spider from the house.

~

I CONSUMED FAR TOO many cups of coffee while formulating my plan. If they taught proper murder investigation procedures to ladies, I had missed it sometime between fleeing France and charming the beau monde.

Still, the difficult part was already complete. I had my culprit. I would simply work backward to find the evidence.

What that evidence looked like and how I would find it... Surely those details would work themselves out during the investigation. What I would do with the evidence once I found it... The answer would present itself at that time.

I was under no delusions about my husband having been a good man, but he had been the best husband. He had loved me deeply, fiercely, passionately.

I also knew that I had not known him at his worst.

"I do not seduce innocents. Not anymore."

That had been his one rule, the same rule that nearly ended our romance before it began. Until I made him see sense, made him understand that I had seduced him and he had no say in the matter whatsoever.

The "anymore" held a great deal of significance and weight. Nothing could have prepared me to meet that frail, deathly ill innocent a few months into our marriage. Nor could anything have readied me for her companion, a man who wore his heart in his eyes and gifted insults the way other men gifted flowers.

Gabriel had been in town when Adriane stumbled across me in the country. After our meeting, I stewed for days, alone in the family estate, waiting for Gabriel's return. That was the night he finally told me the worst of it.

I had known, of course, about the mistress, the gambling, the brothel he owned a stake in, and the scheme with the horse breeding. But she had been his greatest sin. He felt no guilt over the rest, but *Adriane*, she was his one regret.

In confessing that sin, he had told me the story of William and Adriane. The details were foggy from that emotionally fraught night. The most devastating argument Gabriel and I ever had.

Now, I racked my brain for threads of a story relayed to me nearly a decade ago. Anything, the slightest tidbit could be the key to it all.

William had been a steward's son, or possibly a tenant of Rose Hall. The two boys had been close in age. Gabriel's father was fond of William and paid for his education alongside his own son and heir. But unlike Gabriel, William had been studious and mild-mannered and planned to go into the law, or perhaps the clergy. It reached a point where His Grace preferred William to his own son.

At some point, Adriane's family had let the estate nearby. Gabriel was certain that William loved her at first sight. Gabriel was equally certain that she preferred him to William. But William didn't see it and had set off to university to earn a living to support Adriane.

And then came the event. Gabriel spoke in the vaguest of self-deprecating details. His Grace was upset with Gabriel for some reason and spoke of wishing William was his son and heir, not Gabriel. That was when Adriane had found him. And he took her, in a horse barn of all places, laughing when she asked him to speak to her father. It was the worst thing Gabriel ever did, to seduce and abandon a gently bred lady, and he regretted it always.

Several months later, William tracked Gabriel to town. He raved that Adriane was ruined by Gabriel's actions and had been thrown out by her own family. The conversation ended in fisticuffs. It was then that Gabriel swore never to touch another innocent. But he still didn't look for her. He learned later that William had incurred the duke's wrath and been cut off when he left the study of law to enlist in the army.

That had been the entirety of the story until that unseasonably warm day in Yorkshire. I could only surmise that William had found her in France while in His Majesty's service. If her bawdy, disconcerting speech from our one meeting was any indication, he hadn't found her in Versailles, but a back alley somewhere.

The story picked up again only after Adriane's suspected death, when William found Gabriel at the races and requested a meeting. Gabriel had assumed it was for assistance with funeral expenses. I knew better now.

To think, I had felt sympathy for the wretched man. I had even once found the notion heartachingly romantic. For a man to leave every privilege he'd worked for to join a war for the sole purpose of finding his lost love, only to find her lost to madness.

Fury now burned where pity had once flourished.

That wretched man was my primary suspect—my only suspect. I needed to know him better than I knew myself if I was to bring him to justice.

He spoke excellent French and made free with his insults while using it. He had eventually gone into the law, and he worked with Kate's brother. His left hand was stained with ink, indicating a preference. He'd carried a sword that day in

Yorkshire, and it was safe to assume he'd learned to use a rifle in the military.

William was also shy or skilled at feigning timidity, and he was certainly not often in society or I would have stumbled across him years ago. And he kissed like he would never get another opportunity.

So little information to proceed with, especially since much of it was likely not pertinent to my investigation.

I needed more.

I could set up a meeting with Lord Leighton, but he likely shared an office with William. And Kate would certainly begin wedding planning if asked her to arrange a less formal meeting between me and her brother

I could not ask Her Grace. She was unobservant at the best of times. If she even recalled William's existence, it would be a small miracle.

Davina was much too young to remember details.

That left only Xander as a source of intelligence. I set off at once to Rycliffe Place. And if Xander was unavailable, I could search for anything I might have missed when I packed up.

Investigating was not so terribly difficult after all.

Eight

CELINE

BY THE TIME I finished readying for the day, it was a reasonable hour to meet with my brother-in-law. Xander was a notoriously late riser, but that would merely leave me my window of opportunity.

The sun was bright and warm when I stepped out of my carriage. But my stomach sank when I realized I had forgotten one thing. To visit Xander, I would have to enter the house. The facade of Rycliffe Place was as lovely as ever. It was still painted a creamy, buttery yellow with a bright red door. And the three stone steps leading up to that door remained. My heart gave a painful wrench at the sight.

With a fortifying breath, I ascended and knocked purposefully. I knew better than to look down. The last time I had looked, the stains from my husband's blood remained. If not precisely in reality then in my mind. No matter how hard the servants scrubbed, the red ring from where he'd fallen remained. I could still see the gnarled iris petals trapped in a bloody prison.

After an eternity, the door opened to reveal Reeves. "Lady Rycliffe! How good to see you. What an unexpected pleasure."

Reeves had served as butler even before my tenure as mistress of the house. I liked the man a great deal. But his voice, no matter how warm, never failed to remind me of that day. I fought my instinctive revulsion and gave him an appreciative, if brittle, smile.

"*Bonjour*, Reeves. I was hoping to meet with His Grace this morning if he is in. I have something I wish to discuss with him."

"I will see if he is available for visitors. Would you like to wait in the drawing room?"

I handed the man my bonnet, then stepped around him and wandered down the hall rather than turn into the drawing room off to the side.

"I think the study would be best today, Reeves," I called back. "Please let His Grace know I will meet him there."

He sputtered after me, crying something about protocol, but after two years with me as mistress, he knew I could not be stopped.

This house... I had nearly forgotten how the memories warred here.

Gabriel's mouth on my neck, a hand up my skirts as his broad form pressed me against that wall.

His blood trailing down this hall.

A late afternoon spent teaching him to play on that very piano bench.

Pressing myself back against that door as I fought for breath, jostled by frantic servants as they worked to stem my husband's bleeding.

They each fought for prominence in a way that left my stomach churning.

The part of me that was given to poking bruises paused

outside the open dining room door. The table was gone, replaced with something darker in color and lighter in form.

I had shuttered that door in the final months I lived here. Even this hall, the main thoroughfare through the house had been avoided at all costs. But I abandoned this room entirely to his ghost.

I was given to understand that his blood had pooled for so long that it warped the table irreparably. That information had been relayed by the late duke with a tone that left little doubt as to whom he assigned blame for the desecration of the fine mahogany piece.

He had informed me in no uncertain terms that my unwillingness to move, to leave Gabriel, for hours after his passing had ruined a perfectly lovely dining table. One that had to be replaced at great cost.

Never mind that no one else in the family could stomach the sight of it, let alone consume a meal at it. I was responsible.

No one, save Her Grace, mourned overmuch when the late duke passed. Xander, by all measures, was a much better man—and duke—than his father had been.

Finally, I reached the study at the end of the hall and slipped in, shutting the door behind me. It was different. More modern, full of darks and lights that warred for purchase. Xander took after his mother in his interior decorating tastes.

His choice of art, however, was lovely. Where Gabriel's grandfather's portrait had once hung, now was a painting of a girl in blue looking out from a gazebo at the bright countryside below. The image was equally full of hope and longing, entirely inappropriate for a study, and completely perfect for this one.

But I could not allow myself to be distracted from my efforts. I had no idea what I was searching for, what I might have missed, but it certainly wasn't the painting.

I pulled out the notes I'd roughly sketched from my pelisse. No doubt Reeves was peeved I hadn't handed over the cloak. When I glanced around the room, my eyes landed on the shelf behind the desk.

Ledgers!

I scurried around the desk and fell to my knees. They were organized by year and then by month for years that had overfilled the first book. But there were no more than five years present, certainly nothing that had once belonged to Gabriel.

I could not help but laugh at the last one on the shelf labeled simply "Davina." She would require her own ledger.

"Can I help you?" A perturbed male voice came from behind me. *Drat*, hadn't that door squeaked?

I spun around, clutching my notes in hand. My eyes met Xander's, his brows quirked in amusement and lips gathered to one side in his trademark expression. It was intended to demonstrate irritation, but his amusement was plain for all to see. His sister was a frequent recipient of the look.

"Xander! How are you this morning?"

"I'm— I had an eventful night. What are you doing?" He gestured toward the seat intended for visitors, before taking the one he called home.

"Oh, you know. I did not get to speak very long with you last night. I wished to see how you were doing."

"And you could not have done that in the drawing room?" His hands danced while he talked, flitting toward the door. I'd never seen another person speak with their entire body the way Xander did.

"Well, no because…" My investigation was proving slightly more awkward than I'd originally thought.

"Reeves is under the impression that you have overspent your portion, and you are here to beg for pin money. That seems unlikely to me."

"I..."

"Weren't you once skilled at manipulating men?"

"Well, yes. But you do not count. I cannot use my feminine wiles on you." That earned me a burst of laughter, and the feigned disapproval vanished.

"Tell me. It cannot possibly be worse than Davina's latest debacle."

I hesitated for less than a second. The truth was on the tip of my tongue, dying to burst forth. "I know who killed Gabriel."

He froze, brown eyes wide and dark, heavy brows raised. "I beg your pardon?"

"I know who killed Gabriel. I met him last night."

"You met him last night... and he told you he murdered your late husband?" He was speaking slowly now, as though speaking to a child who could not understand.

"Well, no. Not exactly, but—"

"Celine, you know I loved Gabriel, and I love you. But it's been seven years..."

"No, I know what you're thinking, but I'm not crazy. I saw him the day before at the races. I forgot until I met him again last night—"

"You saw a man at the races the day before Gabriel died, and you think that makes him the killer."

"Would you let me finish?" I snapped, the irritation, the guilt, the sleeplessness all boiling over.

His palms flitted up in front of him in pacification. "Right, sorry. Tell me everything."

I blurted all of it. The entirety of my knowledge escaped in unending sentences, delivered without breath.

Xander sat before me, eerily still. "Celine... That's not evidence of a murder. That's barely evidence of a possible connection. To be honest, I'm not even sure half of what you said were sentences."

"You don't understand!"

"I do, Cee. I really do. I want to find his killer as badly as you do, but... I remember William. He was kind. He wouldn't have hurt Gabriel. His office handles our estate business. He is always welcoming and affable. Not the attitude of someone who murdered my elder brother."

"But wouldn't you, if someone hurt someone you loved? Not just hurt, but destroyed? Imagine if it were Davina?" He considered me carefully, his gaze flicking to the ledger with her name on it.

"All right, say I believe the motive. You have no evidence."

"No, I do. I have this." I opened my reticule once again, handing over the note I grabbed from the trunk this morning.

"Celine, this is nothing. *W* could be anyone. And it's not even dated. Who's to say this is from the day before?"

"But look at the slant of the writing, and the smear. It was written by someone left-handed. And William is left-handed."

"How do you know that?"

"He had ink stains on his left hand." I waved my left hand in demonstration.

"When were you close enough to notice stains on his left hand? I do not even recall seeing him last night."

"That's not important." *Why could he not focus on the things of import?*

"And where did you find this note, for that matter?" His voice rose in pitch, the same way it did when Davina was being particularly vexing.

"It was in Gabriel's ledgers and things."

"Why do you have Gabriel's ledgers?"

"Oh, the second ones, not the official ones."

"Gabriel had secondary ledgers?"

"Xander, that isn't the point!" My hands had started to dance the way his did, but mine were more irritation than expression.

"I rather think it is. What was he involved in that he needed second ledgers? And why did you take them?"

"There was some nonsense with horse studding that wasn't strictly legal. And he owned a stake in a brothel. Also some gambling." I waved the reasons away. "And I took them because he wouldn't have wanted you or his father to know about that."

"And you think his murder has to do with an affair he had years before but not whatever nonsense he was doing with the horse studding, the brothel, or the gambling?" His hands grew more and more agitated.

"He stopped all of that when he met me. Please, Xander? I know it's him. Something isn't right about William. I can feel it—in here." I pressed both palms to my heart, one atop the other. Willing him to understand, to believe me.

He was silent for a beat, two, three. Studying me. "Say I agree that it's an unlikely *possibility* that he *might* have been involved. What do you plan to do about it?"

Finally! "I'm investigating him. I was hoping you could tell me more about him. And then I intended to have a sneak through his office for anything incriminating that I didn't recognize then."

He sighed. "I don't remember much. I was very young. I did not like Adriane—she stared through me all the time. But Will was nice to me and Davina. He would slip us the frosting off his cake—said he didn't like it. Which was a lie, everyone likes frosting. Now, I use his services. He and Mr. Summers—Lord Leighton—own a practice and they manage the legal business and finances for the estates. He's... nice."

"He was in the army, though. He must know how to stab someone. That's not the sort of thing nice men know how to do."

"Celine, you've spent the best part of a decade learning to fence. I rather think you know how to stab someone too. That doesn't mean you've ever done it. And I know you're not suggesting that army men cannot be kind."

I was left with no alternative but to release a frustrated, "Agh!" at his deliberate nescience.

"*Agh* yourself. You sound like Davina." The last bit was muttered under his breath.

"Xander, please!"

"*If*, and I do mean *if*, I help you, we need to agree on some things."

"Anything."

"No running off by yourself. In the unlikely event that he did murder Gabriel, we're dealing with a killer. I won't have you getting yourself hurt."

"Unnecessary, but agreed."

"No telling anyone and everyone you meet your suspicions. Not until I agree that we're certain. I won't have you ruining the life of an innocent man. An accusation from someone of your station could put him in the gaol at best, the noose at worst."

"Fine." As irritating as it was, I could see the advantages of prudence.

"I want you to remind yourself every day—no, three times a day—that he is likely innocent."

"But—"

"No. Your evidence is flimsy and circumstantial."

"Fine."

"And I want you to do me a favor," he leaned forward, ensuring my gaze met his. "I want you to start to move on. Gabriel was a selfish man, but even he wouldn't have wanted you to mourn him this deeply for this long. I don't need you walking down the aisle tomorrow, just... Promise me you'll cut down your visits to once a month. You cannot possibly move on when you talk to your husband's grave nearly every day."

"How do you know about that?"

He merely shot me a look from under his brow that clearly stated what he thought of that question.

"Fine, I will try. I do not promise to succeed."

"That's all I can ask. Now, what is the plan?"

Nine

HART AND SUMMERS, SOLICITORS, LONDON -
JUNE 6, 1816

WILLIAM

THE STRANGEST THING about the sun was that it kept rising. It gave not a fig whether a man's entire life was torn asunder mere hours before dawn. The sun still rose and contracts still needed to be reviewed.

A quick glance in the glass told me what I ought to have guessed. My curls were loose and tousled in the way Mother scolded me over before she passed.

My lips were a bit redder than usual as well.

Carding my fingers through my hair solved the first problem. Time would manage the second. I strongly suspected no one would notice anyway. For all that the little slip of a marchioness had ruined me, physically I was unchanged.

Though Kit had promised to take yesterday's stack for me, I was in need of the distraction that only the examination of property records and financial transactions could provide.

After trudging down the stairs and out to the street, I unlocked the glass door below the weather-beaten wooden sign reading, "Hart and Summers, Solicitors." It needed to be replaced, but I had a strong suspicion that in a few months' time, I would need a version that read, "Hart, Solicitor."

Kit may pout and stamp his feet now, but he was a good lad and would step up to the earldom eventually. Much as he did not want it, it had its advantages.

I was making progress with the stack when Kit arrived, the bell above the door signaling his entry. His frown was even more prominent than usual.

"Kate couldn't find a woman willing to put up with your sullen face?" I asked.

"How would you know? I never saw you after ten." His scowl deepened with disapproval. "If you think I'm taking your entire stack for an hour of hiding upstairs, you've another thing coming."

"It was an educated guess."

"She paraded me about like a prized pig at the fair. And I mingled with clients, unlike some people."

"Right, sorry. Would you double-check those?" I gestured toward the stack I had reviewed yesterday. I was not prepared to field questions about my whereabouts, but I was more than prepared to hand him work until he moved on.

"All right. But I'm still cross."

"You're always cross about something. Your displeasure is noted for the record and overruled."

And so passed a relatively quiet morning. Mornings typically went that way with patrons generally arriving after tea and social calls. There was an occasional ding of the bell as the clerks we employed arrived—Matthews, Bates, and Williams. The repetitive scratches of quills on parchments, the taps on inkwells. Rarely, a cough from one of the men. But all was as usual.

So it was something of a surprise when the little bell chimed again, signaling a new arrival only a few hours after we opened.

I glanced up through my office door as one of the clerks greeted the unusually tall gentleman. I recognized him as one of Kit's brothers-in-law. Not Wayland, the youngest one.

"Tom, good to see you. What can I do for you? You didn't mention anything last night," Kit called from his office as he stood and went to meet the lad in the main room. Kit directed him back into his own office and shut the door, leaving behind only the scribbles of the clerks.

I was even more startled when the bell rang a second time not even a quarter hour later, signaling the arrival of yet another visitor.

What is Rosehill doing here?

Immediately, all my efforts to forget the woman with hair of spun gold and lips of sin were abandoned at the sight of her late husband's brother. There were only two possibilities: Lady Davina was in trouble again, or he had talked to Lady Rycliffe. The odds were a coin toss from where I sat.

In spite of his relations, I liked the man a great deal. He had still been in school when I left Yorkshire. After his father's death, he generously moved his accounts to my fledgling practice, proving to be one of our most loyal—and profitable—clients.

He often required our assistance to rescue his sister from whatever absurd misadventure she'd found this week. Kit usually handled those. He was more willing to work with foreign governments than me.

But Rosehill didn't spare a glance toward Kit's closed door. He was here to deal with me then. There was every possibility he was Lady Rycliffe's closest male relation.

Rising, I gestured him into my office and moved to the door while greeting him. I didn't need the staff overhearing my dressing down, or worse, a challenge issued.

"Morning, Will. Oh, there's no need to close the door. It's a bit warm today. I could use the airflow. In fact, would you mind opening that window?" He gestured in that exaggerated way of his, toward the large window on the side wall of my office.

He was acting strangely, but I had no reasonable excuse to refuse, so I made the effort. I returned to my seat across from him just as Kit's door opened. Tom peered his head around the corner, hand raised in a wave.

"Sorry, Will. Didn't realize you had a client. Oh, Rosehill! Repurchasing your sister from the pirates?"

Rosehill straightened, alarmed. "What? She's been consorting with pirates again? Which ones?" His voice had risen in panic.

Tom laughed, resting heavily against Bates's desk in the main room just outside my door. "I was joking. She's been ransomed before?"

"Why would you joke about something like that?" Rosehill's tone was clipped and horrified in a way he usually reserved for Lady Davina.

"Well, I thought it was too absurd to have happened previously. What are you doing then?"

"Oh, I was planning to do a bit of traveling, and I wanted Will's advice first."

He wants to travel? That did not follow my experience with him.

"Where are you going?" Tom asked.

"I do not know. Yorkshire? Scotland? I'm still considering my options. That is why I'm here."

"Right, apologies. I'll just leave you to your considerations... Kit, see you tonight." Tom rose, nodding to his brother-in-law before heading out the door, bell announcing his departure. Bates adjusted his stack of paperwork irritably.

Kit wrapped himself around the door, peering his head in my office. "Sorry to interrupt, Your Grace. Will, I need to leave a few minutes early tonight. Kate wants a family dinner."

"And she wants you there? Did she find you a wife?"

"Funny... No. Tom thinks Jules is expecting and Kate wants to have the whole family there for the announcement."

"I hope you're right. If that's the case, congratulate them for me. Tell Wayland he can come in if there's anything to discuss. Or one of us can call on them." Kit nodded, returning to his office and paperwork.

Turning back to Rosehill, I said, "Apologies. You said you wished to discuss travel plans?"

"Good for Juliet," he muttered, seemingly to himself. That was when I recalled the marriage settlements I had drawn up and destroyed some weeks later. She had been Rosehill's wayward fiancée.

"I'm sorry. We should not have been discussing that in front of you."

"No, it's just... She worried she wouldn't be able to have children. I'm pleased for her. Regardless, I suppose that is none of my concern."

"So, travel?" I asked, trying to drag us back to a more appropriate subject. "You do not usually consult me on such matters." *Especially not the morning after I ravished your late brother's wife on the balcony of a gaming hell.*

"Well, I've been meaning to travel for some time, and I expect I may settle more permanently at one of the estates. I would need to set up provisions for Mother and Davina. Gabe traveled a great deal. Did he have anything in place?"

What is he up to?

"Not that I'm aware of. But I was not his solicitor, your father was still alive, and your sister was still a child. I imagine the arrangements were somewhat less complicated."

"Right. It's been so long I nearly forgot. I'm so forgetful. You were friends, right? You and Gabriel?"

"*Friends* is a strong term... Why are you asking me about your brother?"

Out of the corner of my eye, I caught a flash of something gold through the window. It was not possible. There was absolutely no way she was outside, eavesdropping.

"Oh, you know, just reminiscing."

"Right. You mentioned Yorkshire and Scotland? If you're looking to make improvements, I would recommend the Scotland property. It has been left relatively untouched and could probably use some work. I think it would be well worth your efforts. If it were in better repair, should you choose to take a wife, you could summer there. Or you could sell it at great profit."

Just outside the window, a commotion sounded, and a distinctly male voice all but shouted, "Bonjour, madame!" His accent made my eye twitch.

A sharp cracking noise was followed by a *thunk* against the wall.

Perhaps a feminine form breaking a milk crate she was leaning on, startled by the greeting.

I rose and moved to peer through the window.

"Will?" Rosehill's tone was high-pitched and when I turned to him, he was striding toward the window as well.

The source of the *thunk* answered, drawing my attention once again.

"I donna know who ye think I am, but I'm no Madame. Please leave."

It had to be the most abysmal Scottish accent I'd ever had the displeasure of experiencing.

The man's response was startled and unintelligible, each word more distant than the last.

Dragged away then.

I turned back to Rosehill, brow raised as I waited for an explanation. He was backing slowly out of the room.

"Well, that was strange. You've given me a great deal to think on. I should be going now. Do you think you can draw up some paperwork to keep Mama and Davina from bankrupting us if I travel for an extended time?"

I turned to follow him out. "I can— You're really not going to address that?" I asked, nodding toward the window.

"I have no idea what that was about. Some poor Scotswoman accosted on the street."

"Right. I'll draw up some paperwork, perhaps daily and weekly spending limits with the most likely culprits, modiste and such. You go see to your poor Scotswoman." We continued walking, predator and prey, through the main room.

"Yes, perfect. Thank you!"

"Of course. Rosehill?"

"Yes?"

"Next time, come alone?"

His shoulders fell a bit at that. "All right."

"Have a nice day," I said, holding the door open. After closing it behind him, I turned to face all the clerks and Kit observing me with interest.

"What was that about? Is Lady Davina in trouble? Do you need me to contact anyone about it?" Kit asked, feigning disinterest from his office.

"No, as far as I can tell she's fine. I think that was about me."

His shoulders dropped with something like relief.

"Why would it be about you?" he questioned.

"It's a long story."

"I have nothing but paperwork and time."

"I think I have a spy? It's unclear." An enemy with haunting, horrified green eyes—burned in my memory.

"You? Who would want to spy on you?"

An excellent question, if somewhat insulting in tone.

"I suppose we'll find out."

Ten

OUTSIDE HUDSON'S BAKERY, LONDON - JUNE
12, 1816

CELINE

XANDER REFUSED to sustain our ruse, citing a humiliation so severe he would never recover. It was a fair assessment. Fortunately, his abandonment of our shared cause allowed me to continue the investigation on my own.

Even I had to admit that my first attempt resulted in a poor showing. But I was nothing if not adaptable.

I adopted a disguise, borrowing my maid's uniform. It was a bit too long, but otherwise did the job credibly after she pinned the hem. It also hid my dagger easily. I'd taken to strapping the bejeweled knife to my thigh each morning. Gabriel had gifted it to me on our honeymoon. What a poetic sort of justice if I ended up sheathing it in the back of his killer.

With no other ideas, I'd taken to studying the man, following him. Day in, day out, I watched—his own personal phantom. Unfortunately, I had found little in the way of incriminating evidence, but I had learned a great number of interesting facts about William Hart.

That very morning, for example, he abandoned Lord

Leighton to open the office alone and made his way down the street to Hudson's Bakery. I watched from across the cobblestone path as Mrs. Ainsley handed him something delectable and shoved him to a corner table. She returned with a stack of ledgers that she plopped down before him.

Mr. Hart reviewed each of them in a precise fashion, checking numbers against one another with a finger on each. Presumably, he was reviewing the various contracts required to supply a bakery.

Occasionally he would take a distracted bite of a... tart? Cake? Something equally delightful? I had not eaten that morning and Mrs. Ainsley's creations were always mouthwatering.

Though I had found little to incriminate him, I had gleaned information of interest. He wore spectacles while working. When something in the ledgers did not match his expectations, he would remove the spectacles and rub them against a sleeve. Then he would return them to his face and sigh when the information remained unchanged.

His left shoulder plagued him when he sat too long in one attitude. He would tense and massage it with the other hand.

When the ledgers contained something particularly offensive, he would drag a hand through his hair, ruining his halfhearted effort to tame it as it returned to the wild mess of curls from the masquerade.

Lastly, I learned that he was adorably uncomfortable with infants. No, not adorable, just uncomfortable. A few moments ago, Mrs. Ainsley pressed baby Emma into his arms with a laugh. At first, he held the tiny redhead an arm's length away from him with both hands. After a moment, he pulled her closer to his chest, freeing one of his hands to catch her tiny fist. She shook it with all her might and he smiled.

"He is likely innocent." Xander's directive ran through my mind once again. I had expected that rule to be more difficult

to follow than it was proving to be. William Hart did not act like a murderer. Not that I knew many—or any, for that matter. But he did not fit any of my expectations.

Eventually, he handed Emma back to her mother with some reluctance and packed up his copies of the documents, then returned the bakery copies to Mrs. Ainsley and accepted a basket of treats. He slipped Mrs. Ainsley the funds to cover the baked goods in spite of her protestations and stepped out of the shop onto the cobblestones.

I followed at a distance, just near enough to hear him hum something indistinct. His voice was smooth and he was sure of his pitch.

He arrived at his office, and I took the place that had become mine over the past several days—the bench across the street.

Through the glass door, I saw him set the treats on a desk and all of the clerks rose to select a pastry before going back to their desks. Lord Leighton came out of his office to retrieve one as well.

Did killers give their staff baked goods?

WILLIAM

The thing about knowing I was being followed was that it threw into sharp clarity the tediousness of my everyday life. If she was to spend her days staring at me, the least I could do was make them interesting. The only problem was that my attendance at the masquerade was, quite literally, the most interesting evening I'd had in years, perhaps ever.

After Rosehill chose not to drag me down the aisle or call me out, I found myself at a loss. The chit clearly did not intend to force me into matrimony, in spite of her abysmal taste in husbands. I could admit that it would not have taken much effort to convince me. I'd loved one woman who lived and breathed for Gabriel Hasket, what was a second?

But that fact left the question of what she wanted with me. She followed me for hours each day. A woman of her station with seemingly no demands on her time was unlikely. Which meant she was abandoning those obligations in favor of watching me.

She was perched on what had become her bench across the street wearing her usual ill-fitting maid's uniform. Who she thought she was fooling with that was anyone's guess. An ugly dress and a dowdy cap were hardly enough to detract from the bewitching beauty she radiated.

The line of sight from my office to her bench was direct, presumably her purpose in selecting it. I found her position was more than a little distracting. My nights were filled with little beyond memories of her sweet lips, soft hair, and delicate curves. And my days were filled with the sight of said lips and hair and curves.

She was everywhere. Every minute of every day she surrounded me. I could not escape her and worse still, I couldn't decide if I wished to be free of her. The last minutes before midnight that night were a revelation. If time hadn't interfered, I would still be worshiping her. I gladly would have kissed her until the sun ceased to rise.

"Your shadow is getting wet," Kit said, startling me from my efforts to look busy. There had been a lot of that the last few days—staring at paperwork without really seeing anything.

He was propped against the doorframe again, munching on a tart.

"What?"

"Lady Rycliffe. She's getting wet. It's raining, or didn't

you notice? Or did you finally manage to pay attention to your work for the first time all week?"

I glanced outside, confirming his intelligence. It was raining, rather heavily, and Lady Rycliffe made no effort to abandon her vigil. Instead, she merely hunkered down slightly to present a smaller target for the offending rain.

Without pausing to consider the ramifications, I rose, snatched my umbrella, and trotted out to meet her. Her gaze was downturned, avoiding the drops splashing across her face, sacrificing her coiffure instead.

She missed my arrival and startled when I sat beside her. I opened the umbrella and held it over us both without a word.

Her eyes shot to mine with precision. I offered a half grin and a shrug. "Didn't want you to catch a chill. If you took ill, who would supervise my daily activities?"

"You..."

"Me. You can come inside if you like. It's not much, but it's warm and dry. Or you can stay here. But please, take the umbrella if you want to stay out here."

"You're inviting me in?"

"Well, yes. But decide quickly, please. I don't fancy spending the afternoon in a damp coat."

"All right." She stood, graceful even in a too-long dress that was quite soaked through. She brushed past me on her way through the office door, smelling of vanilla, rain, and something richer I couldn't name.

"Lady Rycliffe, good to see you," Kit said. He'd moved from my office door to his own and grabbed another tart in the process. He spoke with the bemused tone he usually reserved for me.

I shot him a look as I shook off the umbrella and set it beside the door to drip dry.

"Lord Leighton," she nodded. His eye gave the requisite twitch at the mention of his title, but he didn't protest. It was a depressing kind of progress. It signified yet another step away from this office and toward his new duties.

"Kit, would you grab one of the blankets?" We used them on particularly cold days in winter when no amount of firewood could keep out the chill. He wandered off in search of one. Hopefully they were not too terribly musty.

The clerks made a valiant effort to ignore the magnificently beautiful, incredibly damp woman in the room, but I doubted they could feign disinterest much longer. If Bates was making any effort to hide his interest, it wasn't a very impressive one. I could hardly blame the man though. I was no better, noting the enticing way her damp skirts clung to her legs.

Kit returned and started to hand her a bundled blanket, but I grabbed it from him. I unfurled it and shook it for any dust or debris—or worse—that might have made its home there in the last few months. Satisfied it was passably clean, I wrapped it around her shoulders, only realizing the intimacy of the gesture when my hands met over her heart. We found ourselves so close, our breaths mingling in the space between us.

A pointed cough from Kit's direction had her jumping away as my hands released the edges of the rough, dark wool.

"Will's office is the warmest. You should settle in there. You can discuss any issues you might need a solicitor for while you're in there," Kit said, nodding toward my doorway, as though everyone in the room was not perfectly aware of which was mine. As if we all hadn't watched eagerly as she stared at it for days.

She chose to follow his suggestion and led the way. Kit waggled his brows in a ridiculous manner behind her back. Mentally devising tortures for him, I followed her into the room and shut the door behind us. She made herself comfortable in one of the chairs reserved for guests.

I took a minute to appreciate the flush on her cheeks and the way her lashes clung together from the rain as I sat before her. Her coiffure was sad and half escaped, and she was all the lovelier for it.

When it became apparent that she would never break the silence, I finally spoke. "Do you wish to tell me why you've been following me?"

Her teeth caught her lower lip. Devil take me if that wasn't the most fetching sight I'd ever seen. "Not particularly."

"Shall I guess?"

"I wish you wouldn't." Her accent was different from the night of the ball, and our one prior conversation. Neither distinctly English nor French, it swirled like half-mixed paint.

I refused further musings on that point, for that way lay danger. Instead, I debated pressing her. She was more or less captive in my office.

"Very well. Would you like a tart?"

"I beg your pardon?"

"A tart, from Hudson's. Would you like one? We have raspberry, apple, and lemon, though Kit may have taken the last of the apple."

"Lemon please." I stepped around her and into the main room, grabbing the basket so she could select one herself. She probably did not wish for inky fingers all over her pastry.

"Do you work with Mrs. Ainsley?" she asked.

"I do, have since she opened the place, actually. She could pay me solely in those tarts and I would die a happy man."

At my prodding, she took a bite. Her eyes slid closed and a small smile crossed her lips. Considering Mrs. Ainsley's tarts tasted like a warm hug, the reaction wasn't unusual.

Distracted as she was by delectable treats, I pressed my advantage. Perhaps if I side-stepped the issue I could determine her purpose. "Is there anything you wish to ask me?"

"You'll answer? Just like that?"

"I have nothing to hide." Her eyes widened inexplicably at that. What did she think I was hiding?

"You grew up with Gabriel?"

"Unfortunately." She made a go-on gesture between bites. "My father was His Grace's steward. We played occasionally, when he was in Yorkshire."

"His father funded your schooling?"

"This might be easier if you tell me what you already know."

"I'm searching for discrepancies in your story."

Perfect, now I was expected to match my story to the great bull calf's.

"I don't remember when we met, probably too young. Unlike Rycliffe, I was studious. And polite. And decent. His father took notice, decided to fund my education. Less out of fondness for me than a desire to shame his son into becoming a contributing member of society, I expect. Anyone who had met Rycliffe could have told His Grace that it would have the opposite effect. They would have been right."

"Tell me about Adriane."

Adriane. I hadn't heard that name outside of my mind in years. I braced myself for the instinctive pang in my chest, but it never appeared.

"Adriane was... everything. It was more than love, it was... obsession at first sight. Just—I could *feel* her whenever she was near. I was so aware of her. Always. And I was not subtle in my interest. I wrote too many bloody poems before she had the heart to inform me that it was not a strength of mine. I bought her flowers. I did all of it.

"She was just so—not even beautiful, exactly—but magnetic. Bewitchingly beautiful too, of course, but she just drew you in and once she had you, there was no escape. I didn't want to escape either."

"I know it, that feeling." Her voice was tentative, small, hollow. Gabriel.

"She wasn't interested in me. Only had eyes for Rycliffe. But it amused her to toy with me. Particularly around him." She was still watching, listening attentively. I had never once concerned myself with disparaging Rycliffe to all and sundry, but to her?

"He told me the worst of it. If you'd like to skip over that part."

She could not possibly know the full truth of the matter. No one could know what he had done to Adriane and still have married the man.

"He discussed it with you?"

"Well, I did not request details, but yes."

"What did he tell you?" I leaned forward, the effort to control my burning fury leaving me uneasy. I glanced away, searching for something, anything to lessen the tension.

"He was different. When I met him. We— He rejected me because he refused to be with an innocent. He regretted it— what he did to her."

My stomach turned viciously. This was the woman I had worshiped with my hands and lips days ago. She sat before me now attempting to justify what that monster had done to my Adriane.

"Oh, well if he regretted it, then it's all fine. Her life wasn't destroyed. She didn't die sick and in pain."

"I didn't... That is not what I meant."

"People don't change. Not that much. And some things are unforgivable. To think, I had convinced myself... I felt sorry for you! I thought perhaps he had seduced you and someone had to drag him down the aisle at the end of a pistol. Or perhaps you didn't know. But to think, you knew what he was from the beginning, and you married him anyway. You are as bad as he was."

"I—"

"I think you should go." I rose, reaching my office door in two harsh steps, ripping it open with enough force to test the hinges. "You can have the umbrella. Whatever reason you have for following me, it ends now. You are clearly not intending to force me to wed you. And frankly, I would rather meet Rosehill at dawn than marry you."

She stood slowly and turned to me, then dropped the blanket on the chair before stepping toward me. "You thought... You thought I wanted to *marry* you? There is not a man on this earth I would rather marry less than you! I loathe you. You disgust me." Her venomed verbiage was delivered at a whisper, but it echoed as though she had screamed it.

"Wonderful. Now that is cleared up, glad you could stop by." With a wordless grunt of frustration she stomped through the office, wet slippers squelching with every step. She grabbed the umbrella and threw the door open with as much force as her tiny form could muster, the bell clanging its irritation at her abrupt manner.

The clerks, who had been staring with interest, immediately dropped their attention back to their paperwork, feigning ignorance. My return to my desk was less satisfying with nothing to slam or stamp. I collapsed in my chair, dragging fingers through my hair, breathing too heavily.

"So, I don't need to book the chapel?" Kit asked, once again leaning heavily against my door frame. His arms were banded about his chest, and he wore an infuriating smirk.

"Get out...." It was less of a demand than a weary sigh. The fight had well and truly abandoned me, and I was left shrunken and drained.

"Go home. Better yet, go get a drink. You'll be useless this afternoon anyway." The idea was tempting—not home, of course—but a visit I'd been pushing off since the masquerade.

"I think I will."

His jaw hinged open. "You? Leave work? Get a drink? Inconceivable."

"Kit..."

"Lucky for you, the rain has stopped. Especially since I don't believe you'll see that umbrella again."

"If I leave, will you stop talking?"

"No, but you won't be here to hear it."

"Goodbye."

Eleven

CROSS BONES GRAVEYARD, LONDON - JUNE
12, 1816

CELINE

THERE WERE A THOUSAND—A thousand, thousand
reasons really—to stop following William Hart. I was wet and
disheveled. I had just berated the man quite thoroughly in
front of the entirety of his staff. He had proved entirely
cognizant of my surveillance. I was enraged and embarrassed.
The last time I was this angry, Gabriel had been alive to infuriate me. But William had never left the office at this time of
day, at least not since I'd been observing him.

I followed at a greater distance than I had in previous days,
hoping desperately I would not be caught. His pace was brisk
and he moved with purpose, his arms swinging at his sides. It
was almost a swagger. After days of observation, I would not
have thought him capable of such confidence.

He clearly had a direction in mind, turning down first one
side street then another. He kept to the edge of the Covent
Garden hustle and bustle all the way across the river. With
each turn, the area of town became more questionable.

Just when I was beginning to suspect he knew of my pres-

87

ence and was attempting to lose me, he came upon a short wrought iron fence.

He strode to the gate with intention, lifted the latch, and tugged at the gate itself. He wiggled it in its hinges until it slid open with an irritated creak. The motion was familiar to him. I approached at a cautious distance, slipping through unnoticed before the breeze blew the door closed.

The sign above the gate was worn with splinters missing and peeling paint. But it read "Cross Bones Graveyard."

This was nothing like Gabriel's carefully tended resting place. The graves here were marked with weather-beaten wooden crosses. Some were simply vertical sticks where the horizontal piece had fallen off. Several mounds of earth had no markings at all, though they bore all the indications of an inhabitant. Few and far between were the occasional headstone.

My stomach twisted in guilty revulsion, but I pressed forward. I slipped behind one tree until he passed the next, then I scurried to reach that one before he turned. Finally, he slowed, his gaze fixed on a headstone. I did not need to press closer to read it. I knew the name I would find there.

Adriane.

"Hello, sweetling." His baritone was thick with emotion as he knelt before the stone, heedless of the damp earth. He brushed some of the decaying growth off the top before tracing her name with his fingertips.

I could not make out details from my hiding place, but the stone was certainly nicer than any of the others in the vicinity. It still stood straight, proud, and was not overly worn. He was a regular visitor.

"I've been meaning to come by and see you, but I've been busy. It's no excuse, though, is it? The weather has been nice here, more sunshine than usual. I'm sure you would have something to say about that. But the clear skies mean it's easier to see the stars. I hope you can see them, too, where you are."

My heart twisted. I was not alone in my peculiar little habit. William Hart also spoke to his late love. Could he have his own little bird? Did the breeze answer him too?

He continued, "I'm being evasive, I know. I'm not here to chat about the weather. I don't suppose you remember that morning in Yorkshire? You went wandering in your bare feet and made it halfway to Rose Hall. Scared the life out of me. You came across Rycliffe's wife. The woman with the shite French accent?"

I bit back a laugh at the insult. There was no heat behind his words, if anything his tone carried amusement.

"I met her again. Only I didn't know it was her, I swear it. I kissed her, too, before I knew who she was. It was… it was a revelation. I'm sure you're cackling away right now. This is the sort of thing you would find hilarious.

"The next day, Rosehill paid me a visit, the beetle-headed ballock's brother. I thought he had come to drag me down the aisle, just for a moment. For that minute I thought… Well, that might not be such a terrible fate. She has unbelievably tragic taste in men, but so did you, and it doesn't make you a jot less lovable.

"But I was wrong. He was helping her in her bizarre endeavor to follow me indefinitely until she discovers… something. Haven't the foggiest what she's after. Something to do with Rycliffe, I expect.

"I learned today that she knew what he was and she still married him. She's still defending him. She knew how he hurt you the way he did. What is it about him? Why do you love him so much? Why can't you see what he is, what he does?"

This man… These were not the words of a killer. Were they? Even the hurt and outrage I heard in his rusty, bitter tone contained nothing of violence, nothing of death.

"It is damn ironic, is what it is. The first time in ages that I saw a woman and thought... well, anything really. And she's already his. Just like you were. Doesn't matter though. She was sure to be a disappointment. No one can hold a candle to you, sweetling."

It was such an intimate moment—one I had no business witnessing. But for the first time in seven years, I did not feel so alone. He loved her the way I loved Gabriel. And if I ever found his killer...

He was talking about Kit—Lord Leighton—now, inconsequential things about various clients. He was not going to confess to Gabriel's murder—not now. I followed my tree line back to the road as the sun began to kiss the horizon. After wriggling the gate in the same manner he had to get it open, I exited the graveyard and made my way back out to the London streets.

Few lamps were lit in this part of town. The buildings cast impossibly long shadows in the setting sun. It seemed later than I knew it to be, with the darkness spilling across the walkway.

I hadn't intended to be so far away from home, hadn't meant to follow him to such a distance. This was precisely the sort of situation Xander warned me to avoid. Not only had I intruded on a very private interaction and learned nothing of value, but I was going to get myself killed for my efforts.

I stepped quickly, with purpose, moving as fast as I could manage without drawing undue attention. I was grateful for the maid's uniform; it was certainly less conspicuous than my usual apparel. In my haste, the umbrella I still carried bumped against my shin occasionally. I was not used to traveling with such an item.

Already fewer people were on the streets than had been perhaps an hour before. The ones who were out seemed less savory in appearance than those I'd observed earlier.

I hadn't paid as much attention to the route as I should have. I was too occupied with my pursuit and had planned to follow him on his return journey. Now, I was less confident of the direction.

Two men rounded a corner just ahead. They were huddled together, sharing confidences. My steps slowed without permission, an unwitting demonstration of weakness that drew their attention.

My heart skipped with instinctive unease. Even from the distance of a few hundred paces, their interest was unmistakable. One took a step toward me. The other joined his advance, and they hurried to close the distance.

I could not continue forward. To my left was a blind alley. I could turn down it and hope they lost interest. That would leave me no escape if their excitement did not wane with lost sight.

While I considered my options, they had already halved the distance.

Two options left. I could gather my skirts and pull out the dagger strapped to my thigh—I could fight. Or I could run.

Gabriel's graveled voice rang through my mind. *"Always flee. If you have a choice between fighting and fleeing, flee."* Pulling the knife would leave no time for flight.

Decision made, I turned back toward the cemetery and took off, sprinting faster than I ever had before. My feet pounded on the pavement.

And they weren't alone.

I didn't dare look back. The men were close enough to hear their harsh breaths. They were going to catch me. They would grab me. They would do unspeakable things to me.

The second half of Gabriel's instructions flicked through my mind between breaths. *"If you can't flee, then fight, and do not fight fair."*

The move was instinctive. My feet planted and I spun, the

umbrella I had nearly forgotten about clasped in both hands. *Whack!* My blind swing made contact with the side of a man's head and he went down. He landed in a crumpled heap at my feet.

Unfortunately, the hit jarred my grip and the taller man caught my weapon and tugged. I tripped over the injured one and stumbled forward but managed to retain my hold. Tightening my hands with everything I had, I yanked and twisted. I pulled it free and floundered backward slightly.

By the time I righted myself, the first man was staggering to his feet, his cheek bleeding. My heart was pounding too harshly in my ears to make out his words, but they weren't pleasant.

My gaze darted between them. I had never fought two men. Hell, I had never fought a single man with the intention of wounding him. And certainly never with an umbrella. My decade of fencing was only slightly better than useless.

The wounded one. Instinct told me to incapacitate him first. Suddenly, hours of foil practice came back to me.

Without warning, I thrust the point of the umbrella straight into his gut. There was nothing to foreshadow my motion. I managed to pierce flesh.

The umbrella tip wasn't sharp, not like my small sword, nor was it tipped like my practice foil. It hit the mark, and what followed wasn't pretty. My weapon dragged through the man's belly with a sickening squelching sound before my motion was aborted by the fabric, a few inches along the shaft.

It was a severe wound. It might even kill him. But it would be a slow death, infection rather than blood loss. All it would do now was slow him down.

I'd never had to pull my blade free from sinew. The umbrella didn't pull free the way I expected. Instead, his skin closed around it and it stuck. I had to yank much harder than intended to free it.

A rough hand grabbed my shoulder and yanked me back, distracted as I was by the unfamiliar feeling of pierced muscle and organ.

My other assailant. How had I forgotten him? It would be a costly mistake. I was left with my umbrella clasped in only one hand. My other arm was trapped in his hold.

My victim righted himself, hand clasped against his wound. The men were too close now. I couldn't get my arm back far enough to thrust.

This was it.

Time slowed and everything sharpened. Heavy breathing filled the air. Their scent filled my nose and lungs—liquor, piss, blood, and bile. They shared greasy brown hair, brown eyes, and a ruddy complexion. Brothers perhaps.

My rapers—murderers?—closed in on me.

Not like this.

I went limp, becoming dead weight in the uninjured one's grasp. My shoulder slipped through his hold, and I landed at their feet. I was grounded, but free, and I had space.

And a clear shot at a man's most vulnerable part.

I grabbed the umbrella with both hands and slammed it up decisively between the uninjured man's legs. The angle wasn't the best, but he crumpled at the waist, hands cupping his genitals.

I was lining up for another hit when the bleeding man was wrenched backward with a grunt.

Before I could decipher what had happened, a familiar baritone rang out.

"Evening, gents. What might you be up to?"

William.

Relief poured through me. Somehow, I knew without a doubt that I was safe.

Twelve

WILLIAM

THE HOUR WAS LATER than I'd intended when I left Adriane to her stars. The sun had just dipped behind the horizon. I would need to hasten my pace to avoid unsavory elements. My sweetling hadn't been allowed a decent burial in a respectable cemetery, not after her time in the brothels of Paris.

Predictable as the rise and fall of the sun, I came across two men having a bit too much fun with a tempting armful. They hovered menacingly over the girl. She was little more than a heap of skirts on the pavement.

I sighed. This was precisely the sort of thing I'd hoped to avoid.

I snatched the nearest one by the shoulder, wrenching him back to me and meeting his face with my fist. He crumpled forward gracelessly.

"Evening, gents. What might you be up to?"

"William!"

Bleeding hell! Not her again. Sparing a glance at the heap of skirts confirmed what I knew the moment I heard my name. Lady Rycliffe, holding my own umbrella out to me.

"It's not raining, and I'm a bit preoccupied at the moment." The man I struck managed to right himself, and the other had rounded on me.

"You can hit them with it. I've done it." Now that she said it, the men were rather disheveled.

"Well, keep it then!" Each man took a swing simultaneously.

I blocked the one intended for my face instinctively, leaving my gut open for the other. Though painful, it lacked the force I would have expected of a man his size. Still, it knocked the air out of me.

"I have a knife," she cried.

Another fist rained down on me and I ducked. It continued on its trajectory into the other man's face, knocking him to the ground. At least they were somewhat inept assailants.

"Then why the hell are you hitting them with the bleeding umbrella?" On further inspection, it was obvious she had managed more than a few hits on at least one of them. He was bleeding from his stomach and the side of his head. He was the more unsteady for it, and I aimed a blow at the wound on his stomach. It earned me a devastated grunt.

"It was tucked under my skirts." I heard a *thunk* followed by a groan behind me. I spun in time to see that she had made it to her feet. The taller man collapsed at the waist. It seemed she'd hit the man's kidney with the umbrella.

The aforementioned knife was tucked uselessly in her hand.

"Keep the umbrella. Give me the damn knife!"

"Oh!" She had enough sense to give it over, handle first. Now that we were armed and standing together, the men eyed us wearily.

She had caused a fair amount of damage with her makeshift weapon. The man holding his bleeding side was unlikely to forget her if he survived.

The slightly less injured one struck with very little warning, but I caught the slight dip in his shoulder and met his fist with the knife. He yowled in pain and pulled away, damaging the hand further.

His compatriot joined him in his cries when she whacked him about the knee. He was on the ground writhing. She'd broken it then. Good.

This was our opportunity. We would likely win if the fight continued. They were badly injured, and she was a crack shot with an umbrella.

Or we could run. I didn't fancy waiting to see if they had friends. I grabbed her hand and tugged her away from the scene, urging her into a run.

We turned down the nicer side streets, doubling back every so often to be sure we weren't followed. Finally, we reached my office and the little apartment above them. Fortunately, I managed to retain my keys in the scuffle, and I ushered her inside and out of the night.

I finally released her hand when we reached my door at the top of the stairs. My hands shook as I fought to get the key in the lock. When I managed to open the door, I gestured her in front of me, then I pressed the door closed with my back.

She stood stark still in the center of my entry. Her arms were wrapped around her waist. The umbrella lined her side, supporting her, keeping her upright. The golden glow of her skin was gone and in its wake a sickly pale.

"Are you injured?"

"What?" she asked, her tone small and far away.

Shock then. I grabbed her by the shoulders and directed her into the chair by the hearth. I tugged the umbrella from her grasp and nestled it against her knee. She would want it within reach.

That she allowed me to take it without protest was proof enough of her distress. Her shuddering form was unnecessary evidence.

I pulled away to light the fire. When that task was completed, I retrieved a blanket from the bedroom and wrapped it around her still-trembling body.

I had seen men in shock on the battlefield. I don't think she would appreciate my usual method of reviving them.

No, a sharp crack on the cheek was not likely to please the marchioness. Quite frankly, I was somewhat afraid of her wrath if I displeased her.

My instinct was to make her tea, but I preferred coffee and my selection was pitiful. It would take time to heat the kettle as well.

I puttered about the kitchen, keeping an eye across the open room. My selection was truly pitiful. Kit and I typically dined together in the evenings. In the mornings, I often broke my fast at my desk.

I managed to procure a loaf of bread and some butter. I did not wish to overwhelm her, lest she be sick, so I ignored the cheese and dried meats.

I checked the last cupboard, desperately hoping for something edible to appear by magic. My prayers were answered in the form of drink rather than food. Whiskey.

I poured a finger into a teacup and brought it to her. I had to press it into her palm and curl her fingers around the cup before they responded.

"Whiskey. Kit left it, so it's likely terrible, but it's all I've got. Unless you'd like tea?"

She took a mindless sip with none of Kit's usual fanfare.

"I've got bread as well if you think you can eat something? It might help with the shaking."

She straightened a bit. "Do you have any cheese?" With the request, her tone returned to something of the usual warmth and vibrancy.

"I think I've got some North Wiltshire."

"Really? But it's so…"

"Expensive? That's why I live in this hovel. Must save money to afford cheese." That earned me a giggle and the sound warmed my chest in a far more pleasant manner than the whiskey could have.

"You don't mind sharing?"

I gave a disinterested shrug as I returned with a cheese plate as requested and perched on the arm of her chair. "I'll overcharge Rosehill this month. He'll never notice."

She took a healthy bite of bread and cheese, her eyelids fluttering closed with an appreciative groan. It sent a shiver down my spine that had nothing to do with our fight.

We ate without words, and her trembling slowly subsided, and her coloring was restored. The brightness returned to her eyes as she peered into the fire. She was still a mess, her hair tangled and mostly undone, the ill-fitting dress wrinkled and caked with mud and Lord knew what else. But she was an unbearably beautiful mess.

"How are you feeling? Bit better now?" I asked.

She turned to face me and answered with a prim, "Yes, thank you."

"Good. So… you followed me to the cemetery?"

She ducked before mumbling an affirmation.

"Why?"

"I don't wish to say." Her answer was directed to her lap and the empty plate.

"Should have thought about that before you followed me and nearly got yourself killed."

"I was defending myself admirably!" Her tone was indignant and utterly charming.

"You were. I'll be asking about that next. But I've been more than patient with this nonsense. I think I've earned the truth."

At last, she looked up, her eyes catching mine. They were a mossy green in the flickering firelight and the steady gleam from the streetlamps outside. She was searching for something, an answer to a question I couldn't begin to guess.

She released a great breath, her chest dipping with the effort. "Did you kill Gabriel?"

"No!" I shot up from my seat to face her. Immediately following the instinctive, incredulous denial, the implications of the question filtered through slowly. Each more horrifying than the last. "You think I..."

"I do—I *did*. But I think perhaps I was wrong."

"You believe I murdered your husband, stabbed him in the back on your front steps, and you decided to follow me?"

She rose, prim, ladylike, and a touch wary. "Yes, I—yes."

My hand fisted in my hair. "You thought I was a murderer, and you followed me? Are you daft? Are you trying to get yourself killed?"

"No!"

"Truly? Because it seems you deemed it sensible to follow a murderer around for the best part of a week. You brought nothing but a knife to defend yourself with. One you couldn't even reach, I might add. Do you realize how dangerous that was? You could have been killed! And that is not even considering tonight's scrape, which could have left you bleeding or dead in an alley. You thought you were chasing a murderer!"

"I am perfectly well."

"That is hardly the point! What if you had been hurt tonight? How do you think Rosehill would have felt? And me! Do you suppose I could live with myself if you were hurt recklessly chasing after me?"

"You can barely tolerate me. I think you would have managed just fine."

"Of course I can barely tolerate you! You're infuriating, breathtaking, and charming. You can do things with an umbrella that would make an intelligent man wince but are certainly not having that effect on me. And you have a bleeding death wish! Lord, this must be what Kit feels all the time. No wonder he refuses to do anything about it. Is that what ladies do? They just gallivant wherever they please with no regard for their personal safety and expect the people who care about them to clean up whatever mess they make?"

"You care about me?" She took a step toward me, one hand reaching out. She froze just before she reached my chest.

"No—yes—I don't bloody know! I can't stop thinking about you. Dreaming about you. You're everywhere. All the time. And you're out there convinced I'm a murderous monster. How am I supposed to feel?"

"I didn't know." The hand brushed my chest through the thin fabric of my shirt, immediately igniting the fire within. Her delicate fingers rose and fell with my ragged breath.

"Of course not. Regardless, it doesn't matter how I feel. You clearly find me repugnant."

"I don't..."

"Don't what?"

"Find you repugnant. I never did." The way she said it, softly with wide, earnest eyes... as though repugnant was the opposite of how she felt.

The sight had me clutching at the hand that sat like a brand over my heart. I pressed it tighter, preventing escape.

"How do you feel then?" I breathed.

"I... I don't know either. I was so sure. But you were so... And I couldn't believe that someone could be that... Would do that to him."

"That didn't make a lick of sense."

She took a deep breath, held it, and released. "I don't know how I feel. I think it's fair to say that I've thought of nothing but you since that night."

"So where does that leave this?"

"Two people, who feel something other than hatred."

"And what do two people who feel something other than hatred do?"

Her tongue darted out, brushing between parted lips, and I could not be held responsible for my answering groan.

"I think they kiss. They definitely kiss."

And so they did.

Thirteen

CELINE

A REVELATION. That was what he had called our last kiss. If that was a revelation, this was earth shattering.

All the eagerness and enthusiasm from the balcony, now with an added confidence. And, oh he had been paying attention. Somehow, some way, he had learned every single thing I loved. Memorized them. Things I hadn't even known myself. And he was trying them all. He used every bit of knowledge he had gleaned to take me apart, piece by piece, until all that was left was a puddle of desperation at his feet.

William's groans caressed my neck, sure as his lips. There was something heady in it—the knowledge that he took so much pleasure in the taste of my skin. His breathing was harsh and ragged, whispering along in a sensuous glide along my flesh.

His hand knotted in my hair, tugging enough to feel but not hurt. His other arm wrapped completely around my waist, solid and steady and *there*. He nipped my lip gently and soothed it with his tongue. Before I could accustom myself to a sensation, he had moved on to the next mind-blowingly sweet torture.

Breathlessly, I slipped one hand up to cup his cheek and trace the sharp corner of the bone. The one I hadn't been able to appreciate fully under the mask. The muscles beneath my fingers worked with each kiss.

His groan was sharp and needy when I wrapped my other hand behind his neck to pull him to me tighter, closer, harder.

I never wanted his kisses to stop. At the same time, other parts of me were crying for attention. If he could do this to my lips, what could he do with my neck and breasts and the space between my legs? The effect would be devastating.

As if sensing my thoughts, his lips slipped from mine, traveling along my jaw and finding a space just below my ear to ravish. Bolstered by the warm reception his lips received, the arm still wrapped around my waist made a brave dip to grip my bottom. A moan ripped from him at the touch.

He hitched my leg up around his waist and dragged his hand along my skirt-covered thigh. Even through far too many layers of skirts and breeches, there was no mistaking his appreciation.

With a reluctant groan, he pulled away, setting me back on two feet before stepping back. His lips were swollen from my attentions and his eyes hazy with lust.

My confusion must have read on my face because he answered my unasked question. "We need to stop."

"No, we don't." My answer came from someone else's lips. It could not have sprung from me with so little thought. Wherever it came from, it settled into the space between us, quivering there.

His throat bobbed and his cheek worked as he bit back whatever instinctive response my comment elicited. Azure eyes closed and he took a deep breath, releasing it before stepping forward.

He cupped my jaw and tilted my gaze to meet his. "Not tonight, love. It's been quite a day for the both of us. Lots of excitement, passion, and frights. Don't want to do anything you'll regret."

Delight at the endearment warred with undeterred and unabated lust, fighting for prominence against the instinctive pang of rejection.

"But you want to?" I asked, sounding pathetic even to my own ears.

He chuckled. "Wanting has never been the problem in our situation. I didn't want to want you. But... Every time I see you, every time we talk, every time we touch, every time we fight—I can't think for wanting you. You're in my blood, spreading through every inch of me until all that's left is you."

Oh... Oh my.

My stomach flipped as I stared into his eyes and my heart slipped out of rhythm in a way that was at once familiar and entirely new. I was not there. Not even close yet.

But it was within my grasp—that thing that I wanted most in the world and feared more than anything else. The sentiment that would leave me drowning and needing—not air—but *him*. My heart pounded out a staccato rhythm.

Could I do this again? If I did, would I survive the fallout?

"Told you I was a terrible poet..." He took a step back and his hand fell away from my cheek. It found the back of his neck in a sheepish scratch.

"No! That was beautiful. I just think you might be right. About tonight. It was an eventful day."

"Right. I should see you home."

"You don't have to, I can manage."

"Celine—Lady Rycliffe, I mean. If you think I'm allowing you to walk home by yourself after the events of this evening, you are sorely mistaken."

"I think we can dispense with the formalities at this point, don't you?"

"All right. *Celine*, I will be escorting you home. Now, gather your umbrella and your knife."

"It's your umbrella, *William*." His eyes, midnight blue in the dim firelight, softened at the sound of his name. Even as a smirk crossed his lips.

"Not anymore. You got viscera on it."

I could not have contained the burst of laughter that broke from my chest for all the world.

"I really did, didn't I?"

He handed me his overcoat and I slipped my arms inside. It hung too wide and too long, but it was warm and smelled of sage and old books.

"You did. Is it strange if I tell you I found it rather attractive?" He led me down the steps and out into the night before hesitating.

"Left. And probably. But I rather like the idea of you being attracted to me." He turned, guiding me along with a protective hand hovering behind my back. It never found its place, but I could feel the warmth through the dress and coat and chemise.

"Are you going to tell me where you learned to do that?"

"Gabriel taught me to fence. I used it like a foil."

"Don't know why we sent an entire army to France. We could have sent you and your umbrella and the whole war would've been finished in an afternoon."

"It was mostly luck. They didn't expect me to fight back. Right here," I directed.

"No one would have expected you to fight back like that. You were glorious. Remind me to stop upsetting you."

We reached an even safer area of town than the merchant row he lived on. His hand dropped to his side. I found myself missing the warmth. During a furtive glance in his direction, I caught his gaze on my hand swinging softly at my side. He stared at it for two paces, three, four before taking a deep breath and wrapping his hand around it. Rewarding him for his bravery, I slotted our fingers together and he gave a gentle squeeze.

"Left, Cadieux House is just up there." I gestured with my chin, unwilling to let go of his hand for the sake of clarity. "The one with the white pillars and the wrought iron fence."

He nodded thoughtfully, then took another fortifying breath with a glance at our entwined hands. "Would it be presumptuous to ask if I could call on you?" He must have read my hesitation because he continued, "Just to see that you're all right, I mean. Sometimes bruises and such take time to develop."

"Yes, you may call on me. But I have to make a visit tomorrow morning. Perhaps in the afternoon? Or another day?"

"Tomorrow afternoon."

"You aren't needed in the office?"

"I'm the owner. I'm simultaneously always needed and never needed depending on who you ask and which moment you ask them." I rewarded his white lie with a genuine laugh as we reached the door.

"Goodnight, William," I whispered as Bouvier opened the door behind me with a disapproving tut.

"Goodnight, Celine." He turned and scampered away, likely eager to avoid whatever menacing expression my butler had donned.

"What on earth?" Bouvier stared, jaw slack at my frightful state.

"Not now, Bouvier."

"In the morning then. You had us all worried sick."

"I'm sorry to have upset you. You may lecture me at your leisure in the morning."

"Very well. I'll have a bath drawn for you. May I take your... men's great coat?"

"Please, and the umbrella as well."

"Of course." I wandered down the hall, eager to be elsewhere when he inspected the item.

"What did you do to this?" he called after me.

"You really do not wish to know."

"You will be the death of me, you know that don't you?"

"Goodnight, Bouvier."

"Goodnight, madame."

Fourteen

WILLIAM

THE MORNING after the strangest day of my life, I woke surprisingly refreshed. Considering the sheer number of things I was studiously *not* thinking about, it was a wonder I found sleep at all.

My back, shoulders, and bruised midsection protested when I moved wrong. Remnants of the scuffle last night. That fight... She could have been seriously injured, or worse, killed. And she held them off with an umbrella. I still couldn't decide whether to kiss her or scold her. When I considered for too long, terror and lust swirled in a bizarre combination that left me entirely discomfited.

I was dressed and downstairs far earlier than was my custom. My desk was relatively clean when I settled in my chair with my coffee. Kit really had taken care of things yesterday afternoon. That would certainly cost me.

Though not as much as the questions I had for him.

A brief glance through the main room and out the door revealed an empty bench. That caused a pang of disappointment. My little shadow had been annoying, amusing, and intriguing. But I felt her absence keenly.

I hadn't missed her in my dreams at least. In sleep, she was glorious, all gilded hair and skin, delicate curves, and sweet sighs. And desperate for me.

The kissing had gone well—more than well. But she wanted more last night. I'd never done more. Hell, I'd never had a kiss like the one at the masquerade. And unfortunately for me, my only friend was Kit.

Summoned by my reluctant thoughts, the bell chimed against the door. His usually dour expression was nowhere to be seen, and in its place, amusement.

"You seem… refreshed this morning."

"Smug does not become you, Christopher." He wandered off to the side table where we kept treats. I had not gone to Hudson's this morning, worried about the work that awaited me. His disappointed groan echoed through the empty room.

"I gave you the afternoon off; the least you could do is bring tarts."

"My name is above the door, same as yours. But I appreciate your efforts yesterday all the same."

"You can appreciate my efforts with pastries. Or one of those fancy little cake things she makes," he said, stripping his coat off and tossing it over Matthews's desk for the sole purpose of irritating the man.

Gathering my courage and dignity, I made what was sure to be a terrible choice. "I'll go now. Come with me? I have something I would like to discuss."

"I just took off my coat. What is it that you cannot discuss here?" He whined at me from across the office.

That is precisely why I want to be elsewhere, Christopher.

"I could discuss it here, I just prefer to discuss it elsewhere. It's not strictly related to our work."

"Fine, but you're buying three of those little cake things."

He appeared in my doorway, his coat halfway on. I followed him out and locked up behind us.

The bakery was just down the street, and we had traversed nearly a quarter of the distance before he goaded me. "Are you planning to discuss whatever it is sometime before we get there?"

I hesitated, uncertain of where to start. Coward that I was, I started with the easiest. "I will need to step away for a few hours this afternoon."

"Again? You couldn't take care of whatever it was yesterday?"

"The circumstance only arose because of my afternoon off yesterday."

"I can manage the office. Are you going to tell me what it is? Or am I to guess?"

"I am calling on someone. A lady."

He actually froze on the pavement. When I turned, he was staring at me wide-eyed and open-mouthed. I would feel somewhat resentful of his astonishment, but even I had to admit the situation was worthy of such a reaction. "You... Who?"

"As I said, a lady."

"A... Oh! Oh! You're calling on Lady Rycliffe?" He nearly shouted the comment and several nearby heads turned.

"Keep your voice down."

"That's not a 'no,'" he said, more sedate this time. Finally, he lurched forward to join me and continue to Hudson's.

"Yes, but you needn't tell the whole *ton*."

"How did that happen?"

"That is not relevant nor is it something I will be sharing. You will manage the office?"

"Yes, of course. Anything for true love. You're perfect for each other. I don't know why I didn't see it yesterday when you were hissing at each other in your office like angry cats."

We reached the shop and tucked inside to wait in the substantial line. Hudson's had become a destination for the rich and beautiful, but that was in the afternoon. The beau monde came to sit in front of the curved bay windows to be seen while they enjoyed mouthwatering tarts and delightful cakes.

In the mornings, the peasants like me stood in an infinite line, taking our treats with us. Each and every bite had been worth the hours of my life spent in this line.

Kit had the good sense to set the conversation aside while we were inside. When, at last, we made it to the counter, an exhausted Ainsley slumped against it in his wife's usual place.

"Oh, it's you two. Anna was wondering why she hadn't seen you this morning. She set aside the usual assortment of tarts for you so we wouldn't sell out. Let me grab them."

"Thank you. And thank Mrs. Ainsley for us. Is she with little Emma?"

"Yes, Em is cutting teeth and has no interest in anything except being bounced by one of us. My stomach has decided that there shall be no more bouncing for a bit." I winced in sympathy.

I spent little time in the company of infants, but there had been nights when Adriane required constant stroking of her hair so she could sleep. That was probably somewhat easier on the stomach than the bouncing.

"These are perfect. We're going to need one of those little cake things for Kit over here. He was a very good lad watching the office yesterday."

Kit turned, glaring with indignation. "Did you not, just two minutes ago, ask me for a favor? Do you really want to press this?"

I turned back to Ainsley. "Right, one little cake thing. No irreverent commentary."

Ainsley added one to the basket with a raised brow and

grin. We usually ended up with four or five empty baskets before one of us remembered to return them to the shop, but Mrs. Ainsley was overly indulgent with us.

With an exchange of thanks and well wishes, Kit and I set off once again. Having used my easy question for the walk to the shop, I was left with the more uncomfortable one.

"Kit?"

"Yes?" He answered, his mouth full of cake thing. Impatient, that one.

"I need your advice. Not because I think you're the best person to offer it. But because, as it turns out, you're my only friend."

"I don't know who should be more insulted by that statement, me or you?"

"Me, certainly."

"All right, out with it."

I kept my voice low. "How does one go about... pleasing a woman?" My efforts at subtlety were destroyed when he choked on his bite of cake thing. Great heaving coughs racked through his chest in an attempt to expel the crumbs from his lungs, drawing the gaze of everyone on the street. Were he not turning a purplish-red shade, I would think it purposeful.

At length, he righted himself and asked in a hoarse croak, "Come again?"

"You heard me the first time." We continued down the street.

"I assume this has something to do with your call this afternoon with a certain stunning Frenchwoman of our acquaintance?"

"It does."

"You know she's a lady? She won't want to be pleased without a ring on her finger."

Well, that was certainly not the case with Celine. Now I

was faced with the challenge of providing the necessary information without tarnishing her honor.

My lack of response must have caught his notice because he turned to look at me, catching my arm and pulling me to a stop. "Unless.... William! You did have a pleasant afternoon, didn't you?"

"Do stop talking." I turned back, hastening my strides toward the office.

"No, no. In all seriousness, Will, are you not five and thirty?"

"Six and thirty. What has that to do with anything? I was at war, in case you forgot. And Oxford. And there was... someone. But she was unwell, and we never..."

"And you didn't... in France?"

"No."

"Right..." We had reached the office. Fortunately none of the clerks had arrived in our absence. Once inside, Kit set the basket at the designated table and nodded toward his office. Shutting the door behind us, he gestured to the chair across from his. "So, obviously, this conversation never happened."

"Obviously."

He sighed, leaning back in his chair to prop his feet on the desk. The chair tipped up onto two legs, balancing precariously. I couldn't help but hope he fell. "I don't exactly have hands-on experience. So to speak."

"Brilliant."

"I'm four and twenty, you can hardly be disappointed that I cannot offer advice when you have more than a decade on me."

"No, you're right. I'm sorry. I just..."

"Don't want to disappoint?"

"More or less."

"Well, I did not say I'm without advice. Just nothing first-hand." At my raised brow, he continued. "You should have asked Ainsley back there. Mrs. Ainsley always seems to be in a pleasant mood."

"He is a client. She is a client. That is wholly inappropriate."

"Excellent point. Well... you could always just ask her—Lady Rycliffe—what she likes. If the time comes, I mean. She is a widow, so it's not as though..."

"That is... not the worst possible idea."

"Thank you. I'm quite known for my mediocre notions."

Just then the bell chimed, signaling either a clerk or a patron and the end of our conversation. I rose and poked my head out of Kit's office to see Rosehill wringing his hands in front of him.

Before I could dissolve into a fit of panicked explanations for last night, he spoke. "Good morning, Will. Do you have a few minutes later this morning? I wanted to discuss my trip. But unfortunately, Dav is making a nuisance of herself. As I understand it, Davina's concerns are Mr. Summers's to solve."

"Of course. Just stop in when you've sort—"

"She was caught trying to sneak aboard a ship to France. She was dressed as a lieutenant." The shamed exasperation with which Rosehill spoke was equal parts amusing and endearing. He could not be accused of failing to love his sister.

"Right... I'll leave that to Kit." I turned back to see the man collapsed onto his desk, his face buried in his palm. "Good luck!"

My only answer was a pathetic groan.

THE KNOCK STARTLED me out of my contracts. Rosehill appeared somewhat less high-strung than earlier.

"Come in, come in. Everything sorted?"

"I think Mr. Summers is going down to the docks." He

settled in his usual chair with far fewer concerns about the windows and doors this time.

"Better him than me. So, Scotland? Yorkshire? Somewhere else entirely?"

"Scotland," he nodded. "Is the place inhabitable?"

"Your steward seems to think so. How long are you planning to stay? You may wish to arrange some improvements if you're to be there the rest of the summer."

"That was one of the things I wanted to discuss." He studied my desk with interest, his finger tracing the grain along the wood. "I would like to settle there. For that to be my primary residence."

"I beg your pardon?" The words were out of my mouth before my head considered the rude tone.

"I would like to move. To Scotland. Permanently."

"But, with all due respect, Your Grace…"

"It's Xander, Will. You've known me forever." His lips pursed to one side of his face in a manner I'd only ever associated with him. That expression meant a whole host of things, but it was usually in the vicinity of a smile.

"What about your mother? And your sister? And a wife?"

"It's time for me to leave. I— It's for the best." His eyes found mine, so brown they were almost black and filled with an exhausted heartache. It was the closest he'd ever come to acknowledging—confirming my suspicions.

Still, I could not allow him to make such a decision without considering the implications. Surely there were other ways. "And your family?"

"That's why I have you. I need to set up provisions for Mother and Davina. Celine too. How much control are you able to give Celine? She's the only one with a lick of sense."

I would beg to differ on that point after last night, but I could hardly tell him that.

"I'll need everything that isn't entailed to be split between

Mother and Dav if anything were to happen to me. However, I do not think they would do well with immediate, unfettered access."

"Well, the Yorkshire property belongs to the dukedom. The Scotland property is yours outright, though it doesn't bring in a great deal. The houses here in town I'll need to look into. The Rycliffe house, at least, may not be entailed. But, Xander, are you certain this is what you wish to do?"

"I have a great many wishes. Unfortunately, wishes cannot change reality."

"Right. Well, you're young. You should have many years before the entail becomes a concern for your family."

"Gabriel was a year younger than I am now. He had many years to live and a wife for that matter. I was never intended to inherit. If I do not wed and have children, the dukedom will go to some second cousin. Is the income from the unentailed estates sufficient to support Mother and Davina? I do not want to rely on a second cousin's goodwill."

"For any other mother and sister, I would say yes, more than. For yours..."

His mouth quirked to one side in that way of his. "That is what I feared. Is there any way to take income from the entailed estates and set up accounts for them now that cannot be accessed unless something were to happen to me?"

"Well, the dowry should be untouchable."

"Who, exactly, do you believe willing to marry Davina?"

I rather thought Kit would, if he ever gathered the courage. Though whether the girl would have him was a different matter entirely.

"I'll need to review and see exactly which properties are entailed to see what will need to be done."

"Very good. Can you look into dowering Celine as well? Obviously, we could not guarantee it if the title changes hands. But while I'm able, I would like to offer her that option. She has her own funds, but I do not want her limited in her choices. Also, can you determine what authority she could be granted to manage things?"

Suddenly it became very apparent that, in addition to managing Lady Davina's adventures, Kit ought to handle conversations about Celine. Because this was entirely unethical.

The urge to argue that any dandy who would require a bribe to wed *Celine* did not deserve her was nearly overwhelming. Suddenly, the image of my mother's ring on her delicate hand flooded in and took hold. Entirely inappropriate.

Forcing myself to attempt a veil of professionalism, I answered. "The dowry should not be an issue. Authority may be. Also, I hate to bring this up, but... Lady Davina? I cannot imagine she will stop her... adventures when you are away."

"Mr. Summers will be given carte blanche to use whatever funds necessary to get her out of whatever scrape she has gotten herself into. That is one of the things I hope Celine may be able to manage in my absence. And if my sister is still finding mischief after my untimely demise, she will have to find her own way out of it."

"Well, you've given me a great deal to consider. To be quite honest, I thought the trip was a ploy to get into the office. I haven't been as thorough as I ought."

"Ah yes, I owe you an apology for that."

"Unnecessary. It was certainly amusing."

"Well, apology issued, nonetheless. My departure does not need to be immediate, but I should like to be settled in Scotland before the weather starts to turn."

"I will have answers to your questions by next week, and contracts drawn up just as soon as we discuss my findings. Would that suffice?"

"Perfect. Thank you, Will. I could not trust just anyone

with this. I appreciate your discretion. Now, I should head down to the docks and retrieve my recalcitrant sister."

"Good luck!" He merely offered an exhausted chuckle in response on his way out. And I was left with a great deal of research to distract me from the even greater list of things I was decidedly not thinking about.

And another damn favor to ask of Kit. Perhaps Mrs. Ainsley had not sold out of the little cake things yet.

Fifteen

CELINE

I WOKE with fewer aches than I deserved but more than I wished. My hip was home to a truly spectacular bruise, the result of landing on the pavement. My neck was home to a wholly inappropriate one, the result of one William Hart.

I could not bring myself to lament it, not when the brush of my fingers across the mark served as a reminder of citrus and sage and heated sapphire eyes.

I did not favor the fichu as a rule, and it took some time for Jane to locate one to cover the mark. It would certainly attract notice where I was going, but it could not be helped. While I broke my fast, I endured a lecture from Bouvier that was more severe than I wished but well warranted. Afterward, I set off into the morning sun.

For the first time in days, I did not have a bench to occupy. Instead, I made my way to Mama's.

Presently, I occupied the home that had once been ours. After the late duke demanded I give up Rycliffe Place, I moved back in with her. For over a year, she and I lived together before she left the house to me and moved into Monet Manor with our dear friend Marie.

There was something about young widowhood and the violent death of one's husband that only my mother could understand. It was a peculiar bonding experience. Our relationship shifted irrevocably that day—the day I fell apart in her arms with Gabriel's blood still staining my hands. That was the day we became equals in grief.

Though he had known me for nearly two decades, Marie's butler was ever the professional. He directed me to the drawing room as though I were a lady he'd never met before. Mama found me a few moments later, midsip of my tea.

"*Chérie*, you look well." She whispered after a warm embrace. My mother's French never failed to cause a pang of guilt and longing for the country I barely knew and the language I hardly recognized.

"Merci, Mama. You as well. How is Marie?"

"She is lovely as always. She is still abed, but I'm certain she will join us soon." Her dark eyes surveyed me. Perhaps it was my imagination that they caught on the mark through the gauzy fabric covering my neck. There was no way she could see it through the fabric, I was certain. But her gaze lingered in the space on my neck where the mark lay.

"Is there something you wish to tell me, *chérie*?"

"How do you always know?"

"You are here before midday. You're wearing an ill-suited fichu. And I've loved you your entire life. It makes one observant."

"I may have feelings. For a man."

She studied me thoughtfully before answering. "And you are worried. About what, precisely?"

"Anything? Everything? I've entertained the thought, occasionally, over the years. I considered, perhaps, moving on, finding someone whose company I could enjoy. In wistful moments I've even considered the possibility of falling in love again. But..."

"Faced with the possibility you are terrified?" She always knew. How did she always know?

"Yes. I do not even know precisely why."

"Oh *ma fille chérie*... In losing Gabriel, you endured pain beyond words. To love someone the way you loved him, and to lose him—in such a sudden, violent manner as well. It is more than anyone should have to endure. But I know you. You are not capable of loving by half measures. To let someone in, truly in, you risk that pain again."

I remembered little of the months after Gabriel passed. But I would never forget the agony of each breath. My chest fisted in an angry knot, each and every inhale feeling like death. Worst of all was the knowledge that I would have to make the effort all over again in mere seconds, endure the torment again and again and again.

Eventually the pain lessened, or perhaps I became accustomed to it. But the memory of it was still sharp and bright. And that was the essence of it. Because when I had been with Michael, we shared an amicable friendship alongside our arrangement. Feelings had never gone deeper than fondness and attraction. That would not be so with William.

From the start, every interaction between us had been the highest of highs and the lowest of lows. I wanted to kiss William as often as I wanted to kill him. And he made no secret that he felt the same. Already, I could feel myself being swept away. I could fight the current and perhaps survive. Or I could give in and drown in him. And each was its own kind of terror.

I had not noticed the tears start to fall, not until my mother brushed them away one by one. "You are brave, *ma chérie,* to even consider it. And I am so proud of how far you've come. No matter what you decide."

"What about Gabriel?"

"If it had been you who passed and not Gabriel, what would you have wanted for him?"

"It is different. He had responsibilities."

"Not so different. He would want you to be happy, certainly. Now, tell me about this man."

"Mama!"

"What? He must be an interesting fellow."

"He... He fascinates me. The way Gabriel did, but... different? Every time I learn something new about him, I like him more because of it."

"Is he very handsome?"

"He is... sharp, all extremes. Not classically attractive, but I find him handsome."

"Sharp?"

"It fits him. He has an edge, quick to irritation but softens easily. His face fits as well, his cheeks and jaw are finely honed, and his eyes are the bluest I've ever seen."

"Not charming then?" she asked.

"On closer acquaintance, yes."

"He need not be charming to others. How does he treat you? You said he is easily irritated?"

"He is unwilling to suffer my very occasional nonsense. But he is considerate and brave."

"Do I wish to know how you determined he was brave?"

"No, certainly not." That earned me an indulgent chuckle, the same one I used to receive when I was caught sneaking biscuits from the kitchen.

"How does he support himself? Does he own property?"

"He is a solicitor. He works with Kate's brother, Lord Leighton. You remember Kate, Viscountess Grayson?"

"Vaguely. The pretty one whose aunt put her in the unfortunate gowns?" she asked before waving the thought away. "A man who knows the value of hard work, that is not to be underestimated. Life itself can be hard work, and a man accustomed to it will be well served by his experience in those times."

"Yes, that is her. But I must admit, I expected a bit of disapproval for his position."

"Perhaps at one time. But having seen how you suffered these past years, I rather think that anyone who makes you happy will delight me. Regardless of his circumstances. I would like to meet this man. Have him come for dinner?"

"But..."

"Celine Cadieux... if you are considering this man with any kind of seriousness, I wish to meet him. If you prefer, you may host." My mother had never adopted the Hasket name when scolding me. Nothing made me feel quite so young and insolent as being addressed by my maiden surname.

"I do not know if I am considering him. I do not know if he is considering me."

"Well that is ridiculous. Every man with a pulse has been considering you since you were far too young to be considered." I merely rolled my eyes, something Mother was kind enough to indulge.

"I should be going soon. He will call this afternoon and I have another stop to make. Is Marie still abed?"

"Oh, likely so. She is a late riser. I will give her your good wishes. And you can see her when you bring your young man to supper."

"Yes, Mama."

"Celine? Say hello to Gabriel for me."

"How did you know?"

Her eyes softened when she replied. "I always know."

THE WALK to the Hasket family home was more than warm —it was sweltering. The sun was high and bright, and the temperature was unseasonably hot for so early in the summer.

The past week was the longest I had ever gone without visiting Gabriel. The oppressive heat and more oppressive guilt slowed my pace. Each step was a fight, as though I walked through mud.

The trip took nearly twice as long as it ought to due to my theatrics, but eventually I made it to the plot outside of Hasket House. The family was used to my visits, and I was free to slip through the wrought iron fence without announcing myself.

Unlike the Cross Bones Graveyard, the fence and grounds were well-tended and maintained. The contrast between Gabriel's final home and Adriane's was more stark than I ever could have imagined. Brushing away that unhelpful comparison, I found myself at my usual spot in mere steps.

Usually on a day as warm as this one, I would sit on the ground, my back resting against the cool stone. Sometimes if I closed my eyes I could pretend I was in his arms. Today the bench was more tempting. It had the irrational effect of making me feel that I was facing him.

I began my ritual as I always did, my fingers pressed to my lips before dropping them to the headstone with a whispered, "Bonjour, Mon amor." My voice was thicker this time than it had been in years. In lieu of the intimacy of resting against his stone chest and the perceived distance of my bench, I sat on the grass facing him.

"I am sorry to have left you so long, but I have much to tell you. And ask you."

A leaf from the nearby oak tree escaped and brushed my cheek on its fall.

"I missed you too. I... I know you are not here, not really.

But I need to ask you something. And I need you to give me a sign. Please. Anything."

The breeze gave a gentle waft, ruffling my hair.

"You were not killed by William, were you?"

An unnatural stillness surrounded me. For an unending moment, nothing happened. I waited, too afraid to breathe, to create an unnatural sign. Then a butterfly flapped delicately into view before finding perch on the nearby irises. Orange with black-tipped wings that fluttered easily. It was soon joined by a brother, small and white. Then a blue and a red friend came too. Dancing around the flowers as they swayed in the breeze.

"That's a no?"

The littlest blue one flitted over and settled itself on my knee. This one was familiar. I had seen it, or one like it, last week and in years past. But he had never come close enough to touch, to land.

"Thank you." The words came out of me in a rush. Tension abandoned me, leaving me boneless with desperate relief.

"I... I have... feelings for him. Not love, but... it could be. Maybe. And I don't know what to do with them."

My little companion gave a graceful flap of his wings.

My throat tightened as I tried to find the words. "I feel as though I'm betraying you. What we had. What we could have had."

The grass beside my feet rustled with the breeze. The tears were there now, just hovering, waiting for the right moment to escape.

"I could not possibly have found someone you would hate more."

Somewhere high up in the oak tree, the great tit that called it home let out its laugh-like call.

"I don't know how to do this. If I'm even capable of it. If I fell in love again. And lost again... I would never recover. I'm not sure I know how to stop anyway. Nothing could have stopped me from loving you, not even your own efforts."

With a last agitated flap of his wings, the small butterfly returned to the irises with his friends.

I rose and settled my back against the familiar stone. In Gabriel's arms again, I let the tears go. One became ten became ten thousand. Tears for all the memories we would never make, for the kisses we would never have, the days that were stolen from us.

I made no effort to wipe them away. There was no point. Eventually, minutes, hours, days later, the world came back to me. Blue iridescent wings waving back and forth in the breeze on my knee, the great tit sitting on its lower branch, laughing at me, a breeze brushing through my hair, and his cool stone at my back.

I sat, enjoying the sights and smells and sounds and touches I had attributed to my husband over the years. Appreciating each and every one of them for their efforts. Thanking them silently.

"Thank you, mon amor. I do not think I will be by to see you quite as often anymore. I think it is time I make some new memories instead of mourning the ones we will never have. I will never, not if I live to see the end of time, love anyone the same way that I love you. I want you to know that."

One by one, the butterflies flitted back to wherever they came from. The bird offered one last forlorn chirp. A bit of dandelion fluff whispered past me in the great gust of wind that pulled a few tendrils from my coiffure.

And then all was silent. And I rose with one last press of lips to fingers and fingers to stone. And I made my way out of the cemetery and into the sunshine.

Sixteen

WILLIAM

Six and thirty and I'd never called on a woman, not with courting in mind anyway. And I was starting with *her*.

Kit returned from retrieving Lady Davina at the docks dirty and exhausted and more than a little irritated to work on my behalf this afternoon. His mood was much improved after I sent him to clean up. He yelled something about flowers in my direction as I was leaving.

I purchased a few blooms at a stall on the way, making an effort not to crush the stems in my fit of nerves. The walk was pleasant and the breeze offset the sun's potential to overheat.

Grosvenor's Street. Was it possible to more clearly illustrate the futile nature of this endeavor? Half a mile. Half a mile and a few thousand pounds separated me from Celine.

Her home was not part of the Rosehill portfolio, I knew that for certain. She had money of her own, independent from her marriage to Rycliffe.

It explained some of her difficulty blending into the background in her maid's outfit. Her manners were innate, born of decades of practice. It was a part of her now, her frame, the way she moved.

She hadn't looked in askance at my little one-bedroom apartment above the office. But how much of that had been shock, how much good breeding, and how much was a genuine lack of concern?

I found her house by the columns and the fence, just as she had directed last night. She had a well-manicured little lawn behind the fence that I hadn't noticed.

Her little off-white house was more modest than the homes surrounding it. Only four stories whereas the surrounding homes had six. Hers had a delicate balcony that wrapped across the second story.

Balconies and multiple stories, I never learned...

Still, I promised to call. And I'd never been able to think with my head when beautiful women were concerned. Why start now?

After a deep breath, I knocked on the black double doors. The butler I hadn't caught a good look at last night answered. "Mr. Hart, do come in. She is expecting you."

"Thank you..."

"Bouvier. She is awaiting you in the drawing room. At present, she is free of blood and soot. Please see that she is returned in the same state."

"I... I will. I—is it customary for staff to scold guests?"

"Lady Rycliffe is a well-loved employer. There are more than a few of us who would be willing to do far worse than scold." Of course she would be a good employer. It was not as though she could be wretched to her staff or anything else that would make her even somewhat dislikable. There was nothing about her that I could cling to as a balm when this foolhardy endeavor ended spectacularly at my feet.

"Noted..."

"I trust you will have her home at a reasonable hour."

"She is widowed and in her thirties. Also, I don't know that we are intending to leave."

"I fail to see what that has to do with the matter."

"Have you met her? I doubt God himself could take or keep her anywhere she did not wish to be." That earned me a laugh that was poorly covered by a cough.

"She is in the drawing room. This way." Light poured from the windows behind me, casting long beams down the hall. The entry space was open and airy with golds, soft greens, and creams.

I followed the butler to the drawing room. He'd returned to his solemn professional countenance.

He announced my arrival to the occupant with more than due ceremony. Even from the hall, I could hear the smile in her answer.

"Bouvier, I told you I was expecting him and you could just direct him here. Did you use the time to lecture him as well?"

"I would never, madame. That would be impertinent."

"Oh, of course. Send him in, will you? And tea, I think. When you have a moment." He turned back to me with a warning eyebrow, then gestured to the opened doorway.

And there she was, bathed in the afternoon light pouring through the windows. Impossibly, she was more beautiful than the night at Wayland's. With her face unencumbered by a mask, there was nothing to distract from her expressive eyes and button nose. Today, she wore her own gown instead of a borrowed maid's uniform. She was herself for the first time since we'd met. And she was breathtaking.

"Hello, William," she said, forcing my frozen feet into action. Her lips curved into a delicate, pleased smile. At least she appreciated the effect she had on me. If she found it off-putting this would be a very unpleasant afternoon.

"Good afternoon, Celine. I brought you these." I thrust

the flowers, clasped too tightly in my hand, toward her in the least gentlemanly manner possible. Gone was the easy familiarity brought by danger and darkness. In its place, an awkward solicitor with ink still smearing his wrist.

She stopped a few feet from me and tugged the flowers gently from my grasp.

"Irises... Thank you." Her voice was thick as her eyes widened and welled slightly with tears.

A poor choice indeed. I hadn't studied the language of flowers—what on earth had I given her? I made to pull them back, but she refused to release them.

"I am sorry. Are you not fond of them? I do not know flower meanings. Are they offensive?"

"Not at all. I love them. It's difficult to explain. But they're good. Trust me."

"But you're crying. I've made a right mess of this."

"No, no. I talk to Gabriel sometimes. The way you talk to Adriane?" She flicked the tears away, drawing an elegant finger beneath her lashes to collect the last of them. "He used to bring me irises, and I had them planted near him. It feels a bit like permission. But I'm always assigning meaning where there is none. At least when it concerns him. It is surely a lovely coincidence, nothing more."

I was not quite certain how to feel about that. It seemed a bit doltish, bringing her the same flowers as her late husband. And being compared to Gabriel in anything was sure to find me wanting. But... permission. Permission for what? That was certainly an inappropriate question.

"Truly, William," she assured me. "They are my favorites. Well, anything purple."

Purple, that made sense. She wore purple that night, and she wore it now. And the room around us was draped in purples, mixed with the same soft green from the hall. I could remember purple.

She returned to her place on the settee near the window, leaving me with the awkward choice of chairs placed slightly too far and the space at her side, far too close. Coward that I was, I chose the chair.

"I'm glad you like them. How are you feeling? Are you well?"

"Quite. Only a few bumps and bruises from our adventure. Nothing too serious."

"Bruises? Where? How bad are they?"

"Well, the worst of them is right here," she said. She pointed to the slope where her neck met her shoulder.

There, faint and small, was a red mark. What had happened in the fight to cause that? Was that truly the most serious of her injuries? I glanced up and caught green eyes full of mirth I couldn't explain.

"I suppose it's lucky that is the worst of it."

My comment was met with a feminine giggle. Clearly I was missing something.

"William, that one is from you."

"What?" I could not recall hitting her accidentally last night. When did that happen?

"When you were kissing me..."

"Oh! Oh no. I am so sorry, Celine. Believe me, I had no intention of marking you..."

"Do not apologize, it made me laugh. Though I did have to wear a fichu to visit Mama, and I despise those. I suppose you may apologize for that."

Asking what a fichu was seemed to be the wrong course of action in this situation. "I am truly sorry."

"It is no matter. Speaking of my mother... She wishes to meet you."

She wished... But that meant... "You told your mother about me?"

"It was more that she looked at me and knew. But I would

have gotten around to mentioning you before I left. It just would have taken longer."

"What did she say?"

"That she wants to have you over for supper. Or that I could host if I preferred. Is there a day that would be best for you? Or, I suppose, would you be interested in dining with us?"

Did I wish to dine with her mother? Not particularly. It sounded like an unusual form of torture. "I am available at her convenience. But was she not... concerned about my situation?"

"Oh, not at all."

Every time I thought I understood this woman... Certainly she misunderstood. "Celine, surely she was not pleased. She understands I am not titled, and I have no lands or property?"

"I told her you were a solicitor. That you worked with Kate's brother. She was pleased that you know the value of hard work. The implication being that courting me might be difficult work. I found the notion somewhat insulting, though not entirely inaccurate."

"She knows that I am a solicitor? Does she think I am an earl like Kit?"

"Not at all. She merely wishes me to be happy. It is not so complicated as all that."

Such a stance went against everything I had ever known about the beau monde. Oh, there was the occasional member of the *ton* who was pleasant enough. But that certainly did not extend to courting a member of their family. Adriane's family had been landed gentry, not even titled. It hadn't stopped her father from slamming the door in my face at the mere mention of a courtship. Celine's mother could not be encouraging this.

"There are no distant uncles to leave me their fortune. No titles to be found anywhere."

"I promise I've not misunderstood this. Please, would you join us for dinner? It would mean a great deal to us both."

Her lower lip dipped out in the slightest pout and I was finished. "Of course, if it would make you happy." Though, perhaps I could take up drinking before the evening arrived.

"It would, very much. Thank you. How are you feeling? You received a hit or two."

"My ribs are a bit sore, nothing terribly painful."

"I am glad of it."

The butler arrived with a tea tray in hand and placed it on the mahogany table in front of us.

"Thank you. Please have these brought to my rooms?" She handed him the flowers from beside her. He bowed, overly formal, and tossed a warning glare in my direction before sweeping out the door. "Oh, Bouvier. Would you be a dear and close the door, please?"

"Madame?"

"The door, if you please."

The glare turned from disapproving to murderous. It was in the eyebrows, it had to be... But he bowed in acknowledgment and shut the door behind him with a decisive, judgmental click.

"You didn't have to do that."

"I know," she said. "Sometimes I just like to make his eye twitch." Her laugh joined mine, bright and easy. "How do you take your tea?"

"However you take it is fine. I'm not particular."

She studied me, her eyes narrowing slightly. "It's just tea, William."

With a heavy sigh I answered, "Three sugars and a splash."

"Was that so difficult?" She plopped the sugars into the delicate cup one at a time before tipping the perfect amount of milk, and then making her own. Two sugars and a healthy pour. We would go through far too much sugar if we—

Too fast, much too fast.

"It's good, thank you." I spoke before taking a sip and she raised a brow. Rather than commenting, she turned to the plate of tarts.

"Which do you prefer?"

"Hudson's?"

"Of course. Which tart would you like?"

"It's no matter."

"There are plenty of all the flavors. Pick one."

"Blackberry, please." She settled it on the plate before taking a lemon one. That was the one she chose in the office that day as well. *Lemon, remember lemon.*

"I know what you're doing. You should know, it won't work on me."

I was doing something? "I don't know what you mean?"

"You think if you have no opinions or preferences that inconvenience me in the slightest that I will keep you around longer. I am an expert on the subject."

"Who would wish you away?"

She smiled, catching her lower lip between her teeth to stifle it. The effort was ineffective, it still warmed me all over.

"You did, yesterday if you'll recall. And you're not alone. When Mama and I came from France, we had only what we could carry and sewn into our clothes. We relied on charity for years before her mother passed and left us an inheritance. I became very good at being exactly what everyone else wished. Retaining the favor of whoever took us in for as long as possible was how we survived."

"I didn't think... I am sorry for mocking your accent, when we met that first time."

"I did not realize you recalled that much."

"I remember the breeches. Quite clearly."

"Do you know? I still wear them quite often." She timed the comment perfectly with my sip of tea.

I nearly choked trying to keep from spitting the sweet brew out with my laugh. "Where? When? How?"

"Here, usually. I prefer to practice my fencing in them."

Would it be worth selling my soul to watch that? Probably, but best not to ask. "That explains why you were so good with the umbrella, and so annoyed by the skirts." She took a dainty bite of the lemon tart in agreement. "Rycliffe taught you to fence?"

"He did."

The question was there. Waiting. The one that hadn't been explained away last night. "Why... why did you think I killed him?"

She sighed heavily. "With Gabriel, I tend to react first and think later. Much later on occasion. I did not remember that I saw you the day before he passed. At the races, you caught my gaze across the field. Seeing you again at the masquerade sparked the memory. In a fit of pique, I went digging through some of his papers. I found a note that I thought was from you, calling him out. And I... that was all I needed."

"He died the next day? I didn't know. We were to meet later in the week."

"About Adriane?"

"Yes. I was hoping he could put the title to some use. Get her a proper burial. Was right furious when he never came. Until I heard..."

"He would have. I think he would have. He— I know you hated him. And I know that what he did to her was unforgivable. But he really did regret it."

"Think this might have to be a thing we agree to disagree on, love. You said there was a note?"

"Yes, in his things. He was involved in some... less than ethical dealings. I took the secondary ledgers and anything else he would not have wanted his father or Xander to see."

"You... you have a secondary set of books?" And now I

recalled why I found her so infuriating. "With information in them that may have gotten your husband killed. Does anyone know you have them?"

"Well, Xander as of earlier this week. And now you. You think they had something to do with Gabriel's death?"

"It's possible. And this note?"

"It just said 'Hyde Park 6:30, *W*.' But it looked as though the writer might have been left handed."

"May I see it? And the ledgers? I... If there is something in there that was worth killing over, it is perhaps worth consideration."

She hesitated, and for a moment I thought she was not entirely certain that I hadn't killed her husband. But then she said, "Yes. You won't tell Xander about what you find? Gabriel would not have wanted his brother to know this side of him."

"I won't."

"All right, they're in the study. Bring the tarts?" I grabbed the tray at her direction and followed her down the hall to the last room on the left.

Seventeen

CADIEUX HOUSE, LONDON - JUNE 13, 1816

CELINE

THIS WAS NOT GOING AT ALL the way I had intended. Not in the least.

He was *supposed* to be worshiping me in the boudoir, not digging through dusty old documents between bites of tart.

Though, if I was being honest, he looked... rather adorable. He hunched over my small, feminine desk with his hair mussed and the spectacles slipping down his nose as he paged through yellowed ledgers.

I admired him freely from my perch, resting against the edge of the desk beside him. He was too distracted to notice my indulgent smile.

"If you told me what you were looking for, I might be able to help."

"I'm not certain what I'm looking for. I'll know it when I see it. Do you have that note you mentioned?"

I pulled it from where it was bookmarking one of the more recent ledgers and handed it over.

He studied it with interest, holding it up to the firelight as if there were secrets to be gleaned. "I see what you mean, about the writer being left-handed. But the smudges go the wrong way. When I write, the ink smears to the right. This goes to the left, like they set something damp on it and pulled it out from underneath it."

The easy refute had me feeling more than a little silly. He wasn't irritated. He didn't lecture. He wasn't looking at me at all, but rather studying the page for clues. He treated it as though it was more than a random slip of parchment, tucked into a random ledger nearly a decade ago. The fact that there was no date and little more than an initial didn't lead to an outright dismissal.

I had followed this man around for a week. I had all but branded him a murderer. And he took my evidence seriously? He was helping me?

"There's no date. But you said it was tucked into the most recent ledger when you found it?"

"Yes, just under the cover."

"Do you know of any other Ws he might have known? The names in here appear to be false names your husband chose in jest. Unless there is a lord of 'unfortunate toupee,' that I am unfamiliar with."

"That will be Lord Weatherby. I hadn't considered others, but yes, certainly."

"We'll need to consider given names and surnames, titles as well. Can you make a list of any that you can recall? I can try to match them against the official copies of the ledgers that we keep in the office."

He plucked the spectacles off and cleaned them absent-mindedly with a cloth he magicked out of some pocket or other.

"You're really just helping me with this?"

"Of course. Why wouldn't I?" He finally turned his magnetic gaze back on me. The question was clear in the tilt of his brow. He genuinely had never considered an alternative.

"I accused you of murder..."

His lip quirked up in a self-deprecating smile. "I am hardly a saint, Celine. It's not as though I never thought of calling Rycliffe out. The night I learned what he had done, the day I found her, the evening I lost her. A few thousand times in between. It was a good notion, in truth. It's lucky you never went to the authorities with your suspicion, or I'd surely have been hanged. Now, can you recall any names?"

"I... you're a strange man, William Hart. You know that, right?"

"I do." He tapped the parchment spread before him with an impatient finger.

"I think he had occasional dealings with the Earl of West-field... There was Sir Wilhelm Jacobs."

This was more difficult than one would believe. To recall the faceless masses of the ton.

"Adriane's brother, Weston LaMorte. I suppose he might have been angry enough. Though I'm not certain he was overly invested." William added him to the list.

"His Grace the Duke of Sutton–his Christian name is Winston, Mr. Wesley Parker... Lord Wyatt..." He wrote each with a decisive hand while I racked my brain, searching for the names or faces of anyone who could have known Gabriel. "There was a woman who owns a brothel. Victoria. I don't know her real name or her surname. It's possible she was involved."

His gaze snapped to mine, ink spilling across his list. "Gabriel was visiting a brothel? While you were married?" His tone had turned sharp, snappish, and his eyes darkened.

"No, he stopped all that after we met."

"Right," he agreed, disbelief clear in his voice.

"He did!"

"I'm sure he did. I'll see what I can learn about a Victoria who owns a brothel."

"He truly did stop, William."

I could not explain why it was so essential to me that he believed me, that he understood. Perhaps I did not wish him to think me so naive. Perhaps it was the undertone of pity that had joined the note of irritation at my insistence. My marriage was not something to be pitied.

He caught my hand in his, thumb tracing my knuckles. "No, you're right. No man in his right mind would visit a brothel when you were waiting at home." His eyes and voice had softened.

I swallowed thickly, pushing down sentiments that were entirely inappropriate for the setting. Honestly, lusting after a man while digging through my deceased husband's ledgers, searching for his killer. What had gotten into me?

I settled for a simple, "Thank you."

"Of course. It's the truth. Are there any other names you can recall?"

My gaze cast to the side of the desk as if the answer was to be found there. In fairness, William's eyes were unbearably distracting. Naming the color was quickly becoming my favorite pastime.

That was when I caught sight of the invitation for last week's masquerade, not yet properly disposed of. The masquerade at Wayland's, named after its proprietor. A man Gabriel occasionally had dealings with.

And my former lover.

My stomach twisted into a knot in rebellion at the thought. I could feel my lips moving, attempting to say the name, to add him to the list. But no sound came out.

"Celine?"

Still unable to give voice to that name, I tugged my hand free, grabbed the invitation, and handed it to him silently.

"Oh, love, no. He's aboveboard."

"Now. He's aboveboard now. He began building after receiving funds in 1809. The same year Gabriel was killed."

"He's a friend. I know him. He would never."

"He was my lover for two years. Do you think I wish for it to be him? It's entirely likely that Gabriel's death was the result of some sort of gambling dispute. Michael is the king of gambling in this town."

"He was?" William asked, his voice soft.

"Was what?"

"Your lover."

My eyes found his, and I saw something unreadable in them. "That is the part you found to be of import?"

"Yes—no—right. No, that is not the important part. I apologize. I was just… I don't like to think him capable of it. But you're correct. He should be on the list."

"I think, perhaps, we should be finished for the day." Even I could hear the hollow, tinny quality to my voice. It was fitting when mixed with the metallic tang filling my mouth.

"Right, yes, of course. I… I am sorry. I was distracted by the excitement of a good mystery, and I forgot myself. I forgot that it was real and he was real and that this would all be so very painful for you. That was badly done." His hand caught mine once again. He peered up at me from beneath his brow, his eyes a soft cornflower blue and full of concern.

"It's not your fault. I just, with the masquerade and my ridiculous plan… And then last night… And today I saw Mama and Gabriel, and now this. I am just… I am just a bit overwrought."

He rose, his free hand finding my chin and tipping it up so my eyes met his, concern still etched in their downturned corners.

"You have nothing to apologize for, love."

"I was convinced you murdered my husband. I followed

you for a week in an ill-fitting maid's uniform. I went so far as to spy on you during private moments."

He cocked his head to the side with a smile in acknowledgment. "You have a few things to apologize for. Not this though. I've mucked this up quite thoroughly to be honest. I intended for there to be a great deal more kissing and a great deal less paperwork. I... you— I get quite nervous in your presence. And I do and say the wrong thing. But I'm good at this." He gestured at the pages strewn about my desk. "Can't say the wrong thing to ledgers and contracts."

"You're quite good at the kissing as well. In case you were unaware."

"I'm glad to know you think so. Especially since I quite enjoy kissing you." I tilted my head, awaiting his lips. "Oh, I'm not going to kiss you tonight. As you said, you're overwrought and I would like to be certain that the next time you're feeling unstrung, there's no question that it's due to my kisses."

I blinked, slowly coming to terms with the realization that I was not about to be ravished.

"William! That was quite... charming."

"It's been known to happen on very rare occasions. I think the knowledge that you're so exhausted that you likely won't remember any of this is making me brave." He brought my hand to his lips and pressed a delicate kiss to the knuckles. "I would not become too accustomed to it if I were you."

"I like it. I like you shy too. But you should be brave more often."

His only answer was a chuckle as he bent to place one last kiss on the place where my neck and jaw met. The place that already bore his mark.

"Goodnight, Celine. Sleep well."

I was left standing alone in my study, once again finding my world shaken to its foundations by this man. And I had nothing but warring feelings of arousal, trepidation, and exhaustion for company.

Eighteen

WILLIAM

WHAT I WAS DOING WAS unethical in more ways than I could possibly count. I absolutely should not be digging through contracts and ledgers from clients on behalf of my... whatever she was. Not in the harsh light of day and certainly not in the middle of the night like a common criminal.

I laid abed for an hour, perhaps two, before I could take it no longer and snuck down to the office to have a hunt. No matter how many times I told myself I was only using the Rosehill ledgers for the research Xander requested, it was impossible to separate the tasks. Particularly in the silence of my candlelit office.

Thus far, all I'd gleaned was that Lady Davina had been causing expensive mischief since before she left the nursery and that Her Grace's modiste bill was large enough to fund a small principality. As a courtesy title, the Rycliffe documents, properties, and contracts were so wrapped up in the rest of the Rosehill estate that separating them was nearly impossible.

I managed to discern which Hasket man's abysmal handwriting belonged to Gabriel and made a list of those entries. I created a separate list for any dealings with anyone whose name or title began with a W, regardless of the handwriting. The effort was unlikely to be sufficient and my complete disinterest in the *ton* was serving me poorly in this venture.

It didn't help that I was seemingly permanently distracted by thoughts of Celine. Of her shining hair and sun-kissed skin. Of her eyes, kind with a lived-in sadness behind them. Of the spiced vanilla and floral scents that wrapped around her, drawing me in. Of her graceful form wrapped in silk more luxurious than any I'd touched. Of her seemingly endless patience with my foibles.

The feeling was a strange one, this stirring of attraction, interest, longing. Seemingly reciprocated for the first time in my life. Which was absurd. I had more than a decade of experience loving Adriane. But even at the end, she never loved me. Not really. She loved to toy with me. She loved to use me to attract Gabriel's attention. She loved that I came for her, saved her, cared for her. But it was never real love, desire, or yearning. Not for me.

Only now, years later, could I see the cracks. I suspected the experiences gleaned over a lifetime were to blame for my perpetual astonishment at Celine's easy affection. I could not reconcile this woman, with her friendly open demeanor, against Gabriel as I knew him.

She loved him though, that much was clear. That knowledge chaffed more than I would readily admit. Another woman that I— another woman I had tender feelings toward who loved that man. Jealous as I was, it was nowhere near enough to prevent me from seeking her out, courting her, and anything else she might deign to allow.

But I could ruminate on my burgeoning infatuation without wasting every candle in the place, so I gathered the documents into a haphazard pile. I doused the candles and bundled the paperwork in my arms, then locked the door behind me before making the trek upstairs to my apartment.

As usual, the lamplight from the open window was sufficient and I did not bother with a candle. I tossed the paperwork on my desk next to Celine's mask, the one I really ought to return the next time I saw her.

I collapsed on my bed, still in shirtsleeves and britches. And promptly fell asleep, my dreams filled with sweet laughter and eyes the color of the forest.

I STARTLED awake at an irritating and incessant pounding at my door.

"Will!" Kit's voice was muffled through the thick wood. "Will! Open up!"

Rolling to my feet was more instinct than command because the fog of sleep still hung heavy.

I ripped the door open with an irritated, "What?" Only to be met with a frazzled partner, his dark hair disheveled and eyes wild.

"Thank the Lord. You're all right?"

"Of course, why would I not be?"

"You're usually downstairs by now, and when I got in and saw the place had been ransacked..."

"I didn't sleep well— Wait, what?"

"You better get dressed. I'll meet you downstairs."

"Ransacked?"

"Get dressed. Now. Come downstairs immediately after." He spun on his heel and went back down the stairs.

"Right." Something of Kit's urgency finally penetrated my thick skull and I tossed last night's clothing into a pile to be dealt with later. I struggled into fresh breeches and tugged on a clean shirt as I made my way down the steps, two at a time.

I turned the corner too quickly and nearly smacked into the door as it opened. I glared at Kit, who held it open for me, before I stepped around him. Finally his frantic banging and harried countenance made sense.

My office was... destroyed. Pages were tossed about, the cabinet knocked over and smashed open.

And it was only my office. Beside it, Kit's was untouched. The trunks we kept behind the clerks' desks, too, were unscathed.

There was no telling what they had taken, or if they had taken anything at all. I could barely comprehend the sight before me. My entire life's work... It was more battlefield than office.

"Will..." Kit began from behind me.

"I don't— I have no idea. It was fine after I left last night."

"Someone was looking for something, Will."

"I suppose we'll find out when we determine what's been taken."

Nothing was left to do but settle on the floor and begin stacking documents by account while Kit moved around me, picking up the scattered pieces of the broken cabinet.

The clerks began to arrive, one irritating clang of the bell after another. Each had his own astonished exclamation before Kit directed them to account for all of their files.

"What happened here?" Bates asked, bolder than the others. He peered into the office with interest.

"Break-in," Kit answered from behind him. "Will, can you take a quick look at the overall list of accounts to see if it's up to date?"

"Of course, anything." I scrambled off the floor with what was left of my dignity, ignoring the ache in my ribs from two days past.

"You can use my office. Sorting out this mess is going to

call for a whole batch of those little cake things." He tossed a coat on and set off toward Hudson's.

"Do you want me to continue sorting, sir?" Bates asked, toeing my pile.

"No. I need to see it all if I have any hopes of finding what they took. If anything, I suppose."

I shut Kit's door behind me, taking his usual seat, and cracking open his ledger. He returned shortly and set a little cake thing on the corner of his desk.

"How are you getting on?"

"I think we're all accounted for."

"Good," he said, licking the excess frosting off his finger.

"Can you use a napkin?"

"And waste perfectly good frosting? I think not... I locked the door last night, Will. I know it."

"I know you did. I couldn't sleep. I came down to do a bit of work and all was well."

"What time was that?"

"Twelve thirty, perhaps one. But I locked it too. I'm certain of it. Why would someone break in?"

"Will, they didn't."

"What?"

"The door, it's not broken. They only broke your locked cabinet and desk. If you're certain you locked it..."

My stomach sank. Either a skilled lockpick worked on the door but smashed anything locked in my office, or more likely, they had a key to the front door.

One glance at Kit made it clear he had reached the same conclusion.

"Do you suppose we should call a constable?" I asked.

"And tell them what? Someone made a mess? They only consider cash, jewels, that sort of thing. They won't see the value in information. Not that Bow Street has ever found anything of value anyway. Or returned anything they did find."

"So, proceed as usual? Keep an eye for anything suspicious?"

"Seems to be the best plan. We could revoke everyone's keys, but I'd rather find out who did it."

I sighed and headed back to my disaster of an office. No sooner had I opened the door than I found Bates on his knees on the floor, sorting away.

"Bates, I asked you to leave the mess to me."

"Right, sorry, sir. I just wanted to be of service."

"I appreciate the sentiment, but back to your desk, if you please."

"Of course."

I settled back on the floor with a repressed groan. Bates had fussed with my piles, and I had to start them all over again. In an impressive display of control, I managed to refrain from commenting about it. It took hours to finish, and I wasn't entirely confident that everything was perfectly returned as it should be. But there was nothing missing that I could recall off hand.

I called Kit in to join me on the floor with a sigh.

"Can you grab my accounts ledger, it's in the bottom right drawer," I told him, digging my key out of my pocket and holding it to him.

"Don't need it," he muttered, reminding me of the smashed lock.

He spread the book out before him and grabbed the first half-sorted stack.

"Right, we've got paperwork for both the Ainsleys. The apartment, the club, and the bakery. Everything looks to be in order for the apartment." He muttered, mostly to himself, before making check marks or notes while I continued to sort.

"Is the Hasket paperwork missing?" Kit asked.

Everything stopped. Ice filled my veins.

There were still any number of possible explanations. But my blood had always been right on the battlefield. I wasn't about to question it now.

They knew.

I had no idea how, but they knew we were hunting them. Gabriel's killer knew.

Which meant...

"Celine!"

Nineteen

CELINE

Just how early was too early to bother a man at his place of business? And how exactly did one go about that if she wasn't staring through his office in a borrowed uniform?

Such were the essential questions I pondered between bites of toast and sips of tea. I made a half-hearted effort with the morning paper, but it was a thoroughly wasted exercise, distracted as I was.

I rarely bothered to dress before breaking my fast, and this morning was no exception. Instead I wore only my night dress and wrap. It was, after all, one of the greatest advantages of my solitary lifestyle. Even in spite of Bouvier's most fervent insistence on the inappropriateness of the habit.

I was, however, planning to wear a fetching sage morning dress for my visit, whenever I deemed it late enough. I was all but certain it would be thoroughly appreciated by a certain shy, occasionally charming solicitor.

I couldn't help but imagine the way his eyes would crinkle in that astonished way. I'd never seen another like it. The naked admiration was clear in that expression. I found it made my heart give a little skip every time I saw it.

My reverie was interrupted by a fierce pounding at the front door. On instinct, I rose and walked to the hall, heedless of my state of undress. All I could see was the back of Bouvier as he tried to keep someone out. My stomach dropped before I heard the familiar tenor of his voice.

"Let me in, damn it! It's urgent!"

"Sir, it is not an appropriate hour for callers. If you will wait—"

"What part of urgent are you not understanding? I need to see her. Now."

"Let him in, Bouvier," I called down the hall. Both men froze before turning. Bouvier offered me nothing but a disapproving tut and raised brow. There was an "*I told you so*" about my state of undress just as soon as we had a moment alone. Little did he know, William's reaction was hardly a deterrent.

He was frozen in eye-crinkle astonishment and, if I was not mistaken, a fair bit of arousal, given the severe bob of his throat as he stared at me. It was a heady thing, to be gazed at with such adoration.

That was the only explanation I could offer for my next suggestion.

"Come with me?" I asked with a nod toward the stairs. His head dipped with no real thought behind the gesture. All of his former urgency seemed to have died away at the sight of me. I ought to be concerned about whatever had him so distressed, but really, how was I to think of anything other than the reverence with which he stared?

I didn't know if I had ever been more conscious of the way I moved up the stairs. Or the footsteps behind me. At the landing, I turned, waiting for him to join me. When he did, I grabbed his hand in my own and tugged him along to my dressing room.

There, I found Jane laying out my recently pressed gown and stockings. She was startled at the sight of my company but made an exemplary attempt at a curtsy when I dismissed her. Though it had been some years since a man had been in my dressing room, she wasn't entirely unfamiliar with the concept.

William, on the other hand, *was* entirely unfamiliar and quite uncomfortable with the concept, given the stiff way he held himself and the way his eyes darted from object to object around the room.

"Would you care to sit?" I asked with a gesture toward the settee. He approached and sat with a stiff sort of formality, his back ramrod straight and jaw clenching and unclenching with uncommon regularity.

After several minutes, I broke. "Are you quite all right?"

"No. Yes. I don't know." I bit back a smile. It would not do to find amusement in his discomfiture, no matter how endearing.

"You said you had urgent business?"

"Yes—well, no—I mean, it is urgent, but not so urgent that it could not have waited for you to dress."

I stifled a giggle at his expense. "It is not as though I am naked, William. Honestly. I'm more clothed than Adriane was when she found me. Clearly you've seen women in their night dresses before."

"No—I mean, yes. I have. Obviously. But not like that." He nodded toward my form.

"I'm not certain I followed you around that bend..." That was a lie, I was baiting him for compliments in the worst possible way.

"Lord, I'm such a..." He tossed his head back on his neck and stared at the ceiling as though it had answers to all of life's questions. As if the Lord would actually answer him. "I can't do this."

"What? No! William, I was just teasing." He lolled his head back down with some effort, his sharp eyes finding mine with a haunting intensity before slipping closed with a shake.

"I— We— She was sick. She was unwell, and I never... And she didn't look like that, and her gowns weren't so... It wasn't so terribly difficult not to... And you're..." He abandoned yet another sentence with a sigh before bringing his hand to his forehead and dragging it across his face.

Somehow, I was fairly sure those half-finished sentences were compliments. They were certainly more intoxicating than the most poetic declarations of love and lust could ever be. And if I was understanding his statement fully, he and Adriane had never... Had *he* ever?

Each time we kissed, it was like a revelation to him. But the way his lips worked over mine... Surely such a thing could not be achieved on instinct alone. Right?

Regardless, he came here on an errand of some urgency. If his words and demeanor were to be believed, the urgent matter was not in his breeches, however much that fact might disappoint me.

"All right, what I'm gathering from that is that you would feel more comfortable if I were fully dressed. Yes?"

He exhaled a shaky breath between nods.

"Very well," I whispered. Unable to resist, I leaned down to him. His eyes slipped shut and his chin tilted up, still eager for my attentions in spite of his discomfort. I pressed a soft kiss to his lips before dropping one, then another on his closed lids. My efforts earned me a quiet gasp as I pulled away, thrilling me in an entirely self-satisfied way. "I am going behind the screen. Don't peek."

I slipped behind the screen with my gown and stockings.

This would have to be done alone since I had dismissed Jane for the morning.

I could not resist the urge to let the fabric of my wrap brush against my night dress as loudly as possible in the silent room. I made no claims of sainthood after all. I pulled my chemise from its place on the hook and donned it. My stays proved more challenging. Fortunately, I wore half stays *a la paresseuse* with this gown and could fasten them well enough myself. Stockings and petticoat donned, I slipped the sage muslin overtop.

That was where my talents ended. The long line of dress hooks would defeat me.

"William?"

"Yes?"

"I need some assistance."

"Would you like me to call your maid back?"

"Or you could..." I trailed off. Confident now in the numerous layers of fabric between us, I stepped from behind the screen. He still had his eyes respectfully shut. "It is merely the dress, if you don't mind?"

He swallowed, his throat bobbing enticingly. "No. No, I don't mind."

"Very well. You'll have to peek I suppose." And he did. His eyes found mine with astonishing accuracy. They had hardened to the darkest of navies. He rose slowly, stretching his limbs out while I turned to offer the line of hooks down my back for his fingers.

He started at the bottom, near the base of my spine. Though there were at least three layers between my skin and his hands, and his fingers did not stray, it felt as though there was nothing between us.

Nearly halfway up, he ran into the obstacle of my hair. His touch was featherlight as he gathered it and swept it across my shoulder gently. He continued on, his feet pressing closer with each hook. By the last one, I could feel his warmth against my back and his breath caressing my neck.

I had lost the upper hand in this. And I was fairly certain I did not want it back. Far too quickly, he finished the last hook. His hand slid around my shoulder, holding me steady while he dropped a fevered kiss to the back of my neck, just above the line of hooks.

"There," he breathed.

Uneasily, I pushed my hair back and moved to attend to my coiffure, to add some distance, to gain my bearings. I reached for the silver brush resting on my vanity as I sat. His hand found it seconds before my own.

"Let me?" His voice was low and graveled and oh so delightful. If he spoke like that always, I would be able to deny him nothing.

Even as I nodded, I expected him to start from the top of my head and rip the brush through, taking all my tangles with it. Instead he grabbed a curl, pulling it through his fingers, studying it.

"Spun gold," he whispered, more to himself than to me. He settled the brush at the end of the lock, pulling it slowly through before moving up an inch and repeating it.

And then I remembered where he likely gained familiarity with the care of long hair. The hurt for him was overshadowed by the warmth I felt at such reverence. And both were dwarfed by the bone-melting satisfaction that came with each pull of the brush.

Far too soon, he finished. He pressed a gentle kiss to the top of my head as he set the brush aside before turning back to the settee. He left me at the vanity, bereft and desperate for more.

I spun on my stool and caught sight of his back—an enticing back at that. His shoulders were tight and unnaturally high on his frame. I caught my lip between my teeth to keep back the pleased grin at the way I had discomfited him.

Shaking the thoughts away, I recalled the reason for his presence. "Downstairs, you said you had something urgent to discuss?"

It was as though I had doused him with water. The languid, calm, sensuality disappeared. In its place the distressed posture and expression.

"Celine, love. Someone broke into my office last night. I think— I suspect— The killer, they know we're searching for them."

Twenty

WILLIAM

BRINGING her to the office went against everything in me. Presumably they were watching this place, or had someone doing it for them. And I brought her right into the line of fire.

The distraught cry at the sight of my office nearly did me in. If that hadn't done it, the way she inspected me, with her eyes and hands, for injury that could not possibly exist, certainly did it. Her concern melted the last bit of resistance in my heart. No one had ever... cared before. Not like that, to the point of irrationality.

Oh, Adriane had cared in as much as I kept her fed, housed, and clothed. And she enjoyed toying with me. The late duke had cared as long as I continued to function as an example to hold up against his wastrel of a son. Mother cared, but my only memories of her were of her wasting away to illness. She hadn't enough left to worry after me. Kit cared, as a friend, a companion, perhaps even as a brother.

But this was different. I was enjoying it in a purely selfish way that I would never willingly admit. And when her hands ran over my torso, searching for nonexistent damage, it took more will than I thought I possessed to catch her hands in mine and reassure her.

I had bundled her into Kit's office for the three of us to talk. She wasn't listening, her gaze kept darting to the wall between his office and mine. Of course, I was too focused on her to listen to Kit's prattling either.

"Lady Rycliffe?"

"Celine, please. You've prevented Davina from being sold to a Prussian prince. I think we can dispense with the formalities. And I apologize, it has been something of a morning. Could you repeat that?"

"Austrian," he replied.

"Excuse me?"

"It was an Austrian prince."

"Well, that might not have been so bad. The gowns are better in Vienna," she retorted.

"I— But— She..." Poor Kit, he wasn't prepared for the full force of Celine.

"That was a joke. I appreciate your assistance in all of her scandals, even the ones that have the potential to end with tiaras."

"Right," he said. "Will seems to think this break-in was possibly related to your late husband's death. Is there... Are you able to tell me what you remember from that time?"

"You do not ask the easy questions, do you? Where should I start?"

"The beginning, I suppose?"

With a weary sigh, she began. "I had been out for several seasons when Gabriel and I met. After Mama and I left France, we relied on the generosity of the *ton*. My grandmere passed a year or so before I was presented, and for the first time since we left France, we were independent. I enjoyed the feeling of being beholden to no one, and I was in no hurry to wed.

"It made me very popular, you see. Men would trip over themselves for a dance. It's a flattering feeling. But Gabriel was different. He knew immediately what I was doing. It's difficult to describe—that feeling of knowing something—someone— is dangerous but wanting it more desperately than anything."

Celine was far away, back in 1806 or 7. Back with the man who still held her heart. Mine twisted uncomfortably, even knowing that the information might be essential.

"He tried to stay away, tried to drive me away. He insisted he didn't seduce innocents any longer. But he couldn't— I couldn't—wouldn't. I even allowed others to court me, Leopold Bennet, Earl of Champaign, specifically. But one night, Gabriel and I slipped out onto the terrace and walked back in engaged.

"After we wed, everything was wonderful. For a little while. Then he started arriving late, missing engagements entirely, that sort of thing. When I confronted him about it, he told me about most of his dealings. Before me, he had an exclusive relationship with a madam. Victoria was her name. They were... close. He even went so far as to invest in her brothel."

"Victoria White?" Kit asked.

"I do not know. It's possible."

"How do you know that?" I interjected.

"You stare at gentlemen's finances all day long. How do you not know the most popular brothel in the city?" I winced before shooting him a glare. He should not be discussing such crass matters in front of my—Celine. And she certainly did not need to know I was quite as inexperienced as I was.

"He said her benefactor was the most powerful man in the city. Because she knew all the secrets, you see. He had a few other less than honorable activities, boxing matches he fixed, that sort of thing. He also told me about a scheme he ran with his horses. He had one that was a particularly popular stud, and sometimes he would use a look-alike instead and collect the fees anyway. Then, a few years later, he would place wagers against that horse in races. But he said he stopped all of that when we met."

"And you believe him?" Kit voiced my thoughts, with much less incredulity than I could have managed.

"I do. I know I sound naive. But he loved me."

"All right, anything else?"

At his question, her eyes shot to mine. Adriane then.

"Might as well, love."

Her tongue darted between her lips before she began to tell my piece of this sordid tale. "Later, in Yorkshire, I met a girl. She was unwell and..."

"I believe the word you're searching for is *mad*." She shot me a look for the interruption.

"William came and got her and took her away. And I knew she was the girl Gabriel meant when he said he didn't seduce innocents *any longer*. We had quite the quarrel about it."

They fought about it? She was upset about what he had done to Adriane?

"After we came out on the other side of that, things were good. Wonderful, really. In retrospect, something was off the day before he was killed. But at the time I didn't notice anything in particular. I tried to convince him to practice fencing with me. He managed to talk me back into bed instead." She muttered that last part, staring at the floor.

"He was your husband, love. Nothing wrong with that." It was the truth, though it felt like a lie on my lips. I was proud of how steady my voice was, barely reflecting the way I wanted to lay claim to her.

"We went to the races that day. We didn't go often, at least not together. But it was his mother's ball that night. We took

Xander and Davina to keep them out of the house. He disappeared for a bit, and I saw him talking to someone, who turned out to be Will.

"When I asked Gabriel about it, he told me he thought Adriane had passed and that he and Will would meet later in the week to sort out funeral arrangements. We went to his mother's ball that evening. He disappeared for a while with some of the gentlemen, but that wasn't uncommon. That night when we went to sleep, everything was well—wonderful, even. The next morning I woke up in hell." Her voice had gotten thicker with each passing word.

I moved to stop her, to offer what little comfort I could, but she shook her head.

"I woke to a shout. By the time I made it downstairs, there was already a trail of blood to the dining room. He was stabbed in the back. On our front steps. He— I— We didn't have much time. He told me he loved me. He told me he knew I loved him when I couldn't get words out. And I kissed him. And he was gone."

My heart lay cracked open before her. For the way she wrapped her arms about herself. For the small, hollow, wooden quality of her voice. For the sobs I could hear in her words that she was bravely keeping at bay.

I didn't notice my own tears, not until the first one made its track down my cheek. Never in a million years had I thought I would shed tears for Gabriel Hasket.

I suppose I wasn't. Not really. I was shedding them for her. For the unendurable pain that was clear in her shuttered eyes.

Without warning, she bridged the gap between us and wrapped her arms around my waist, burying her face in my shoulder. Nothing could have stopped me from banding my arms about her shoulder blades. Her tears were silent, but the dampness spreading through my shirt was evident.

Between kisses pressed to her hair, I caught sight of Kit handing me his handkerchief with an uncomfortable shrug.

Eventually she pulled away, drying her tears on the aforementioned handkerchief. "Apologies," she whispered.

"We do some work with wills and such. It's not an uncommon occurrence." Kit's lie was a kind one. While it wasn't unheard of for someone to shed tears in our office, it certainly wasn't a regularity.

"A few months after Gabriel passed, His Grace demanded that Xander take over Rycliffe Place. I took some of Gabriel's documents with me, the ones I didn't think he would have wanted his father or brother to see. That's everything. All I know."

"I think Will is right. I think the break-in was tied to Gabriel's murder. I'd say it's most likely due to the nonsense with the horses. There is a great deal of money to be made in his scheme. And the timing of his death... I'd say the temptation to wager on one of his horses was too great. That he hadn't been gambling as regularly probably made the choice more noticeable," Kit said.

"We'll need to take a look at the General Stud Book. See if we can trace some of them."

"Dance something..." Celine interjected.

"What, love?"

"The horse that lost that day... It had *dance* in the name."

"That's helpful. Anything else?" Kit asked.

"Not at the moment. Maybe if I have some time to think."

"All right, I'll go hunt down the book. Will, do you want to stay with me tonight? Or I'm sure Kate could put you up in Grayson House."

"Beg pardon?"

"You can't stay here, Will. It's not as though they don't know where you live. It'll be the next place they check for the documents."

"He'll stay with me," Celine said.

"I will?" I asked at the same moment that Kit's incredulous "He will?" rang out.

"Yes. I won't be able to sleep otherwise. Go pack your things."

And just like that, I was staying with Celine. In her house. Where she lived. Without a suitable chaperone.

Suddenly the house that had seemed so overwhelmingly large yesterday felt impossibly small in my memory.

Twenty-One

WILLIAM

There was something unbearably vulnerable that came with crying in front of someone—with someone. It left both of us a bit stilted at supper that night.

Supper.

At Celine's house.

Where I would be staying overnight.

Across the hall from where I remembered her dressing room to be.

The damned guest room was nearly as large as my entire apartment. Aptly named the blue room, it overlooked a little terrace that opened out onto the second floor. Perfect for making my escape when her proximity drove me out of my mind. There was even a helpful trellis running up the wall beside my window.

The entire house smelled of her—vanilla and spice and some ridiculous flower I couldn't name to save my life. How was a man to think of anything else when all he could breathe was her?

I hadn't the time to thoroughly examine my feelings about this morning either, my livelihood tossed about like trash. Kit had been kind, but word of the break-in would certainly impact our clients. After all, privacy was of the utmost concern to them.

And then there had been Celine in her sheer nightgown like a female being out of mythology—a nymph, a goddess, Aphrodite herself. All golden skin and loose curls.

She made a joke in the hall before slipping into her boudoir that evening, promising to be fully dressed at breakfast tomorrow. It was a miracle I managed to refrain from begging her to change her mind. To wear that slip of purple silk and lace—it and nothing else. Always. To burn the rest of her clothing. I could help her. There was space on the terrace for a bonfire.

I was going to wear a hole in the carpet, pacing between window and door as I was. It was a tetchy combination of exhaustion, anxiety, anger, and arousal, and with no other way to release it, I paced.

Phantom curls trailed through my fingers, and my lips longed for the ghostly brush of her skin. And the knowledge that I carried all day, of exactly how many layers of fabric stood between me and miles of sun-kissed skin, was a kind of torture I had never known.

The whisper of a door moving against carpet came from the hall. Certainly a figment of my imagination. Or, I *was* certain until a breath of candlelight seeped under the crack between my door and the floor. Light and shadow.

Unwittingly, I found myself in front of the door, my hand hovering above the brass knob. Waiting for a nock, a sound, a sign.

A minute passed. Two. I stared at the rich wood inlaid with delicate florals. The shadow never moved. If I closed my eyes, I could almost hear the soft breaths of my visitor. My hand slid to the door, gliding up to press against it.

I had a vision of Celine's hand pressed against mine through carved, stained mahogany, separated by nothing more than wood and nerves. Each of us waiting for the other to gather courage.

With a fortifying breath, I broke first. "Are you going to knock, love?"

"I don't know yet." Her answer was softly delivered and muffled through the wood.

"Your decision, what is it based on?" Slowly, she set the candle down on the floor, just visible through the crack. It cast a clean semicircle on the carpet beneath my feet. Then came the brush of silk against wood. I could picture it, her back pressed to the door as she slid to settle on the floor. Her chin would be propped on her knees.

I had no way of knowing how accurate the image in my mind was, but her shadow offered no counter. I found myself mimicking her presumed position, back against the door. One leg sprawled into the room, the other bent and serving as an armrest.

"The way I see it, there are three possibilities if I knock. I'm not certain whether I can live with all of them. And, of course, the fourth, where I don't knock at all."

"Tell me?" I begged.

"If I step away, door unknocked, we continue as we have been. We dance around whatever it is between us until one of us breaks."

"I don't particularly fancy that option."

"I don't either."

"What's behind the door then?"

I caught the ghost of her sigh. "I could knock. You could open the door, laugh in my face, send me away."

I felt the laugh bubbling up. Fortunately the sincerity in her tone stopped me before it could escape. The idea was so absurd...

"You really think there's a situation in which you knock on my door, that you come to me, for anything, and I would send you away?"

She was quiet for an overlong moment. I held my breath, waiting desperately for her response. She was silent long enough for me to feel an impassioned declaration bubbling up inside, struggling to break free.

"It was the least likely of the options. Still, it's a possibility to be considered."

"It's not." I insisted. "What are your other possibilities?"

"If I knocked, and you invited me in, one of two things would happen. We could kiss, and kiss, and kiss until the world fell away. Until your coat and shirt and trousers fell too. Then my night rail. One thing would lead to another, and we would fall together."

Christ... My breathing was heavy and quick, and if the sounds through the door were at all accurate, it matched her own.

Swallowing some of the lust, I answered through the door. "That sounds like an excellent option."

"Oh, it is. For now. You would certainly fall in love with me. But what would happen tomorrow?"

"You seem very sure of yourself."

"Tell me I'm lying."

She wasn't. And I couldn't. I was half in love with her already. If I were with her, inside her, I would be lost.

"Oh, you're not. I'm a little disappointed in how transparent I've been."

"You saved me, that night when those men attacked. And you came for me, when your entire professional life had been ransacked, you worried after *me*. And you held me this morning, while I cried over another man."

"So entirely obvious..." I lamented.

"Yes."

"And the third option?"

"You invite me in. And we fall into bed, same as before. Except this time, you wrap me in your arms. You hold me, and run your fingers through my hair, and watch me sleep until you can't stay awake any longer. In the morning, I wake before you and do the same. And I fall in love with you as the sun rises."

It was, apparently, possible to be reduced to trembling desperation by mere words whispered through a door. I didn't need any help falling in love with her, the possibilities she offered were more than enough.

"Also an exceptional choice." My voice was rusted, broken, and it was all her fault.

"Except for the problem of tomorrow again."

"What happens tomorrow?" I begged.

"I don't know how to be loved any longer, or be in love. I — It nearly destroyed me. Losing him. Every single breath was a white-hot knife in my chest. For years. I don't know how to risk that again. And... if I don't risk it, how could I possibly be what you deserve?" Her voice was strung tight as a bow, anguished tension in every word.

But she was there with me. She may not know it yet, but the fact that she was considering it, contemplating it, she was there.

I choked back the whispers of love and reassurance. Those would only ensure she left without a knock. "Why don't you let me worry about what I deserve?"

"Would you? Really? Because I don't know everything about your relationship with Adriane, but I don't think she loved you as she ought."

In one sentence, she summed up years of my life.

"It's still my cross to bear. What do you want, Celine?"

Behind the door, I heard the gentle rustle of fabric. The candlelight dimmed. I, too, rose to face the rich mahogany. My hand slid along the frame, waiting as I held my breath.

And then, there was a knock.

 Twenty-Two

CELINE

A STREAM of sunlight woke me from the most restful sleep I'd had in years. Probably since the morning I awoke, alone, in hell.

This wasn't hell. Far from it. Here, I was safe, warm, loved. There was no confusion. I needed no moment to place myself, even though I was in a foreign bed.

It should have felt wrong—wrong room, wrong lighting, wrong scents, wrong arms around me. But it was so right. Everything was perfect. The bicep I rested on, the hand laid high and possessive on my thigh, the soft puffs of air against my neck, synchronized to my own, even in sleep.

Finally, I was free to peruse him without his notice, and without the distraction of his unbearably blue eyes. Instead, I traced knife-point cheeks, a full lower lip, and a chiseled jaw. Unfairly long lashes dusted across pale skin. The shoulder under my fingers was far harder than it ought to have been for a solicitor. His hair was a riot of short curls. The shade was somewhere between blond and brunette and sprinkled with the suggestion of gray around his temples. He was a man. There was nothing boyish about him.

Even after a night's rest, he smelled wonderful, some sort of citrus and herb combination. I had the silly notion to see if I could find his soap while he slept. It would be a thoroughly invasive idea but, then again, I had acted on more incredibly inappropriate thoughts where he was concerned.

Yesterday's clothes lay rumpled and tugged uncomfortably across his shoulder and waist. After an endearingly awkward explanation of his preferred sleeping attire—nothing at all— he had settled into the bed after me in his shirt and breeches. His toes, free of stockings, were tucked between my calves, unconsciously seeking my warmth.

I had been right last night. This man would certainly be the end of me. Far beyond the handsome countenance and alluring scent, underneath the sharp edges, was perhaps the sweetest man to ever live.

I ran from him, followed him, eavesdropped on him, accused him of murder, crawled into his bed in nothing but a silk nightdress, and my troubles had him evacuated from his home. Yet he merely wrapped me in his arms, humming something unfamiliar, until the soothing vibrations of his chest lulled me to sleep.

The fear I expressed last night, that I was no longer capable of love, that it would destroy me—it all seemed so inconsequential in the moment. I knew, once I left this bed, though, they would seem all the more terrifying for their proximity.

A part of me thought to rise, to break my fast downstairs. But that part of me was quickly silenced by his sleepy snuffle, that and the memory of awakening alone that terrible morning.

"'Lo, love," he mumbled.

A bleary eye flickered open, the other still trapped in the pillow. How was it possible to be shocked by the exact shade every single time? It was cornflower this morning. Or perhaps sky. My rusty heart gave a little pang, something more than affection flowing through my veins. The eyes, they were the last boyish remnant of him. I had forgotten while they were hidden from me.

Nothing in the world could have held back my smile at the sight. I pressed a quick kiss to his forehead and he pulled me tighter with another tired sound. His lips found the hollow of my neck and pressed his answering kiss there.

He settled back into the ray of sunlight that had awoken me. It must have found a home in a puddle or the pond on the terrace because a small band of color landed in the hollow of his cheek. I traced it delicately and it moved to my hand before I settled it back on his shoulder.

"Good morning, *mon arc-en-ciel*," I whispered between us.

His answer was a sleepy chuckle, his single eye tracing me with the same intensity I had surveyed him with earlier. I was unused to such perusal, particularly at such an early hour. It was discomfiting, allowing such admiration with no preparations. Surely, I looked as though rats had nested in my hair, and the pillows had likely creased my face. The naked appreciation in his gaze slowed my instinct to fuss and correct. Against every impulse, I forced myself to allow his perusal, focusing on the adoring crinkle at the corner of his eyes that appeared once again.

"*Votre français est toujours terrible,*" he answered, voice sleep graveled.

"*Sois gentil ou je me lève.*"

His hold on the place where my hip, thigh, and bottom met tightened, and he dragged me closer. He hauled a leg over mine, trapping me in his embrace.

"I take it back. Your French is impeccable," he said, the words pressed into my shoulder to hide the laughter. His smile more than gave him away.

"Quite right."

"Why rainbow?"

"You're wearing one," I answered, gesturing to the tiny ray that had migrated to his shoulder with the sun. "Do you object?"

"No, there is nothing about you to object, *mon rayon de soleil*."

"Not 'love'?"

"Just slipped out the first time. And you didn't say anything, so…"

"I do not mind it. But you know, I cannot reciprocate it. Not yet."

"I know, love. Truth be told, I was expecting a bit more panic this morning. Especially after all the warnings last night."

"I'm too comfortable to panic. Perhaps after breakfast."

"If you think I'm letting you out of this bed to break your fast if you plan on overthinking this as soon as I let you up, you have another thing coming."

"Kidnapper! I knew you were a blaggard!" I could not keep the giggle at bay long enough to issue the accusation with the seriousness required for the jest.

In answer, he rolled me to my back and rose to hover above me on his forearms, pinning me loosely to the bed. He was sleep rumpled, adorable, handsome, sensual, seductive… everything.

"Right, you are. I'm a terrible, very bad man. You're trapped here until I tire of you."

"Such a horrible fate. When do you suppose you might tire of me?" I ran my free hand through wild curls, carding them between fingers. They were softer than they had any right to be.

"Never, I expect." He was inexplicably serious for such a

playful moment and my heart gave another jolt of something I wasn't yet ready to name.

"Are you certain? I don't know if you've noticed, but I can be a great deal of trouble."

The burst of laughter that escaped him startled us both. His head fell to my shoulder where he gave a gentle nip, before soothing it with a kiss.

"Aye, I've noticed that you're nothing but trouble. But you're the very best kind of trouble."

"What kind is that?"

He pulled away from where he was doing incredibly terrible, very bad things to my neck. "You're trouble for all the right reasons, love. You're brave, and you're funny—even intentionally on occasion. You're passionate and determined. Stubborn as hell, really. Every time I think I understand you, you just... you show me something completely new and unexpectedly wonderful. You're so damn beautiful that it hurts to look at you sometimes; it's like staring into the sun. I could spend the rest of my life getting into trouble with you, and I wouldn't regret a single second of it."

"Will..." There weren't words to respond to such a speech. Not in English or my rusty French.

"I know last night you were worried about tomorrow. But it's here, love. It's the harsh light of day and nothing has changed. I'm every bit as in love with you as I was last night. I know you're not ready to hear that. And I won't say it again, not until you are. I just needed you to know that I love you and the world isn't ending because of it."

It was entirely overwhelming. He was everything, everywhere. Surrounding me, in the air I breathed. And in that moment I wanted desperately to be able to say the words. The ones making a home at the tip of my tongue. The answer to his.

"Will, I..."

"Not yet, not until you know it. Don't say it until you mean it."

"How will you know when I mean it?" I asked, somewhat petulantly.

"Trust me, I will know. Now, I suppose I have to feed you. That's what a good kidnapper would do, right?"

"I thought the point of kidnapping me was to keep me in this bed forever."

"It was. Aren't you fancy folk supposed to have servants with trays of tasty things?"

"We do. The bell is over there. Or are you too much of a plebeian to pull the cord?"

"Minx..." he pressed his lips to mine before rising. "Don't move." It was easy to watch him saunter over to the rope and pull. To appreciate his form. And to refrain from thinking and just *feel*.

Twenty-Three

WILLIAM

BREECHES. It was the breeches that would do me in, in the end. Celine in breeches specifically. All long lines, and gentle curves. The sight was certainly going to be the death of me.

I had been too distracted that day in Yorkshire to notice how fetching the woman in front of me was. I wasn't distracted now. Not from the breeches anyway.

"Let's fence," she said. All warm and sweet-smelling in my arms and in my bed between nibbles of biscuits and sips of coffee. The excitement in her eyes had been intoxicating, addicting. What kind of monster would decline an offer that made that delight line her face? Not this one.

Of course, now she would kill me, and it was entirely due to the breeches. Somewhere, filed in the back of my mind, I understood on a purely intellectual level that she was certainly good. She had already stabbed one of the men who attacked her with the umbrella before I even arrived. But this... She was incredible.

And incredibly distracting. Curls piled on top of her head,

clad in a shirt and breeches that were almost certainly made specifically for her. Specifically for her to torment me to death. The linen of the shirt, though fine, was thin and nearly transparent. It made no effort to conceal whatever stays or corset or frilly underthings she had on.

She was clearly aware of the effect she was having on me if the self-satisfied smile on her lips was any judge. That was fine. I was out of practice, but I had done more than my fair share of fighting in France. True, my opponents had never been quite so lovely, but even as talented as she was with an umbrella, I didn't anticipate a serious challenge.

She tossed me a foil with a familiar ease. It was finely crafted.

"The smith near Rose Hill?" I asked.

"Indeed. Gabriel always said he was the best."

"He is. This is a fine sword." It was too. I was unused to fighting with a foil in general and a tipped one in particular, but I could recognize fine craftsmanship. I took a few practice slashes and thrusts to adjust to the lighter, thinner weapon.

"I'm glad it meets your approval." There was just the slightest bite in her tone, a hint of sarcasm I shouldn't have found attractive. She fell into formation with a practiced ease and raised a brow expectantly.

I suddenly felt every one of my years behind a desk. And my years as a soldier. And all the years between when I learned how to follow the rules she knew well. And this moment, bathed in sunlight on the terrace of the goddess in breeches before me.

I made the perfunctory salute, following her lead. She made the first attack, thrusting with the point of her foil. It was unexpected and I was barely able to sidestep. This was how she had wrought such damage the other night. I was making the same mistakes those devils did. Underestimating her.

She recovered quickly, slashing back. I blocked it, lamenting my choice of right hand when I was met with more force than anticipated.

She was good. She was more than good. I was suddenly incredibly grateful she had chosen the blunted weapons. That being said, she'd done more than a fair bit of damage with my tipless umbrella.

After parrying yet another attack, I made my first move. I went for a slash, changing my mind when she anticipated it and aborting it for a thrust. Still in motion, it grazed her arm, harmless. It must have startled her though because she began to attack with a frightening rapidity.

Her expertise was clear. She must have practiced regularly. Her motions were thoughtless, effortless. I was more than certain she knew the appropriate term for every step she took, every motion she made.

There was a grace to her, unlike anything I had ever experienced. It was a dance.

I blocked and sidestepped, the tip of her blade whispering past my ear, catching on the loose fabric of my shirt, meeting air an inch off my flank. She was exceptional.

And still she couldn't get a touch. I could see the irritation mounting with each miss. It was an enticing look for her, frustration mixed with exertion. Her cheeks flushed while curls escaped her coiffure and stuck to her glistening skin. She was breathing heavily, panting between reddened lips.

I saw the exact moment when vexation won out.

"How are you doing this?" she demanded.

God himself could not have willed me to ease her annoyance, not when her bosom rose so enticingly with each irritated breath. Not when she made adorable little grunts with every unsatisfying attack.

"Doing what?"

"You're not following any of the rules."

"I don't remember the rules, love. Told you as much." My own thrust hit her shoulder before she flicked it away with her blade.

"But you were a soldier, you fought all the time." I thrust toward her throat, freezing an inch away.

"No rules in battle."

"But…"

"No, remember the other night? You weren't following the rules then? Or perhaps I missed when they added 'grab an umbrella with both hands and whack a man upside the head as hard as you can' to the guidelines." She lowered her foil and I followed suit, our harsh breaths in perfect synchrony.

"That was life and death."

"Right. Why are you practicing as though it isn't? Those men the other night, they weren't going to salute you."

"No…"

"Exactly. You were brilliant. You are brilliant. Better than I am, certainly. But if someone wants to hurt you, they're not going to follow the rules. You want to fight, you should practice the way you intend to if you're attacked. Years on the battlefield and not once did anyone wait for someone to keep score. Those points, they're not just points, love. They're wounds. Wounds that can maim, wounds that can kill."

"I've never… I wouldn't know how to."

"Of course you would, you did the other night. Just have to stop thinking so hard. Now, attack me. I won't attack, only block. But I want it all, everything you have."

"But I'll hurt you."

"No you won't, love. Dulled tip, remember?"

"Still…"

"I'd rather you hurt me than be unable to defend yourself if you need to because you're used to fighting nice. No saluting, attack when you're ready."

And she did. Somehow, with the shackles of civilized

sportsmanship removed, she was even more graceful, more ferocious, more beautiful.

Finally, she caught me in the ribs with the tip and wore a pleased smirk.

"Good, love. That was good. Next time, aim for the eyes though, or the uh... delicate areas. Feet can be good too, slow a man down to give you time to run."

"You want me to—"

"*Want* is... perhaps the wrong word. But if you're being attacked, those will shut a man down faster than the torso. They may not be as deadly but they're damn painful."

"I'm not certain Monsieur Jereaux will approve."

"You can do things properly for your lessons. Though I think it's a travesty that he's teaching you to fight politely."

She pulled the foil from my grip, set it aside with her own, and dragged me toward the nearby bench with enticing kisses.

Twenty-Four

CELINE

APPARENTLY, I was fond of spectacles on a man. Who could have known? Also, how was I expected to concentrate on anything after the showing Will made on the terrace?

I had such plans this morning. I was going to trounce him thoroughly and he would fall to his knees, impressed with my swordsmanship. Instead, *he* trounced *me*, and he was entirely too handsome while he did it.

Now he was reviewing ledgers while wearing spectacles which was astonishingly something I found attractive. So far, we'd managed to determine that the horse was likely bred sometime in the three or four years before Gabriel was killed. That was before my time with him, so I was proving to be of little help.

Of course, the longer and more in-depth our search into Gabriel's less than gentlemanly occupations prior to our marriage, the less I was enjoying the results. Thus far, nothing had been a shock. But the reminder of just how much of a degenerate he was in the years before we met stung.

And I was not alone in my irritation. Oh, William was being nice about it, but both of our frustration was mounting. He'd removed the spectacles at least three times, cleaning them on a handkerchief before returning them to the bridge of his nose. And my lip was certainly reddened from biting back my annoyance.

I was fairly certain we were reviewing transactions from around the time Gabriel had seduced Adriane. It was not exactly a delight to find out just how much money my husband had spent at the local brothel before we met. Still, unlike William, I managed to refrain from clenching my jaw. Each time he did it, the motion emphasized the chiseled angles of his face.

I shouldn't find it attractive. My new suitor's annoyance with my late husband was absolutely not something I should take pleasure in, no matter how enjoyable the resulting view.

"What do you suppose is offered at a brothel for ten pounds? Surely nothing should cost that much." His question was distracted and likely rhetorical though it still hit a mark. Gabriel had never touched another woman after we wed, I had no question of that. But such an astronomical sum... What services could garner that? Certainly nothing we had done together.

"I have no idea."

"It's just... I see gentlemen's finances all day long. I've never seen anything close to that amount."

"Well I do not believe that overpaying at a brothel is what got him killed." The snappishness of my tone must have registered finally because he broke free from his ledgers, startled.

His eyes, like the sky after a rainstorm in the afternoon, widened with something like regret. "Sorry, I didn't mean to..."

"It's fine."

"No, it's not. I forgot for a moment. Do you want me to

set this aside? I can continue tomorrow, or this evening after supper."

"No... No. I just, Victoria was a point of contention between us. This is... more difficult than I expected. And for you as well, I expect."

"You're not wrong. He... he could have saved her. He was spending more than a hundred pounds per annum at a brothel, but he could not provide for Adriane? And that does not even consider what he lost regularly at the card table. He wouldn't even have had to marry her. She could have lived comfortably with less than half what he was wasting. But I should not be speaking so, not to you."

"It's in the past, it hardly signifies."

"I think we should set these aside for today. We've made quite a bit of progress. Mr. Wesley Parker seems to be a recurring name in the official ledgers that coincides with funds from 'Cock-sure Blunderbuss.' The notes, 'flush' or 'in quite deep' seem to indicate whether Gabriel is paying or receiving funds. 'White's' clearly refers to the brothel, not the club. 'Puff Guts' seems to be the Earl of Westfield, who has yet to win in the year and a half we've made it through. 'Hell's Own' seems to be Wayland to whom Gabriel seems to lose somewhat consistently. In fairness, a lesser sum than I've often seen men owe Wayland. That's a great number off our list that we've at least identified in the secondary ledgers."

"Very well."

"Celine, love. I am sorry. I can try to review these without your assistance."

"It's not that... Gabriel was not a good man. I know that. I knew that then as well. But I suppose time had dulled the painful sheen on the knowledge. Still, I want to help. I need to help."

"Of course, anything you need. I will try to be less obtuse."

"It's all right, William. Truly."

"It's not."

"I just, I think I could have borne it. If it were accident or illness that took him from me. But this… It was all so senseless. My husband died over a horse, or a game of hazard. Xander and Davina lost a brother, Her Grace lost a son, and for what? At least if you had killed him, you would've had good reason."

He huffed a laugh in response. "I've never understood the gentry. Not really. Even the late duke. I knew what I needed to do to curry his favor. I knew the consequences of failing to do so. But I never understood him."

"Even though I'm one of them, I find it baffling. All those years, singing and dancing and performing exactly as they wished to keep a roof over our heads. I never felt like I belonged, not really. Not after we fled. And now… Now I do what I wish."

His blinding smile and the crinkles at the corners of his eyes illustrated his delight more than words could have.

"What is it that you wish?" He gazed up at me from beneath his spectacles. His hand made a tentative movement toward my own, pressed to the desk. When he glanced down at his destination he paused, reconsidering. Ink? At that moment I could not have cared less about stains.

I caught his fingers, denying his retreat, tangling them with my own. The ink on his fingers smudged onto mine. He made a half-hearted effort to separate, but I merely tightened my hand, keeping him in place. There was something about the sight… I had a rather inappropriate vision of that ink staining other areas of my person, far more scandalous places than fingertips.

Just then, I wanted it desperately. My cheeks, my jaw, the bodice of my gown, my waist, my bottom, every inch of me covered in ink, stained fingerprints marking me for the world as his. And the smudges underneath my gown too, but those would mark me as his for the two of us alone.

If he knew the direction my thoughts had taken, he gave no sign of it. He studied me with curious eyes and an air of uncertainty. It was so different from the confidence I was accustomed to. He was so hesitant to press for more, even after the morning we shared. Yet, none of my actions had been unwelcome.

Summoning my courage, I pulled my hand from his and he dropped it at the first indication of resistance, releasing it as though it were on fire. It was both refreshingly endearing and the tiniest bit heartbreaking. I wanted him to feel sure in touching me.

I could continue to lead in this respect, though. I pushed his chair away from the desk and settled myself astride his lap with a confidence I did not feel.

His eyes widened in something that was either panic or arousal. Before I could question it too much, his hands settled about my waist, pinning me in place. And conveniently fulfilling my earlier fantasy. I would never draw his attention to it, he would certainly stop to fuss over the ink. It was an issue for future Celine to explain to future Jane before readying for dinner tonight. There was no place for stains here.

"You."

"What?" His voice was strangled and discomfited. I had to bite the inside of my cheek to hide the smile. It was intoxicating, the ease with which I overwhelmed this man.

"You asked what I wish. I wish for you. You seem to like me just as I am. I've made no effort to curry your favor. You're helping me for absolutely no fathomable reason, at great personal cost. You're not afraid to put me in my place. You're unbearably handsome, particularly in your spectacles, if I do say so myself. You're what I wish."

His throat bob was his only reaction. He seemed to have forgotten how to blink. It was... sweet. I'd never entertained a sweet man before, deeming them too easily manipulated to be of any interest. But I was finding that I liked it quite a lot.

"What would you have me do?" He finally managed to offer up the question, slightly wary.

"Whatever you wish. There are no rules. A benefit of widowhood."

He removed the spectacles distractedly, decidedly avoiding my gaze.

"I'm not—surely you know—you must have gleaned by now—I'm not very skilled... with women." My heart clenched, warmed by his admission. There was guilt too, at the pleasure I took in something that took so much fortitude to admit.

"I don't need you to be skilled with women." His eyes shot to mine with confusion written across his brow. "I want you to be skilled with one woman—me. And I am more than happy to teach you."

"Celine..." His admonishment was halfway between a growl and a purr, and it had me clenching my thighs.

Determined to retain the upper hand, I retorted, "Not now, of course. Now we need to dress for supper. With my mother."

He blinked slowly, his thoughts returning from soft sheets and even softer caresses. "You're a minx. You know that?" The question was half under his breath and entirely distracted as I rose and offered him a hand up.

He shook his head. "Need a minute. I suspect I'll take less time to dress than you as well. I'll have another look at the ledgers and be up in a moment."

"All right, but do not think I will allow you to miss this supper."

"Wouldn't dream of it, love." I pressed a quick kiss to his

temple and gave his shoulders a commiserating rub on my way out the door.

Twenty-Five

WILLIAM

I COULDN'T REMEMBER the last time I was so nervous meeting a member of the gentry. Perhaps Adriane's parents. And given how well that went... Mayhap my apprehension was warranted.

Celine was seated across from me in her well-sprung carriage draped with rich blues and silvers. Even the fetching sight of her in violet silks was not enough to distract from my dread. Particularly when combined with the blatant pity in her eyes. Her repeated assurances had done nothing to assuage my fears.

Frankly, this carriage was traveling much too fast. It was certainly not safe to be speeding along at such a great gallop through the city. When I said as much, she merely offered me an indulgent smile.

"Will, I promise she knows the entirety of your situation. She is unconcerned."

That opened a new set of fears. "The entirety?"

"Well, not that you're presently living with me. And I had

hoped to hide the full extent of the kissing—for propriety's sake only. But that is likely wishful thinking. Mama knows all."

"That does not cheer me up. In case you were wondering."

"I was not trying to make you feel better. I was trying to be honest with you. Mama and Marie don't often receive visitors, particularly male ones. I imagine the novelty will last until at least the second course."

"And they know each other how?"

"Marie is a family friend. We stayed with her for a number of years before Mama received her inheritance."

"Surely it is not usual. Having a house guest for so long."

"I suspect Mama hoped I would begin to move on from Gabriel if I had more autonomy. And I rather think they missed living together." She hesitated a moment, sizing me up. "Mama is Marie—Madame Bosarge's—houseguest in the same way you are mine." She waited, brow raised in anticipation.

It was overwhelming how much I wanted to kiss her for that revelation. She had shared so much of herself with me. That she trusted me with an additional secret, something that had nothing to do with Gabriel's murder and our present danger... That she knew, without question, that I would keep her family safe—that was more than enough to ease my nerves.

Fortunately and simultaneously unfortunately, we arrived outside the house before I could make good on my desire to demonstrate my appreciation. It gave no time for the trepidation to return.

Handing her out of the carriage was a privilege I hoped to soon repeat. That she slipped her hand into the crook of my arm was an equal delight. We were met at the door by an impossibly thin butler and a ruddy-cheeked maid who took our things. We followed the butler down the hall though Celine more than knew the way.

"Damn," she whispered under her breath.

"What?" I hissed back.

"I forgot about Lilibet."

"Who is Lilibet?"

"The maid. I hope you're prepared for the whole of the *ton* to know you were here tonight. Her sister is a nurse in many homes and a notorious gossip." Celine tipped her face to mine, checking for unease.

Her expression was all concern—for me. There wasn't a hint of worry for herself that I could identify. She would be the one to bear the gossip and snide comments.

Satisfied with whatever she saw, she pressed closer to me while entering the drawing room door after the butler's announcement.

There was no mistaking which of the two women was Celine's mother. She had the same green-hued eyes and pert nose. Though paler and with slightly duller hair, she was beautiful. Her face bore the faint creases of age with grace.

The other woman had a rounder face with a sharp chin and dark hair. She, too, wore the signs of maturity with pride.

The drawing room was decorated in the French style, the actual French style and not the Anglicized version of it, papered in tasteful creams and bold scarlets.

Celine abandoned me to my perusal in favor of embracing her mother. Madame Bosarge studied me. The effort required to avoid fidgeting under her pointed gaze was significant. My unease was interrupted when Celine turned to greet her friend. Of course, that left me to be measured by Madame Cadieux instead.

"Celine, *il est plus beau que vous ne l'aviez dit. Ces pommettes...*" Her mother spoke boldly.

Obviously, Celine had neglected to mention my fluency in French. I had to bite back a smile when I caught the flush on her cheeks.

"*Oubliez les pommettes, regardez ses yeux. Si bleus,*" Madame Bosarge added. Well, this was just... delightful. *By all means, ladies, please continue to enumerate my many fine qualities.*

Celine appeared moments from passing away in shame for their naked admiration. "*Il parle francais, Maman.*"

"*Est-ce un vrai, jeune homme?*" she asked in a sharp tone.

"*J'en connais, Madame.*"

And that ensured the rest of the evening would continue in French, much to Celine's consternation.

"I apologize for our rudeness, Monsieur Hart. We often forget ourselves."

"No need."

Celine wandered off to a sideboard and poured a glass of something amber. She drank it quickly and refilled it before filling a second one with water and bringing it over to me where I remained haunting the entry. She handed me the glass, then grabbed my arm, dragged me to a settee, and manhandled me next to her in the seat. Her mother's lips pursed concealing laughter—poorly.

"So, Monsieur Hart. My Celine tells me you are a solicitor. Was that always your chosen profession?"

"For the most part. I had a generous patron for my schooling in the late Duke of Rosehill. But I briefly paused my studies to fight abroad."

"And that is where you learned to speak better French than my native-born daughter?"

"Well, we studied it in my courses as well."

"You know, I don't believe I agreed to be the subject of ridicule this evening," Celine said. No real irritation showed in her tone or manner though.

"You need not agree. It is my right as your mother to shame you. And I do it far too infrequently."

"I strongly disagree."

Madame Bosarge interjected, "You could always attend soirees dressed in the same style as the Duchess of Rosehill. That would prevent shame befalling your daughter"

I tried to picture the elegant, understated woman before me dressed in the ostentatious gowns and hairpieces favored by Her Grace, and the image was so laughably incongruous that I had to bite the inside of my cheek.

"That is an excellent idea, Marie. Or perhaps I might ask Lady Agatha Grayson where she purchases her signature scent. Then I could be less embarrassing to my daughter."

"If you wish to ever be in my company again, you will refrain. I do not love you enough to subject myself to that decaying lilac essence," Celine added.

I was suddenly exceptionally grateful that I had never been in the woman's company. I thought Kit had been exaggerating.

After a chuckle at Lady Grayson's expense, Madame Bosarge turned her attention back toward me. "I am given to understand your business is very successful, Monsieur Hart."

How was I meant to answer that? How did she even define success? Knowing the dire straits that some gentlemen found themselves in, I could be considered more comfortable than they were. Though I was certainly less comfortable than the likes of Wayland and Ainsley.

But it was very likely I would lose Kit in the coming months to his new role. That would impact my situation in unforeseeable ways. Without him, I would likely have to refer out some of my work. But I would not have to pay him either.

"He does very well, Mama. Everyone who's anyone uses his services." Celine caught my hand in hers as she spoke, tangling our fingers together for all to see.

My heart found its way to my throat. This was it. Surely, faced with incontrovertible proof of our affection, Madame Cadieux would voice her objections.

"I did not ask you, I asked him," Madame Bosarge insisted.

"I—" My voice was hoarse with nerves, and I had to clear my throat before continuing. "My partner and I do well. There may be some changes in the coming months that could impact my situation, but I am well-positioned to weather that."

"What changes?"

"Kit—Mr. Summers—my partner—his uncle and father recently passed, leaving him an unexpected title and estate to manage. I expect he will take his place in the coming months. His work is far too essential for me to manage on my own. I will have to refer out some of the accounts."

"Oh, the new Earl of Leighton. That was such a terrible accident. How is he managing?" Madame Cadieux asked.

"He works too hard and has chosen to pretend nothing has changed." The words slipped out far too easily and unbidden. "That is— He is managing by immersing himself in familiar pursuits."

"I heard there was a break-in at your office the other day. Was everyone all right?" Madame Bosarge questioned.

How on earth had she—

"Lilibet?" Celine asked the woman.

"Lilibet."

At my questioning look, Celine answered, "The maid. From earlier."

"Right. Yes, there was a break-in. No one was harmed and nothing was taken."

"Were they searching for something, do you suppose?" Madame Bosarge asked.

"I have my suspicions. Fortunately, what they were looking for was not there at the time."

"I'm glad all was well," she said. "Celine, darling, I heard the most interesting rumor about you, you know."

The woman in question took a hearty swig of her drink. "Falsehoods, the lot of it."

"Really? So you weren't seen sitting outside Monsieur Hart's office every day for nearly a week? And he is not currently living in your residence?"

"How does she always know?" Celine asked her mother.

"I would like some clarification in that regard as well," Madame Cadieux said.

My mouth opened to offer a pathetic explanation, but Celine squeezed my hand and shook her head.

"He is. His residence is above the office that was broken into. And I was, for reasons that are not for the whole of the *ton* to concern themselves with, worried about his safety. Also, you absolutely must tell me which of my staff I need to dismiss."

"The Lord himself does not know all of Lilibet's sources," Madame Bosarge mused.

I was equal parts tempted and terrified to ask what else the woman had disclosed about me. Did they know about Adriane? About the animosity between Gabriel and me? Before I could ask, the same maid from before entered and announced supper.

The dining room was as sensibly elegant as the drawing room. Were the table of lesser quality, it would have sagged under the weight of all the food. Roasted duck, macaroni a la reine*, custards, chicken pie, and more covered every available inch.

I could not recall the last time I had been seated at such a table. The mouthwatering scents overwhelmed my senses. It was nearly enough to distract from the pang of distress that arose when Celine released my hand to be seated across from me.

"Monsieur Hart, tell me about yourself. What of your family?" Madame Bosarge asked.

---

* Historical version of Mac and Cheese

"My father was steward to the late Duke of Rosehill. My mother was a governess to the children. They passed before I left for France."

"Oh, of course, so you know the family?"

"I did, yes."

"And you were familiar with Celine's late husband, Gabriel?"

"I was."

Celine took a hearty sip of wine, shooting me a sympathetic glance over the rim of the glass.

"Was he an unrepentant rake in his youth? Or did that come with age?"

I choked slightly on a bite of pie before Celine rescued me from that line of questioning. "Marie... You know as well as anyone that Gabriel came out of the womb an unrepentant rake. Do not force William to disparage the deceased."

"And yet you wed him..." Madame Bosarge pointed out.

"And yet I wed him. You wed an octogenarian so you could spend as little of your life with him as possible. I hardly think either of our choices are appropriate conversation for the table."

"Very true, Celine. William, I understand you are unwed?" Madame Cadieux said, diffusing some of the tension.

"I have never been married, no."

"Do you suppose it was a lack of opportunity or a lack of interest?" Madame Bosarge cut in again.

"Marie..." Celine warned.

"I was never given the opportunity to properly question the last, and look how that turned out," Madame Bosarge countered.

"It's quite all right, Celine." I cut in. It was something of a shock that a family friend would so freely disparage Celine's beloved late husband—and in company. "A bit of both, I believe, Madame. I formed an attachment when I was young.

Unfortunately, it was not to be. And, well, I was in France for some time. Then I spent a few years caring for an unwell family friend before finishing my schooling and setting up my practice."

"This attachment, what happened?"

"Her family did not approve of my position."

"And where is she now?" The woman fired questions, hardly allowing me breath, let alone a bite of my meal.

"She passed away several years ago."

"Of w—"

"I believe that is enough interrogation, Marie," Madame Cadieux interrupted. The women shot each other looks that were indecipherable to my ignorant masculine brain.

Celine's mother turned back to me. "What do you do to amuse yourself, monsieur?"

"My occupation does not leave me much time for relaxation, but when my situation allows for it, I read or fence. Occasionally I am invited to the country estates of clients, and I enjoy a good walk on a fine day."

"Celine loves to fence. I know it is not an appropriate occupation for a lady, but I cannot see the harm in it," her mother explained, a hint of pride in her tone.

"Oh, I know. She is quite good."

"What about other gentlemanly pursuits? Do you enjoy the gaming tables or the races?" Ah, so the interrogation had not ceased, merely shifted to a slightly more subtle line of attack.

"I do some work for Wayland's, but I do not partake in the games myself."

"That is good," Madame Bosarge added. "I don't believe in gambling. Do you know, a few years ago, Lilibet told me of a man who lost so much in a single race he had to give up every piece of property that was not entailed away."

"That could be a great many men, Marie," Celine said.

"Yes, but he was demonstrating interest in a lady and had to drop her in favor of a larger dowry. What was her name? She was quite pretty, but her dowry was only modest and she had been passed over once before. The one that played that awful joke on Miss Summers before she was wed."

"Charlotte James?" Celine supplied.

"That's the one. Oh, what was his name?" Madame Bosarge asked.

"I do not know. It's possible I was on my honeymoon at the time."

"Is that Baron James's widow?" Madame Cadieux asked.

Though I was entirely superfluous to the conversation, it was something of a relief from the pointed questioning. And it allowed me time to stuff myself with more of the decadent food.

"Yes, Mama."

"Lilibet told me some weeks ago that there is a rumor that she is increasing. And, if I recall correctly, the baron passed nearly half a year ago."

Celine sighed. "I should not be petty, but she is so wretched. I suspect it was one of those gentlemen who were always surrounding her like flies. I noticed at the masquerade they were avoiding her with some determination."

"Surely whoever it was will take responsibility?" Madame Cadieux asked.

"Certainly not with a wedding. Not with the way they were speaking at the masque," Celine added.

"I cannot help but feel badly for her." Madame Cadieux said. "The baron had gambling vices of his own from what Lilibet told me."

"Oh, she will find some relative or other in the country to visit and return as if nothing ever happened next season," Madame Bosarge added. "Monsieur Hart, we must be boring you quite beyond belief."

"Oh, not at all, madame." It was the truth. Watching Celine interact with her family was fascinating. And truthfully, I quite preferred it to them questioning me.

This was nothing like the stilted dinner parties I had attended before where all one discussed was the recent weather. Weather that was always *too* something. It was a recitation of some lady's predictions for the future weather—always hopeful for improvement. A gentleman would opine on whether the weather was more or less pleasant than last season—always less. Someone would muse about the coming season's weather—it would always be an improvement to the current. I was always certain that they would have had the exact same opinions last week, last month, last year. And they would have them next week, month, and year.

Permission granted, the ladies volleyed back and forth about some gossip or other. I half listened, frequently distracted by the bemused glances Celine shot my way. Rolled eyes, pursed lips, bitten back grins—they were all part of her repertoire, and each was more endearing than the last.

It was some time later, after the dishes were cleared away, a game of whist was played and won, with Celine curled against me in the carriage, that I realized my nerves had faded away. Once home, Celine and I parted ways briefly before a familiar knock sounded at my door.

Celine, just the slightest bit in her cups, tugged me to the bed, both of her hands wrapped around mine. I followed in after her. She curled against me before sitting up and adjusting my arm into a position that better suited her. Once she settled, she grabbed my other arm and pulled it to her hair, silently demanding that I run my fingers through the curls. It was nothing like a hardship to acquiesce.

As she slept against me, snoring daintily, I realized she was right. Even Madame Bosarge's questioning had not been related to my situation but my character. And wasn't that a revelation? This miraculous woman beside me might not be so far beyond my reach as I once thought.

Twenty-Six

WILLIAM

IT WAS UNBEARABLY difficult to leave Celine's warm feminine curves the following morning.

Still, I could not abandon Kit for yet another day.

I arrived after a much longer journey than usual to an undisturbed office. That was more of a relief than I'd anticipated. I was deep into my search for answers to Xander's questions from the week before when Kit arrived.

He wore his teasing smugness like a coat and propped against my doorway with a pastry in hand. "So... How was your Sunday?" He asked the question with an amused lilt to his voice, taking a bite to hide his smirk.

"Better than yours, obviously."

"I'm sure it was. How is the lovely Celine?"

"As you stated, lovely."

"You're not going to tell me anything, are you?" he asked, annoyance written in his tone.

"I dined with her mother and a family friend last evening."

"Really? I take it by your sanguine demeanor that went well?"

"It did."

"And..."

"And what?"

"And am I to ask you for advice with women yet?"

"Women? Or Lady Davina?"

"Fine, I'm going to my office. I have more than enough work to do. Before they arrive though, keep an eye on the clerks. Bates specifically. He's been jumpy since the break-in."

"You don't mean..."

"Well, whoever broke in either picked the lock or used a key. It's possible one of them was involved. I caught him trying to 'help' tidy your office or search for documents in here no less than three times the other day."

"Perfect..." I sighed. "Thank you for the warning, I suppose."

"Of course," he mumbled with a mouthful of tart.

One by one the clerks arrived with Bates making a concerted effort to come into my office to welcome me back to the office. I noted a less than surreptitious glance at the documents on my desk. Lord, I hoped Kit was wrong. The man had a family to feed. But if he had information that would keep Celine out of danger—

The bell at the door rang and in stalked Wayland, shooing Lady Davina ahead, half-garbed in what was clearly her brother's clothing. Wayland's youngest brother, Mr. Tom Grayson followed, trying and failing to keep his laughter to a minimum.

"Kit! I understand you're responsible for this nuisance?" Wayland hollered from the main room. Grayson propped himself against one of the clerk's desks to enjoy the show as Kit stumbled out of his office. I made my way into the main room to see what all the commotion was about.

"I would hardly say I'm responsible for her. That would be her brother."

"Yes, well, I did steal Rosehill's fiancée from under him. So if it's all the same, I'd rather deal with you."

"Ugh! No one is *dealing* with me. I won! What is there to deal with?" Lady Davina demanded.

"Right. My office then," Kit said, gesturing distractedly behind him while gaping at the sight of the lady in breeches. She sauntered up to him, paused to adjust his cravat in an overly familiar way, then continued inside. Wayland followed, and Kit stood frozen, blinking dully for a moment until she called his name. He turned and joined them, closing the door behind him and leaving a bemused Mr. Grayson and the rest of the office thoroughly distracted in his wake.

I selected a tart from the nearby table and nodded toward my office when I had Mr. Grayson's attention. "Have a seat and a tart?"

He agreed and settled himself with his pastry across from me at the desk, his boot-clad feet promptly hitting the wood as he leaned back in the chair. It creaked in irritation but held fast and apparently Mr. Grayson was unconcerned with the protest.

"So, she was gambling then?" I asked, hoping for an amusing story for my morning.

"She won some three thousand pounds off Lord Montrose before anyone caught on. Now, of course, he's refusing to pay like the little weasel he is."

"Do we need to send a note to Rosehill?"

"Augie went to fetch him before he went home to Anna and Emma," he explained as he polished off the tart.

"Very good. Were you at the club?"

"I was. Michael was having one of his usual crises. He's convinced he cannot be a good father to his child since our father was shite. At least he's decided working far too many hours is preferable to running to Piccadilly and losing thousands like he did last time."

I left the majority of that statement lying, instead inquiring after the lady's health. It was a safe enough topic and one we covered quite nicely by the time Xander stumbled through the door, disheveled and underdressed.

I rose to greet him, and Mr. Grayson followed me into the main room.

"Is she in there with Mr. Summers?" Xander demanded.

"And Wayland. I'm sure they'll be out in a few moments," I explained.

"She was gaming at the club?"

"That is what I'm given to understand. I believe she won, at least. Have a tart and a seat. Catch your breath," I suggested, gesturing to the additional chair in my office before taking my own. Both men entered and settled beside each other, Mr. Grayson with a second tart in his hand. Without a word he passed it to Xander, who tore into it unthinkingly.

"So," Mr. Grayson started. "I was wondering something," he asked, his full attention on Xander.

"You need her permission," the duke retorted, looking up from his tart, peevish.

"What?" Grayson's brow furrowed.

"You need Davina's permission. To court her. The Lord himself could not force her into a courtship she did not wish. I'm certainly not going to attempt it."

"I wasn't going to ask to court your sister," Mr. Grayson explained slowly.

"You weren't?"

"No. I envy the men brave enough to court Hasket women. I'm not one of them." He turned in my direction to deliver that last little quip. *Well struck, sir.*

"Well, what did you want then?" Xander demanded.

"I was just wondering where you decided to go for your trip."

"My trip?" Xander asked, distracted once more by the tart.

"You were planning a trip the last time I saw you." Mr. Grayson leaned toward him, biting back a grin.

"Oh, I'm for Scotland."

"Scotland... Highlands? Lowlands? For how long?"

"Lowlands. And I'm planning to make it my primary residence. Why do you have so many questions?" Xander snapped back.

Mr. Grayson's teasing smirk fell from his face and his eyes widened in something like distress. "I—you—Nothing. Just making conversation."

"Apologies. I'm a bit... distracted at the moment. What with my sister," Xander explained, his hands brushing away the distraction.

"Of course. When, uh, when do you leave?" Mr. Grayson asked, picking at an invisible piece of lint on his waistcoat.

"That depends on what Will has managed to find out for me. Hopefully within the next several weeks."

"I suppose I should leave you two to it then." Mr. Grayson said, stumbling up from his chair and walking back out to the main room. He leaned against the tart table, picking at his thumbnail.

"Have you had the opportunity to find any answers? I know there was a bit of a situation here the other day," Xander said.

"I have answers for some of the questions. Surprisingly enough, neither the Rycliffe residence nor Hasket House is entailed, only the Yorkshire property. If you wanted to sell the Rycliffe residence after your departure, you could, and the money would be yours to do with as you see fit and untouchable by an heir. You could stay with your mother whenever you return to town."

"I can sell that house? You're certain?" It was impossible to discern whether he was distressed or excited by the idea. His tone and expression were on edge.

"Yes. Your father treated it as though it was a part of the courtesy title, but it was only purchased by your grandfather for your father."

"I do not have to live there? Where he died." There was a desperation in his tone.

My heart broke a little for him.

"No. If you would rather, you could use the funds to purchase a different house in town. I did not realize you wished to give it up. I deeply regret that I did not look into that earlier."

"No. Thank you. Thank you so much."

"Yes, well. Lady Davina's dowry, such as it stands, is untouchable, even if she remains unwed. I could set up anything additional you wish to add to it for her to have access to at an age you deem appropriate. Normally I would suggest twenty-five, but..."

"Thirty? Do you suppose she will mature by thirty?"

"It's possible. You can also have it released to her in installments, rather than a lump sum. You may wish to do the same thing with your mother."

"Yes. I can dower Celine from those funds as well?"

"Yes, if you wish."

"And what do you wish?" He grinned and steepled his hands under his chin.

"I beg your pardon?"

"I heard an interesting rumor last night. You are staying at Cadieux House?"

"I am..."

"Mr. Grayson out there claims not to possess the bravery necessary to court a Hasket lady. Do you?"

"Whether I possess the bravery is neither here nor there. I

believe she has determined that I am to court her. I've simply chosen to accept my fate."

"Good man." He offered a genuine smile. "Is she able to manage some of the funds?"

"Yes…"

"You do not sound overly certain."

"As long as she remains unwed, she can manage the funds. If she were to take another husband, they would become his. We could write the contract such that it would terminate at that time. But that would leave you with the same problem you are currently facing, no one to manage them."

"Why is that the case?"

"When a woman is born, she exists under her father's identity. When she weds, she and her husband become one in the eyes of the law, and that person is him. It is only if he precedes her in death that she becomes her own person, legally speaking. If she weds again, she accepts her new husband's identity."

"Well, that is patently absurd."

"I cannot disagree with you."

"And there is no way around it?"

"A vote in parliament…"

"Oh, well, there is no problem then." He rolled his eyes demonstratively.

"You can still manage everything by post. There just may be some difficulties. What those might be, I have no way of knowing."

"Right. Let me discuss selling the house with Celine. She should have a say as well. Do we need to have a purchase in place to draft the documents?"

"No, I can get them started and we can determine what funds should be placed where before signing."

I heard Kit's door open from the hall. Xander turned as all three former occupants came around the corner.

It was Wayland who broke the silence. "Rosehill, I trust you are well."

"I am."

"Good, that's... good." He turned his attention to Mr. Grayson, still awkwardly perched next to the tarts in an ungainly pile of too-long limbs. "Tom... Off the furniture. How many times must we have this conversation?"

"Everything sorted?" Mr. Grayson asked.

"It is. Let's head out." The men turned, heading for the door. The bell chimed behind the brothers, leaving a stilted silence in their wake.

It lasted only a moment before Lady Davina stomped into the room and fell into the empty chair beside Xander with an indelicate plop.

"I assume you two need to have a discussion?" I asked Kit.

"Only if you're finished. It can wait."

"I believe we're sorted for now. Do you want to use my office?" I asked.

"If you do not mind, while everyone is comfortable."

"Of course." I rose to leave and perhaps find a tart before they were all gone.

"You can stay. Our discussion impacts the rest of the estate," Kit added. Drat, no treat. I left my seat vacant for Kit and leaned against the wall.

"So, Lady Davina won some £3,250 this morning off of Lord Montrose. Michael is determined that he will pay it. However, he is equally determined that he cannot have young ladies sneaking into the club dressed as young men."

"It would serve you right, you know. If he had you arrested for public indecency," Xander scolded.

"He would never. He still feels badly for stealing Juliet from you."

Xander tutted. "A person cannot be stolen. She made the choice that would make her happiest and I am glad for them both. You are not to exploit any feelings he has on that subject. Do you understand?”

She crossed her arms, her lips twisting into something akin to a pout. The effect was somehow endearing rather than irritating. On anyone less beautiful, it would come across as childish and petulant, but on her it merely... was. When Xander remained unmoved by her display, she answered with a sullen, “I understand.”

“We can set up an account that will be for Lady Davina’s personal use. It will be under your name of course, if you agree,” Kit explained.

“Her own account? Is that necessary?”

“It might be good practice,” I offered.

“She also won £575 from Mr. Wesley Parker and £250 from Baron Thurston Lucas.”

“Davina...” Xander sighed.

“Why are you scolding me? I did well!”

“You could have just as easily done poorly,” he snapped. “Did she bankrupt anyone else? I thought Parker was more fond of the tracks than the tables.”

“No, Montrose was the most substantial gain,” Kit said.

“All right, have the accounts drafted, I suppose. I’ll call for the carriage. You stay right there.” He directed the last comment to Davina.

She watched him walk out before turning to me with narrowed eyes. “What are your intentions with Cee?”

“I beg your pardon?”

“You understood me perfectly,” she insisted.

“I...” I was saved from further interrogation by Xander’s return and subsequent dragging of his sister into his greatcoat before he stuffed her into the carriage.

“Well, this has been quite the morning,” Kit said to no one in particular.

It really had been.

And why did these women insist on traipsing into our office in all manner of ridiculous dress?

Twenty-Seven

DALTON PLACE, LONDON - JUNE 16, 1816

CELINE

APPARENTLY THE MOMENT of panic was instinctive. That one where I woke alone and shut my eyes against the burning sunlight to a vision of a blood-soaked hell. It came first, before last night's conversation about William returning to work in the morning fought its way through.

His scent, lingering on the cool fabric of his pillow helped stem the tide of terror when I buried my face in it. I could breathe properly here, inhaling the woody, herbal, and citrusy aroma with a hint of parchment and ink.

A brief glance at the clock told me what I already knew. Far too late to still be abed. Particularly with my morning's destination in mind—the one I hadn't told William about.

I ate quickly and dressed with precisely as much care as usual, no more and no less, before setting off on foot. My destination was not far, and the day was fine enough. I arrived more quickly than I would have liked at the house a few blocks from my own.

I hesitated longer than I would care to admit outside the

white house with the cheerful yellow set of doors. Baskets of flowers hung from the iron fence, and the door bore a wreath. All new additions in the last few years. Signs of new ownership.

Finally, I knocked and was led into a recently refreshed sitting room bathed in shades of blues and purples. Over-stocked bookshelves lined two entire walls, and several tomes sat on side tables throughout the room. Every furnishing bore a hand-embroidered cushion, save the gaming table in the far corner by the unlit fireplace.

I was inspecting a truly exquisite piece of embroidery when I heard the rustle of skirts behind me. I turned and found not the person I requested but his wife, Lady Juliet Wayland.

"Good morning, Lady Rycliffe." Her tone was pleasant as always, betraying no ill will, despite our unusual circumstances.

"Oh, good morning, Lady Juliet. How do you do?"

"Juliet, please. I am quite well. I understand you wished to meet with my husband. He has gone to manage something or other at the club, but I expect him back shortly. Can I bring you a cup of tea while you wait?"

"If it's no trouble, that would be wonderful. Or I can return at another time if that would better suit."

"Of course not. Please, make yourself comfortable. I will be back in a moment." I dropped onto the nearby settee. The fabric was luscious and hinted at rather than announced the wealth of the couple that occupied the modest home.

It was apparent now, seeing how Juliet spent the vast wealth available to her, just how poorly she and Xander would have suited. She would have shrunk under the oppressive force of Her Grace as her mother-in-law. And Xander's fine taste, though more subdued than his mother's, would not have allowed for the homey atmosphere she had cultivated.

She returned shortly and settled beside me. A maid set a tea tray before us and fussed with the offerings. It was overflowing with various treats from Hudson's.

For an overlong moment Juliet and I stared at each other, each hoping for the other to provide a topic to be seized.

"Rumor has it that congratulations are in order."

She flushed in response. "Yes, thank you. Michael and I are very pleased."

"When is your confinement?"

"It is still early days now. Four months, perhaps five? I hope you do not mind if I have ginger tea; it's the only thing that seems to soothe." Now that I knew to look, her usually rosy cheeks bore a sallow tinge.

"Of course not."

"Kate made this entire process look so easy. Anna as well. I am having a slightly more difficult time with it all."

"I am sorry to hear that."

"Do not let them convince you it is a simple matter. They're dreadful liars."

"Oh, I am not so easily fooled as all that. Besides, I am one and thirty. It is probable I may never be in such a position."

It was a fact I had come to accept. Since the years of Gabriel's frequent attentions were unfruitful, it was entirely likely that I would never reproduce. If that fact pained me at all, I had more than enough experience appearing as though it did not.

Something about the look she gave me told me my acting was somewhat lacking. Or perhaps she simply understood the notion.

From out in the hall, I heard the door open and close, and a familiar tenor called out, "Duchess, I'm back. You will not believe the morning I've had."

"In the drawing room," Juliet answered—apparently the

duchess in question. The name made little sense to me, but the love behind his tone was apparent.

Michael sauntered in, tugging his cravat loose in irritation. He froze the moment he recognized me, his eyes darting to his wife.

"Bonjour, Michael."

"Celine, good to see you." His eyes flicked cautiously between the two of us, searching for signs of distress, presumably. It was somewhat offensive, his concern that I would visit his home and upset his wife.

"You as well. It seems you've had quite the morning. Do you have a few moments? Or should I return some other time?" I only had to bite off one habitual term of endearment.

He glanced at Juliet, apparently determining her sanguine expression to be legitimate, then nodded. "Here or?"

"Your study? If you do not mind?" Once again his gaze shot to his wife.

"Oh, for heaven's sake. You do not require my permission," the lady snapped. He eyed her warily before nodding toward the hall. I followed him down several doors to a study.

Like the drawing room, it was filled with bookshelves. Though not as overfilled, and primarily populated with ledgers rather than novels. It suited him. Also like the rest of the house, it seemed every piece of furnishing was new, and though tasteful, of exceptional quality. He gestured toward a chair and poured himself a drink of whiskey before opening the gin and pouring a glass for me.

He was every bit as handsome as he had been when we first met. Perhaps more so. His dark hair was longer and less styled. And there were a few lines around the corners of his warm brown eyes. But he moved with ease, a languid peace to his motions that had been absent before.

When we knew each other, he wore his unaffected demeanor like armor. At some point, he had set it aside.

"So, are you going to tell me what this is about? Or am I to guess?"

"Good to see you too."

"I love to see you, you know I do. But you haven't been to visit me since that day."

"I... I have an uncomfortable question to ask you. I'm not quite certain how to ask it."

"Never known you to shy away from anything," he remarked, taking a sip.

With a deep breath, I started. "What I am about to ask is incredibly offensive. And I already know the answer. But I just —I need to hear you say it. I hope you can forgive me for asking."

"The curiosity is eating me alive. Out with it then."

"Did you kill Gabriel? Or have him killed?" The words spilled forth, slurred and desperate.

His brow hit his hairline in an almost comical way. Or it would have been in any other circumstance. He blinked slowly, once, twice, three times. "No—God no—Celine. I would never. I've never..."

The sincere desperation in his countenance and tone was enough. I felt a tension loosen and dissipate.

"You—you don't really think that? Do you?" He continued.

"No, not truly."

"What made you ask?"

"I— Oh Lord, this is embarrassing. I met someone, and it reminded me of the day before he was killed. And I found a note."

"I'm going to require a few more sentences."

"We went to the races the day before. And I saw someone from Gabriel's past, and it reminded me of a note I found in his possessions. It was signed from *W*."

"A threat?"

"More or less. 'Meet me at dawn,' that sort of thing."

"Who did you meet?" His brow furrowed for a moment, as he studied me. "Oh..." he drew out that syllable with a knowing tone and I was caught. "You've met a man."

"I have no idea what you mean."

"Liar." There was no accusation, just an infuriating smirk. "Who is he? Do I know him?"

The stubborn part of me considered insisting on my ruse, but really, what purpose would it serve? "William Hart."

His eyes widened in response before settling into a studious squint and he added a circumspect, "Hmm."

"Hmm, what?"

"Nothing."

"Michael..."

"Nothing, truly. At first it seemed a surprising choice, but then I considered it further. He's a good man. You would be good for each other."

"Why surprising?"

"You like to see and be seen. He prefers a more solitary life. Also, the difference in stations. But I'm not one to speak in that regard. I expect you complement each other." He was perfectly sincere, earnest and genuine in expression and voice.

"You truly think so?"

"I do. Of course, I think any man you grace with your affections is lucky. But there are certainly those less worthy." He took a sip of his drink before continuing. "Do you ever wonder? Why we never considered making our arrangement more official? I cannot regret it, of course. I would not give up Jules for the world. But we could have been good together. We were good together for a time."

"I hadn't given it much thought, to be quite honest."

"I suppose I always knew that. It's why I didn't contemplate it either. Neither of us was ready, perhaps. I was still angry with my father and Hugh. You were still grieving Gabriel."

"You're not wrong. Though I think it was always friendship, not romance, between us."

"Of course, I never meant otherwise. But there are marriages built on less. Or maybe we both knew there was someone more *right* out there for us."

"You think so?"

"You don't?"

"Oh, I mean, of course, Lady Juliet is wonderful and you both seem so happy. I just meant..."

"For you?"

"Yes."

"I always have done. I want it for you. If anyone deserves happiness, it's you, Cee. I hope it's Will. But if it's not, then there's someone else. Your life didn't end with Gabriel's."

"I know it. I do. It's just..."

"Risky?"

"Yes."

"Did I ever tell you what I did when I realized Jules and I were falling in love?"

"You know that you did not."

"That was rhetorical, and you know it. We were in Kent, with Hugh and Kate. I knew I was nearing that point—love— but when I tipped over the line... She was glorious. And I ran —ran all the way back to London, where I lost a small fortune in the hells of Piccadilly. It was a desperate attempt to outdrink and outgamble my feelings. Didn't help. Not for one second. All that to say, I understand. Love—it's absolutely terrifying. Scariest thing in the world."

"It is—absolutely terrifying."

"Right now, I'm completely petrified. Our child isn't even here yet, and I love them more than life. And I'm panicked for Jules too. She's being brave, as usual. But her mother passed in childbirth. And her stepmother never recovered from her still-born. We're both pretending, all day every day, that we're not terrified."

"How do you do it?"

"I tried being without her. *That* was the only thing that felt worse."

"You think so?"

"I know it. And you do too."

"I do?"

"All the agony of losing Gabriel, but you would do it all over again if you had the chance. You would choose to fall in love with him again, every single time. Even knowing how it would end. Wouldn't you? Because the only thing worse than losing someone you love is never having had them at all."

It wasn't until he handed me a delicately embroidered handkerchief that I noticed the tears on my cheeks. The material was far too fine to use. Juliet was incredibly talented. One corner bore his initials with little forget-me-nots woven around them.

"Now that I've made you cry... What's this about the note?"

Twenty-Eight

CELINE

THE AIR WAS thick and heavy with humidity that night. Or perhaps it was anticipation. Michael's words still rang in my ears and my head. He was right. I would do it over again. I would choose Gabriel every single time, even those last moments holding his hand. Even the agonizing, devastating weeks, months, years that followed.

It had been worth it.

If I was honest, I had suspected for several days that William would be worth it too. Or he could be. I would have to take the risk to be certain. But as he babbled on across the table about Davina's latest escapade at Wayland's, his eyes a bright cobalt blue and razor cheeks flushed with delight, I rather thought that I knew he was.

He was such an intriguing combination of discrepancies. Sharp, hardened angles softened by a warmth within. Familiar in death and loss and naive in love and lust. Guarded and blustery before opening up with naked, earnest vulnerability.

I was a rather poor conversationalist. Though my artless,

wordless study of him was sufficient to encourage his story. It was charming, what little of it I was listening to. It would not be such a terrible fate, watching his animated face retell stories at the table night after night, year after year. In fact, I was hard-pressed to consider a fate I would enjoy more. This kind, loyal, intelligent, witty, handsome man for company? It would be no hardship at all. There was no better fate.

There were things to discuss. The conclusion of my discussion with Michael being nowhere near the bottom of the list. But quite frankly, those didn't interest me at the moment. No, at present, I was aware of my body in a purely feminine way. And I was aware of his body in that same way. I had mapped the distance between our angled seats.

In my mind, I had yanked him to me with a handful of cravat and fallen into his arms. Unfortunately, if he knew the direction my thoughts took, he gave no indication of it.

Which left me in the awkward position of trying to implement my plan. The one that involved the rest of the evening luxuriating between the sheets and exploring all the different ways to bring each other pleasure. Not separating until the sun rose and set and rose again—perhaps thrice more.

What this man lacked in experience, he more than compensated for in enthusiasm when he'd kissed me. I had absolutely no reason to suspect the boudoir would be any different.

He was midsentence when I interrupted, unable to stifle the want careening through my blood for a moment longer.

"William?"

His pause was lengthy, likely parsing his last few words for the offense. "Yes?" he asked cautiously, drawing the word out. Waiting for a reproach.

"Have you given any more thought to our conversation that first night? In the hall?" By the way his jaw ticked, he more than understood me.

"Have I given any thought to... Constantly. Every moment. It's quite thoroughly driven me to distraction. A man does not forget a conversation like that, love."

"And are you opposed to exploring our other option tonight?"

He swallowed thickly before answering—not with words but with a kiss, wild and hungry. Evidently he found the possibility of exploring that option more than favorable.

His lips fell against my own with a breathless groan. Fingers tangled in my hair, pulling me close—closer. It wasn't close enough, not for either of us.

The clatter of dishes and silverware echoed through the room as he rose and hauled me out of my seat and onto his lap without breaking contact. His warm, William-scented frame bracketed me against the table. I tugged his unfairly soft curls and traced that blade he called a cheek. I tasted the lemony dessert on his tongue. He was delectable.

The edge of the table ground into my lower back. I didn't mind the bite, but when his hand found a home there, serving as a cushion, I *loved* that. He was all thoughtful consideration, even in the fog of lust.

His hand fisted in the tendrils at the base of my neck, somehow managing not to tug on the pins. The other hand tightened on my waist, even as his forearm was sacrificed to the table. He took full control—there was no hesitation when he tilted my head the way he wished and chased my tongue with his own.

A teasing nip to his tongue was answered with something akin to a growl that was far more arousing than it had any right to be. He pulled me even harder against him, my skirts pushing up against his hips. The movement left me directly over top of his growing hardness.

He abandoned my lips with a groan and found his way to that magical place where my shoulder met my neck. I was left unable to do anything except clutch his neck, moan wantonly, and press myself closer to him in any way possible.

His hands slid boldly down to my bottom. Assisting me, rocking me harder against him. Then, in a movement that left me gasping and clinging to his shoulders, he stood, supporting me with one hand on my low back and the other gripping my backside.

With a grace and confidence I never could have predicted, he strode purposefully down the hall and up the staircase. I clung to him, my legs wrapped low around his waist. When it became clear that he was in no danger of dropping me, I used the opportunity to loosen his cravat and take the fullest advantage of the newly revealed skin. His throat bobbed enticingly, and I nipped playfully there, earning a groan.

He navigated the first staircase without trouble, only stumbling when my teasing ministrations became too much. At the landing, he pressed me into the wall, taking the opportunity to find my lips with his. With a nibble on my lower lip, he pulled away, growling, "Behave."

"If you wanted someone who would behave, we wouldn't be here right now."

He pulled my lips back to his, slightly more tender. "Behave enough that I don't drop you at least," he said, trying and failing to bite back a grin.

He hauled us both away from the wall, continuing up the steps, down the hall, into my open bedroom.

~

WILLIAM

I had never been so close to heaven and so near hell in the same breath as I stumbled, my arms full of Celine toward the bedroom.

I was going to die—it was an absolute fact—if I didn't do

something right this second. What that something was, I hadn't the foggiest. Every single idea that flitted through my head was the best I'd ever had. Tear her gown off, yes. Kiss her *everywhere*, certainly. Bury myself inside her and never leave, unquestionably the best notion anyone had ever had.

The problem was that I wanted—*needed*—this to be good for her. Better than good.

I was man enough to admit I was a jealous arse. I wanted to be better than Gabriel. Better than Wayland. I wanted to make her forget their names and any others that had come before me.

Unfortunately I had nothing to go on but instinct and the little whimpers, mewls, and groans that escaped her. And I had enough sense left to know that this was not likely to be an impressive performance. Nights of holding her in my arms with no release meant I was wound tauter than a drum. If there was to be any hope, I would need to slow this down.

I set her on her feet reluctantly inside her bedroom. She was rumpled and more beautiful than she had ever been. Her eyes burned an olive in the firelight. Her cheeks and neck were flushed from my attentions. In short, she was perfection.

Why had I stopped kissing her again?

"You missed the bed..."

"I didn't. I want to take your gown off first."

"Unnecessary." She grabbed my hand, trying to tug me to the bed but the temptation of her bare form before me in the candlelight was not one I would forgo willingly.

"Very necessary. I want to see you, love. All of you. Let me? Please?"

"How do you always say the exact right thing?"

"I have never in my life said the right thing, as you know better than most. Now turn around." I started with her hairpins. Plucking the decorative little pearls tucked into her silken champagne waves. Lord, this hair... One by one the curls tumbled down into a rippling curtain of sunshine, glittering in the shadows cast by the flames. There were so many shades of gold, some near white, some strands a darker sun-kissed bronze.

"William?" She turned back to face me, all flushed and lovely.

"Yes, love?"

"I thought you were going to take my gown off." I pulled her hair to one shoulder, freeing the other for my lips. I received a small sound that could only be named contentment as her tiny fist found my shirt and tugged.

"So impatient... Want to savor this. Savor you."

"But..."

"Celine, love, I want to do this properly."

"And slowly is properly?"

"Hush and turn back around." She did with a raised brow as the only comment. My hands shook slightly as I studied the hooks.

I had faced a damn army and I was intimidated by some dress hooks. A little curl at the base of her neck swished back and forth in time with my harsh breath. Swallowing my nerves, I started at the base of her neck.

The hooks came free with ease, one after another. The lavender silk parted to reveal a fine petticoat underneath. It was decorated with enticing bits of lace. She raised her hands and tugged the straps off her shoulders. It loosened suddenly in time with the gown. Both fell off her in waves to pool between us.

She was still wrapped in a chemise and stays, and I still wore my waistcoat and shirtsleeves. I traced the laces with my fingers, a perfect row of straight lines down her back ending in a delicate bow. Without giving myself time to think, I tugged one of the strands and the knot slipped loose. I was not entirely unfamiliar with women's undergarments; my past interactions with them had been substantially less erotic.

Celine was so vivacious it was easy to forget just how tiny she truly was. Not now, not when my hands fit over her waist with room to spare. She was so damn small. So damn fragile. And so damn brave. I could have lost her that night, before I knew her.

And I never would have known *this*.

Shaking away the intrusive thoughts, I loosened one row of cording, then the next. It only took a few before that layer joined the others on the floor. That left only her chemise. A whisper-thin scrap of delicate muslin, entirely transparent in the firelight, silhouetting her, was all that stood between me and her bare form.

"'Lo, love."

She smiled, turning to face me as she tucked her fingers into the top of my waistcoat and tugged. "My turn?"

"I'd rather continue my turn, but I suppose." She gave me a whisper soft kiss to my chin, playful and pleased when she pulled back.

Turning her gaze to my waistcoat she slipped the buttons free with ease. She pushed in close, shoving it off my shoulders to join her frippery. Before I could make for the delicate bow mocking me between her breasts, she slid her hands to my loose cravat. She tugged one end free, looping it around my neck. Just when I thought she would pull the other end free, she instead fisted one end in each hand and tugged me down to her. My lips tasted her self-satisfied grin.

Celine took control of the kiss, holding me where she wanted, directing me. It was as comforting as it was arousing. With her instruction, perhaps my showing would not be as poor as I feared. Hands knotting in my hair and my shirt, pulling me ever closer. I understood the desire, the need, the absolute loathing of the space and fabric between us.

She broke free for a gasping breath, yanking my shirt over my head with no ceremony whatsoever.

Rather than returning her lips to mine, which was my preference, she dragged her hands across my chest and stomach. Her expression was entirely unreadable. Unease began to fill me, was I not what she expected?

"Love?"

She blinked back to me, her eyes finding mine. "Apologies, I just... Solicitors don't look like *that*."

"Like what?" I asked, making a rather poor show of hiding my distress.

"Will— I've never... You're a damn statue."

"I don't know what that means."

She shook her head, at last smiling slightly. "It's good. Don't worry about it."

When I had no response to that she decided there should be more kissing. That was good—more kissing was always good.

Somehow, she managed to maneuver us to the bed. I only noticed when my knees hit the edge and buckled. Celine, beautiful, clever Celine set first one knee, then the other on the bed outside of my hips, straddling me with ease. She pulled back against the fist I had tangled in her curls, keeping her lips pressed to mine.

"Relax. There's no one here but us," she whispered. Her lips brushed across mine with assurance.

"Love..."

"We've talked about this. Anything you wish to know, I am more than happy to teach you." There was no guile in her expression, and when I cupped her cheek, she leaned into the touch.

"It's... overwhelming. In the best possible way. And I want you to feel as I do. But everything I know about pleasing women comes from conversations with an unwell adventuress or braggarts in the army. It seems safe to say that neither is a reliable source."

"That—I have to agree with that assessment. So ask. I am all yours. Anything you wish to know, anything you wish to try, you need only ask."

"You're all mine?"

"I'm sorry, was that not clear? There's only you. In here, out there. Just us."

"Celine..." I could only kiss her for that. There was no other response that could possibly convey the way her words wrapped around my heart and squeezed, nearly painful, but lovely all the same.

She made a pleased little hum against my lips, pressing herself closer. I could feel the ghost of her breasts brushing against my chest through the impossibly fine fabric of her chemise. A promise of something more.

"Tell me," she murmured in my ear before tonguing the lobe in a way I never would have thought to enjoy, but now couldn't imagine life without.

Summoning courage I did not know I possessed, I slid a hand up her thigh to cup the crevice between her legs. The place I wanted to live in, die in, be buried in for eternity.

"I want to taste you." My request was an ineloquent blurt, but there was no mistaking my meaning.

A pleased groan burst from her before I had a moment to second guess myself. Her assent was more moan than word.

Swallowing harshly, I tugged eagerly at the hem of her chemise. She pulled the tie of the bow holding the scrap of fabric on her frame. The widened neck slid off one shoulder instantly, revealing a pert breast.

Before the thought was fully formed in my head, my lips found her nipple, tonguing, tasting, worshiping. Her back arched as she pressed herself closer with an encouraging moan.

Between the two of us, we were able to remove the fabric

entirely with minimal interruption to my efforts. That, of course, left her bare for my gaze. Her need directly above my own, separated only by my trousers.

I was going to die. There was no way I would survive the night. My heart had ceased beating and was certainly not going to start again.

I was more than all right with that.

To die with her taste on my lips, her silken skin under my fingers, the sight of her unclothed and mussed in my arms—it was a privilege I did not deserve.

Her curls were tangled from my hands, hanging in luxurious waves around us, shrouding us. My kisses had left her lips, neck, and chest reddened, and I felt a purely male pride at the sight. A few yellowing bruises decorated her abdomen, remnants from that awful night. Stark reminders of how close I came to losing her, my Celine. Inches away, from never having this or any of the thousands of other moments I wanted in her arms.

I ducked, pressing the gentlest of kisses to each one of her battle wounds.

"Will," she whined, trying to guide me by my hair back to her lips or her breasts or her neck, I doubted she knew which either. In a superhuman feat, I refused her, instead catching her waist and flipping her back onto the cloud-soft bed beneath me.

She gave me an arch grin in response, one I could not help but reciprocate before taking her lips with my own. It was impossible, of course, to express my feelings for her in words, or even in kisses. But I was never one to give up without trying.

She tasted of sunshine, and hope, and something warm, sensual, spicy. I could only imagine the desperation she tasted from me.

Far from repulsed though, she clawed at me, dragging me closer still.

"Will, I want to feel you." She clung to my back with surprising strength, pulling herself off the bed to where my chest hovered over hers.

"You'll be crushed. Do you have any idea how devastated I would be if I crushed you now?" I answered, inspecting her jaw once again with my lips.

"Please?"

"No, 'm busy." I had every intention of finding my way to her feminine folds any moment now. But there were a great number of curves to map with my lips and tongue, lest I be lost forever in the heaven that surely awaited between her thighs. Of course, that would be no great hardship.

The divot in her clavicle, the mound of each breast with their very distracting peaks, the valley below them. The river between each of her ribs where the lightest glisten of sweat clung for me to taste. The cleft above each hip bone. Each and every one was charted and explored until her hands fisted in the bed coverings and every exhale was a pant of my name.

There I found it, my destination, my shelter, her surely delectable center. Instinct drove me. All enthusiasm and no finesse when I found myself buried between her thighs. Here was ambrosia, manna, something better. She was hot and wet and all mine, all for me.

I was lost to her, the only grip I had on reality was the hand that somehow found its way tangled up in hers.

It was a gloriously fortunate thing that she was so damn expressive. Whimpers and sighs escaped her lips. Fingers threaded through my hair, fisting when I moved just right. Her hips chased my mouth, directing me to the places that were most pleasing to her. She was a symphony, a ballet, a revelation.

After a close call between her hips and my nose, I pressed

our joined hands low on her belly to keep her where I wanted her. With each passing swipe of my tongue, my confidence grew. I drew her leg over my shoulder with my free hand, spreading her even wider for my appreciation.

Following the instruction of her hand in my hair, her stilted movements, and her whimpers, I was fairly certain she was closing in on release. Finding herself ever closer to that peak where she would collapse into a beautiful heap in my arms. I slid one finger, two, into her channel where she welcomed me eagerly.

Her whimpers and moans were gaining in frequency and pitch, and her fingers tangled in my hair were hovering on just the right side of painful. Not that I would have complained. That would have required stopping and I had no intention of doing that, possibly ever.

Sooner than I hoped, her core tightened on my fingers with a keening gasp. Her back bowed and her thigh shook by my ear. It overtook her with such a suddenness that I froze, unsure if it meant what I thought it might. Seconds, perhaps minutes later, she collapsed into the covers, boneless.

Indecision clouded my mind once more. I did not know the protocol for this. I knew I wanted to keep going, to drag her up and over the crest again and again until time ran out.

Before I could revel too far in my discomfort, she tugged at my hair once more, this time purposeful. Following her instructions, silent or otherwise, had served me well thus far so I followed my map back up. If I took detours to see my favorite sites once more, Celine certainly wasn't complaining.

Twenty-Nine

CADIEUX HOUSE, LONDON - JUNE 16, 1816

CELINE

He prowled up my body, cat-like in his grace. It was without a doubt the single most erotic view of my entire life. This man, all sharp, lithe, corded muscles, with chiseled cheekbones shining in the candlelight from my offerings, slid up my form with an expression that very much said he was not finished feasting.

I would not soon forget it.

His lips found mine and all I could taste was me. All the tentative softness was gone, in its place a worshipful confidence. Well-earned confidence—I wasn't certain my legs would regain feeling ever again. That was perfectly all right. I was never leaving this bed anyway.

When he pulled away for the benefit of my breathing rather than any particular desire to do so if the heat in his eyes was any indication, I wiped away the last of my spendings from his lips. He caught my wrist in a tender gesture and pressed a kiss to my pounding pulse.

"Who... are you?" I panted.

"What do you mean?"

"You've just killed me. I am dead. This is heaven. I thought you said you had little experience."

"I do. That was the first time I've done that." He had never... How?

"You're a savant... Also, you live here now."

"Already live here, love."

"In this bed. I'll tie you here if need be."

His answering smile was infectious, and he pressed a gentle kiss to my nose. "If 'm tied to the bed, what'll I eat?" His hand found my entrance at the exact moment he finished the sentence, leaving absolutely no doubt of what he intended to eat.

Summoning all the strength I had managed to regain after he wrung it from my body, I curled a leg around his hips without warning and rolled him over onto his back.

As he lay prostrate before me, I caught his hands and pinned them above his head before he could regain my newfound control.

Dipping down, I pressed a kiss, nearly as gentle as the ones he'd bestowed on me, to the gray-green bruise marring his ribs, just below his heart.

His eyes burned blue in response, that shade where flame met candlewick and was just as bright. Brighter even, when paired with the affectionate crinkles at the corners of his eyes. The crinkles I was slowly coming to realize were reserved for me. For when I did something he found charming, or amusing, or arousing, or loving. Those crinkles were at their best when I did something that made him feel loved—like right in this moment.

If there had been any doubt of his feelings for me, that look would have banished them. No one could adopt that expression of awe, reverence, astonishment, and wonder without the sentiment behind it. Surely men looked upon angels with less adoration.

It was a heady thing, being the recipient of such an expression. It filled me with a confidence I hadn't known in so long. I hovered over him, just out of his reach, curtaining us beneath my hair.

Teasing him, I brushed my lips across his—a breeze rather than a kiss. He made a valiant effort to chase my lips while still abiding to the shackles of my hands around his wrists.

His upper arms strained against my pitiful bonds, tensing and releasing in the most intriguing of ways. I had no idea that all of *this* was underneath those stodgy woolen waistcoats and scratchy linen shirts. He shifted slightly under my perusal, drawing my attention back to his impossibly warm eyes and unbearably soft lips.

I settled back onto my knees and released his wrists. The movement brought me in perfect alignment with the hardness threatening to escape his trousers. A stark reminder of the fact that, while I was more than sated—though rapidly regaining interest—he had not been.

I braced myself, my hands on his cool, slate chest. Careful to avoid the bruises earned in defense of me, my fingertips ghosted over wiry, corded muscles, divots, and peaks, each just as sharp and steep as his cheeks and jaw. He tensed and relaxed in rhythm beneath me, clearly desperate for more but unwilling or unable to ask for it.

"What do you want, William?"

"I..."

"Do you want me to taste you? Do you want me to ride you? Do you want me clawing at your back from beneath you? Tell me what you want, and it's yours." His pupils dilated, swallowing all of the blue until all that was left were fathomless black depths.

"Yes," he choked out.

"Yes, what?"

"All of it."

He earned a kiss for that. His hands, now free from their imaginary prison, banded about my waist and fisted in my hair.

"You have to pick one. I'm not flexible enough to manage all three at once."

"Above me, where you belong, Aphrodite."

"I don't know about that. But I'm happy to oblige."

"Goddess."

There was a moment, however brief, where I considered simply... not uttering the question, however necessary it was. Where I just let fate, or God, or the gods, or nature decide.

But it was not my choice to make, not alone, and not without vows. "Do you... you will let me know when it is time? So there are no... surprises."

He considered my words with all the severity they were due, regardless of their vagueness. Shifting beneath me, seeming to test his resolve. "Yes, I... yes." He pulled my lips down to his, pressing them simply, earnestly, against my own.

I settled back, resting on his thighs, working on the falls of his trousers. I had a suspicion that what I would find under there would be thoroughly distracting. So distracting that I would never get his trousers off if I didn't remove them entirely before sitting back to admire him. I forced myself to slide to the side, yanking them all the way and flinging them elsewhere.

Obstacles gone, I settled back into my spot resting on hard thighs to admire. I was no blushing debutant, but I felt it now. He was hard and proud, and I was suddenly, achingly empty.

"You cannot look at me like that and expect this to last for more than a few seconds," Will groaned.

My gaze found his. He wore a hungry expression that was entirely reflective of my own need. Bending down, I offered him what I intended as a gentle kiss. He had other ideas. His tongue slid along mine, becoming downright filthy with ease.

This man... This man who had been infuriating me, saving me, cherishing me, pushing me, arousing me, loving me from the moment we met. This man who took me apart, piece by piece in this very bed mere moments ago... Oh, I was going to destroy him. I was going to send him to the same euphoria he sent me to.

I pulled away, running my hand up and down his length a few times, twisting on the end for good measure while he cursed and thrust to meet me.

"Yes?" I asked, waiting for his clenched eyes to open and meet mine.

"Yes, love—Always, yes." Permission granted, I lifted myself, more awkwardly than I wished, overtop him. He caught my hip in one hand, steadying me, as I sank down, down, down on him.

Breath left us both, my lungs refusing to cooperate, while his worked too well. After a moment, air came back to me and I rocked gently forward and up, back and down. That movement earned me another curse and Will's free hand pulling me forward.

Our lips crashed together. He used teeth and tongue and that full lower lip to convey all the emotions I wasn't quite ready to hear aloud. There was no doubt though, what he meant. Admiration, adoration, lust, love, all poured through his lips to mine. My hips stuttered at the overwhelm of it all, but his hand tightened on my waist, adjusting the rhythm.

A peak was building again, one I hadn't thought to expect. Certainly not after the one I just had, but it was growing, over-filling with his feelings and my own. Higher and higher with each thrust, his free hand found my bud between us, pressing against it in a way that left me shattered without warning.

I collapsed atop him, boneless and sated and heaving great

gulps of air. Lost in another world entirely. Seconds, minutes, hours, years later, I found myself sprawled above his cool chest, his member still hard inside me.

Languidly, I rose off him and slid down his form, and swallowed him down. He was too much for me to take in his entirety, and I caught the rest of his hardness in my hand. It took mere seconds before he was babbling words of adoration, encouragement, and curses mixed with groans. His hands threaded through my hair, directing my rhythm, still exceedingly gentle.

"Celine, love, I'm going to..."

I didn't care. Not anymore. I wanted it.

I met his gaze and he cursed above me before his release filled my mouth. After swallowing, I crawled back to my place on top of his chest and curled against him. Somehow even now, damp with perspiration, he was cooler than I was. His body was a soothing balm against my own.

I rose and fell with his heavy breaths. His hand, still tangled in my hair, extricated itself and began the impossible process of smoothing out the snarls.

Eventually my breathing returned to something close to normal and I made to move off him. His arm tightened around my waist, pinning me in place.

"Where do you think you're going?"

"A few inches to the left?" I asked, propping my chin on his chest to peer up at him.

"Right here is perfect."

"I'm crushing you."

"You couldn't crush me if you tried. Stay."

"But..."

"Stay, love. Not ready for you to be that far." There it was again, that little crinkle in his eyes that said *"I love you"* without saying a word. And somehow, his protests made perfect sense. Pressed along his side, a few inches to the left, was much too far away.

I made his wish come true, sprawling out across his chest like a star, purposefully taking as much space as possible.

"Charming," he murmured.

"You adore me."

"Not the word I would have chosen, but yes."

"How do you feel? About everything?"

"Feeling lots of things... adoration as mentioned. A surprising amount of lust considering I may never regain feeling in my lower extremities. Other things I promised not to say until you're ready to hear them."

"No regrets?" It wasn't until I gave voice to the question that I recognized the tightness in my lower spine for the anxiousness that it was. He'd waited years for this moment. A moment he almost certainly planned to have with Adriane. I wasn't sure I would recover if he regretted having it with me— now—instead.

He pressed a kiss to the top of my head. "No, love. A few moments there, I was wishing I had a bit more experience, that I knew how to make it good for you. But I wouldn't be anywhere else."

I propped my chin on his chest. "It was good for me. It was incredible."

I felt more than heard his chuckle. "Know that, love. Nearly yanked all my hair out enjoying yourself."

"Sorry..."

"Don't be. Turns out I like that."

"What else do you like?"

"Everything. As you well know. Did you— do you like everything?" There was an unasked question behind the words. A vulnerability I wished to soothe. It was not a case of better or worse than Gabriel, but different. A different time, a different place, a different set of circumstances, and most significantly of all, I was not the same girl I had been.

"I *loved* it." His eyes—closer to navy now—widened, reading the significance in my phrasing. "I'm not ready to say it, not just yet. But I..."

"You're all right hearing it?" I nodded, my chin resting atop my folded arms on his chest. "I love you, Celine." It slipped from him in a rush, as if the words were all that was keeping him filled. Now that they were free, he could collapse into the bed beneath him and watch me with soft, loving eyes.

I pressed a kiss to his heart in answer, resting my head above where each beat was infinitesimally slower than the last. They finally leveled out just before I fell asleep in his arms.

Thirty

WILLIAM

The sunlight was an unwelcome intruder. I had my very own sun, wrapped naked in my arms and half buried under a blanket. What use had I for the one intruding on our morning?

I threw an arm over my head to block the irritating rays. That did nothing for the infuriating little bird outside that was determined to remind me I should be dressing for work at that very moment. The least it could do was learn a third note. Perhaps Celine would like a cat, one that ate whatever specific bird that was.

Beside me, Celine stretched languidly, her curves pressed all along my side in a way that was definitely not encouraging me to get out of bed.

"Hush you," she murmured. To my great astonishment, the bird listened, ceasing its infernal two-toned chirp instantly.

"You're a magician."

I felt, rather than saw the self-satisfied smile cross her lips as she slung an arm low on my waist. "The bird and I have an understanding."

"What?"

"Don't worry about it. How are you feeling?"

"Like I never want to leave this bed. Here is perfect. We don't need to go out there, do we?"

"I don't... At least not yet. You, on the other hand, seem to feel that your attendance at your place of business is necessary."

"Cruel."

"You've just now noticed?"

"Noticed last night when you were trying to kill me."

"Only a little death..."

"Misnomer, that. One day my heart will stop beating and it won't feel nearly as momentous as that."

"I cannot disagree. I don't suppose I can convince you that work is entirely unnecessary?" she asked.

"You absolutely could."

"And if I wished to set about doing that... How, precisely, should I make it happen? And please do be explicit."

WHEN I FINALLY MANAGED TO DRAG MYSELF from her arms, I was only very, very late.

It took all the willpower I possessed to leave her in that bed, sprawled across it as she hummed thoughtfully. She watched me with hooded eyes as I parsed through my clothes that had miraculously found their way to her dressing room.

I ought to be ashamed of how much her servants knew, but I had a limited capacity for cares and they were all occupied with her.

"Do you have plans this evening?" she asked, nonchalant as she stood to don her dressing gown.

"Planned to ravish you until sunrise," I grumbled as I tugged my fresh shirt over my head. It was nearly impossible to remind myself why we could not begin immediately. The not insignificant risk of my heart giving out from the exquisite bliss of entering her for a second time in an hour was pitifully unconcerning.

"So nothing fixed?" she pressed.

"No, nothing," I said, sliding on stockings while seated at the edge of the bed. She had found her hairbrush and was running it through the ends of her curls carefully.

I wanted to do that. Damnable employment.

"Kate is hosting a ball tonight..."

I groaned. "Please don't ask me what you're about to ask me."

"But..."

"Celine..."

"But it's Kate. And Lord Leighton—Mr. Summers—will certainly be there, so you can complain together." Her lower lip dipped out just the tiniest bit. It was absurd, enticing, and altogether too adorable. I caught it between mine, giving it a nip.

Quite frankly, I did not possess the needed resolution to resist, nor did I wish to. Still, I managed to break away, answering with a flat, "No."

Her jaw fell open and her eyes widened. "You... but..."

"Me—But nothing. You and your feminine wiles are not subtle, minx."

"Will... Please?" It was the please that finally did it. The please and the big downturned olive eyes.

"Fine, but I won't dance." I shoved my legs through my trousers irritably. I didn't want to be putting these on, and in my present state, they were more than a little uncomfortable.

"All right, but one dance though."

"Am I speaking? I feel like I'm speaking and words are

coming out of my mouth and those words have meaning. But you seem neither to hear nor understand the ones you do not like."

"Precisely, so you may as well give in. Two dances, the supper set I think. And the first."

"What happened to one?"

"You know you want to dance with me."

"I want to dance with you between these sheets," I said, nodding to the bed beside us. "I have absolutely no interest in the rest of the *ton's* involvement."

"Oh, very well. I suppose I shall be able to find some other partner."

The sound that ripped from my chest was in the vicinity of a growl. What was this woman doing to me? "You are a tease."

"I am a delight, and you know it. Three dances."

"I don't know three dances."

"I'll lead." She held out my waistcoat for me to slip my arms in. I turned in her grasp and she slipped the buttons through the fabric.

"You will be the death of me."

"Very likely," she answered pertly. She straightened the knot of my cravat and ran her fingers through my curls, smoothing them. "There, all respectable again. No indication that I spent the evening debauching you beyond belief."

That would not do.

I kissed her, hot, hard, fierce, desperate, pouring every ounce of regret, and irritation that I had to leave into her. Finally, I pulled away. She looked thoroughly tupped and, by the way her thumb traced my lower lip with an indulgent smile, I feared I did too.

"Get to work. Before I tie you to the bed."

"Goodbye, love."

"Goodbye, William. Be home by six?" Her lower lip

caught between her teeth and I caught a hint of the vulnerability she was trying to hide.

Home by five then, and perhaps flowers on the way.

"Six."

~

I WAS VERY, very late. And I cared very, very little.

All the clerks were in when I finally walked through the office door after a considerably longer walk than usual. Kit, on the other hand, was not there, though he had been at some point if the tarts were any indication. They had been well enjoyed before my arrival, all but a few were little more than crumbs. I grabbed one without regard for flavor.

I hadn't yet made it to my chair before Bates was out of his and hovering in my doorway.

"Good morning, sir. I'm glad to see you're well. When you weren't in, I went upstairs to check on you and there wasn't an answer. Mr. Summers told me you were staying elsewhere?"

"I am perfectly well, thank you. In the future, you need not concern yourself with my whereabouts."

I was becoming more and more certain that he had been involved in the break-in. He was too young to have been entangled in Gabriel's murder, but surely he knew something.

"Right, of course. Where are you staying? Somewhere nice I expect. You look well-rested. How long do you think you'll be away from home?"

I prided myself on being a kind and fair employer. But even I had my limits. Today of all days most especially, a day when I left a warm, sun-kissed goddess in bed to be harassed by a particularly incompetent, nitwit of a criminal.

Still, I needed whatever information he had, and I wasn't likely to get it by slamming my office door in his face. No matter how tempting the thought.

"I am staying with a friend. And I will be gone as long as necessary. Now, I believe there is work to be done..." I raised a brow in the direction of his desk, and he finally had no other option but to scamper off.

I needed to discuss this with Kit.

I dug Xander's documents out of my satchel, the one that never left my side when I was in the office now. I was nearly finished with some of the contracts Xander had requested when Kit finally returned, looking rumpled and harassed.

"Finally made it in?"

"You're one to talk."

"I was helping my sister and her arse of a husband with her ball, you were... Well, I have no wish to know what you were doing," he said, grabbing the last tart and wandering into my office. He tugged the door shut behind him.

"Are you ever going to forgive the man?" I asked.

"He made Kate sad. Have you met Kate? That ought to be impossible. She may have forgiven him, but I don't have to."

He took the seat across from me and grabbed a scrap of parchment, then scribbled a note.

Bates is listening at the door.

"How is dearest Kate? Prepared for her ball tonight?" I asked, writing my true reply while overenunciating my question.

He knows who is involved in all of this. Should we interrogate? Or try to get him to slip?

"I hadn't thought you were listening when she invited you to the ball," he replied.

There have been no further attempts. We can risk a more subtle approach.

"I wasn't."

Agreed, but we should keep him from more sensitive accounts. He may be after more than the Hasket documents.

"So the lovely Lady Rycliffe has convinced you to attend? What did she offer, I wonder?" He nodded his assent.

"Nothing at all, merely the gift of her company."

"Ah, threatened to dance with other men, did she?"

"You can leave my office now." I held the page over a candle until it caught, then I held the flaming parchment over the rubbish can and watched it burn thoroughly, completely, before pouring the day-old cup of tea on my desk into the bin.

"I could, but where would be the fun in that?"

"Christopher…" I grumbled in mock irritation.

"You should head out early. Kate will have your head if you make Lady Rycliffe late. Kate adores her."

"That is hardly a novelty. Everyone adores her."

"Too right," he said before wandering out the door and into his office.

Reviewing Xander's documents took most of the morning and proved a sufficient distraction. Unfortunately, it left the afternoon without occupation.

The ball tonight was a looming shadow over the day. Nerves and Celine's continued absence from my arms left me tetchy and irritable, to the detriment of all.

It had been so easy this morning to agree to attend this certainly disastrous ball when Celine was all mussed from my hands and mouth. How could I say no when her fingers were tangled in my hair and her lips pressed against mine?

Now, though, I actually had to attend this mess. An event exclusively for the wealthy and titled, of which I was neither and she was both.

Even though her mother hadn't warned her off, the *ton* would certainly set Celine to rights. They would remind her that I was beneath her in appearance, status, rank, and wealth. Below her in even the more subjective measures of desirability —affability and gentility. Tonight would throw into sharp relief just how ill-suited we were.

She would finally see, finally understand, what I had known the entire time. I learned many years ago that affection wasn't enough to scale society's barriers. Love wasn't enough —my love, specifically. And, as easy as it was in her presence, my love alone could not forge a relationship—especially not in the face of such obstacles.

Still, I could not regret last night. I would not trade a single second of it for the entire world. Not even if it was the only night we would ever have.

I would treasure it enough for the both of us.

A million years later and far too soon, Kit popped his head back into my office with a wordless nod toward the door. My forlorn expression, he was content to ignore, but my heaving sigh was not enough.

"It'll be all right, Will. You've got an earl in your corner, remember? Just give me the signal and I'll commit some horrible faux pas that will have them talking for the next decade."

"What, precisely, is the signal?"

"Your complete and utter humiliation. Do not worry, I will know it when I see it."

"Lovely."

"Just hide in the library. That's what Wayland and Lady Juliet do. Probably best knock first though."

"Do I wish to know why?"

"Absolutely not."

"Very well."

The walk back to Cadieux House was too quick, even with a detour for flowers—not irises. I bypassed Bouvier as quickly as possible, desperate to avoid conversations about my whereabouts last evening, I took the stairs two at a time.

"Will?" Celine called from her dressing room. I turned that way instead of toward the blue room I had been using.

Peering inside, I found Celine's maid fussing with her curls at the dressing table.

"'Lo, love," I murmured, leaning against the door. I could only see her reflection in the mirror. Even that sight felt very much like the punch I had taken a few days ago. She was so damn beautiful with the late-afternoon sun streaming through the window.

Her eyes darted to the clock on the mantel before widening slightly. She said six—I was certain of it. I had left at quarter to four, it couldn't be anywhere near six. Still, my stomach lurched with worry as I checked the clock myself—half past four.

"You're early." The statement was simple, but her voice was thick with unknown emotion.

"Too early? I can duck into the study for a bit."

"No, no. Not too early." A sentiment was behind the words that was clearly beyond me and it had me off-kilter already.

Clenching my hands for want of something to do, I nearly squished the purple calla lily stems in my grasp. Trying to affect more confidence than I felt, I stepped into the room and set them on the table beside her.

"You're early *and* you brought me flowers?" she asked, turning toward me in her chair.

"Yes?"

"Jane, would you be a dear and fetch a vase?" Though the question was directed toward the woman behind her wearing a slightly peeved expression, Celine's eyes never left mine.

It was very, very slowly dawning on me that I may not have made a misstep after all. I may have done something very right.

Behind her, the maid tossed a handful of hairpins on the table in irritation before setting off in search of the vase. Though improper, I could hardly blame her for her annoyance. It was entirely probable that Celine's hair would be in quite a state of disarray when I was finished greeting her.

"You came home early."

"I did."

"And you brought me flowers."

"Yes..."

"To attend a ball you would rather chew your own foot off than accompany me to."

"I wouldn't put it quite that way..."

Her hand tangled in my cravat, and she pulled me down to my knees before her. She cupped my cheek with her free hand and traced the bone with her thumb.

"Thank you," she whispered just before capturing my lips in a kiss.

I had absolutely done something right—though what it was, I had no idea. I wasn't going to quibble over details while her tongue was tracing my lower lip, seeking entrance.

I was not unaware of our positions, of my proximity to the heat of her that I was desperate to taste for a... third? Or would it be the fourth time? Last night was a blur of silken flesh, lust-filled moans, and unbearable ecstasy.

If my hands wandered to her hair of their own volition, who could blame me?

Apparently Jane, if the irritated groan from the doorway was any indication. I wrenched my lips from Celine's while her lady's maid stomped over to the table and thumped the filled vase onto it.

"You do her hair then!" The woman whirled around and stalked away, slamming the door.

Celine caught her lower lip between her teeth, desperately trying to hide a smile. My laughter was bubbling beneath the surface, only to escape in an inelegant snort. Celine's quickly followed, although it was more delicate.

Slowly we managed to settle. "Well, I suppose I have a coiffure to arrange." Another laugh burst from her, and I had to duck to hide a pleased smile.

I rose and stepped behind her to examine the damage I had wrought. Honestly, Jane was overreacting. I had left Celine in much worse states than this.

Still, best to start with a good foundation. I slipped out the pins Jane had already placed, and set them beside the others scattered across the table.

"You're not really going to?" Celine asked, her lips pursed in a perfect *O* of surprise.

"Well, I can hardly do more damage than I already have. If it's rubbish we can take them out and beg Jane's forgiveness."

She raised a brow at me in the mirror, her lips pressed into an indulgent smile.

Free from pins, I untangled her curls one by one with my fingers. Celine collected the disorderly pins, topped with glinting baubles, while I worked and dropped them into a little pile.

Task completed, she turned to the flowers. One by one she placed them in the vase, arranging them thoughtfully. It seemed that they were an acceptable choice.

I wasn't entirely unfamiliar with my task. I was, however, extremely out of practice. But Adriane's hair had been much straighter and more resistant to taming. That experience worked in my favor. Celine's waves seemed willing to cooperate when I twisted a large mass of them into a delicate knot at the back of her head. I pinned it in place, making every effort not to stab her scalp. Adriane had wailed when that had happened.

In short order, I had the majority of her strands securely pinned back with a few framing her face. Even I could see the style was not quite right, but I thought it was quite lovely on her. Of course, I was hardly unbiased.

Celine observed my progress quietly in the mirror while I worked, handing me pin after pin before I needed to ask.

"Well, I could have done worse, but I don't believe I shall give up my office in favor of becoming a lady's maid. Let me apologize to Jane." Her hand caught my own as I turned to leave.

"Don't. I like it. We both should apologize, of course. But I will keep it, I think."

"Love, it's not the style."

"But it suits me much better than the style." She slipped one of the lilies out of the vase and sliced the stem off with the edge of a nearby letter opener. After grabbing a spare ribbon, she deftly wrapped the stem, all without a word. Finally, she handed it to me. "Will you add this? It matches my gown."

The desire was there to protest, to argue, to insist. The need to spare her this one humiliation was nearly overwhelming. But I had seen resolve in her countenance before, and I knew what it meant. I would be better off arguing with a tree stump for all the good it would do to try to convince her. I tucked the flower between curls and pinned it in place without comment.

No longer distracted by my task, I was able to appreciate the sight of her in her gossamer chemise and nothing else. Her breasts pulled enticingly at the fabric and I was very much regretting fixing her hair when I could have had it curtaining us atop her bed coverings.

"Just noticed, did you?"

"I was busy. I don't suppose we have time to…"

"No, since someone ran off my maid, I need assistance with my stays and gown."

With a regretful sigh, I turned toward the screen where a purple gown and stays hung. I was prepared to follow instructions, no matter how much I regretted the need for her to wear any clothing at all.

 Thirty-One

CELINE

He was so... sweet—underneath the sharp exterior anyway. And handy with hairpins as it turned out. Tightening the laces of my stays proved to be somewhat more challenging. I could tell the lacings pulled somewhat unevenly, but it was not enough to be noticeable to anyone but me.

William had already proven a deft hand with the dress hooks, but now that I knew how those hands felt on my bare flesh, it was a different kind of torture to add layers between us.

Now I was anxiously applying rouge while he dressed in the other room. It would not do for him to change here—we would never make it to the ball. I was studiously forcing myself not to consider all the ways the gift I had left for him could go awry.

My minimal application of cosmetics usually took no more than a minute. It was difficult to draw it out for the nearly ten before he returned. His long, lithe lines filled my mirror as he pressed against the door frame with an unreadable expression.

"It appears that someone has replaced my waistcoat. You wouldn't know anything about that, would you?" I could not read his tenor. There was, perhaps, irritation. His reflection gave nothing away. He looked terribly handsome in the new waistcoat. I particularly appreciated the wide expanse of chest available for my perusal with his cravat loose around his neck.

"Of course not."

"So the fact that it is the exact fabric of your gown is a coincidence?"

My gown was a dove-gray silk with brushed gold brocade. More subdued than my usual deeper tones or bolder purples. It emphasized the amethyst jewels around my neck and ears and favored the lily in my coiffure.

"Entirely. Are you certain you didn't bring it with you?" My first instinct had been a bright blue silk to bring out his eyes. But I thought this might better please him. If the kiss he dropped to my shoulder was any indication, I was correct.

"Must have."

"You need not wear it if it's not to your taste. I would not be offended."

"'Course I like it. It's the finest thing I've ever worn." He swallowed then, his throat bobbing. "Only this though, yes? I like my clothes just fine."

I had been right. He hadn't mentioned the difference in our stations since dining with Mama. But it was still present, growing and spreading like a cancer. A conversation needed to be had, reassurances made. But this was not the moment.

"I love your clothing too. Though I do prefer them on the floor. I just wanted to... make you mine."

"I'm yours, you don't need to worry about that."

"Will, it is sheer luck that another woman hadn't found you and claimed you long before I did. It's also luck that you seemingly find my particular... quirks amusing. I don't intend to leave anything else to chance. If you prefer I label you as my own in some other way..." I had to bite back a giggle at his utterly baffled expression, it would not do to tease him so.

"I... have no idea what you mean."

"Come here." I stood and met him halfway. Surveying my options, I saw but one choice. I brushed aside the neck of his shirt and freed the skin over his heart from its cloth prison. There I pressed a kiss, leaving a rouge print behind. After righting the shirt once more, there was no outward trace of my claim.

"Right..." he said, his voice thick and eyes crinkled once again. I loved that look. With a finger, I traced his cheek before landing on the outside of his eye. The nearly imperceptible crinkle deepened in favor of the obvious lines that came with a smile.

Now that the rouge once on my lips was marking his heart, I had no reason to refrain from kissing him. Grabbing the loose ends of his cravat in my fists, I pulled him to me, chasing away his nerves and my own.

Eventually, we were forced to break apart. I wiped the residual color from his mouth with a thumb before shooing him back to his room to finish dressing.

In spite of my efforts to soothe him, I was not ignorant to what we may experience tonight. Oh, our friends would be welcoming and lovely. Mother and Marie too. But they did not compose the whole *ton*. Not by half.

I was a questionable marital prospect, with a two-year marriage and no children to show for it, and I was considered advanced in age by men twice mine, but I was not without prospects. Fewer than the early days of my reentry into society, but I was still wealthy enough and—while not strictly fashionable—a noted beauty. Those men would not take kindly to being thrown over—if only in their minds—for a solicitor with no title, no connections, and no fortune.

Ladies, too, who preferred the current order of things, would surely be unpleasant. Agatha Grayson would certainly be in attendance at her son's ball. The woman who had barely forgiven Kate, her son's wife, for daring to wed the man without a title to her name. Lady Charlotte James was possibly brazen enough to attend in spite of the animosity she shared with Kate. Others would also be spiteful.

But if there was one thing I knew, it was the *ton*. Hiding would spark more gossip and cruelty than a brief shameless entrance followed by perfectly respectable behavior ever could. I had once been the belle of every ball I attended. I could resurrect those dazzling skills for one last performance. For William's sake.

He knocked on the open door frame, now fully done up.

"You look very handsome tonight. Are you ready? I believe I heard the carriage."

"I am. You're stunning, love. You always are. Know I've been a bit of an arse tonight, but I'm proud to be on your arm."

"Thank you for doing this. Even though you would rather eat a shoe."

"Celine, there is nowhere I'd rather be than where you are. Would I rather be elsewhere with you? Yes. That bed, specifically. But if you're attending, I want to go with you. Eat a shoe —honestly. It's a privilege being with you. Not a hardship."

His mutterings about difficult, ridiculous women, or a woman specifically, followed us all the way down the stairs and into the carriage. I made no effort to interrupt. It seemed to distract him from his nerves.

And I understood his sentiment. It was certainly no hardship to watch him, listen to him speak, feel his hand along my lower back, and perhaps—probably—almost certainly—even love him.

<h1 style="text-align:center;"></h1>

GRAYSON HOUSE, LONDON - JUNE 17, 1816

WILLIAM

THE CARRIAGE SHUDDERED to a halt in St. James's Square, an unwelcome reminder that Celine was right. I would, in point of fact, rather eat a shoe than attend a social gathering with the *ton*. Much as I had complained about the mask at the last ball, I longed for it now, for the anonymity it provided.

Celine was stunning—not that such a thing was an unusual occurrence. But she was certain to attract the eye of every person in attendance, all of whom would then turn to me with a disapproving glare.

When the footman opened the carriage door, I rose, but Celine caught the hand that had been in hers since we set off and tugged me back.

"Any time you wish to leave, just let me know."

"I... Thank you."

"I mean it. Promise you will tell me?" She straightened one of my out of place curls, brushing her thumb along my cheek. Tender.

"I promise."

"All right. What do you say we start a scandal?"

"May as well. I have no other pressing engagements this evening." I stepped out before handing her out myself.

I had never been inside Grayson House before, but the furnishings were new and quite fashionable. The young viscountess's doing most likely. We followed along the corridor as directed, Celine's hand tucked into the crook of my arm. She smelled of warmth and spice.

"The library is down that hall if you wish to escape. Knock first though."

"Kit warned me to knock as well… What, precisely, would I walk in on if I forget?"

"Michael and Lady Juliet met in that library."

"I don't understand."

"Will, if you managed to get me on the terrace at Wayland's once again, what would you do with me?"

Nothing appropriate for a public— "Ah…"

The receiving line had been short, and we only received a glance or two from the couple in front of us. It was too much to hope that would be the lot of it.

We reached Lord and Lady Grayson at the entry to the ballroom. Even if I had never met her, I would certainly know Lady Grayson by the similarities to her brother. Small stature, pale skin, full lips, dark hair, and wide eyes, though hers were blue whereas his were dark. Her husband, in contrast, was one of the broadest men I knew, and while not the tallest, he was near as much.

Celine greeted her friend with enthusiasm, proclaiming delight at all the decorative things. The ones neither Celine nor I had yet had the opportunity to examine.

Lord Grayson and I knew each other only professionally. Beyond a polite nod, he was content to stare adoringly at his wife. I had only taken over the Grayson books in the last year, and my interaction with the lord had been minimal.

Finally, the ladies finished their greeting, after a pointed cough from another couple waiting behind us.

Celine pressed close to my side as we stepped inside the ballroom. "Well, Lady Charlotte James is not here tonight. That is one unpleasant interaction avoided."

"Lady James?"

"Baron James's widow. She's a shrew under the best of situations. Although her machinations brought Kate and Lord Grayson together, so Kate continues to tolerate her."

"Right." Celine's arm was tucked in mine, and she led a slow saunter around the ballroom, occasionally nodding or waving at someone but never leaving my side.

"The dowager viscountess, Agatha Grayson, is here. We will wish to avoid her."

"Which one is she?"

"You'll know her when you smell her. Xander will be here with Davina and their mother, but they usually arrive later. Over there are Mr. Ellsworth and... Viscount Lucas? Baron Lucas? I can never recall. Lucas is a booby, but Ellsworth is usually acceptable company. He has recently come into an inheritance and is looking to invest in textiles. He could be a prospective client. I could introduce you, if you like?"

"Perhaps later." How did she remember all of these people?

Whispers followed in our wake, but Celine either did not notice or did not care.

"Oh, the Duke of Sutton. He was on our list. Winston is his Christian name. I forgot he was a cousin of Kate's." She nodded subtly toward an indistinct blond dandy who looked exactly like every other dandy here. Beside him was an equally indistinct, mousy blonde woman, his wife presumably. I recognized the name.

"I don't believe he made an appearance in either of Gabriel's ledgers. He's likely not our culprit."

"True. He's too dull for anything as exciting as murder. Oh, there are Lady Juliet and Mrs. Ainsley, we should say hello." Celine dragged me toward the flaming hair that could only belong to Mrs. Ainsley.

She greeted the women warmly. Neither so much as blinked at the sight of me, which was something of a surprise. As a regular patron of Hudson's Bakery, I was relieved at Mrs. Ainsley's easy acceptance of Celine's form pressed along my own.

"Ladies, you know Mr. Hart, I believe?"

"Yes, of course. He and Kit are trying to keep the bakery in business all on their own," Mrs. Ainsley said.

"Evidence of his excellent taste. Mr. Hart and I have met once or twice," Lady Juliet added. Once or twice was her polite way of saying that I helped with paperwork related to her father's arrest and the purchase of his debts. The lady was unfailingly proper.

"Where are the gentlemen?" Celine asked.

"Hiding in the study drinking Hugh's scotch, of course. I'm sure you would be a more than welcome addition, Mr. Hart," explained Lady Juliet.

The suggestion to join them was a temptation—the indistinct whispers had gotten louder. But I was reluctant to abandon Celine. And Kit had yet to arrive.

However, it might afford me the opportunity to gather some information from Wayland—confirm he was not a suspect in Gabriel's murder.

"Go, enjoy yourself. As soon as Lord Leighton arrives, I'll send him that way," Celine prodded. Anticipating all my worries.

"It's entirely possible he is already hidden away in there," Lady Juliet added.

"I thought you had me down for at least three dances," I protested.

"I decided to spare you all but the supper set," Celine responded, prim with a teasing smile.

"There's a hidden door, just behind this curtain. Straight down that hall and the study is the last on the left," Mrs. Ainsley said. At my baffled look, she added, "Maid, remember?"

She pulled the edge of the curtain back, revealing the hidden door. I slipped through and followed her instructions to the end of the hall where firelight poured out of an open door.

It was strangely comforting, the reminder that my marchioness was conversing easily in a ballroom with a former maid. And served as yet more evidence that she was truly sincere in her insistence that my profession did not bother her.

After knocking on the open door frame, I was greeted by the expected parties. Wayland, Ainsley, and Kit. The youngest Grayson, too, was settled on the desk, his feet swinging back and forth.

"Will, come on in!" Kit ordered jovially. He was ruddy-cheeked and, for the first time in recent memory, neither sarcastic nor sullen. Drunk then.

He clambered up from his chair, pressing his half-empty glass of scotch in my hand before wandering over to the shelf filled with different bottles and glasses. He selected something clear and lifted the stopper for a sniff before pouring—sloshing—it into a glass.

Wayland was behind the desk, seated properly and seemingly less drunk than the rest by far. And he was glaring at his brother. Mr. Grayson cradled his drink in both hands before taking a sip, his feet still swishing.

Wayland rolled his eyes before turning to me. "Hart! Cee drag you here?"

"How did you..."

"Oh, she mentioned it when she called. I did dig through a few of my ledgers, and I've got a couple of possibilities."

I didn't know which was worse, the instinctive panicked nausea at the thought of her calling on a potential murderer alone, or the jealousy prickling along my skin at the thought of her calling on a former lover.

"She called?" My lips felt numb, but it had been my voice, hollow and cracking. She could have been killed. That maddening woman with no sense of self-preservation—chasing after potential murderers all the livelong day. First me, now Wayland.

"She didn't say? I've made a right muck of this haven't I?" Wayland had the decency to look chagrined.

"When did she call?"

"Yesterday," he said, sheepish.

Yesterday. She visited Michael and then came home and dragged me to her bed. Was it just because he was unavailable? I wasn't thrilled with the idea of being a substitute for Gabriel. But I could live with it—had done it before. But a surrogate for a dead man was very different from serving as stand-in for someone down the street.

"Right." It was the only word I could muster, and I downed Kit's half-finished scotch in one swallow. It burned and I only just held back an instinctive cough, unwilling to humiliate myself further in this man's presence.

"I'm sure it just slipped her mind. We talked about her... project. And you."

"Of course." Silently, Mr. Grayson handed me his drink too, three quarters gone. I tossed that one back as well.

"Truly, she did me a favor. I was just returning it."

"All right, wonderful."

Ainsley leaned over and feigned whispering to Wayland. "This, what you're doing, is the exact opposite of what Celine did for you when you met Jules."

"Thank you, as always, Augie. I was unaware."

"No, because you must remember, she ended your arrangement *and* encouraged you to pursue Juliet. But you're ruining whatever those two have started."

"Really? I couldn't tell."

"That's why you pay me. Full of insights." Ainsley stood and turned to me. "Do you want another drink, Will?" The temptation was strong, but the first two were doing nothing to settle my stomach. I shook my head and took the abandoned seat he offered.

"Where are you going?" Wayland called as the man stepped into the hall.

Ainsley turned, curving around the door to answer. "Find my wife. Dance with her. Tell her that her hair burns like the last vestiges of the sunlight in autumn. Profess my undying love. Literally anything to convince her I had nothing to do with whatever is happening here."

"So, making it up as you go?"

"Of course. I'll tell Jules and Lady Rycliffe that it's all your fault."

"Augie, no!" Wayland whined.

"Augie, yes. Good luck."

Wayland turned back to me after one last longing look at Ainsley. Whatever he saw on my face had him evicting Kit and the youngest Grayson from the room with a chorus of grumbles.

"Will, I'm sorry. It was truly not what you're imagining. But Cee did put a bee in my bonnet, so to speak. I dug through Juliet's father's ledgers. It's possible it was him, Westfield was certainly losing enough in every available venue. And I wouldn't say he was above murder. But I am confident that he's not managing anything now. He's in the highlands with a distant cousin and no financial resources. I suppose there may be some with goodwill toward him in town, but I doubt it."

I sighed, wishing I had accepted a third drink. "It's probably not. Rycliffe called him Jaundiced Sagging Gooseberries, JSG as an abbreviation, because Gabriel was charming to a fault. There were multiple notes not to wager more than £10 with him."

"That is a surprisingly apt description of my father-in-law. Still, the bet was likely through someone else. The horse's owner may not be the killer, but someone who placed a wager based on the stud," Wayland added.

"I assumed as much, but if we track down the horse, we can search the stud book and follow the trail from there."

"It's a good notion. I went through my documentation on that race. It's limited because the club wasn't open yet. Rycliffe placed an unusually large wager on Peppercorn Junction and a smaller wager on Storm's Kiss. The odds favored Flashdance, but Peppercorn won. Rycliffe was smart. He certainly spread out his wagers. Unlike Westfield. That's actually how I first caught on to the match he was making to fix."

I ignored the insight into the man's relation with his father-in-law. "Did anyone lose substantially on that race?"

Wayland dug through coat pockets, patting them before finding a piece of parchment. "A few, but I was certainly not the only option at that time. Lord Embery Wyatt lost £250, which was a substantial but not insurmountable sum for him. Wesley Parker lost £1,500 which was likely more than I should have allowed him to wager. Sir Wilhelm Jacobs lost £300, but he bet on Storm's Kiss."

"That the lot of them?"

He handed me the parchment. The intelligence was neatly organized in a tidy script.

"There were more, but those are the only *W*'s. I would start with the horses and see where they lead, personally."

"Thank you."

"I'm happy to help in whatever way I can. Or if you need

to find Westfield—I'll have to check with Jules, of course— but I can get you the direction."

"I'm nearly certain it has nothing to do with him."

"All the same."

I nodded, starting for the door before thinking better of it. "How do you do it?" I asked without turning toward him.

"Do what?"

At last, I turned. "Watch these people behave like this?"

"Ah, the excesses of the *ton*. I manage with the love of an incredible woman. Also scotch." He lifted the referenced glass and emptied the dregs. "And I do enjoy relieving them of a great deal of their money."

"Right. So I merely have to be blind drunk to tolerate them."

"Tell me she's not worth it." He took my silence as confirmation. "I could abide far worse if it meant I retained the privilege of going home with Jules at the end of the evening. If you cannot say the same about Celine, then you do not deserve her, and I was wrong to encourage her your way."

"You—"

"Yes, I did. Now, you are more than welcome to stay here if you wish. I have a rendezvous next door." He pressed himself out of the chair before wandering over to the second door I hadn't noticed. It opened into what seemed to be a library. That was all I could glimpse before he shut and locked the door.

Thirty-Three

CELINE

"CELINE!" Mrs. Ainsley dragged me closer to her by the elbow.

"Yes?"

"I didn't know Mr. Hart could look like *that*."

"Like what?"

"I believe she's referring to the expression of adoration and lust on his face. It brightens the eyes," Juliet added. "And they're already distractingly lovely."

"He is quite handsome, isn't he?"

"Handsome and besotted," Mrs. Ainsley said. "I didn't know you were looking for a new companion."

"I wasn't. Nothing about Will was planned."

"You mustn't let Kate take credit for it," Lady Juliet said. "She claims credit for every relationship that forms in her vicinity and it's tiresome."

"Will is a bit apprehensive about our attendance tonight. I know the dowager Lady Grayson will be here tonight. Is there anyone else to avoid?"

"The Duchess and Dowager of Sutton can be difficult," Mrs. Ainsley said.

"And Mrs. Courtenay will be snide if her husband remembered he has a wife long enough to stuff her into the carriage tonight," Lady Juliet added in what might have been the most unforgiving speech I'd ever heard from her. I raised my brow in feigned disapproval, but it lasted only as long as my next breath before the laughter broke free. "Kate has pared down the invitations primarily to the most tolerable."

Nodding in agreement, Mrs. Ainsley's gaze flicked to the entrance, then returned to us before darting back to the door behind me. Her eyes widened and her jaw dropped slightly. "Oh, good Lord." The way her eyes softened in my direction made me absolutely certain I was in for a headache this evening.

In turning, I was proved entirely correct. My mother-in-law, wearing a gown that was either twenty years out of date or twenty years too early with a circumference that was surely visible from the heavens, was attempting to navigate the stairs without injury. The shoulders of the gown were truly unique. Rather than puffed, as was common, they rose like two sheer cliffs, knifelike in black taffeta. Apparently she had decided to continue with the wigs as well. This one was only slightly more sedate than the one she wore to the masquerade. It still rose nearly six inches off her head in an alarmingly dark shade.

Behind her, Xander escorted Davina in. As always, she was dressed far more appropriately. After all, it was difficult to get away with mischief when someone stood out the way her mother did. Her simple white gown trimmed with green ribbon belied her vexing ways.

Xander, too, looked very fine as always, his head held high despite his mother's entrance. That was one of the things I appreciated most about him. His refusal to be anything other than supportive of his mother's ways, even when the rest of the *ton* found them odd or off-putting.

I had always suspected that one of the reasons Gabriel always returned home late for evening engagements was the desire to arrive after the whispers about his mother had died down.

With a fortifying breath, I took leave of Mrs. Ainsley and Lady Juliet. Approaching Clementia and her children, I greeted her with warmth and a kiss to the cheek as always. Her jewels were more sedate than the rest of the ensemble, and I complimented those. I tried to give her sincere compliments on her gowns whenever possible, but this one was a touch too far.

My greeting was often enough to break the spell cast by Her Grace's gowns, and tonight was no different. Lady Grayson, the dowager viscountess, all but raced to her side. That odious woman would keep Clementia occupied for some time with her sycophantic adulations.

Davina was scooped up by some young buck I did not recognize before I could greet her. I would need to keep a close watch on them to ensure they did not run off to Gretna Green by morning.

At last, I was left with Xander who took my hand in his for the first dance without a word. It was not an unusual practice for us, even from his first ball, and I always enjoyed myself.

He was light on his feet and confident in his direction.

"Surprised not to see Will here," he said at a turn.

"I sent him to the study before Lady Grayson—the dowager—noticed him."

"So, that courtship is going well?"

"I don't know that we're courting. We're merely... enjoying each other's company."

Xander merely hummed pointedly in response.

"What was that for?"

"Oh, I just wonder if he knows that."

"He does." *Doesn't he?*

"Of course, my mistake." His tone told me plainly that he was certain he was not mistaken. "I did have something I wished to discuss with you—to ask really."

We were briefly interrupted by a twist in the dance.

"I'm intrigued."

"A ballroom may not be the best choice for this, but I had thought to sell Rycliffe Place."

If I'd had a lifetime, I never would have anticipated his words. My stomach lurched uncomfortably at the thought for reasons that weren't readily apparent. I was so shocked I missed a step in the dance and had to perform a little skip to right myself.

"I— Why? Are you purchasing something else?"

"No, I thought to move."

"To Hasket House?"

"No... No. I think I have, perhaps, overstayed my welcome in London. Gabriel gifted me a small estate in Scotland. But since it was your home too, I know it holds many memories for you." My thoughts swirled in too many directions. In the years after Gabriel's death, Xander had become one of my dearest friends. There was a sudden, sharp stab of hatred for the cruelty of the world toward him. "Celine?"

"I beg your pardon, I'm feeling unwell. If you don't mind, I will step off for a moment."

"Cee..."

"I need a moment, Xand. It's not you, I promise. It's them," I whispered, catching the beady gaze of Mr. Parker across the room. Beside him, still fawning at Xander's mother, was Lady Grayson, now joined by the Duchess of Sutton and her son. They debased themselves before Her Grace, and not one of them would hesitate for a single second to see her son hanged.

"May I escort you?"

"Best if you don't. Find Davina? Surely she's eloped by now, it's been nearly seven minutes."

"I wish you were jesting."

"I never jest about Dav." I squeezed his arm reassuringly before escaping in the direction of the ladies' retiring room with artful composure.

Freed from the crush of the ballroom, I fought to maintain the air of indifference, making my way sedately down the hall. I slipped into the drawing room reserved for such a purpose and pressed the door shut firmly behind me. Scanning the room, I found it to be blissfully empty.

No sooner had I sighed in relief, than the door opened and another person entered. My jaw clenched in instinctive irritation. I made no move to turn around, unequal to the requisite platitudes.

As such, when she spoke, my spine stiffened with native disquiet.

"Celine, I've been waiting to meet you for a long time."

There was no earthly reason I should know that voice. I'd heard it but once, across a ballroom at that. But I knew it.

I spun slowly, very much wishing I had brought my knife instead of relying on the intrinsic safety of a ballroom.

Victoria.

She was still lovely. The years had brought no particular signs of aging. Her hair still shone a flaxen gold. Her complexion was still fashionably paler than my own. Her form and height, too, remained very much reminiscent of mine. It should have been upsetting, seeing her. I was distantly aware of that fact. But instead of the jolt of hurt and jealousy that had accompanied her last appearance, there was... nothing.

Victoria. Gabriel's mistress. His mistress of nearly twice the length of our marriage was here before me, and I felt nothing but dim irritation at the interruption. And more than a little curiosity.

"Victoria. You needn't have waited. I've been here the entire time."

"I see you've abandoned the feigned accent." Her voice was high with a contradictory raspy quality. Childlike in tone with an exhaustion that only came from use and age. She took a step closer, quartering the distance between us.

"You too."

"Just for you." Another graceful step.

"Are you here to kill me?" There was no tremor in my voice. I was proud of that.

I gave no quarter. Offering her nothing to indicate that, despite the eerie calm that overwhelmed me, I knew on an intellectual level I was in grave danger. And I was. She halved the remaining distance between us in a single step. My feet were frozen to the carpet with both stubborn determination and a vague notion of holding my ground.

"So you know what's going on."

"Something of it. Are you?"

She took the final step, now close enough for her breath to brush my face. She cupped my cheek in a cool, patronizing hand.

"That's precious. If I wanted you dead, I would have killed you in 1807." She flashed a sinister, fangy smile. "What would be the point now?"

"You tell me."

"Ah, you haven't figured it out, then. I suppose intelligence wasn't what he wanted you for." I held her gaze, unwilling to be the one to break the tentative hold. My heart beat as harsh as a drum in my ears and still I didn't *feel* the terror I knew was there. Somewhere.

"So he wanted me for my beauty? My wit? My charm?" It wasn't strictly the wisest move, insulting her. Her hand slipped off my cheek, brushing a fictional piece of lint away from my shoulder.

"Your breeding and your birthing hips. Like a cow." I had never been accused of having a form suited to childbearing. In that respect, her insult rang hollow. But it did prick at the certainty, the truth I had accepted as fact, that I would never have need of birthing hips because children were not in my future.

"If I'm a cow, what does that make you?" Not my best, but given the situation, it would need to serve.

She stepped back, half a pace, perhaps less. "I will never understand what he saw in you. If he were pursuing you now, I could at least intellectualize the appeal. But a virginal little debutant, self-important and fickle... There's no accounting for taste, I suppose."

Her fingers caught a loose curl from my coiffure, she slipped a finger inside, smoothing the ringlet with her thumb.

That, more than anything, made me feel slightly sick. That she was running her fingers through curls William had placed with care mere hours before. And still I did not look away.

"And your... charms, to the extent they exist, were less than those of a virginal little debutant. What do you suppose that says about you?"

"You have more spine than I credited you with. Believe it or not, I didn't come here to trade barbs. Or blades." She released her finger from my hair and perused me, toes to nose.

"Why did you come?"

"Settling a debt."

"A debt?"

"Surely you know your husband was a frequent purveyor of my establishment. He paid in advance, of course. I owed him a tup or two before he passed."

She was good. She was very, very good. If I hadn't known with a surety that was etched on my bones that Gabriel hadn't touched her after our marriage... It would have been a devastating blow.

"And you're here too, what? Give me a farthing? After all, that's certainly what a roll with you is worth."

Her smile was cruel. "Do you know, I think in a different world we would have been friends."

"I'm glad to live in this one then."

"I cannot disagree. He's going to kill you. And your studious new friend. And anyone else you've dragged into this —the grumpy solicitor, the molly, Wayland, everyone. He'll leave a trail of bodies in his wake."

"Who?"

"I can't tell you that. No one likes a chatty whore. It would jeopardize my position and the safety of my girls."

"So you came here to, what? Insult me? Tell me things I already knew?"

"The attack the other night, those men. It wasn't random." That was new. I fought to keep the surprise from my eyes.

"Why now?"

"You started investigating, acting strangely, asking questions. Word travels quickly in this town."

"Do you have anything useful to tell me?"

"Your little solicitor, the break-in at his office. If you're going to continue *investigating*, if you can call it that, pull that thread. Not too hard of course, it will snap."

"Anything else?"

"Enjoy the rest of your evening. Do try not to look too distraught. He'll consider moving up his plans. And we both know how that ends."

An image of Will, bleeding and broken on the dining table at Rycliffe Place flashed through my mind and I had to bite back the bile. It was enough of an occupation, to resist the retching sensation growing in my gut, that I allowed her the last word.

Victoria slipped seamlessly through the door and into the hall, leaving me more distraught than I had been when I entered.

Thirty-Four

GRAYSON HOUSE, LONDON - JUNE 17, 1816

WILLIAM

CELINE WAS NOWHERE to be found when I returned to the ballroom. Not that I knew what, precisely, to say to her when I did find her.

The last lingering burn of jealousy warred with worry and fury. This woman was determined to give me a fit of apoplexy, rushing around confronting absolutely everyone she suspected of murdering her husband—alone and unarmed. *A bleeding death wish.*

Unlike at Wayland's, there was no second level of this room to hide away in. Instead, I made my way to the drinks table. It seemed safest over there with the spinsters, chaperones, and wallflowers. There was still another set before the supper set, but I hadn't the slightest interest in dancing with anyone but the infuriating woman my heart had claimed.

Distractedly, I rubbed my chest where she had branded me with rouge and lips. Surprisingly, the motion did soothe my worry—just a little. Not as much as if it had been her delicate hand instead of my own, but enough.

Rumor must have circulated through the room because no match-making mamas or debutants found their way to my side. That, at least, was a relief.

I was left to sip my lemonade in silence and prop up the wall alone. Or as alone as one can be in a ballroom.

It took no more than a minute before I was joined by the oversized form of Lord Grayson. He was tall, dark, and broad in every way that ladies swooned over. Physically, he reminded me very much of Gabriel. How he and his diminutive wife managed was the subject of occasional musing. Where he was imposing physically, in personality he was more restrained. His wife, though tiny in form, was bold and vivacious in manner. It was an intriguing pairing to be sure. One that vexed her brother to no end.

"Hart," he said. We had spoken on a few occasions, but certainly not with any regularity or particular friendship.

"Grayson."

"You lose your lady?"

"Something like that. I was in the study with your brothers drinking your scotch. I assume she's off with the ladies now."

"Not the good scotch I hope."

"No idea."

"Remind me to rap Tom against the head later. Do you have brothers?"

"Just me, I'm afraid."

"Consider yourself lucky."

I had no response to that. I didn't consider myself lucky or unlucky. It was difficult to miss what you did not have.

He continued. "So, I'm trying, very unsuccessfully I might add, to discuss Lady Rycliffe."

And there it was... The beginning of the disaster I knew was coming. "What about her?"

"My wife wants to know your intentions."

"I beg your pardon?"

"Kate. She is very fond of Lady Rycliffe."

"And she wishes me to leave her alone?"

"Certainly not. As long as your intentions toward her are honorable."

"Has your wife met Celine?"

"Yes?"

"Then your wife would know precisely who is managing this situation. And your Lady Grayson would also know that it is entirely impossible to meet Celine and not love her."

"So... I should tell her your intentions are honorable." It was inappropriate to roll one's eyes at a viscount. Wasn't it?

Glancing the other direction, I caught sight of Kit across the room, staring forlornly at Lady Davina dancing with some dandy I didn't recognize.

"Yes," I snapped. "Shouldn't Lady Grayson be worrying about her brother? Instead of me?"

"She does. Constantly. No one has caught his eye."

"I don't know about that," I countered.

"What do you know?"

"Officially? Nothing. Unofficially..."

"Tell me."

"I didn't say a word. But he's brooding in the direction of a certain Lady Davina."

"Lady Davina... That is a... bold choice."

"A choice that might keep your wife occupied."

"Might indeed."

"Will?" A familiar husky feminine voice called from the other direction. "Oh, Lord Grayson, good to see you. I don't suppose I could borrow Will? He promised me the next set."

"Of course. I believe I'm due on the floor as well." He nodded to me. "Hart."

"Grayson."

Celine's warm hand found mine, and she pulled me brazenly to the floor with little concern for the spectacle. Couples were lining up for the waltz, eyes fixed firmly on us instead of their partners. Confidently, she settled my hand on her waist before grabbing the other and lacing our fingers together inappropriately.

My person and her gown fussed with to her satisfaction, she finally met my gaze. Something was wrong. Something about her eyes, perhaps a bit more downturned than usual? Or the divot between her brows? Her lower lip worried slightly more? Maybe the prissy way she adjusted her gown? Or the tight way she held herself?

It was very, very wrong.

"Love?"

She swallowed, shaking her head. "Not here."

The music began and as promised, she led me through the rusty motions.

"Just tell me you're all right," I begged.

"Physically, I'm unharmed. But not here." Her words were low under her breath. Barely audible over the orchestra. She caught my eyes once more, holding them, willing me to understand.

It went against every instinct I had. To let her distress lay there, untouched. It was a near physical ache. But I nodded. I clenched my teeth and swallowed the knot in my throat before I managed the motion, but I did.

"Thank you," she whispered, pulling me closer. The unfamiliar steps were loosening once more and I was able to take the lead. Breathing her in helped. She was safe, warm, and vanilla-scented. She slipped her hand from my shoulder to rest above her mark on my chest, and my heart gave an approving thump beneath her hand.

With a deep breath, she rolled her shoulders back slightly.

It did nothing to improve her already flawless posture but seemed to fortify her.

"Do you know, I think this is the grumpiest anyone has ever looked dancing with me."

"Lies. Gabriel was always brooding. And Wayland? Certainly grumpier than me."

"I never danced with Michael."

"No?"

"Never. I can't remember the last time I waltzed. It seems too... intimate for someone I don't particularly care about."

"Don't know if what we're doing counts as a waltz, love. It's a miracle I haven't crushed your foot."

"If you do, it will be a worthy sacrifice. But I doubt it. You're quite good actually."

"Not too embarrassed?"

"Never." That was enough to pull a smile from me. "Would you be devastated if we left before supper?"

"I've never wanted anything more."

"Nothing?" She raised a teasing brow.

"I've only wanted one thing more."

"We can slip out when everyone heads for the dining room."

"No one will mind?"

"All the better to gossip about us."

"Wonderful."

The dance came to an end eventually and gentlemen escorted ladies into the dining room. Celine led me, her arm tucked in mine, to follow at the end of the pack. Once we escaped the room, we turned the opposite direction.

The carriage awaited us just outside the door. At my questioning glance, she explained, "I didn't think you would object. I had it called before I found you."

I handed her in, then followed and clambered onto the

seat across from her. No sooner had the door shut behind us than she was in my arms.

She was in my arms and she was *frantic*. There were a thousand reasons this was a terrible idea. The practicalities of a moving carriage. The intricacies of our apparel. The fact that I was still somewhat infuriated with her. That I had no idea what upset her so earlier. All very valid justifications to stop her.

But her fingers were clenched on my jaw dragging my lips to hers and the other hand was knotted in my hair, pinning me in place.

There was nothing tentative, sweet, or gentle in her touch or her kiss. It was hard and fast and ferocious. In an instant, it went from the bearable, everyday arousal I had come to call a friend in her presence, to an inferno. I caught her knee where it was braced on the edge of the seat, and yanked it to meet my hip. She collapsed in a desperate heap on my lap, her lips never leaving mine.

I pulled back to taste her jaw while she panted my name. Her hand finally left my jaw, dropping to the nonexistent space between us, industrious fingers searching for the falls of my trousers. Her obvious intent was the only thing that could dampen my lust even slightly. Catching her fingers, I laced them with my own and distracted her with a nip to the freckle behind her ear.

That earned me a whimper as her hips rocked against mine. The free hand left my hair to continue its twin's efforts. I caught that one too.

"Will..." It was a beautiful and far too loud whine that certainly left no doubt as to our occupation at the moment—if there had been any before.

"Not here, love."

"But..." It was an impressive feat, to claw my way through the fury of lust to deny her. I pulled away from the tempting curve of her neck to meet her eyes. Her pupils were blown wide, her cheeks flushed, her lips swollen. She stopped struggling to free her hands and resumed her effort toward my trousers with a squeeze of my hands.

I released her hands, trusting the promise in those clenched fingers. "You're fine, sweetheart. I've got you." I caught the back of her neck with one hand, dragging her décolleté to my lips, the other found her hip. She had managed to create her own instinctive rocking motion, and I made it ours.

Her hands still clutched at me desperately, hair, jaw, back, shoulder, arm. But she allowed me the control. With each jolt of the carriage and our bodies, she gifted me a new whimper.

I slipped a hand underneath layers of skirts and petticoats and delicate fineries and drew a finger across where she was aching for me. Oh, that was a heady thought. An equally heady sound ripped from her mouth, caught by mine, as I slowly continued my ministrations.

"Will, please."

"What do you need, love?"

"You."

"You've got me."

"Don't stop," she begged.

"Never." She was close to her peak. Her hands clutched my hair and my shirt—right over her mark. Her hips stuttered. I rocked against her once, twice, three times before she cried out into my shoulder with a shudder.

One by one her fingers unclenched and her breathing slipped back to normal. I slid my hand free and straightened her gown, then tucked both legs over my waist.

It only took a minute, perhaps two, before the carriage stopped outside her house. The convenient timing was more than a little suspicious, and I wouldn't have been shocked to learn that the driver had gone around a time or two.

Celine was still flushed and tired, and she whined a bit when I jostled her. But she stepped willingly out of the carriage.

I was forced to rip off my great coat and hang it awkwardly over an elbow in front of me while I valiantly strode into the house, her arm in mine.

Thirty-Five

CELINE

UNDER THREAT OF DEATH, I could never explain how I ended up pressed between my bedroom door and William, his trousers shoved down and my gown rucked up. And for the life of me, I could not care. I could die, right here, in his arms, with him moving inside me and it would be worth it.

He was everywhere, everything I could see, taste, smell, feel. Oh, how he felt. Moving against me, with me, for me. Everything I gave him, he returned tenfold. Every kiss, every caress, every touch, every thrust, he was a man possessed, starving, and I was his for the taking.

Raking my nails down his back just made him groan and the onslaught between my legs harder. And his strength, so deceptive and so damn erotic.

This wasn't sweet or gentle. It was hot and hard and desperate and loud, so loud. The door rattled against the frame. Great rasping gasps broke free. The groans and grunts and whimpers, the slickness between us, it was all a symphony of lust.

The man was a prodigy, a savant, a revelation. And then he pulled his lips off my neck, cupping my cheek with one hand until I met his gaze, hips never missing a beat. There it was, his heart in his eyes.

"Love this. Love you."

I bit my lip to keep from screaming it to him, the world, the heavens. My head slammed back against the door with a painful *thunk* as we crashed over the peak together.

I love you. I love you. I love you.

Awareness returned slowly, first the bite of copper from my bitten lip, then the pull of hair caught in the door, the plop of tears dropping from chin to breast, the racing thump of his heart beneath my ear.

The heart I was about to shatter.

With a great shuddering breath I willed back the tears, determined that he know them as nothing other than perspiration. It was certainly not an implausible excuse, here on the floor before the door where we had collapsed during our little deaths. His legs must have given out. Mine were no more functional.

That was good. As long as I couldn't move, I couldn't do this. This terrible, unbearable thing that made my chest hurt and my stomach revolt. This thing that would confirm every one of his worst fears. That would make him hate me.

And keep him alive.

He slipped the pins out of my hair, one by one. And I loved him. The row of dress hooks popped open. And I loved him. The petticoats and stays fell by the wayside. And I loved him.

I loved him. And everything I feared was coming true. Even now my lungs protested every inhale with a sharp, disgruntled stab and the knot in my throat was so thick I couldn't have swallowed if I tried.

He was going to hate me. *I* hated me. But if he knew, if he had the slightest idea, he wouldn't leave. He would stay and he would try to defend me, and I would be left with another grave to visit.

He guided me up, supporting me with cool hands clutching the backs of my thighs. Still kneeling at my feet, he pressed cool kisses to my stomach. Not now. Not tonight. I was wrung like a sponge; I couldn't manage it. Not tonight.

I pulled him to his feet, ducking his gaze, distracting, evading, dancing away. I led him to the bed where he shucked the wreckage of his clothing and curled up behind me.

Flipping over, I found my rouge mark still covering his heart, a bit smudged now but no less vibrant.

His arm banded about my waist, pulling me in tighter.

"Are you ready to tell me what had you so upset?" His voice was strained but warm. He didn't attempt to pull me from my hiding place either, buried next to my mark.

"It was nothing. Xander told me he intended to leave London." It wasn't even a lie, at least not entirely. I felt his muscles relax even further.

"'M sorry, love."

"Don't apologize." *Please, I could not take it.*

"Not sure what I did to earn the welcome I got in the carriage..." I pressed a kiss to my original print, feeling his heart give a thump beneath my lips.

"I just—you were..."

"Jus' needed me?" The tiniest hint of hope peaked through, and I knew. I knew I should crush it. Discourage it. Anything but what I wanted, which was to wrap my hands around it and breathe life into it. To tell him that I needed him, wanted him, loved him; then and always.

"Something like that." His chest rumbled beneath me in some kind of contented purr and apparently my response was sufficient.

I was a monster. Right now, right this second. I was using

him. I was weak. And greedy. And I was leaching everything from him. His comfort, his vulnerability, his warmth, his love. I was taking it all and leaving him with nothing because it was the only way I could find the strength to do this.

He played with my curls, tracing one with a deceptively delicate, ink-stained fingers. It was soothing and loving and all the things I didn't deserve. The motion, combined with the steady beat of his heart was almost enough to lull me to sleep.

Almost.

Because then he plucked the same one Victoria had, and the image of him bleeding beneath me flashed before my eyes. The sick feeling rose again, and it took everything in me not to tense, not to roll off him and heave.

After a moment, he moved on to the next curl, none the wiser. Eventually, his motions slowed, the gentle tugs on my hair weakened and stopped. His hand fell to his chest with a curl still trapped underneath.

Deep, even breaths and the rhythmic *thadump, thadump, thadump* of his heart were the only things keeping me sane. The images of him bleeding underneath me were too real and too close to the surface for my own rest, especially once his soothing touch was abandoned to dreams.

Thirty-Six

CADIEUX HOUSE, LONDON - JUNE 18, 1816

WILLIAM

FOR THE FIRST time in recent memory, I woke alone. I didn't like it. I hated it, in fact. I hadn't felt her leave my arms and that was a terrible shame. She should be here, warm, sleep-rumpled, and sweet. Instead, the bed was cold.

A *tap, rap, tap* sounded from the window. The same infuriating tit from yesterday. "Hush you," I said, feeling every bit the fool. It ceased its tapping but gave an indignant chirp as it stared at me. Good lord, I was talking to a bird.

Something was... not right. I could not point to it and name it. But something was coming.

My clothes from last night were folded neatly at the foot of the bed. I grabbed my trousers and stuffed in first one leg then the second, then I rose to fasten the buttons. And still no sign of Celine, just the two-note song of the damn bird.

Tossing on my shirt, I made for the door only for the handle to twist of its own accord under my hand. Celine stepped inside, a tray balanced against her hip as she shut the door behind her, my position unnoticed. She turned and jumped like a startled cat, her free hand pressed to her breast. Her clothed breast.

Notably, she was fully dressed for the day. Hair tugged back and up. She even wore slippers. Not once, since I joined her here, had I seen her dressed before half past ten. I hadn't glanced at the clock this morning, but it was certainly earlier than that.

"William! You startled me."

"You're dressed."

"Yes?"

"Why?" She set the tray on the edge of the bed before straightening. Her shoulders rolled back nearly imperceptibly with a heavy but delicate breath. And her eyes met mine.

And I knew.

"Do you want something to eat?"

I considered the bed for a moment. I wasn't entirely certain my knees would hold for the blow that was coming. But the bed... the bed where, for two perfect nights I had loved her and she had loved me... No. Standing was better.

"If it's all the same to you, I'd rather not." *I'd rather not have this moment at all. I'd rather still be in that bed with you snoring softly in my arms. I'd rather still be at that ridiculous ball with my ridiculous attempt at waltzing. Anywhere else.*

I had the brief notion at the start of whatever this was, that this moment might be easier for knowing it was coming. It wasn't. If anything, it was worse. Because even knowing it was inevitable, even though I was ready for it, I hadn't seen it coming. Not really. Not like this. Not when I had the vague notion to sneak upstairs at the office and find my mother's ring.

"William..." There was no warmth, none of the usual affection. I hadn't noticed until just this moment.

Part of me wanted to urge her on, to force her hand. But the petty, jealous, broken part of me wanted her to suffer for it.

To drag it out. And the rather delusional part clung to hope, desperate to give her one last moment to change her mind.

"William, I..." Her gaze cast about the room as she searched for the right words. Anywhere but at me. "I think it's time you returned home."

A fist tightened around my chest, heart, lungs, esophagus, all of it. The tears were there, of course they were, but that—that was the one thing I would not do.

"I see." The words ripped from me, my tone far steadier than I felt.

"I-I've been using you." Even now, even in this, she was beautiful. It wasn't fair. That the sun should halo her so, that her cheeks should flush that delicately—it was cruel. "I've been using you. I don't love you. I can't love you."

There it was. The crack. The physical agony that burst from my chest. I tried to swallow it but it lodged there, suffocating me.

"I'm sorry, William."

And with that, she turned and stepped out, leaving me open and bleeding on her frilly purple carpet.

I took a great ragged, rasping breath. There was pain, Lord there was pain. At some point after the door shut, my knees gave out and I landed in a ragged heap. Ironically in very much the same position I had found last night with her in my arms.

But I felt relief too. The waiting was over. No more worry over whether this thing, or the next, or the one after that would be the one. The thing that did it—that reminded her how far beneath her I was.

This feeling, this bone-deep agony, this was the worst it would be.

I didn't know how long I sat there. Not crying, surprisingly. My eyes were dry. But breathing. It was a difficult enough task at the moment, each breath taking consideration and will. But eventually I managed to stand.

When I slipped into the hall, I found my bag packed. And wasn't that just charming? Had she informed the entire staff this morning? Or merely the essentials? The snap of irritation was a balm against the devastation, and I clung to it, fed it. I grabbed my bag and hurried down the stairs to the door.

Bouvier hovered uncomfortably there, a carriage waiting through the doors. "Monsieur... I'm—"

"Don't. Please." I could not manage the man comforting me.

I could feel wide, downturned green eyes behind me. It took everything inside me not to turn and beg, scream, cry, anything.

"Would you prefer the carriage, sir?"

The carriage... The carriage with a desperate Celine whimpering for me. Certainly not.

"I think I'll walk. Can you have my bag sent at your convenience?"

"Of course."

I nodded and set the bag aside. I stepped purposefully through the door when he opened it, out into the deceptive sunlight. On the little railing sat the damned bird, silent for once in its damned life.

CELINE

The ease of it was the worst part. Not on my end, of course. I felt an agony that was at once the same and entirely different from the torment of Gabriel's death. That I managed to get the words out with any semblance of steadiness was owed entirely to determination and the numbness that had settled over me.

But his acceptance—that was a pain I would not soon

forget. There was no fight in him, not a single word of protest. Even beneath the hurt in his eyes, a shade of ice blue that was entirely new to me. There was no steel, merely resignation and almost... relief. And wasn't that a sickening thought?

The man had worked his way into every facet of my life within days. My bed smelled of citrus and sage and him. His cravat and waistcoat were still spread on the edge of the bed. The lilies he brought me were still in bloom on my bedside table. Everywhere I turned, reminders of William. My door reminded me of him. My flesh was a reminder. Under my skirts, sets of five finger-shaped bruises lined my upper thigh. My neck bore similar marks. He was everywhere.

And gone.

I climbed into the unmade bed in a pathetic ball. The fabric was cold and stark, wrinkles the only reminder of his presence, that and the divot from his head on the pillow.

I wrapped the bed coverings around myself, swaddled tight like an infant. That was when the tears began to flow, fast and hot in enduring rivulets down my cheeks. My breathing, too, came ragged in harsh pants that filled the silent room.

There were no sobs. Those were for people who were not the cause of their own suffering. They were a relief to the knot in my throat that I did not deserve.

I must have fallen asleep eventually because I woke, still bereft of his warmth, to an irritating chirp outside the window.

Damn bird.

"Go away," I mumbled, my throat raw and sharp, in the direction of the bird. If anything, the chirping increased in volume and frequency, with an added tap on the window between each two-note repetitions.

Over and over again he continued, chirp twice, tap, chirp twice, tap. I ignored it. I yelled at it and ignored it again in a similar rhythm. Eventually, I could take it no longer and flopped my way out of my pile of bedding to yank the window open with no ceremony and far more irritation than the situation deserved.

Far from startled by my efforts, the bird made two little hops to sit on the inside of the sill. It tilted its head, staring at me curiously, judgmentally.

"What?"

Chirp-chirp, it answered. It hopped over to the side of the sill where a pile of pebbles sat. After grabbing one in its little beak, it bounced over and dropped it in front of me. It was bizarre. I would have thought I'd imagined it if a tiny pebble didn't sit before me.

I glanced about the room, searching for something, anything. My eyes fell on the breakfast tray still on the opposite side of the bed from where I cried myself to sleep. I stepped away and grabbed the pastry and the empty teacup. I tore a tiny bite off the edge of the pastry and handed it to the bird. He ate it in one, two bites with a pleased two-note chirp.

Skipping back, he grabbed another pebble and set it next to the one in front of me. I traded him for a piece of pastry. This continued twice more until he returned, looked at the bite, looked at me, sauntered over to the empty cup, and tapped it.

Taking it to the basin, I filled it and returned and watched in awe as he flitted to the rim and dipped down to take a drink before returning to the pebbles and bringing another one to me.

After that trip, he took no more bites and drank no more. Instead, he tapped the sill next to his stones.

"Yes, it's a nice pile." He tapped it again with his beak. "Thank you."

Three quick hops and he found my finger resting on the wooden frame and gave it a sharp peck.

"What?" He pecked at the finger once again before

returning to his pebbles. He straightened one or two before stepping away and quirking his head at me.

Finally, I looked, truly looked at the pebbles. They were arranged in a *W*.

"I'm losing my mind. This is what going mad feels like," I muttered under my breath.

Chirp-chirp.

"Gabriel?"

Two chirps.

"I don't know what this means." He pecked my hand and tapped his pebbles again.

"I don't know what you want from me. I don't understand." He grabbed the tip of a finger in his beak, dragging my hand to the pebbles. "You want me to find *W*?"

Chirp-chirp.

"I can't. They'll kill William. I can't let that happen. I'm sorry, Gabriel. I would give almost anything to find out what happened to you. Anything but him." That statement earned me a flurry of angry cheeps and taps and a slightly more vicious peck at which point I pulled my fingers away.

"I'm sorry. But no. Not him. I won't let anything happen to William."

He gave one more irritated series of chirps before he flew off, leaving behind a thousand questions and no answers.

Anthropomorphizing a bird who wanted breakfast, that was madness. No question.

Thirty-Seven

CELINE

THE NEXT SEVERAL days followed a depressing pattern. Wake, cry, argue with a bird, pay calls, cry, attend dinners or dances, perhaps the theatre, and repeat. My very public, very concerted effort to demonstrate that I was not investigating anything and that I had nothing to do with William was both time consuming and exhausting.

I hadn't been out in society in such a bold way since I was a debutant. I was feeling my age and recalling every single reason I detested half the *ton* in the first place. And, of course, the half that I could stand were infrequent in their attendance.

That was certainly the case tonight at the Montrose ball while Mr. Wesley Parker spoke directly to my décolleté. I had been forced to choose my most scandalously cut gowns for these events in order to ensure that I escaped no notice. It had the unfortunate side effect of attracting leches like Parker. The repugnant oaf made my stomach lurch and my flesh crawl even more than the rest of them.

Every single time someone placed my hand in the crook of

their arm, every time someone handed me from a carriage, with every insignificant brush, it was all I could do not to scream at them all. "*Not for you! Not for you to touch, not for you to stare at, not for you to smile at. No!*" Instead, I merely smiled demurely, looked away, and swallowed the knot in my throat.

"So, what happened to the solicitor who was courting you? Did you finally see reason?" Parker asked.

My fingers positively itched for my long discarded fan to hide behind.

"Our friendship ran its course."

The first time I had said something to that effect, the words produced a physically painful effect. Now the phrase was rote.

"Peculiar arrangement, that," he replied. Mr. Parker was, however, the first person to press beyond my vague comment. Interest sparked anew in my chest. Could he be?

That spark was doused as quickly as it arrived. Whether he was responsible for Gabriel's death or not was irrelevant. Because I was finished investigating.

Nothing was worth William's safety, not even the truth.

That fact had become its own kind of truth. I had lived for years without knowing, and with no answers in sight. I could do so again.

Ironically, I had also lived for years without William. But his continued existence—even if I never saw him again—was as essential to me as breathing.

In the end, it had come down to William's life or Gabriel's memory. And I had chosen.

"I hadn't realized my comings and goings were of such interest."

"Indeed, they are. Would you care to join me for the next set?" A waltz. With Mr. Parker. Every part of my being revolted.

"I thank you for the offer, but I don't waltz." I turned and stepped over to the drinks table before he could protest further, though he muttered something about waltzing with Hart under his breath.

And so my days and nights continued, mind-numbing monotony after mind-numbing monotony.

A change in pace finally came nearly a week later with Xander's summons to Rycliffe Place.

It was eerie, stepping inside the house nearly packed up. Great sheets covered the furnishings, and some of the wallpapering revealed darkened rectangles where paintings had protected the paper from the sun's displeasure.

"Cee?" Xander called from down the hall in the study. I had to press myself along the wall twice to avoid a servant carrying some large trunk or painting. Finally reaching the study, I peered in.

There was Xander, ever dignified even with an undone waistcoat and cravat, plopped on the floor surrounded by books and ledgers in various piles.

"Well, isn't this cozy?"

"You're not as charming as you think you are," he retorted as he flipped through a ledger with disinterest before adding it to a stack.

"Lies. Can I help?"

"Actually, I was hoping you would take a look upstairs and see if there's anything you wish to keep. You have most everything by now, but I wouldn't want to dispose of anything precious."

"Thank you," I said, pressing a teasing kiss to the top of his head.

The stairs proved to be nearly as treacherous as the hall, but I made the journey without injury. I turned down the hall to the rooms that were once my own. Memories danced through my mind of these halls, more loving and less bloody than the moments that haunted me below.

There, at the end of the hall, was a set of three open doors. These had been closed up longer than the rest of the house, seven years, or thereabouts. The same white sheets covered the furnishings, gray for the thick layer of dust.

There was the massive bed where I fell in love with my husband, right in the center. Under the window was my dressing table, long ago emptied. I started there, yanking the sheet and releasing a storm of dust. Nothing rested on top except the large vanity mirror I had no need of. As expected, the drawers were bereft.

I tried to right the sheet, but it slid off the other side, once, twice, three times before I realized it needed a second hand to reach over the top of the mirror without pulling away from me.

Feeling rather guilty that I had caused even more work for the already overwrought servants, I approached Gabriel's dresser with more caution. I lifted one edge and folded the sheet carefully in half over the top.

Gabriel had always kept the top clear of clutter, but the drawers had been an organized chaos. Over the years, the contents had spread their way across London, to Xander, Davina, and Her Grace—to me. The first drawer had little but a quill, an inkwell, and some parchment.

I slipped that one closed, content to leave those items to a future owner. The sheet caught in the edge of the drawer. Pulling it back open, I gave a gentle tug, but the sheet didn't budge. A harder yank revealed that it was caught. One last jerk and the problem exposed itself. A false bottom.

My husband had a false bottom in the drawer by his bed. I supposed I ought to have some sort of feeling about that, but it was entirely unsurprising. After slipping out the quill and other items from the drawer, I lifted the wood piece.

Below it was a stack of parchment. And right on top was a yellowed banknote.

WILLIAM

It was a wonder how quickly someone could become essential. She went from stranger, to nuisance, to friend, confidant, lover in days. Now all that was left behind was a dull ache in my chest and a throbbing behind my left eye.

A few days of my foul temper had been enough to scare off even the most determined visitors to my office, Bates included. It had, however, been a very productive few days.

That, of course, led to its own pitfalls. No sooner had Xander's documents been completed than Kit shoved me out the door toward Rycliffe Place to gather signatures.

In fairness, I had made no fewer than three clerks cry just that morning.

When I arrived, the house was in a state of organized disarray. Servants scurried about with various trunks and paintings, covering furnishings and the like. One of them merely grunted with a head nod down the hall when I asked after Xander.

Peering in a drawing room, I found no hint of Xander. But there was a sense of Celine. In the curtains and settee that hadn't yet been covered—purple damask in the same tones she still favored. It was the slap of a reminder that I didn't need.

Next, I passed a music room and a dining room. At last, I found Xander in the study at the end of the hall. This room bore no evidence of Celine. Xander had made it his own. And he was currently hunkered on the floor in a little fortress of documents and ledgers.

Though I favored my desk, I was no stranger to the looming and foreboding presence of a perilously stacked document tower. I knocked on the doorframe and he invited me in, not glancing up from his project.

"Xander?"

"Oh," he said, whipping around to verify the identity of his intruder. "Will! I thought you were... someone else."

"Just me, I'm afraid."

"Are those all the documents I asked for?"

"They are."

"Help me up? I believe I've been bent in this position so long that I have lost the ability to stand."

"Wait until you see the other side of thirty."

"Oh, good Lord. With any luck, Davina will have given me a fit of apoplexy and put me out of my misery by then." I pulled him to stand. He had managed to surround himself with piles and spun once, twice for an escape before deciding to step over gingerly.

"Alas, I've yet to find anyone who manages to have their apoplexy conveniently timed."

"If she doesn't, my mother will manage. She's been detailing every ridiculous fairy story she can find about Scotland. Did you know that I'm certainly going to be mangled by wulvers and drowned by kelpies?"

"I hadn't heard that. I'll miss you dearly."

"See that you do." He wandered over to the desk that remained uncovered. It was blanketed by yet more documents. He made a half-hearted attempt to shuffle the piles before picking up the one directly in front of his chair and dropping it to the floor with a decisive *thunk*.

"Do you need... help? With all of this?"

"I need a drink with all of this. And a large fire. Also, a new sister. Dav is responsible for at least half of these." He lifted the corner of a stack, letting the pages snap from his thumb in rapid succession. "Do you suppose she's a changeling? Mother was concerned for my future offspring as well, but perhaps she should look to her own."

"It might explain a few things…"

"Oh!" A soft, startled, feminine voice came from the doorway. *Celine.*

The single syllable was a punch to the gut. I turned, slowly taking her in. She was so damn beautiful it hurt. Still all honey curls, golden skin, and wide downturned olive eyes. She wore a simple gray dress with blue flowers. The cut was modest, merely hinting at curves I had caressed. She held a thin file in her clenched hand, insignificant in comparison to the deluge of paperwork in the office.

"Cee, glad you're here. We've some documents that require your signature."

"You do?"

"I do. I didn't get a chance to mention them at the ball the other night. Will and I have made some… arrangements for you."

"I beg your pardon?"

"Oh, damn, Cee! Nothing like that. I've just arranged for an additional dowry if you choose to wed again. And we're giving you some authority over funds in case Davina boards a boat to the Americas and you need to send someone to fetch her back before she weds a Puritan."

"She would hardly wed a Puritan. She's flighty, not a prude."

"I just need you to be able to authorize the funds for someone to fetch her before she develops the abhorrent accent."

"And a dowry? What precisely made you and William believe I required a dowry?"

"Oh, Will very much didn't. I did. I want you to have any option your heart desires, Cee." He turned to me. "She is able to spend it as her own if she does not wed, correct, Will?"

"Indeed." I sounded as though I swallowed a frog and it was stuck halfway down. I cleared my throat awkwardly.

"Very well, which documents do I need to sign, surely not all of these?" She gestured to the whole of the room in a teasing manner.

"Hilarious. Will, can you go over them with her? I'll go see if I can harass someone into tea." He slipped out of the room, entirely oblivious to any protests. She released a weary sigh as he darted down the hall.

"William."

"Lady Rycliffe," I answered. It may have been my imagination, but I thought I caught a flinch as she passed me to take Xander's seat. She settled her folder on top of one of the piles and directed her attention to the stack before her.

Proximity was a necessary evil since I needed to flip through the pages and point to places for her signature. Unfortunately, the closed distance made her warm, sensual scent all the more noticeable, distracting, arousing.

"This one gives you control over the dowry Xander is bestowing on you."

"Do you mind if I read it?"

"Of course not. You should. I just find that it's rare that people do." She read silently before signing her name with a flourish.

"This allows you to manage some additional funds that Xander is bestowing on Her Grace and Lady Davina."

"He probably should have mentioned that..."

"I think he's a bit distracted." And so it went. Explanation, reading, questions, signatures, desperately resisting the desire to bury my face in her silky curls.

Xander took an extraordinarily long time with the tea. By the time he returned, she was on the last swirl of her name on the last document, and he was bereft of tea.

"Couldn't find anyone with a spare moment. I hope you don't mind," he muttered, navigating his piles of parchment.

"Not at all."

"I think I will be going. I've found everything I need, Xander," she said, grabbing a file off one of the stacks.

"Celine..."

"Goodbye, Xander. Mr. Hart," she said my name as if it was a curse, before vanishing through the door as if she'd never been there at all. Xander sighed after her, slipping around to his seat behind the desk.

Before he could sit, a knock sounded, startling us both. He turned, brushing one of the top folders off his pile.

"So sorry, Your Grace," the footman said. "Did you still wish for tea?" Xander turned to me, seeking a response. I shrugged, entirely without preference. It was unlikely to taste less like ash than anything else had for having been in her company for nearly half an hour.

"No, thank you." The footman nodded and scurried off back to trunks or sheets or whatever else was needed.

Xander bent down to gather the scattered contents of the folder. He flipped through them, his brow furrowed. "These must be yours, Will. They're not mine." He handed them over.

"I didn't bring a..." Suddenly, I recalled Celine setting the folder on the stack before signing documents. She had grabbed the wrong one.

I took the file from Xander and flipped it open and there, right on top, was an old banknote. Made out to Gabriel Hasket, Marquess of Rycliffe.

From Mr. Wesley Parker.

Damn.

Thirty-Eight

WILLIAM

I LEFT AS SOON as it was feasible after Xander signed the documents. The entire process was a blur as was the walk back to the office, Celine's file clenched tightly in my grasp.

I slipped into the office quietly. Everyone was industriously occupied as usual. And as had become standard, Bates's chair was empty. I glanced to my office. The door was mostly closed.

With a sigh, I handed Xander's signed documents to Matthews for filing. Celine's folder was still pinched tightly between my fingers.

I stalked silently to my office and peered in the gap of the open door. There was my missing clerk, crouched behind my desk trying unsuccessfully to work a letter opener into the locked drawer.

I pushed the door open forcefully so it banged against the wall. From the other side I heard an irritated "Oi!" from Kit. Of more interest to me was Bates spinning around toward me and shoving his hands behind his back in the flurry.

"Oh, sir. I didn't realize you had returned, and I was checking to see if there were documents that needed to be filed."

"And you needed to break into my desk to do that?"

"No! I-I beg your pardon?"

"Which is it?"

"What?"

"Are you denying the accusation or are you confused as to the nature of it?"

"Both?"

"Get out." He shuffled past me, trying to press himself to the wall to get as far from me as possible while still escaping through the door. He started for his empty desk before I interrupted. "Out!"

"Sir?"

"Your employment is terminated—without severance and without a reference. Get out."

"But…"

Kit, finally sensing something amiss, popped his head out. "Will? I thought we discussed—"

"Caught him going at my desk with a letter opener."

He froze for a moment before turning to Bates. "Right, you heard the man. Gather your coat."

"But…" The man protested, his eyes wide and skin a pallid with a clammy sheen. At the sight of Kit's frown, he abandoned his protestations. I had been on the receiving end of it so often that its foreboding nature was somewhat lost on me, but Kit could glower a man to death.

Bates grabbed his coat and stumbled toward the door, yanked it open, and rushed away.

The rest of the clerks returned to their paperwork simultaneously, feigning disinterest with impressive alacrity.

"Will, are you all right?"

Wasn't that a question.

"I don't rightly know."

"Go on then. I can find something to keep this lot busy."

"Really?"

"Bring me a little cake thing in the morning."

"Done."

I followed Bates out to the street. Every part of me wanted to trace the now familiar path to Celine's house. Instead, I returned to my apartment above the office, folder still in hand.

THE SUN HAD JUST BEGUN to set when I finished sorting the entirety of Gabriel's deception.

I wasn't overly knowledgeable about horse racing or breeding. I'd only attended the one race and only because I was certain to find him there. But he had charged obscene studding fees.

And they were more than enough to put a dent in Parker's annual income, if not outright obliterate it.

The scheme was clever. Two similar looking studs, one with a pedigree to put royalty to shame, the other just slightly above average. Charge a small fortune for studding the exceptional one. Occasionally use its inferior twin instead. Keep exceptional records, reap secondary rewards in two to three years betting against the inferior's offspring when they debuted. Collect an even larger fortune.

Parker was one of the unfortunate souls Gabriel had duped twice. I hadn't studied the man's finances, but certainly the banknote was enough to ruin him and his offspring for generations to come.

There were other drafts in the folder as well, but only one with a signature that matched the flourished *W* I had studied so closely in recent weeks.

I knew I ought to go to Celine with this. To see how she wished to proceed.

But I wanted to confront the man. Toss him into a cell and throw the key in the Thames. Demand to know why he hadn't just made his suspicions public and shamed Gabriel into returning the funds. Hurt him the way he hurt my Celine.

Except she wasn't mine. Not anymore. If she ever was. She had found the answers on her own, she had no need of me now.

Idly tracing my finger along the *W* while I considered my options, I was startled by a *tap, tap, tap* at the window. There, perched on the sill was Celine's damned bird. He gave his usual disgruntled two-tone chirp before tapping at the window once again.

"Shoo!"

Tap! Tap! Tap! More rapid this time.

"Begone you. Go bother your mistress."

The tapping increased in pace and intensity, threatening to break the window. I rose and strode over to the window, yanking it open with a force that should have sent the bird skyward.

Instead the beast flitted up to my hand for a peck. The nip of its beak was severe, drawing a drop of blood. *Could birds have rabies?*

It did a little loop in the air before coming back down on the sill and tapping the glass hard once again.

That motion did it. Just in my periphery, I saw movement. Below my window, I found a new pile of straw, and the familiar form of Bates as he knelt fussing with something.

It took a moment to fully grasp what I was seeing. It was only the damn bird pecking me again that launched me to action.

I sprinted through the door and down the stairs, half-tripping in my haste. I rushed around the side of the building to see Bates fanning the familiar spark of a tinderbox.

Then I was before him, kicking the box out of his hands without conscious choice. It landed with a clatter a few feet away. Grasping him roughly by the neck with both hands, I hauled Bates to his feet. With one hand, I reared back to deliver a blow to his face.

Thunk!

I registered the sound of the board that slammed across the side of my face before I felt it. White hot agony burned through my skull a second later. Before I could right myself, the board rained down another blow, this time on my side. I heard the snap of my rib before the pain registered with a great choking gasp.

Blood streamed into my eye from the first hit as I tried to roll over onto my knees. To do what—I hadn't the slightest idea. Bates pulled his foot back to deliver a kick to the same ribs.

Air abandoned me. My head was screaming for air, but my lungs wouldn't obey. Every attempt led to a choking sound that would have been frightening if I could think on it.

My vision darkened at the sides with yet another kick, this one to the stomach. And then I heard the sweetest and most terrifying sound in the entire world.

"Will!"

And then the blackness took her too.

Thirty-Nine

HASKET HOUSE, LONDON - JUNE 28, 1816

CELINE

I LEFT Rycliffe Place fully intending to return home and prepare for a dreary whist party at some lady or other's house. But when I rounded the corner that would take me home, I spotted Gabriel's resting place ahead.

I slipped in through the side gate and found him much the same way I left him last. My fingers found my lips for a kiss before I recognized that I was not quite interested in offering that kiss today.

I dropped my hand with a sigh and settled onto my bench with the folder beside me.

"I'm unbearably cross with you right now. Did you know?" A warm breeze rustled through my hair.

"Of course you did. It's been seven years, Gabriel. It's been seven years and I'm lonely. I found a man who loves me. He adores me. And I ruined it because your senseless schemes are still haunting me. I have it right here," I said, lifting the folder at him. "You ruined him. You promised me you were done with all of it, but you couldn't help yourself. One last bet.

Look where that got you. Banknotes hidden in a drawer for seven years. Was it worth it?"

I sniffed pathetically. "I love you. I wanted to find justice for you. I put William in danger too. He's in danger right now, because of me."

A little blue butterfly flitted over from the irises, surprisingly still in bloom, and landed on my knee once again.

"It's enough now. I know, and that has to be enough. Because I can't lose him too.

"So I'm going to burn these. Find some way to let Mr. Parker know they're gone—I'm finished. And I'm going to beg William for forgiveness.

"Because I love him. I'm in love with him. It's not what you and I had. It's different, softer, steadier. But I'm different now.

"You died that day. You were the one who died, but I've been acting like I died too. I didn't. I'm still here and I deserve to live. If that means the truth never comes out, that you never get justice, then so be it."

The sun dipped below the horizon when I stood on spindly legs and walked over to him, then dropped the belated kiss on his stone. The breeze returned, rushing through the tree again, leaves chittering above me. The folder blew to the ground, scattering the documents every which way.

"You're an arse, you know that?" I muttered to the wind as I bent to gather the papers and froze. My veins turned to ice.

Not a one of these documents were the ones I took from Gabriel's bedside table. Instead, they were from one of Davina's exploits. I took the wrong folder.

Surely Will or Xander had noticed by now. My plan lay in shambles at my feet. Neither of them would let it rest, I was certain.

Picking up the pages, I had every intention of yelling at

Gabriel more when I heard the distinctive two-note chirp of the great tit.

He flew at me, squawking his song with greater urgency than I'd ever known. He flitted around me, agitated. His circles constricted tighter and tighter until he was right in front of my face.

Then he flitted away, darting back to check on me, and flitting toward the gate once more.

The chirps, so frantic, so repetitive, began to form a single word.

"William, William, William."

THE RACE to his office was a blur. A blur of desperate attempts to convince myself that this was insane. Will was fine. There was no world in which a bird was the spirit of my late husband, warning me that the man I'd fallen in love with—quite against my will—was in danger.

I had almost managed it, to believe I was insane, when I heard the *thwack* and grunt.

Will's grunt.

The bird stopped midflight just before I rounded the corner alley beside the office, and I nearly crashed into it. Another *thunk*-grunt. I tried to pass the bird, but it wouldn't allow it. Instead, it flitted toward my leg.

All confusion, I tried once more but it flew back in front of me, blocking my path, before returning to my skirts, tugging at them with its little beak. *My dagger.*

"Thank you," I whispered, then winced at another grunt while I crouched to pull the knife out. Armed now, I was allowed to turn the corner, the knife tucked tight against my skirts.

And once again, I walked into hell.

Will was broken and bleeding on the ground as a man kicked him in the ribs. Another watched with a long wooden board in hand. And to make the situation worse still, a small pillar of smoke rose from straw bundled against the building.

The man rained another kick on Will, this time to his stomach, and I couldn't hold back my startled gasp of his name.

Will turned toward me, blood streaming from a cut on his brow. Too much blood. His head drooped, crashing to the pavement as he lost consciousness.

My outburst hadn't been missed by the other men. They turned, advancing toward me. A chirp at my side drew my gaze to the broken milk crate. The very one I stood on, listening outside William's office all those weeks ago. I grabbed a sharp piece in my free hand. It wouldn't be much use against the longer, heavier plank, but two weapons were better than one.

The first man had reached me and a sick sense of familiarity crashed over me. The taller man from that horrid night.

"Not so brave without your umbrella are you?" The scent of his breath, far too close, sent a wave of nausea through me. Unfortunately, I needed him close, closer even, if I was to use my weapons.

"Where is your friend? Still recovering from that umbrella?" Another step. I kept the wall at my back. It left no retreat but no room for an attack from behind either.

"You killed him, you spiteful shrew."

"Oh dear... Did you want to join him?" He pulled his arm back, ready to swing the board and I ducked, thrusting my piece of crate toward his privates with all my strength. He turned at the last moment and it glanced off his hip, but his blow missed too.

With my knife hand, I slammed down into his foot, cutting through his boot with ease. His shout echoed through the alley. Could no one hear this? Why was no one coming? I yanked it out, earning another yell.

Just as I heard a shaky groan behind the men.

Will stumbled to his feet. He distracted the other man, who turned his attention back to Will's prone form. *No!*

A fist found my throat and squeezed hard enough to bruise when the man yanked me up, up, up, off the pavement. My feet kicked uselessly, half a foot above the ground. He tightened his hand. My breath grew weaker by the second.

Black dots filled my vision, I was so close to unconsciousness that it had to be a delusion—the flit of wings past my ear.

Suddenly, the man dropped me and I crashed to my knees with great heaving gulps.

The damn bird.

The ridiculous little bird attacked the man's face with a ferocity it shouldn't have been capable of, pecking and diving and squawking. The man flailed at it, swatting furiously.

I stumbled to my feet just in time to see a hit land and the little bird flung to the ground. Frenzied violence ripped through my chest at the sight, and I reared back to slam my shin into the man's groin.

He collapsed in a moaning, whimpering heap, and I gave another kick to his prone form for good measure.

The sound of Will's gasp drew my attention, and I saw the other man advancing on him. Worse still was noxious black smoke and flames blowing up from the straw.

"Fire! Fire! Fire!" The scream ripped from me on instinct as I clambered on the other man's sweaty back, knife to his throat, still shouting.

Seconds—it only took seconds for the people, the very ones feigning ignorance of the fight in the alley, to respond to my cries. They swarmed with buckets and water like cockroaches.

Their presence was enough. A burly man pulled me off

William's assailant while another grabbed the man, the other still groaning on the ground.

I wrestled free from the unfamiliar grasp and collapsed next to a barely conscious William while men, women, and children filled the alley and passed bucket after bucket, tossing water on the flames.

Desperately, frantically, I dragged his body away from the flames. One of the men paused to help me pull him farther to safety.

I fell against the wall, William's head cradled in my lap and his hand clasped tightly in mine. I watched in horror as the flames grew higher, hungrier. Tears clouded everything, and as I blinked them away, my eyes landed on the still form of my bird.

And I choked on a sob.

Forty

OUTSIDE OF HART AND SOLICITORS, LONDON -
JUNE 28, 1816

CELINE

FOR YEARS AFTER GABRIEL DIED, I had nightmares of that morning. Almost daily, I woke on a tear-filled gasp convinced my hands were still dripping in his blood.

This was nothing like that yet somehow... exactly like that. The acrid smoke burned my lungs. My throat revolted with every breath, a combination of bruising, soot, and the agonizing knot that called it home.

I didn't know how long I sat on the pavement with William's head in my lap, brushing bloody curls away from his face and counting each and every precious breath.

"Celine?" A worried voice came from above me. I was unwilling to look away from William's face to confirm, but it sounded like Kit.

He knelt before me—it was Kit, wearing a look of horror. "Is he..."

"He's still breathing," my voice was hoarse and unrecognizable. "Can you go fetch a doctor?"

"Right, yes." Awkwardly, he clambered up and raced off without another word.

Dimly, I recognized that the heat from the flames was lessening, that the smoke was dissipating somewhat. The shouts from the bucket line dulled.

Another person collapsed beside me. Orange hair, the color of the now subdued fire—Mrs. Ainsley. Wordlessly she pressed a cloth to the wound on William's head, holding pressure. My stomach dropped with the understanding that I should have been doing that.

"What can I do?" someone asked from above me. The voice was familiar, but I couldn't place it without looking away, and I couldn't—wouldn't.

"The bird," I croaked.

"What?"

"The bird," I tried again, nodding toward where he lay. "Is he... is he alive?"

"Uh... it's trying to get up, but it looks like it's got a damaged wing. What happened to it?"

"He saved me," I whispered through tears. "Can you bring him over?"

"I— Should I touch— I don't know..."

"Augie," Mrs. Ainsley snapped, confirming his identity. "Pick up the damn bird."

"Yes. Sorry." Large hands appeared before my face, clasping a struggling, ruffled, but very much alive bird. He hopped out of the hand with an irritated flap of his unaffected wing and flopped on the ground beside me. Using his beak for leverage, he pulled himself onto my knee, where he nudged my arm with his head.

"Thank you," I breathed.

Chirp-chirp.

We sat in vigil, the four of us, for some time before Kit

returned with a doctor who joined us on the lamplit walkway with his bag.

"What happened?"

"He was attacked. I didn't see it, but I think he was hit with a board over there somewhere," I nodded. "I saw him kicked in the stomach or the ribs... It was from a distance."

He pulled Mrs. Ainsley's hand away from the wound. No gush of blood came forth and that was a relief.

"Just the one blow to the head?"

"I don't— I think so."

"Was he unconscious when you found him?"

"No, and he woke up for a moment."

Nodding thoughtfully, he reached down to probe Will's ribs. A quiet groan came from deep in his chest, and it was the sweetest sound I had ever heard.

Still hovering above us, Kit asked, "Will, can you hear me?"

"Shh," Will murmured through closed lips. I lied before— *that* was the sweetest sound. I choked on something that might have been a laugh or a sob, it was impossible to tell.

"All good signs," the doctor added. "As long as he does not take a turn, he will likely recover to some extent."

"To some extent?" I demanded, panic flooding me again.

"Head injuries are tricky business, miss..."

"Hart," I lied, needing to say it—at least once.

"He may be completely fine. He may never be the same. He may never wake up. The only way to know for certain is time. There are a few broken ribs here too," he prodded Will's ribcage, earning another groan. "They don't feel out of alignment though. Those aren't life-threatening, but they're certainly painful. Unfortunately, anything we give him for pain could make his head worse. He is in for a long few nights."

"There's no way to tell?"

"We'll know more if he wakes fully. In the meantime, we'll need to get a stretcher built and get him somewhere more comfortable. Where are his lodgings?" Everyone pointed simultaneously to the charred second floor of the building.

"Perhaps somewhere else then," he responded.

Mrs. Ainsley slipped her hand over mine and squeezed gently. Offering what comfort she could.

The doctor turned to me. "And you? Is your throat the worst of your injuries?"

"Yes," I answered with a hollow tone.

"Are there any others injured?"

"The man who hit him, I stabbed him in the foot. And I kicked him between the legs."

"Well done!" Kit interrupted.

"I think one of the gentlemen has him and his accomplice restrained over there," I nodded toward the alley.

"I'll take you to them," Mrs. Ainsley volunteered, her tone conveying the displeasure she had with the task. "You two work on a stretcher," she instructed.

One by one, the onlookers dissipated, the darkened alley and street emptying. And I sat there on the pavement as people grumbled while they passed, annoyed that they had to maneuver around us.

William's hand was still in mine, and his chest rose and fell with each precious breath.

"Lady Rycliffe?" Mrs. Ainsley asked. "The constable would like a word. I tried to explain that this wasn't the best time, but..."

"He'll have to come here. I'm not moving him."

"Of course." She wandered off, returning a moment later with a portly gentleman.

"Lady Rycliffe? I'd like to get your version of events if you don't mind."

"It's a long story, and I'm not entirely certain how those

two fit in. Tonight I arrived to see William being kicked and beaten. I pulled my knife and a sharpened piece of wood and stabbed the rotten-smelling one in the foot and kicked him in the privates. I caught the other one around the neck with a knife before realizing the fire was blazing. I called for help."

"And the longer version?"

"Not tonight, please?"

He gave an irritable sigh before agreeing to call on me in two days. By the time he finished, Kit and Mr. Ainsley had returned with a makeshift stretcher and a plan to take Will to Kit's to rest for the night.

Will gave another pained groan when they moved him, but his hand tightened on mine.

I hurried alongside the stretcher down the street, grasping Will's fingers, the bird resting on his knee.

Forty-One

WILLIAM

I'D NEVER WANTED to open my eyes less. My head was big. Surely it hadn't always been this size, so thick and heavy. It throbbed with every beat of my heart. That was how I knew I was, in fact, alive, despite all evidence to the contrary.

My stomach and ribs throbbed with every breath. Inhaling was a chore I wasn't overly interested in. The ribs were broken, I had no doubt of that. It had happened once in France, and what followed was a memorable few weeks. By memorable, I meant agonizing.

Not like this though. I'd never felt like this.

Someone was talking at me, soft and warm words I couldn't fully make out. That was nice. They had my hand wrapped in theirs too. It was the only part of me that didn't hurt and the touch was a comfort.

My memories seemed intact. The damn bird had been there, warning me about Bates and the other one. I remembered the start of the fire. Celine, too, with her knife like an avenging warrior goddess. She was probably the one holding my hand now. It felt right, the way it always did when she touched me.

Liquid dropped onto my hand in uneven drips. My sluggish thoughts took a moment to label them as tears. That was enough for me to attempt to open my eyes.

Attempt and fail.

A single flutter was all that was necessary to determine it was far too bright. Now that I noticed it, the sun blazed, even through my closed lids. Hadn't it been evening?

Also, the left eye refused to obey my commands at all which would be more concerning if I were in less pain.

A sharp pinch to my free hand forced my eyes open. "Ow!"

"Will? Oh Lord, William?" It *was* Celine with her hands wrapped around my uninjured one.

"Cee?" I mumbled through the feeling of cotton stuffed in my throat.

"You know me?"

I squeezed her hand as a yes, hoping desperately she wouldn't ask me to open my eyes again.

"Was that a yes? Can you hear me?"

No luck. "Yes... hurts."

"I know, love. I know. We can't give you anything because of your head. Can you open your eyes?"

"Sun."

"The sun is too bright?" I squeezed her hand again. She rose, leaning over me to close the drapes. Where was I? That was not where the window was in my... Oh, my apartment. Was it even standing?

Her hand settled on my cheek, brushing a thumb against the bone. "'S nice," I mumbled.

"What do you remember?"

"Tired. Later?"

"Oh, yes. I'm sorry, I've been pushing. I'll just leave you to rest."

"Stay?"

"You want me to stay?"

"Yes."

"All right, I'll be right here." She settled back into whatever chair she had been in before I woke.

"Up here."

"What?"

"On bed."

"You want me on the bed?" If I didn't love her so damn much, this conversation would have had me plotting to kill her.

"Yes."

"But... I'll hurt you."

"Don' care."

"But..."

"Cee, on bed," I snapped. It seemed to do the trick because she slid beside me, tentatively curling on her side. She was unbelievably careful not to injure me, resting a hand on top of my heart. The one I knew was still beating because each one corresponded with a throb in my head.

Her soft breath brushed over my neck in even pants as she traced designs over my heart. That was how I fell back to sleep.

IT WAS dark when I woke again, and my head felt less like cotton. I was warm and surrounded by the soft scent of Celine, still pressed against me.

An inconvenient urgency woke me. The minutes stretched, achingly slow. Loath as I was to wake her, it was no longer an option.

All it took was the shift of my shoulder and she darted awake, hovering above me. I could still only see out of the one eye, and I was afraid to ask after the other.

Even so, she was lovelier than ever. Golden curls curtained us and worried green eyes searched my face.

"'Lo."

"You're awake. How are you feeling?"

"Bit better. Need to get up."

"What do you need? I can get it."

"Need to use the pot. Gonna do that for me?"

"I can… assist. If you need it?"

"Lord, no. A bit of dignity."

"Should I fetch Kit?"

"'S'at where we're at?"

"Yes, it was closest." Ah, not good for my apartment. Or the office.

"Have 'im wait outside?"

"Of course," she rose carefully, then found the chamber pot and handed it to me. She slipped out the door, peering around the corner as she closed it.

I managed well enough without assistance, then called out to Kit. He popped his head in, slightly hesitant.

It was good to know where the boundaries of friendship were drawn.

Once I confirmed I was decent, he came in and made himself comfortable in Celine's long-abandoned chair. "How are you feeling?"

"Less like death than earlier."

"That's good. Do you remember anything?"

"Remember everything, I think."

Suddenly a two-toned squawk sounded from the other side of me by the window. I turned, and to my astonishment, horror, and amusement, there was the damn bird. It had one wing bandaged to its side and its feathers were mangled and rumpled. But it still glared at me in irritation with its beady eyes. That explained the pinch earlier. Blasted bird.

"The bird... Celine insisted on bringing it. Said it saved her. I think she might be in a bit of shock." Kit was tentative, trying to warn me without offending most likely. It was the same tone he used when we had bankrupt lords in our office who still spent like kings.

"She's not addled. She and the damn thing have some sort of... friendship? It visits her every morning. And... I think it saved me too?"

"What?"

"Tapped on the window—let me know they were outside."

"So the bird saved you too..."

"I'm not addled either."

"You were hit on the head, quite hard."

I tried a deep breath for courage, forgetting my ribs for a moment. I was punished severely for my forgetfulness with a sharp, stabbing pain.

Forging on, I asked, "Speaking of... my eye?"

"It's not pretty. He hit you in the brow and you've swollen shut. The doc stitched you up while you were out. It'll scar to be sure."

"But 'll be able to see?"

"Oh, yes. He wasn't worried about your vision, mostly your memory, understanding, that sort of thing." That might have been the single most beautiful sentence Kit had ever uttered. "Lucky for us, it seems your head is solid as granite."

The door slid open with a perfunctory knock. Celine. Most likely she had been standing there eavesdropping for a considerable time. I didn't have the energy to tease her about it though. "William?"

She was carrying a tray of something that smelled

delectable, chicken soup perhaps? Until that moment, I hadn't noticed how hungry I was. Now that I did, I was ravenous. If I had ever been this hungry before in my life, I didn't remember it.

Kit helped sit me up while Celine fussed at the tray on my lap with more care than it deserved. Kit stepped away, leaving me to her ministrations.

She pulled the chair up closer to the head of the bed, then ran her fingers through my surely disgusting hair.

Eating proved to be a bit more challenging than anticipated. My hand was unsteady with the spoon, but Celine knew me well enough to let me manage without comment.

It had to be the best soup I'd ever tasted, flavorful, filling, and comforting. I let out an appreciative hum.

"I know, Mrs. Ainsley sent her mother over with it." That explained it then, Mrs. Hudson's cooking was legendary. Far too quickly, I reached the end of the bowl, and she lifted the tray away and set it on the floor beside her.

"Feeling any better?" she asked.

"Much. They didn't hurt you?"

"Nothing like you."

"I should hope not. What did he do?" With a sigh, she pulled back the edge of the frilly thing around her neck. Four perfect fingers and a thumb lined her throat in shades of purple and black. Impotent rage filled me.

"Don't growl—at least not in this context." It took a few seconds to parse her meaning, and I felt my cheeks heat.

"Didn't realize I had."

"Yes, well. I'm perfectly fine. Except for worrying over you to death, I'm the picture of health."

"That you are. Speaking of... Why are you worrying after me?"

"I beg your pardon?"

I swallowed. "Only, I thought you were using me. That you couldn't love me. Don't think most people worry over folks they're using and can't love." It hurt to repeat the words she'd said, to shove them past the knot in my throat that had nothing to do with my stomach or ribs or head.

"Oh, William. I'm so sorry! I didn't mean it. I swear. I didn't mean a word of it! I could never." Her eyes filled with tears amid the incoherent declarations.

"Then, why?" It came out an accusatory croak, more emotional than I wanted.

"She warned me. She found me and she warned me that he knew what I was doing. What we were doing. She said he would kill you if I kept searching. And I knew... I knew you would never stop. You're too stubborn and don't care a lick for yourself. But I couldn't. I... It would have killed me. I never would have recovered from it. I may not recover now, and you're still here.

"But I'm sorry. I'm so sorry. It was lies, all of it. *I love you!* I do. I love you so much. Please, you have to believe me. I know you don't. I've given you no reason to. But I will. You're never going to doubt it. I swear."

My heart lurched, freezing for a moment before sprinting to some unknown destination. Some future where she loved me and I loved her and we were together, in love, forever.

"I caught maybe a third of that, love. Head wound... remember?" It was true, but I caught the essential part. The part where she said she loved me.

"Oh, Lord. I'm sorry. This was too much. I'm here shouting at you..."

"'S all right, love. Think I got the important bits. Maybe we can go over the rest tomorrow?"

"Right, yes. Of course. I'll just leave you to rest."

"Love, is there any world in which you think I'm letting you out that door tonight?"

"No?" she asked, cautious optimism in her tone.

I made a half-hearted effort to shift over, and she climbed back up into her spot and curled along my side.

She whispered, "I love you," once more before I fell asleep again.

Forty-Two

CADIEUX HOUSE, LONDON - JUNE 30, 1816

CELINE

THE FAMILIAR, comforting sensation of fingers running through my hair breached my nightmare. The scent of citrus and William and *home* came second, soothing my racing heart. My hand rose and fell on his shirt-clad chest with each shallow breath—his ribs still plagued him then. He hummed some wordless tune low in his chest, probably some bawdy soldier's tune for all that I recognized.

"Know you're awake, love."

With a dramatic sigh, I abandoned my feigned sleep. He was a beautiful sight. Bruised and battered, eye swollen nearly shut, my beloved cheekbone blackened beyond recognition, but he was alive. So alive. His working eye was clearer this morning, less hazed with pain. Today it was the color I imagined the sea to be on a sunny day in autumn, little sparkles dancing off the surface when the sun hit the waves. Oh, and there was my beloved, adoring crinkle, restored to its former glory.

"You all right? Sounded like you were having a bad dream."

"I am now."

"Yes?" His smile was pleased, no pretended misunderstanding.

"I thought I lost you."

"Oh, love. I'm far too stubborn for the likes of Bates."

"So it would seem."

"What do you suppose my chances are of making my escape today? You and I should talk, and Kit's bedroom is not the ideal place."

"Well, that depends. Your apartment is…"

"It's gone?"

"No, but there was damage. It's mostly to the office. However… I would very much like you back with me."

"Not going to send me packing again?"

I shook my head fiercely and he chuckled before clutching his side.

"Stop being funny, love. Hurts."

I pressed a kiss to my fingers before pressing them to his lips. Just then, the bird at the windowsill gave a chirp of irritation. I suppose I did reserve that for Gabriel's headstone.

"Hush, you."

"I presume the bird is coming too?"

"The bird is coming."

"I don't suppose you can get him to stop biting me."

"After what he did to my attacker, I think you're lucky with a nip. But I'll try."

"Right, can you press-gang Kit into helping me ready? We'll talk when we get home."

"Home." Oh, that was a lovely thought. A beautiful, wonderful thought that I didn't deserve to have but he seemed willing to encourage anyway.

THE MILE or so journey home was long and painful. Though William made a valiant effort to hide his winces every time the carriage jerked, I felt each one.

When he was finally settled safely in my bed, the tightness in my spine lessened. I fluffed the pillow he was resting on, desperate for some sort of useful occupation.

"Don't know what the fussing is about, 'm perfectly well."

"You could have died. Give me a little leave to fuss." I perched on the edge of the bed beside his prone form.

"I just—"

"Will, I already held the man I loved in my arms while he passed once. For too long I thought I might have to do it again. And it would have destroyed me. So if it's all the same to you, I'm going to fret over you for a while now."

"Love?"

"Yes?"

"No—I mean yes, of course, but it was a question. You love me?"

And oh, there it was. That awed look he wore so well, the one that made my heart flutter. His jaw dropped slightly, eyes —eye—crinkled. It was a sunny morning blue just now. The worst of the swelling was beginning to recede on the other one, and I could see the barest flash of blue beneath the puffy upper lid.

"I told you so, last night."

"Thought I might have dreamt that. I was concussed, you know... Were you there with me?" The way he said it, the soft hope flowing through every word. It was a sharp reminder of just how badly I hurt him.

"I was," I whispered. I slipped my hand in his, interlacing our fingers, clasping them tight. He stared at them a moment longer. This man... He had no guard, no guile. Every thought was plain as day, right in his eyes. Even when only one was open.

Slowly, he tightened his fingers over mine and brushed his thumb across the back of my hand. Even now, days after he last held a quill, his nails were stained with ink. The sight made me smile—my Will.

He swallowed, his throat bobbing as he considered his words. "What does that mean?"

"It means... I love you. I'm in love with you. I fought it every step of the way. I thought I wasn't strong enough, brave enough to bear the risk." I broke off, swallowing the lump in my throat.

I turned to our hands. It was easier to get this part out without the agonizing wonder in his gaze.

"When Gabriel died, a part of me died too. Or I thought it had. But you found it. You dug into my soul and you found it, brought it into the light, made it yours. You did it so slowly, I missed the signs. You made me want to live again, love again. You showed me that I am capable of it.

"I knew you loved me. You told me—every second sentence, you told me." He huffed a quiet laugh. "I... I was so scared that I was going to be hurt again. And I was terrified that I was going to hurt you. That I would break you when you found out I wasn't capable of loving you as you deserved.

"You're so courageous, Will. You jump into everything with your whole heart. I knew it even that day in Kent, all those years ago. The way you loved Adriane, it was all over your face and in every move you made. And it was the same way with me. But I couldn't match that. At least, I didn't think so.

"So at the first test, I ran. I ran because I was a coward, and I thought I was broken. But it turns out, I was just bruised..."

"Love..."

"Will, when I thought you had died or that you wouldn't

make it..." I broke off, my voice finally cracking under the pressure of holding back the tears. They fell swiftly, silently, landing on my skirts. "It wasn't any less agonizing for having run. It was worse. Because you would have passed thinking I didn't love you. And that was the thing that was unendurable."

When I finally turned back to meet his eye, his expression was, for perhaps the first time, unreadable. Forging ahead, I continued.

"So, it means... whatever you want it to mean. I love you. I want to be with you. In whatever capacity you'll have me. But I know I was cruel. And I'm an awful lot of trouble. So if you're not ready for that... Well, I'll keep fussing after you while you're trapped here until you fall in love with me again. And I'll feign acceptance of your decision for now."

"Celine, love. You think there's a man with his senses anywhere who could hear a speech like that, from a woman like you, and do anything but fall at your feet?"

"So you—" He cut me off, grabbing the back of my neck with his free hand fisting in my hair and pulling me to him.

I hadn't known it was possible to convey that depth of feeling with nothing more than lips brushing against lips. Even now, William kissed with his whole being. It wasn't particularly involved, no tongues or teeth—he was too injured for more. But there was tenderness, feeling, *love* behind every touch. And it was addicting, I wanted more, more, more, always, forever.

Eventually, his ribs protested and he fell back with a curse.

"So, yes?"

"Yes, love."

With a delighted smile fighting its way onto my lips, matching his contented one, I curled into his side once again.

"Does this mean we're courting?" I asked.

"This means I would marry you tomorrow, but I'm still a touch frightened that asking will run you off."

That had me popping off the bed, hovering over him again. Though there was mirth in his smile, his eye showed no hint of it.

"I'm not running off. But tomorrow seems impractical. It takes longer than that to get to Scotland."

"What?"

"Also, I don't think your ribs will allow you in a carriage for that long."

"You want to marry me?"

"Not tomorrow, as I said, since that's impossible. But by the time the bans have been read, you should be mostly healed."

"You're serious?"

"Yes. Were you not?"

"No, I am!"

"I do have one request."

"Anything."

"When the time comes, you let me die first?"

He cupped my chin thoughtfully, lovingly. "Many, many years from now, you may die first. A century, perhaps?"

"A century sounds wonderful." He kissed me again and I silently cursed his injuries. I settled back against his uninjured side once more while he thumbed through my hair.

"You never did tell me the whole story, you said someone threatened me?"

Forty-Three

RYCLIFFE PLACE, LONDON - JUNE 30, 1816

WILLIAM

"Victoria," Celine answered, tracing a finger over my heart. "She found me at the ball, told me that Gabriel's killer knew we were searching for them. She said they would kill you too. And Kit, and Xander, and Michael, and anyone else who helped me."

Her unease that night made a depressing sense now. My hand, the one not curled around her hip, clenched at my side. I was filled with the impotent desire to hit something, someone.

"I knew you wouldn't accept that..." she continued.

"So you ended things with me."

"Yes. I'm so sorry, Will."

I pressed a kiss to her forehead in lieu of a response.

"She said it had to do with the break-in at your office. I thought... I hoped that if I was seen to... if it was widely known that..."

"You weren't with me?"

"Yes. If that were known, then they would stop. It wasn't

worth it, knowing the truth—the identity of Gabriel's killer—it wasn't worth you being hurt."

If there was anything that would ease the sting of her rejection, the knowledge that she cared more for my safety than the answers that had plagued her for years would do it. Her thumb began to tap against my heart in time with the beat beneath.

My free hand found hers on my chest and traced the elegant lines of her fingertips while she tapped. I noticed that her hand found its way there often, her lips too. I was beginning to suspect it was a comfort to her, to check that it was still beating. Silently, I reaffirmed my impossible promise that she could go first. She should never have to feel my heart stop.

Pulling her fingers up to my lips, I pressed the vow to their tips before returning her hand to its home.

"I found the documents. I know Parker was involved."

Just then, we were interrupted by a polite knock. Rising, Celine found Jane on the other side of the door. "My lady? Mr. Wayland, Mr. Ainsley, and Mr. Summers are downstairs hoping to speak to you and Mr. Hart."

"Just left Kit's apartment, he hasn't seen enough of me?"

"Apparently not," Celine answered. Turning back to Jane, she said, "In my sitting room. If you please, Jane. I don't think it wise to move Mr. Hart all the way back downstairs."

"Quite right. Mr. Ainsley brought some of those fairy cakes and tarts from Hudson's. I'll have those brought up as well?"

"Excellent plan. Be sure to let everyone else know they're available before Bouvier eats the rest."

"Already done, just as soon as I saw 'em. Do you want me to send in a footman for Mr. Hart?"

"No!" I protested. "And I'm right here."

"She's already been warned that you're a bear of an invalid and to ignore everything you say, Will," Celine replied pertly.

"I'll let you two manage?" Jane asked.

"Yes," she answered with a sigh. "If he falls on his bottom, the gentlemen can laugh at him while they help him up."

I waited until Jane slipped out the door before making my reply. "You like my bottom."

"I prefer it unbruised," she said, allowing me to stand on my own. She made her presence known, right beside me for support.

I managed the trip to her sitting room without incident, for which I was grateful. When I was barely seated, the door burst open and the three gentlemen entered with Jane and pastries bringing up the rear.

"Will, you look better than I anticipated. Those two had me convinced you were on death's door," Wayland said, pointing at the others while swiping a raspberry tart before the tray hit the table.

"Share," Mr. Ainsley scolded, placing one on a plate and handing it to me. Meanwhile, Jane slipped out, shutting the door in her wake.

"You're not here for tarts and gossip, I presume," Celine said, slightly peevish in tone.

"Well, I did hear from Kate that that horrible woman, what's her name... Lady Charmaine has taken another husband," Wayland added conspiratorially between bites of tart.

"Lady Caroline," Kit corrected.

"Maybe it's Lady Clara?" Wayland supposed.

"It's Lady Charlotte James, you dolts. You and Hugh ruin her ball every year, Michael. I don't know why you cannot recall her name." The burst came from Augie's corner.

"He's distracted by the bosom," Kit said. From beside me, I could sense Celine's hackles rising.

"Don't tell Jules."

"It is quite impressive," Kit added.

"Is this what men discuss when there are no eligible women around? If so, I should like to return to a state of ignorance," Celine snapped. "And really, Will is concussed. Is this the drivel you dragged him from the sickbed for?"

Now sheepish, Wayland replied. "Well, no. But you mentioned gossip. And Kate knows all."

"Out, all of you!" she insisted. I didn't have the heart to tell her I was rather enjoying myself.

"But they found something! That's why they dragged me over here after I just got rid of him," Kit added.

"Go on," she answered, terse.

Ainsley pulled a stack of documents out of a satchel I hadn't noticed before. "Bates. He's Wesley Parker's half-brother. And the other one, Lloyd Dickens, was a half-brother on his mother's side."

"Was there another brother?" Celine asked, more sedate.

Ainsley flipped through another page. "Samuel Dickens, two years younger. Why?"

"Lloyd attacked us a few weeks ago. With another man. I thought it was random—I was in a disreputable part of town. But I stabbed the man with an umbrella tip. Lloyd said something when we were struggling... that I had killed him." There was a numbness to her speech, delivered to the carpeting. I wanted desperately to gather her in my arms.

"I do not know whether to scold or applaud you, Cee," Wayland replied.

"Neither will do nicely."

"You have all this information on your patrons?" I asked, reaching a hand out for the file. Ainsley passed it and I flipped through it, all astonishment. Bank records, family history, collateral, favored ladies at White's, everything a person could want to know about a man's financial and personal situation was contained in the pages.

"It's astounding what people will eagerly share in exchange

for the prestige of being seen at Wayland's. And the chance of riches and glory, of course," Ainsley explained.

"And we do our own... research. On occasion," Wayland added with more significance than I desired as his solicitor.

The majority of the file was devoted to Parker. Associates, properties, banking details, favored bits of muslin, the result of every wager he had ever made at Wayland's and with Wayland himself before the club opened. It was all there.

Then I reached the section devoted to Bates. He was a less frequent visitor to the club. His financial situation clearly didn't allow for it. But there was information about his start with our office, his wife, his children. There was more in this file than I had gleaned in the years he worked for me. My gaze caught on the start date for a second.

"December 1810..."

"What?" Augie asked.

"His start date with us... That was a few weeks after Wayland's opened. You were my first major client." A sickening feeling bubbled up. All that time...

"Must have been using the position for intelligence. Hand me Parker?" Wayland asked and I passed him the top several pages.

He perused it with interest before handing it over to Ainsley. "His wagers improved substantially a few weeks after his brother started with you. Must have been using the intelligence. Clever..."

I hadn't considered Bates a friend, but friendly certainly. To know that his betrayal wasn't a recent development, that he had been using me all those years, it was slightly sickening.

"Why do you suppose he got sloppy all of a sudden?" Kit asked.

"My subtle and well-conducted investigation obviously spooked him," Celine jested, easing some of the tension.

"Oh yes, you were very subtle. Damn near blended into the walls with how unnoticeable you were," I replied.

"Well governesses don't offer instruction on the best methods to conduct a murder investigation."

"I never would have guessed."

"I feel like I've missed something," Wayland said.

"That should be a familiar sensation," Ainsley added, grabbing another tart, ignoring his friend's glare.

"What about the horse race? Is there anything in there about that?" Celine asked.

"The file you found. It survived the fire." Kit mumbled between bites of tart. "There were banknotes from Parker and Bates in there, Will."

"So Parker wrote the original note calling for Gabriel to meet him at dawn. I would know that handwriting from the bank draft anywhere. Perhaps to get Gabriel out of the house before anyone else was about. He probably never even went to the park. One of the men was probably waiting for him at the house when he returned."

"He was late," Celine murmured.

"What?"

"He was late. He stopped to buy me flowers. If they had found him when they intended, I wouldn't have had time to say goodbye. He would have died on the steps before anyone found him."

My heart ached for her. Even knowing how difficult the goodbye was, how much it hurt her, the idea that she might never have had it... That would be devastating.

"Well, Bates and Dickens aren't talking. Perhaps evidence will make them a bit more loquacious," Wayland said. "No one can locate Parker. I've got one of my best men on it though. We'll find him before too long."

"Please keep me informed?" Celine asked.

"Of course."

"We should be going," Kit added. "Will needs to rest." As soon as he said it, a heavy yawn escaped me.

"We'll be going then. And we'll leave the tarts," Ainsley said pointedly. Wayland and Kit both backed away from the tray slowly. "Will, I wish you a speedy recovery."

"Right, yes," Wayland added, snagging a tart from behind Ainsley's back as they filed out.

Next to me, Celine sighed heavily. She stood and helped me up with gentle hands before allowing me to walk back to the bedroom, unaided.

I settled back into the bed, propped against the headboard. Celine curled herself at my side once again.

"How are you feeling, love?"

"I... I don't know. It's just— It's so senseless."

"An'... about the younger brother? Samuel?"

"Well, apparently your umbrella is deadlier than we first thought." I winced slightly at the memory. That hadn't been a pleasant death. Though, it was not a dissimilar injury to the one Gabriel had received. I could appreciate the poetic justice in that.

Weighing my next words carefully, I asked, "How do you feel about that, love?"

"I haven't had much time to think on it. If he was responsible... I suppose I'm glad he's gone. I wish I hadn't been the one to do it. It's... less satisfying than I had anticipated. And it feels somewhat unreal. I have no evidence, just the word of a criminal."

"'S a lot, taking a life. Your feelings might change on it, and that's all right."

"I'm not entirely certain how I feel about any of it. I do know I made a very poor showing the other night. At least I remembered to get my knife out before I came for them—well the bird reminded me."

I risked the pain of a chuckle. "You did just fine, love. We're both here, right?"

"I merely yelled about the fire."

"Good. You shouldn't have run into danger in the first place."

"But—"

"Remember how you felt at the idea that I would be hurt?" I cut her off sharply.

A guilt-ridden expression crossed her face. "I understand, but I couldn't leave you."

"How did you know to find me anyway?"

"Please don't laugh…"

"Tell me."

She buried her face into my chest before her muffled answer escaped. "The bird."

A burst of laughter escaped me, which was immediately followed by shooting pain in my ribs. Her answering laugh made the pain worth it. She was so damn beautiful when she laughed, bright eyes and sparkling smile and glittering hair in the evening sunlight streaming through the window.

"Serves you right," she teased.

"Where is the bird anyway? Damn thing warned me, too."

She directed a pleased smile to her lap at the thought of our collective savior. "Downstairs. Bouvier is most displeased with him, but Jane has already purchased an extravagant perch. I told her he needs to be released when he's well again, but it may be a fight."

She propped her head up on my chest, careful to avoid my ribs as she balanced her chin on her hand. Inexplicably, she let out a giggle. And another. And another until she was in a full peal of laughter.

"Care to explain?"

Between more giggles, ones she made a slight effort to stifle, she lifted her hand to drag a finger across my newly scarred, swollen brow. "*Mon arc-en-ciel,*" she whispered. Her rainbow...

"Charming."

"I'm a delight."

"That you are, love."

I leaned down to kiss her, making a valiant attempt at ignoring the protest in my ribs. Her sweet smile brushed against my lips.

Slipping a hand to my favorite place tangled in her honey-gold curls, I kissed her with the pent-up desperation I wouldn't be able to follow through with. My lips pulled a desperate moan from her chest and that was worth all the aches.

She moved to pull away slightly, and I made to chase after her. She must have caught the wince I tried to hide because she pulled away completely. If I whined after her, who could blame me?

"Will, we cannot."

"We can..."

"You're hurt."

I caught her hand and pressed it to the newer, more urgent and infinitely more pleasant ache that was forming.

"I am, but I'm sure you can help with that."

"Will..."

"You are too," I whispered against the rainbow bruising decorating her neck. I slipped a persuasive hand under her skirts. My cruel ribs protested the effort. Did they not understand the urgency of the situation? Celine had agreed to marry me, and she had been curled against my side, soft and sweet-scented for days. We were alive.

"But..."

"Celine," I pouted as my hand trailed upward. I was man enough to admit to pouting if it got me what I wanted.

"I don't want to hurt you..."

"I'll let you do all the work. I'll just lie here…"

"Well, we both know that is a lie." I choked out a laugh as I finally reached my destination under her skirts.

With a resigned, pleased sigh, she gently pressed a hand on my chest, pinning me to the bed.

"You're going to lie very, very still."

"Of course, love. Say, if smiles mean a dance, what does it mean when a lady presses you to a bed and tells you to lie very, very still?"

"When *your* fiancée does it, it means she loves you."

"Yes?"

"Yes. Enough to brave anything." Her lips met mine and we were brave together.

Epilogue

WILLIAM

"I'M NOT PRECISELY sure how this goes," I said as I brushed the dust from the bench across from him. It would not do to ruin my best trousers.

For unknown reasons, I waited a beat for a response that wouldn't come before continuing. "I, um... Gabriel, I wanted to thank you. And forgive you. And all that other nonsense."

From the oak tree's branches above me, I heard the familiar *chirp-chirp* of the damn great tit. It fluttered down from its perch, no worse for its injury, before settling atop the tombstone across from me.

"Adriane— Well, it wasn't *entirely* your fault. She could have gone to you. You would have at least helped her. I knew that even then. But she was... She never did things properly. What happened after she chose to go to France, it wasn't on you. And I'm sorry for blaming you for that bit of it."

The damn bird stared at me with its beady eyes before offering a rude double chirp.

I pressed onward. I had a deadline, after all.

"Thank you for helping me. I know you didn't do it for me, but I... I'm so, so grateful that I didn't have to leave her.

"Thank you for saving her, for keeping her safe that night. And thank you for being with her for all those years before I found her. For loving her the way you did. Just... Thank you."

The chirp was more sincere this time, genuine. We sat there in silence, a gentle breeze blowing through the air. I heard the creak of the iron gate before her footsteps.

She came up behind me and dropped a kiss to the top of my head. "You two finished talking?"

"Yes," I croaked, my voice thicker than I would have liked.

The tit flitted over to sit on the back of the bench facing her. She gave his head a little scratch with one finger. "Hello, you. I see you're quite recovered." He gave her a grateful chirp before flapping back up to the tree.

I followed his journey up to a nest. With a female inside who greeted him with a welcoming *chirp-chirp*.

"Oh! Isn't that lovely?"

Celine slipped around me and walked over to the tombstone. In a ritual as familiar to her as breathing, she pressed a kiss to her fingers before dropping them on the stone.

"Congratulations, my love," she whispered. She stepped away, turning back toward me in her lovely gown of mauve silk, a bouquet of calla lilies in one hand.

The bird dove down and landed before the patch of irises planted beside the stone. After tilting its head to the side, it pinched off a stem in its beak, then hopped over to her. Giving it to her.

She bent and took the flower, then tucked it quietly into the bouquet. "Thank you."

Turning back to me, she held out a hand and wiggled her fingers expectantly. My mother's ring glinted in the sunlight.

"Ready?"

"I've never been more ready for anything." I laced my fingers with hers, then turned and ambled toward the gate.

"Let's go get married, William Hart."

"After you, soon-to-be Mrs. Hart."

"Madame! Please."

"*Madame* Hart."

"Perfect."

"I completely agree."

The End

The Most Imprudent Matches series will continue in
A Properly Conducted Sham.

Read the alternative epilogue at https://www.allyhudson.com/bonus-scenes.

Support the Author. Leave a review on Amazon

Acknowledgments

Thank you to my incredible beta readers, Sonia Groupe, and Cynthia Georges. And thank you to my incredible author critique partners, Laura Linn and Ginny Moore. Thank you to Dominique for correcting my rusty middle school French.

Thank you to my friends and family for your encouragement in this and all my projects.

Thank you to my mother for my love of reading.

Thank you to Martha for watching all the period dramas with me.

Thank you, as always, to Bryton for dragging me out of the house on occasion.

Thank you to Mariah for always reading my messy first draft.

Thank you Holly Perret at The Swoonies Romance Art for my gorgeous cover.

About the Author

Ally Hudson was raised in Hudson, Ohio. Currently, she resides in Fort Wayne, Indiana, with a very sassy dog. *Angel of Mine* is the fourth book in the Most Imprudent Matches series. She writes of cinnamon-bun heroes, snarky friendships, and true love. Her other hobbies include reading, embroidery, and re-watching television shows she has seen ten times already.

Also by Ally Hudson

MOST IMPRUDENT MATCHES

Courting Scandal - Book One

Michael and Juliet

The Baker and the Bookmaker - Book Two

Augie and Anna

Winning My Wife - Book Three

Hugh and Kate

Devil of Mine - A Prequel Novella

Gabriel and Celine

Angel of Mine - Book Four

William and Celine

COMING SOON

A Properly Conducted Sham

The Scottish Scheme

A Lady's Guide to Abduction (And Other Legal Matters)